7 DAYS

CARNAL GAMES SERIES
BOOK 1

STASIA BLACK

7 Days

by Stasia Black

© 2025 Stasia Black. All rights reserved.

*For everyone who wanted a
second chance at a doomed first love*

Please note this is a dark romance series with kidnapping, dub-con, and intense themes of trauma and abuse (including references to past childhood abuse). A full list of trigger warnings can be found at stasiablack.com

Playlist

"Nobody" Mitski
"Traitor" Olivia Rodrigo
"Wicked Game" Chris Isaak
"Villain" Bella Poarch
"Arcade" Duncan Laurence
"Unholy" Sam Smith & Kim Petras
"Take Me to Church" Hozier
"Dancing with the Devil" Demi Lovato
"Forever For Now" LP
"You Should See Me in a Crown" Billie Eilish
"Down with the Sickness" Disturbed
"The Family Jewels" Marina
"Who's Afraid of Little Old Me?" Taylor Swift
"Diagnosis" Alanis Morissette
"Silent All These Years" Tori Amos
"Never Felt So Alone" Labrinth
"Only Love Can Hurt Like This" Paloma Faith
"Dandelions" Ruth B.

PLAYLIST

Nobody Mitski
Traitor Olivia Rodrigo
Wicked Game Chris Isaak
Villain Bella Poarch
Arcade Duncan Laurence
Unholy Sam Smith & Kim Petras
Take Me To Church Hozier
Dancing With The Devil Demi Lovato
Forever For Now LP
You Should See Me In A Crown Billie Eilish
Down With The Sickness Disturbed
The Family Jewels Marina
Who's Afraid Of Little Old Me? Taylor Swift
Diagnosis Alanis Morissette
Silent All These Years Tori Amos
Never Felt So Alone Labrinth
Only Love Can Hurt Like This Paloma Faith
Dandelions Ruth B.

ONE

DOMHNALL

I SIP my Jameson and look around the room that's been darkened for ambiance. The event planner did well, and I'm difficult to please.

The gleaming mahogany stage for the auction is the only well-lit spot in the club. They even hung a floor to ceiling burgundy velvet curtain for the virgin and the auctioneer to enter through. The spanking benches and St. Andrew's Cross have been discreetly pushed off to the side. Instead, plush chairs upholstered in dark red fabric are arranged in an arc in front of the stage.

All a little dramatic, yes, but the rich arseholes in designer suits meandering around and laughing too loudly at each other's jokes love this shite.

I ought to be playing my part as host. But one perk of being richer than god is getting to be an anti-social bastard.

"What the fuck, Dom?" Caleb says, suddenly appearing at my shoulder. He's the club's actual owner, and my self-proclaimed best friend. I've told him a thousand time my name's pronounced *Donal*, but he insists on shortening it to Dom. Mostly because he says if anyone should be nicknamed *Dom* it's me, since I'm such a controlling, sadistic bastard. It caught on and now everyone follows suit, even my sister. "I told you, no drinking tonight. Everyone's got a goddamn glass in their hand."

I glance over the rim of my tumbler. "You're welcome. I didn't *have* to organize this little soiree here."

He rolls his eyes. "Thank you, Dom, for helping me pull off this event and inviting your billionaire friends. Now why the fuck is everybody drinking? I know this isn't a ring member event, but I thought you told them the rules."

I scoff even as I finger my platinum-gold ace of spades ring that indicates my top tier membership in *Carnal*. You have to be a member in good standing for three years to qualify and be able to afford the fees. Then it provides entry to the darker, kinkiest events that require the trust of an inner circle.

Tonight, however, is what one might call an invitational event. We're showing off the perks of what being a member of

Carnal can provide. And it's a hell of a fundraiser to inject some quick cash into the club.

"For the kind of money you wanted in this room," I say, "there are expectations. They don't know the rules of the scene. These men assume there's going to be a bar to order top shelf shite from."

I nod towards the sleek bar, the only other source of significant light in the room. The bartender is in a black tux with a gold masquerade mask on. He's framed by a backdrop of hundreds of black and red roses clustered in a living wall.

"Fuck," Caleb runs a hand through his hair.

"Don't worry so fecking much, you'll get a hernia. I had them water the drinks down."

"Even yours?" In the dim light, I see Caleb's eyebrows lift skeptically.

"I'm just the host, remember? I'm not bidding tonight. I have no interest in virgins."

I only want experienced subs, preferably pain-sluts. I want to mark them, fuck them, and then have everyone go on their merry way without ever knowing each other's names.

"You should bid," Caleb says. "Maybe what you need is something different. Someone to settle down with."

I bark out a laugh and look over at him. "Don't be fecking ridiculous. Don't hang that picket fence shite on me. It's a lie sold to muppets like you."

"It's not a lie." His jaw tenses ever so slightly. "Silas and my mom had it."

Well shite. There's no saying anything against his sainted mam, may she rest in peace, his stepdad, Silas. No matter that the man's doing ten to fifteen for bank robbery.

"Plus," I swig down the rest of my drink, "I hardly think a woman getting a paycheck for her cherry's looking to settle down."

"I don't know," Caleb grins at me. "I'd think a billionaire would be a hell of an attractive get for a woman down on her luck."

I give him my deadpan stare.

"C'mon. You're such a closed off prick," Caleb says. "I met the girl. Moira brought her by the club this week. She's sweet. Real genuine."

"Even worse. I don't like sweet. I like silent. Preferably masked and faceless. Fucked up with daddy issues or whatever makes them like getting the shit flogged out of them."

Caleb turns his whole face towards me and frowns. "Dude. That's dark."

I sigh on the inside. It's so tedious to keep up this facade. All this pretending to be something other than what I am, just so I can walk around in normal society. If it weren't for Moira, I wouldn't make nearly as much effort. There's not much I wouldn't do for my sister.

Still, I'm a sadist. Deep in my dark little core, I like to hurt people. It brings me pleasure. Such great, deep-down pleasure, it's the only time I feel alive.

One would think that Caleb, being the owner of the most

exclusive BDSM club in Dallas, would understand people like me. But in spite of the life he's lived, somehow, he's still soft inside.

"Okay, not this girl, but *someone*," he says. "Connection is important. All you do is work and take care of Moira."

Time to don society's tedious mask again. I smile winsomely. "Well, you have met my sister. Over and over and *over*." I mock a cringe. "And too many times in my face at the club. So maybe you're not one to talk about *taking care* of Moira."

His eyes roll. Façade or not, he's at least acquainted with me enough to know that I don't actually give a shit about my sister's sexual exploits at *Carnal*. I'm happy about them, in fact. All I'm trying to do is keep my sister safe.

Moira's what you call an anysexual. Anyone, anywhere, anytime. Addiction runs in families, they say. And our family tree is... well, statistically, Moira and me were fucked before we ever took our first fecking wail.

Carnal is a safe sandbox for her to play in. This world is a fucked ball of death and destruction hurtling towards its inevitable brutal, bitter end. But my sister is somehow still a bright fucking beam of joy and sunshine screaming back into the void. Not that she even knows it. If I have any purpose in this life, it's to never let anything put that fucking light out.

"I'm serious," Caleb keeps at it. "You should at least *consider* taking a short-term sub. You know all the subbies at the club are drooling for you. Why not try?"

His phone buzzes in his pocket, saving me from continuing the useless back-and-forth banter. There's no point in small talk about how I'm not interested in anything even relationship-adjacent. I am what I am and while I will try to present a socially-acceptable facade, I won't apologize for it.

"Shit," he whispers, looking back up at me from the phone. "It's time." Anxiety tenses his forehead. "You really think this will work?"

I lean in and mutter quietly, "You see how *Eyes Wide Shut* we made this shit? These guys are already nutting in their pants to be the one who takes the virgin home."

Well, not home, but to the privacy of the private rooms, with careful monitoring. *Carnal*'s bouncer, Isaak, is bar none. I've seen that guy toss a biker two times his size out of the club for causing trouble.

And for the highest bidder, the bragging rights alone will make him a legend in their little circle for years to come. Obnoxious male bonding and one-up-man-ship rituals are what really get those pricks off.

I clap Caleb on the back. "It's gonna be great."

He nods hard, repetitively for several long moments, then stomps backstage with purpose.

Stubborn bastard. The club is in financial trouble and Caleb refused my offer of the money. Then he refused a no-interest loan. *Friendship and money should never mix*, the idiot kept repeating.

But the club needs the money, and I need the club for

Moira. I even once tried to tacitly explain that I see him less as a friend and his club more as a supply line to what Moira needs, but he just laughed, clapped me on the back—another favorite form of male communication—and said he'd figure something out.

This was his solution. A virgin auction. Apparently, others at the club helped talk him into it. Moira was there and I'm sure she was an *amazing* voice of reason.

Caleb comes through the velvet curtain and strides confidently up to the microphone. All the nerves from moments ago appear to have dissolved. I'm not that naïve. Maybe that's why Caleb and I get along so well. He knows a thing or two about swapping masks.

"The auction is about to start," he announces into the mic, "so have a seat, gentlemen. We have a gorgeous prize to present to you tonight."

Everyone meanders towards their seat while Caleb introduces the evening and tries to get the crowd enthused. I take a chair in the back, watching on with bored curiosity. This is entertaining enough, I suppose, but it's not like being in the club with a whip in my hand and a beautifully pink-assed sub whimpering beneath me.

I can't even take out my phone because Caleb required leaving them at the door. It only seemed sporting to join along, even though I'm just hosting.

I cross a leg and lean back while Caleb settles into salesman mode.

But the other men seem restless too, at least until a woman steps through the curtain wearing a silk negligee with barely any actual material to it, sky high white heels on her feet. A fall of chestnut curls covers her face.

Caleb hurries back to her and they have a quick consultation about something off-mic. Then Caleb lifts the microphone up again, back in ringleader mode.

"Here," Caleb says to the woman, holding out and arm to lead her towards the front of the stage, "come stand right up here."

Her head is dropped, so I can't tell if she's embarrassed, ashamed, or shy.

Finally, she lifts her head, and I'm glad I emptied my glass, because it falls right out of my hand, thudding onto the carpet below.

I can only stare at the ghost standing before me, looking even more beautiful now than she does in my memory.

Too bad the last time I ran across her, I swore I'd kill her for what she and her father did to me.

TWO

BROOKE

FIVE MINUTES *earlier*

I BREATHE out and stare at myself in the brightly lit mirror after the stylist spends over two hours on my hair and make-up.

Like every mirror I've looked at the past eight weeks, a stranger stares back.

Who am I?

My hand lifts unconsciously to the mostly healed bash on the side of my head that landed me in the hospital two months ago with no memory of how I'd gotten there. Or any memory. At all. Even of my own name.

The long, lank dark hair I've been pulling back with a tie is now glossy and slightly curled in a cascading fall over my shoulders. My brown eyes look bigger somehow, with longer eyelashes that make me look startled when I blink at myself.

Virgin. Auction.

Holy fuck, I'm really doing this.

"You look beautiful!" Moira says gleefully, popping up in the mirror beside my face with an excited smile. "Quinn! Look what a grand job they did. She looks so much better!"

I bark out a laugh, grateful for the relief of tension. This past week was a harrying ride of introductions, contracts, and NDAs. And that was all between setting up my own bank account and getting settled in at Moira's apartment, not to mention buying a wardrobe of clothes, which Moira insisted on charging to her card.

I met Moira at the women's shelter—she volunteers there —and she let me crash at her place when they released me. I all but latched onto Moira and *made* her be my friend as soon as I met her six weeks ago. I might not know my own name, but it's been nice to feel like there's still some sort of *me* inside —a personality that lights up when I'm around the right people.

Moira's got these big brown eyes that make her look all innocent and sweet, but she's actually bawdy as a sailor. She loves sex and is unapologetic about it. She's always telling hilarious stories about her latest hijinks—and she doesn't shirk on the details. Turns out I swear like a trucker, so we fit like peas in a pod.

Some people with amnesia wake up and find they still speak a foreign language. I woke up telling people that *fuck, I've got to go shit a cunting brick.*

I didn't have a purse or phone on me when I showed up at the hospital, so they assume I got mugged. I've scoured the thin folder of medical records they gave me like a detective seeking any clues to my own life:

Female. Estimated between twenty-two to twenty-four years of age. No broken bones. No evident sexual trauma at the time of the attack. Good teeth, but no dental records to be found anywhere. That made them think I grew up off grid or abroad, but I don't have an accent of any kind. No surgical scars or anything else that could give them clues about my identity.

I'm perfectly healthy apart from the blow to my temporal lobe that caused significant trauma to my hippocampus. *That* little detail from the doctor's report, I can pull up with perfect recall.

But anything before blinking groggily awake in the hospital in downtown Dallas?

Nothing. Zilch. Blank canvas.

But that's not really true. I *was* somebody. And she's still a ghost inside me. I wake up shaking from nightmares I can't remember, feeling cold down to the bone. *Her* nightmares. I have to turn on all the lights afterwards each time. Whoever I was—whoever I *am*—is scared of the dark.

"Moira," chides Quinn from the corner of the elegant changing room. "Don't make it sound like she wasn't beautiful before they put all that shit on her face." Quinn stands with her arms crossed, intimidating in sleek black head to toe latex.

"Of course she is!" Moira says to Quinn, then makes eye contact with me in the mirror again. "Of course you are. You're just *more* beautiful this way."

She says it so without guile, I laugh again and turn to hug her. "I love you to bits, M." Really, she's made it all feel as smooth a ride as something like this could be.

Right now, we're in a back room of the club, *Carnal*, with tons of bidders from what Moira casually described as "Billionaire's Row" out front.

She seems so unaffected by wealth, but then again, she's around it all the time with her rich brother, I guess. I still haven't met him; everything's been so busy. They weren't always rich, I know from some of the conversations we've had. Moira grew up in poverty back in Ireland, but she still seems at home wherever she finds herself, in some of the fancy places she's taken me this week or back at the women's shelter. She got to the states when she was young, so she doesn't have an accent anymore.

I'm generally so overwhelmed by the details of every room I enter that I'm just wide-eyed wherever I go. I couldn't stop staring at everything at the salon earlier when Moira and Quinn took me to get my long hair trimmed a couple inches.

"You can still back out," Quinn says.

"I'm fine." I suck in a deep breath. "I'm doing this."

"Or at any time," Quinn keeps at it. "You say no, and we call it all off. This isn't like some medieval shit. We're all about consensual play."

I look the stranger in the mirror in the eye and declare, "I want to play."

Yes, auctioning off my virginity is insane. Especially when I don't even know if I *am* a virgin. But as Moira pointed out when she presented the ludicrous possibility to me last week, "Your doctor's report says your hymen's not broken. Not that an unbroken hymen always means anything. But with the amnesia, it's not like you remember your first time, anyway. So, for all intents and purposes," she just kept chattering on, "you're a virgin. It'll be the first time for you, and that's the whole point."

"The whole point of *what*?" I'd stuttered back at her.

"Oh! Didn't I say? My head really has run away from me today. The virgin auction."

She knew I wanted to make big money fast; just like I knew how to cuss and that I'm scared of the dark, I know I need money and that working minimum wage jobs aren't for me. We'd previously been discussing Moira hooking me up with her friend Quinn so I could shadow her and learn how to be a professional domme. But then Moira got excited about this new opportunity that had come along.

The club, *Carnal*, was putting on a virgin auction, and it had a big payday.

I'm not an idiot. Or at least I like to think I'm not. I was skeptical.

But then Moira took me by the club one night last week so I could meet everyone else ahead of tonight. It didn't look anything like it does now. I'm not sure she'd exactly thought through what all the leather and floggers would look like to an outsider, but Quinn saw us walking in and immediately came over. You'd think she'd be intimidating in her shiny black latex—wait, no, it's not latex, what'd she call it? Oh right, PVC. Her black PVC.

But Quinn's so down to earth, she had me laughing in seconds, and when she introduced me to the bouncer and the club owner who'll be the emcee tonight, I felt a lot more at ease.

And then I just thought... Why the hell not? Yes, it'll mean having sex with a stranger. But why *not* do this now, while I don't know who the hell I am? Sure, some part of me wonders—what if there's someone I'm intimate with in the life I lost that I'd be betraying?

But that thought is immediately followed with fury. Because if that was true, then where the hell are they? Why didn't they come looking for me when I disappeared? They obviously didn't look very hard. Even the news picked up the story and broadcast it everywhere.

I might not know who I am, but after waking up terrified and so, so alone, I know if I *did* have someone, I'd move hell and earth to find them if they up and disappeared.

The coldness inside me suspects the truth is far sadder. There was no one. I was alone in the world. Alone and scared all the time. Afraid of shadows. So why on earth was I in a dark alleyway at ten o'clock at night?

With the kind of staggering money Moira says I could make from the auction, I can really, truly start over. I'll make my new life *bright*. Full of light and good things and friends who'd miss me if I disappeared suddenly.

I can start my new life... and hire a private investigator to find out who I was. People don't just *appear* from nowhere out of thin air. While I'm busy starting a new life, I still need to figure out who I was.

Are we really anyone at all if we don't have a past? Everyone I get to know tells me who they are by listing off who they've been. I can't even explain why it's so important to me. But I don't feel... real. To myself, even.

There's a whole person locked away inside me, and I need to know her. I don't know how to go forward without knowing what was behind me.

And I need to know why I wake up screaming most nights, or I'll always be looking over my shoulder. I need to know *why*.

So if I have to fuck a stranger for a chance at all the resources I could ever need to discover who I really am?

You bet your ass I'm going to take it.

Quinn looks at me skeptically from across the beautifully furnished dressing room suite. The whole club is insanely luxurious. There's a sitting area with a couple of couches so elegant, I can't imagine actually daring to sit on them. We're in the open attached bathroom of the suite that's almost as big as the kitchen back at the shelter. There's both a shower *and* a bathtub. I dig my toes into the lush, soft carpet and nod.

"I'm ready to play," I repeat.

"Okay," Quinn says, shrugging. "There's plenty of men out there happy to take you up on it. They're all but slobbering to get a look at you. But just remember," she leans over, and I gasp when she yanks a short, sharp knife out from within the top of her thigh-high boots. "We're all just a room away if you need us."

"Good lord, do you always keep that there?" Moira asks as she brushes past Quinn. "No, don't answer that. Just put it away." Quinn re-sheathes the knife but gives me a significant look.

"Domhn wouldn't let anyone in who wouldn't be respectful of the rules," Moira says. Ah, the famous Domhnall, Moira's brother, who I've not seen hide nor hair of. For as much as it sounds like he dominates Moira's life and decisions, he's been surprisingly absent this week. I expected to see him everywhere for as much as Moira talks about him.

"Show Quinn the outfit I picked!" Moira claps her hands excitedly. It makes her boobs bounce obscenely in her low-decolletage'd bandage dress.

I stand up carefully and unwind my robe. I'm wearing a sheer, white nightie with a collared neck that snaps at the back and has cutouts in all sorts of odd places. Moira had to help me get into it, I could barely figure the garment out. If you can call it clothing at all.

Two triangle silk cutouts completely expose my perky medium-sized breasts. My nipples harden from the cool air of the room. The rest of the gauzy, see-through fabric hangs artfully down my waist and hips, exposing my underwear. The crotchless panties are just as functionally useless as the rest of the garment. Well, I suppose it depends on the function one intends the nightie for...

I feel my cheeks heat at the thought. But then, I've tried to intensely avoid thinking about what actually happens tonight after the auction. I've been singularly focused on the prize.

"Now the shoes!" Moira rushes away towards one of the couches and picks up a shoe box, hurrying back towards me. She opens the box and presents the shoes. "Ta da!"

They're gorgeous: white heels with lace overlay and gauzy straps that Moira sets to tying up my ankles after she waves me to sit back down on the chair in front of the mirror. They look like wedding shoes. I gulp a little and lift my legs to look. They're beautiful and fit well. No pinching.

"We don't even know if she can walk in high heels," Quinn says.

"Let's find out." I grab on to the counter as I stand up, unsure. But it's easy to find my center of balance, automatically leaning a little forward on my toes and clenching my calf muscles. Another clue. In my former life, I must have been comfortable in heels.

I look up at Moira, then over to Quinn. "It's fine."

Quinn just nods and walks towards the door, but Moira's eyes catch mine when I look back at her. She gets the significance and reaches out to squeeze my hand.

Our other occupation this week was skill-hunting. Can I cook? No. Ride a bike? Nope. Paint? I made a disgusting brown mess on the canvas. The only thing I'm good at so far besides cussing is chess. I used to play with Gus, the older maintenance guy back at the shelter.

"We've barely gotten to catch up lately. It's been such a whirlwind," Moira says. She leans in intimately, grinning and all but bouncing up and down. "I've got a seeeee-cret."

"Dear god, I hope it's not about tonight." I lift a hand to my chest. "I'm not sure I can handle much more."

"No, no," she says. "It's just about my dumb life. Never mind."

"Your life's not dumb," I exclaim, turning and grabbing her arm when she starts to pull away. "Tell me! You're right, everything's been so busy with getting ready for tonight, we've barely had time for girl chat. Plus, I could really use a distraction right now," I laugh a little unsteadily. "What's the secret?"

"Wellllll," she says, drawing out the word as she coyly bites at the lacquered nail of her forefinger. "It might have something to do with a mutual acquaintance of ours. I'm being bad and breaking Domhn's rules."

Mutual acquaintance? We don't have many of those.

"Someone from the shelter?" I ask.

"Oh god," Quinn moans, coming up to us. "Don't tell me you're fucking someone outside the club again."

Moira waves a hand breezily. "Oh, c'mon, he's just a side fuck. What fun is following the rules all the time, anyway? And Jesus, I'm a grown woman. I can fuck whoever I want." She grins, eyes glittering. "And you know I can't say no to the thrill of the forbidden."

"Domhn's just trying to keep you out of trouble, babe," Quinn says. "And there's always plenty of men at the club."

Moira rolls her eyes. "The *same* men, usually."

"Well, tonight there'll be all sorts of fresh meat."

"Oh don't worry," Moira winks at Quinn in the mirror, then reaches down for a lip-gloss from the counter of cosmetics in front of me. She applies it, then pops her lips. "All those horny billionaires out there? I plan to get ridden as many times as me-lady can handle tonight." She gives several over-exaggerated thrusts of her hips, complete with accompanying mock orgasmic whimpering.

"How are we friends?" Quinn deadpans as I burst out laughing.

Right then, a ping sounds and Moira looks down, pulling her phone out of her robe pocket. "Oh shit." Her eyebrows shoot up as she looks at me and grins. "It's time. Are you ready?"

I nod, shaking only a little. Her grin gets wider, and she wiggles her hips. "I'll take your leftovers."

I laugh again. I love how unashamed she is with her sexuality. Her and Quinn both. I will say I am... curious. But honestly, there just hasn't been very much time or space to explore myself *that way*, between the hospital and the shelter and the exhaustion of running around the last week.

But being in this outfit and thinking of what's about to happen... I bite my bottom lip. Maybe they'll all be gross old men, and I'll have to just close my eyes and count sheep or something till whoever wins is done with it. Fear and excitement war in my tummy as Moira waves for me to follow her. Because tonight doesn't even matter, not really.

It gets me one step closer to my real life. One way or another, I'll find out who I am.

"IT'S REALLY COOL," Moira whispers as we step into a darkened hallway. "There's a little stage with lights that'll all be on you."

"Cool," I echo her, my throat feeling suddenly dry. Is it too late to ask for a drink of water? Or a shot of whiskey? Would that mess up the artful red lipstick the makeup artist painted on me?

"Here she comes now," I hear a deeply pitched male voice announce loudly as we walk. "Open your minds to what's possible as I welcome you to this unique, one-of-a-kind auction for a sweet, sweet little virgin. She'll never have had any... ahem," he pauses dramatically and waits for laughter, "but yours. You can teach her what sex and pleasure are. She's a blank slate. And she'll never forget her first. Will that be you? Are you really going to miss this one-of-a-kind opportunity? Someone's going to fuck a beautiful virgin tonight!"

I blink as my eyes adjust to the darkness. Moira takes my hand and suddenly we're at the end of the hallway. Except instead of opening into another room, there are steps up to a huge red velvet curtain. Like at a real stage.

Moira urges me towards the steps.

... *oh*. It *is* a real stage.

I guess I didn't think about what the actual event would be like. I was a little more concerned with what comes after to really consider this part. All I can do is nod and keep my balance in the heels as I grasp the railing and climb the stairs.

Then I push through the curtain and step out onto the stage.

THREE

BROOKE

IMMEDIATELY, I'm blinded by the stage lights.

Just like Moira said, they're all pointed directly at me, and I can't see a thing. I put my hand up to block the light, then take an uncertain step forward.

The smiling owner of the club, Caleb, suddenly appears out of the blinding halo.

Caleb leans in to whisper, "Quinn explained what's going to happen, right? That I'm going to touch you to show you off? And ask some personal questions?"

I nod nervously. I've never been on a stage before. Well, that I can remember. The doctor said as I started going back out into the world, familiar things would start coming back to me, but nothing has in the two months since I woke up at the hospital. But every new experience could turn out to be one more clue.

"I need verbal consent," Caleb whispers back.

"Yes," I say nervously. "I consent."

He grins and puts my arm lightly through his as he leads me forwards.

I suck in another breath as I clasp his arm. He helps steady me as we walk up to the microphone. I can only stare out at the murky room beyond the bright stage like a deer in headlights. Everything inside my chest goes tight as a guitar string. The lights are aimed towards me, so I can't see what the men look like beyond shadowed outlines.

"Here," Caleb says, lifting the microphone, "come stand right up here."

I nod, feeling like a bobblehead, and go to stand where he says to.

Caleb lifts the microphone to his lips, holding out his arm towards me. "Here she is, our prize of the night. The beautiful virgin. So ripe and untouched. Do a slow little spin so our viewers can see all of you. Good, good, that's a good girl. Now stand right there in the center and arch your back, gorgeous. Stick out those sweet little tits for our bidders."

I do what he says, a little awkwardly at first. But I finally understand how arching my back makes my nipples point upwards. That's funny. I wouldn't have thought of that. Each thought feels disjointed from the previous one and the next.

Everything's happening so fast. It's like my brain can't keep up.

"Yes. Just like that," Caleb says. "Now turn around and bend over. Touch the floor and give our gentlemen a peek at what they're bidding on."

Really feeling the lights on me now, I turn and start to bend. *There's no one out there*, I try to tell myself. *It's just a dark, empty room.*

"Spread your legs wider."

Oh. I see what he means now. If I stand with my legs open, they can see my—

I gasp a little in shock and shift my legs a little. *There's no one out there. Just a dark, empty room.*

"Wider."

I lift and really separate my legs, spreading them wider than my hips. I bite my bottom lip, feeling the coolness of the room on the warmth of my very exposed sex.

"Good girl," Caleb says, his voice a little caressing. I inhale a little gasp at his praise. "Now touch the floor, if you can with those heels on. Let's see how flexible you are."

Immediately I'm obeying as if on reflex, even though *I* don't even know how flexible I am. I have noticed that I prefer it when people give me direction rather than asking me to make decisions. They were always asking me questions I didn't know how to answer at the shelter. About what I wanted to do next. I felt so choked and panicked each time.

But whenever anyone *told* me what to do, I immediately relaxed.

Even now, calmness settles over me as I reach down further and further until my fingertips, then my palms, rest on the floor. I feel the stretch in the back of my legs and my butt, but it's a pleasant pull. The physical therapists had me do a lot of stretching in the hospital and I kept it up afterwards in the shelter.

Upside down, I look through my legs at the men watching me. My eyes are slowly adjusting to the darkness. I can just barely make out the shape of a few men's faces—enough to tell that they aren't gross old men or like Jabba the Hut in the *Star Wars* movies I watched with Moira this week.

These men all have nice enough physiques, in various dark-colored suits. Like paper-doll cut-outs of each other. All their eyes are glued on me.

"Spread wider if you can, honey," Caleb says into the microphone. "Really give them a look at your virgin pussy."

I gulp and feel a clenching deep inside now that I'm able to see it's absolutely *not* an empty room.

Somehow that makes it real. I'm exposing myself in the most extreme way anyone can be exposed. And unexpectedly... a flooding rush of adrenaline I never anticipated crashes through my body. It's a sparkling electricity that dances across my skin. Especially as Caleb continues to instruct my movements, and I continue to obey.

My face flushes with heat as I lock eyes with one man in

the back who's staring at me so hard, it's like he's trying to drill into me. I can't decide if it looks like he hates me or he wants to fuck me or if he wants to hate-fuck me.

The more I keep staring at him, imagining all the things he might be fantasizing about, I slide my legs further apart like Caleb tells me to. Air-conditioning kicks on then because I feel a draft against my exposed pussy. It makes me shudder.

I break the stare of the man and turn my face shyly into my leg, even as my butt and sex clench, still thinking about him. A couple of groans come from the audience.

"That's good, sweetheart," Caleb says. "You can stand back up now."

I obey, my cheeks wildly hot as I stare at the polished wooden floor.

"Have you ever felt the touch of a man before?" Caleb asks, holding the microphone out in front of my face for my answer.

"No," I whisper, jumping a little at my amplified voice when it comes out of speakers around the room.

"You've never had sex before or been penetrated by a man?"

"Not that I know of," I answer as honestly as I can. "The doctors said my hymen is intact."

"Do you touch yourself?"

I suck in a quick breath. "I— I've thought about it. I think about it."

"What do you think about?"

Oh my god, this is embarrassing. Quinn told me the auctioneer would talk to me on stage a little, but I didn't realize he'd ask about this. She said to just answer everything honestly. To be myself.

"I, uh..." I close my eyes so I don't die of embarrassment. "I think about what it would feel like. First, I think about his arms around me. He's touching my hair. He's heavy on top of me, and I like how that feels. And then I feel his... um, how he gets hard down there. I imagine what it might be like to have him... if I touched him and took hold of him in my fist because I want to know what one feels like—" I pause for a second when more groans come from the crowd.

"Keep going," Caleb whispers to me.

"Um. Then I think about what if he, um, if he put it there and—" I swallow hard. I'm not sure I could do this if Caleb wasn't directing me. "Like, I had a dream the other night about a man pushing me down on the bed and then having, like, um, a thick fullness in there between my legs. And then him pushing it inside me. Like, in the place where it aches."

"How does it ache, baby?" Caleb demands. "Tell us."

My cheeks are red hot. I feel my whole face burning, not just my cheeks but my forehead too.

It feels otherworldly to be up here, baring my naked body that I'm selling, and telling my most intimate fantasies to tempt every man in this room. There's a little bit of shame mixed in, but even that adds to the rushing adrenaline. I might not know much, but I suspect that the big world out there looks down on this kind of thing. I'm doing something forbidden and sexy as fuck, and risky and dangerous. But it's also easy because I'm just giving in to commands.

As for the fact that I'm exhilarated and wet... My eyes open and slide back to the glaring man.

"It aches," I answer, "like this pulsing that starts... down there," my hands caress my body, "and comes up through my belly and then I want... I want to be pushed down and have the heaviness on top of me. *In* me. The heaviness of a man. Like I need something, but I don't know how to get it."

The intensity burning off the glaring man is too much, so I break our stare. Only to find every other eye in the room on me. My eyes have adjusted to the darkness. Some men have their hands down their pants. Others sprout little tents. Then movement and noise in the corner catches my eye.

It's Moira, bent over with a hand against the wall, dress bunched at her waist. A man grasps her hips and enthusiastically fucks her. His pants are shoved down just enough to expose his tan ass.

I gasp a little in surprise. I'm watching my friend have sex.

"Not in the same room as me," barks another man, drawing my eye. He turns away, holding up a hand to block any possible peripheral vision of Moira.

He's the one who locked eyes with me earlier. As I look, he glares my way again.

I frown. He looks angry at me. I look back at Moira as she

lets out a high-pitch groan and wiggles away from the man. Without a word, she grabs him by the front of his untucked button-down shirt while he struggles to yank his pants up, dragging him down a hallway.

"Now," Caleb announces from beside me. "Do we have a bidder?"

FOUR

DOMHNALL

I DON'T KNOW what fucking game this is.

I don't know how she got here or what the fuck is going on. Everything inside me goes cold as all around me, my colleagues start exuberantly shouting bids.

I feel out of control, and I'm never out of control. Not since I was seventeen. Which is where I'm suddenly transported back to.

Seventeen, with my soul broken, in sharp, jagged pieces being sucked out through my arsehole.

Yes, unthinkable as it is, I had a soul once.

But then she left. Without me. She took off with her father and all the money I'd stolen for them. She left me holding the proverbial bag, my digital fingerprints all over data that led right back to the internet cafe where she'd picked me up like the dumb mark I was. Even back to the flat I shared with my little *sister*.

I only had tickets out of town because I'd bought them to run away with her and Moira. We barely got through US customs safe before alerts went out for our names. We had to go with fake ones until I got rich enough to clear up the little problem from my past. Otherwise I would have had to keep running forever.

The sick twist of my guts knows that's only the beginning of the story. Or rather the twisted fucking ending. I never cared about the money.

I care that she served me up on a platter to be fucking destroyed. Just like she did to others before and no doubt after me.

Now, somehow she's here, nine years later. Madison. *Mads*. Though I doubt that was her real name either.

Here with her tits out. She glances shyly around the room of men with those light hazel-brown eyes, fluttering her lashes just like she used to at me when we were teenagers. Rage balloons inside my chest even as, in some part of me, I feel it working.

She's still just as fucking beautiful and alluring.

I want her even as I want to destroy her.

How the *fuck* is she here? And what the *fuck* sorta con is she trying to run now? Moira's told me all about her. A friend from the women's shelter. A sad case.

Sad case my ass. Fury blazes even hotter when I realize she's targeted my sister first, to get to me.

Fuck with me all you want, but my *sister?* Moira's so naïve. It's always been my worst fear that someone will take advantage of her. I only let her volunteer at the women's shelter because I have it guarded twenty-four/seven. I didn't consider that one of the bitches inside might—

My vision goes red and I'm two seconds from yanking Mads off stage by her hair.

Which is when I hear, "Six million going once, going twice—"

"Ten million!" I shout.

I feel the stares of those around me, along with some disgruntled grumbles. I'm not supposed to be bidding tonight. I can see how it might feel to the so-called friends I invited here. As if I'm just artificially driving up the bid, but they'll soon see that no one is walking away today with this so-called *prize* except me.

"Ten million, five hundred thousand," tries one man, a finance bro.

"Fifty million," I say, in no mood.

Everyone turns away, really grumbling now. "If you want to get your dick wet, grab a rubber and go find my sister," I say coldly, "It'll make her night."

Then I'm striding towards the stage.

I jump up on the small platform, ignoring a frowning Caleb.

"Was this your plan all along?" he asks, in some sort of mood. "I told you, I don't want your charity."

I ignore him and snatch Madison's wrist. My fingertips sizzle where they make contact with her skin, and I hate the electricity of our connection that's still here. She looks up at me, her mouth dropping in an O of surprise.

"Hi," she says tentatively.

Always playing her fucking games. I'm torn momentarily from the present right back to the moment I last saw her.

Those big eyes of hers were full of heartbreak and pity. "I know. I saw last night. Oh God, Domhnall. I saw. I'm so sorry. He's a—"

"Don't—" I cut her off. She was never supposed to know. I wanted to vomit. If I thought about it anymore, I would die where I stood. "Let's leave like we always said. Right now. We'll go get Moira and leave right this second."

She shook her head. "We won't make it across the border without money or my passport. You know he holds the passwords. But I know where he keeps them."

It was too dangerous. "No, Mads, you can't, we'll figure a way out—"

But she just grabbed my face, cupping my cheeks with certainty in her eyes. She could always handle intense shit better than I could. "Go get Moira and take her to the airport.

I'll go get the money and my passport. We haven't gone through all this for nothing. I'll meet you there."

She pressed her lips against mine. "I'll meet you there," she repeated, "I swear. We'll start over. Together."

Even after what happened, I convinced myself it had just been a missed connection. Even when I was totally broke and on the run, I tried to find her, convinced we were a tragic pair like Romeo and Juliet or some shit. Until I found out I wasn't the first sucker she'd hooked on the line. Or the last.

My jaw sets tight, and I don't say a word.

Not here. I can't lose it here. I don't know what kind of scene she's hoping to make, but she's not getting it out of me in front of everyone.

I pull her none too gently behind me as I stride off stage. She trips along in her ridiculous heels but finally hurries to catch up.

"Don't ride her too hard," one of the men in suits calls. "Baby, I'll still pay you a thousand for sloppy seconds."

They're crass idiots and now that I no longer need them, they can fuck off.

I pass by the hallway where we'd arranged for the devirginizing to take place. We'd planned a party atmosphere and for Isaak to be nearby as a bouncer. There's also a secret camera set up in the room in case the woman experienced any distress.

But I don't want anyone around us to hear or interrupt my upcoming interrogation. I pull Madison past the room where the devirginization was supposed to happen and down the hall towards the parking lot by her elbow.

"Wait, where are we going?"

"I paid for the night. You're going home with me."

I shove out the door and she only squeaks a little as it shuts behind us.

Madison Harper has things to answer for.

FIVE

DOMHNALL

I KEEP my hand locked on Madison's elbow as I deposit her in the backseat of my car.

"I thought we were just going to another room of the club?" She looks up at me with confused eyes. "And that there'd be a security guard there, too. That's what Moira said."

"Did she?" I mutter, furious all over again that she's targeted my sister. "But that's not what you came here for, is it, Mads?"

Moira called her *Brooke*. I huff out a snort. Probably a new name in every port, right? That's how her kind work.

"Mads? My name is Brooke."

"Is it?"

She shoves a hand out to keep the door open when I try to shut it, and her wobbly voice sounds afraid when she asks, "What's going on?"

It makes that rare flare of joy burst forth in my chest. I'm glad she's afraid. No one ever gets beneath my control, and I'm almost as pissed off at myself as I am at her. Fuck her for showing up here like this. "You tell me."

She crosses her arms over her chest as if covering her peaked nipples will really provide any modesty. "I don't know. I came here for the auction. Moira said that afterwards, we would— That whatever man bought me would take me to a nearby room so we could—"

"Fuck?" I say bluntly.

She nods, cheeks going red.

"And you just happened to be here. In Dallas. Befriending *my* sister. Showing up in *my* best friend's club naked for an auction of your supposed virginity."

The idea that she's still a virgin is fucking laughable. I can't believe she's still using this old shtick. Vulnerable little waif needs a big man to protect her.

Her eyes search my face and the confusion suddenly clears.

"Wait." She sits up straighter, half getting out of the car. She reaches out a hand towards me, stopping at the last moment before touching my suit-coat arm. "Do you know me?"

Her change in demeanor is somehow alarming, and I take a step back. "What the fuck's your game, Mads?"

"You keep calling me that. Who's Mads? Please." She's almost frantic now, pulling at my coat sleeve. "Do you know me? Who am I? I was knocked on the head two months ago. I didn't even know my own name at the hospital after the mugging and I didn't have any ID on me. I thought maybe you were familiar. Almost like I—like I trust you. Please, if you recognize me, tell me who I am!"

It takes me a few seconds before I can make sense of her gibberish.

"Wait." I finally bark out a laugh. "Are you trying to say you've got *amnesia*?"

"Yes! Exactly." She breathes out in relief. "That's it. Amnesia."

I can only stare at her.

Wow.

She must *really* think I'm a total fecking eejit to fall for that one. She's supposedly got amnesia and just happened to be released to the women's shelter where my sister works? I first met her in Ireland. Pretty sure she didn't end up in Dallas, Tx with a magical case of amnesia except by design.

She frowns, head shaking slightly as she watches every twitch of my face. "Why is that funny?"

Because all I can do is laugh. She has got to think I'm the dumbest box of rocks to fall for her sweet-as-all-American-apple-pie shit twice.

"No," I say honestly. "I don't know you. Now get back in the car. I just paid fifty million dollars for your virginity. It's your turn to pay up."

Her shoulders sink and she obeys, sitting down in the seat and pulling her legs back in.

I slam the door on her and sit in the front seat, quickly hitting the child locks on the back doors. I'm not letting her go now that I've got her back in my grasp again.

I never knew her, that's for damn sure. But if she's back, I can play along with her games just enough to tease out what the fuck she's up to this time around. And to get my retribution. Oh yes, I always dreamed about what I'd do if I ever got my hands on Madison Harper again...

"Put on your seatbelt," I bark, then burn rubber pulling out of the parking lot to drive the ten minutes back to my house. There's a little yelp from the backseat, but then a click that tells me she's complied.

I really don't get the play she's trying to make here. Did she think I wouldn't recognize her after all these years? Did she really think just because she left me behind with as little care as every other stupid fecking mark of her and her father's cons, I'd forget her the same way?

I glance in the mirror. She looks almost exactly the same, like she stepped through a time portal. She mighta already had work done. She's two years older than me. But while I look like I've earned every line of my twenty-six years on my face and then some, she's still a dewy-faced debutante.

Maybe I'm the only one who's changed. But she expects me to be the same dumb fuck I used to be, overtaken by lust and nostalgia for the pussy I never got to fuck—as if I'd just invite her back into my life?

That's disappointing, because it means I built her up in my mind as more intelligent than she actually is. In reality, she's just as disappointing and foolish as all the rest of them.

Well, Mads, you might've been expecting the little lamb I was, but I've gone and become a wolf since you last knew me.

Still, if she came for games, I'm suddenly thinking I would very, very much like to play.

She doesn't say a word, and when we pull in my large, four-car garage, I'm all but leaping out of the car to lift her out of her seat, again by the elbow.

"Did you tell Quinn or Moira where we were going?" Madison asks, looking around in wide-eyed wonder at the high ceilings of my mansion as I drag her down one hallway after another toward my elevator.

I hit the down button and the door immediately pings open.

"Come," I say brusquely, and she steps forward onto the elevator with me. My hand's still on her elbow but she's walking forward of her own volition. Which tells me that whatever game she's trying to play this time around, she doesn't mind walking into my trap.

Four-D chess always was her favorite kind. She lets you think you're winning only to go in for the kill once you've exposed your vulnerable belly.

"The bedroom's just in here," I say once we step off the elevator. "But I want you to wait outside for a moment. Will you wait outside like a good girl?"

She pauses, breath catching at my question, but then she nods. "Uh. Sure."

I smile and run the back of my fingers down her cheek reassuringly, giving her a little smile. "Good."

So many years I spent thinking of all the things I would do and say to her if I ever had her in front of me again.

I can't help but stare now that she's here. The cascade of silky dark brown hair over her shoulders makes me want to run my fingers through it just like I used to when the sunlight would hit it as we picnicked by the Dublin River. We'd spend hours just walking and holding hands, barely talking sometimes. It didn't matter how foggy it was out, she made it feel like the sun was shining in that deep, dark, cracked place inside me.

I love you, Domhn, she used to throw her arms around me and whisper. *Swear we'll run away together? Just you and Moira and me.* Her sweet voice in my ear and the scent of her jasmine perfume drugging all my other senses. *I'll love you forever.*

I was such a stupid, obvious, unloved little piece of shit, she and her paps probably scouted me a mile off. The memory creates such a sharp, painful ache, I want to run my fingers through her hair all right. And then yank her head back to demand answers. Will she cry prettily for me? Her uncertain hazel eyes flicker back and forth to check out her surroundings, giving her a Bambi look. I'll so delight in making the mascara run down her cheeks.

Yes, Moira and I had to flee our home country because of Mads but her betrayal goes *so* much deeper.

I know. I saw last night. Oh god, Domhnall. I saw.

I turn away so she doesn't see the gut-churning rage on my face. I slip into a nearby room, and when I come back out, I have a black silk blindfold in hand.

Finally, fate has smiled on me by allowing this foolish woman to dare show her face to me again. I always knew one day I'd find her. I never expected her to surprise me, but oh, how I've waited for this.

Finally, I'm going to take back the power she and her father stole from me.

"I'm going to put this around your eyes now and lead you into the bedroom," I say, offering one of my gentlemanly smiles out of my suitcase of facades.

I'm very handsome, I know. It disarms her.

Does she think I've bought her ludicrous amnesia story? Or does she know *I* know we're back to our old chess games and just think she has the upper hand because she always used to be able to lead me around by my dick?

Her eyes flick to mine uncertainly, but she stands still as I slip the blindfold over her eyes. Only once she can't see me do I allow myself to really smile. With all my teeth like the wolf I am.

Then I open the door wide and lead her inside to my room with assorted whips, cuffs, chains, and cages.

SIX

BROOKE

THE BLINDFOLD IS SO snug and thick, I can't see a thing.

My heartbeat is loud in my ears, at least until the man I'm with flips on a stereo system. Music fills the space with a slow, sensuous beat.

And the elevator went down to a basement. I'm pretty sure, anyway, because there weren't any windows.

Could anyone hear if I screamed? Should I *try* to scream now? For help?

Or is the music meant to cover the sound in case he makes me scream in a different way? Is he interested in my pleasure... or pain? I tremble, suddenly afraid I've been the stupidest, stupidest girl on the entire planet. Moira was nice, sure. But she's naïve and the auction could have had more dangerous bidders than she knew.

Fuck. Fuck, what have I gotten myself into? I try to lift my hands to take the blindfold off, but he catches them and kisses my palms gently.

It reassures me but doesn't stop my hammering heart.

"Are you going to hurt me?" I ask, trembling.

He tugs me forwards. "Sit," he says in his deep voice, taking my hips and directing me to sit on a soft mattress. "Don't take off your blindfold or I'll have to punish you."

"Punish me?" I squeak.

"Yes," is all he says.

His hands slide down my thighs to my knees, then sensuously to my calves, and finally to my ankles, where he begins to untie my shoes. I shiver, at the same time I'm calmed by his gentle touch. Even though he just talked about punishing me.

But I wasn't lying earlier when I said something in me seemed to recognize him. He says he doesn't know me, so is this what people mean when they talk about trusting their *gut*? My gut says he's a safe person. It's why I got in the car. But maybe it was this kind of thinking that got me in an alley with a pipe or whatever to the head in the first place.

"You never answered me," I whisper. "About whether you're going to hurt me or not."

His hands massage my foot and back up to my calf. "Did Moira explain about a safe word?"

"Yes," I hurry to say. "Red. My safe word is red. I saw a woman use it at the club when we visited."

"Good," he murmurs, low and reassuring. "If anything gets to be too much for you, all you have to say is your safe word and I'll stop touching you."

I breathe out in relief, then double check, "No matter what?"

"No matter what."

My breath finishes expelling from my lungs. Safe word. *Safe*. Okay. See, my gut was right.

"In the meantime, I want to play with you. Do you want to play? That's what you came here for, isn't it?"

Well, that's an odd way to word it. I came here to get paid, but I suppose *play* is a nice way to put the act of what it takes to get paid. Quinn used that term upstairs, too, didn't she? Play. That's all this is. Adult play.

And his massaging touch on my calves certainly does feel nice. Really nice, actually. I bend instinctually toward his touch.

It doesn't hurt that he was the handsomest man in the room upstairs. My whole body reacted to him when he came up to me on stage. His first touch on my wrist was unlike anything I've felt in the two months since I first woke up. A zinging chemical awareness of him rushed through my body. I thought it was just a spike of adrenaline from the auction ending.

But after the nerves of the car ride, when I was worried

about his eyes getting a little dark and scary, it's back in full force now that he's touching me again.

And really, it only makes sense that rich guys might be a little intense. He did just pay fifty *million dollars* for a night with me. Holy shit. What's fifty million dollars minus fifteen percent for the club's broker's fee?

I blink beneath the mask. Still too many millions of dollars for me to count, and it'll be all mine after tonight. I've done it. Surely that will be enough money to find out who I am. I frown, thinking back to the moment when it seemed like the stranger might have recognized me. He said he didn't. Was that why he paid so much for me, though? Because I remind him of someone?

He massages back up my legs towards my thighs and I start to have trouble trying to think about why I'm doing all this. All I know is, now that this handsome man is touching me, for once I'm not afraid of the dark.

I inhale sharply as his hands slide up my legs. My insides clench in surprised pleasure. Whatever I imagined whenever I tried to think about what the actual sex might be like... I didn't think— I didn't really think about *enjoying* it.

But the more his strong, expert hands work my legs, thumbs massaging up my inner thighs towards the apex of my—

A stunned, high-pitched little gasp comes out of my throat.

And then his deep voice is hot beside my ear. "Do you

like my hands on you?" He smells so good—some manly scent I can't describe except for how it makes me clench again.

I nod. When I do, my cheek rasps against the stubble on his face. He immediately pulls away.

"Climb on your knees to be fucked doggy style," he says, his voice suddenly harsh.

I blink underneath the mask, startled. Is that it? Are we going to do it now? I'm not sure I know what... doggy style is, but I can guess from the "climb on your knees" part.

Feeling out the mattress with my hands, I turn over and get on my hands and knees.

"Good girl." He spanks my ass, and I let out a startled, "Oof!"

"Did you like that?"

I blink beneath the mask and answer honestly. "I don't know."

"Well, think about it this time."

He spanks me again. I'm just as startled, both by the spanking, and how my ass jiggles in the aftermath. He doesn't stop there, though. His hand slips between my legs and he touches me. On my intimate place.

Red is on the tip of my tongue. But I don't say it. It's enough to know I can.

Instead, I bite my bottom lip and squeeze my eyes shut to think about his question. How does it feel? Not, how do I *think* it should feel? But, how do I *actually* feel, in my body, in this moment?

And I realize...

"Good," I whisper, surprised. "It feels good." Not just because it *feels good*, feels good, either. All my limbs just sort of... relax into his strong, massaging hands. I relax in a way I haven't for the last two months. I've been so stressed for so long now.

After waking up in the hospital, it's been one non-stop sprint to get my life back in order, or rather, to create a life. The paperwork alone almost swallowed me whole. Do you know how hard it is to get a temporary social security card? It's all *exhausting*, and frankly, I expected this to be just as draining. Just another task to check off my list.

But suddenly, like a gift, this stranger has taken the reins, and it feels like for once, I don't have to be responsible for driving.

"How does *this* feel?" he asks as I relax further into him. The fingers that massaged my calves so well now move to explore my... my down-there place.

I gasp out a pleasured noise as his middle finger begins teasing at some spot at the top of my sex. His fingertip swirls gently, teasing it.

I just moan a little in response.

He pulls his finger away.

"Good," I burst out, wanting his finger back. "It feels good."

"That's right. You speak when spoken to or Sir will take the good feelings away."

Sir? *Okay, that's taking it a little far, buddy,* I think, blinking a little out of the pleasured haze he's dropping me into. But then his finger is back and I'm biting my bottom lip again.

"You're getting slick for me already," he rasps. "What a dirty little slut to get so wet for a stranger you've just met. You must really want to get fucked. Oh, I feel your little pussy lips clench at that. You like when I talk dirty."

Fuck, he's right. I really, really like it when he talks dirty.

He runs his finger down the line between the lips of my sex.

I inhale in shock. I haven't had the courage to explore there much beyond a few furtive touches, but he touches me so confidently and commandingly. Duh. He's going to do a lot more before the night is through.

Because suddenly I know this isn't going to just be a ten-minute poke, thrust, and done sort of session.

And instead of intimidating, it feels freeing. I didn't know how to touch myself the couple times I even dared try. But he knows exactly what to do.

My body is more than ready to respond, too. Maybe this is a clue. Maybe this is something else I'm good at—something the *me* from *before* knew how to do, like cussing and chess-playing. Moira and I always knew I might not be a for-real virgin, but that's okay, right? This guy doesn't seem bothered so far by what he's getting.

"What are you thinking about?" he asks.

Well shit. I don't want *him* to know he just paid fifty *million* dollars for a *maybe*-virgin.

"Just that it's a lot," I sputter. "A lot of feelings." There. That's the truth.

"That's so sweet," he says. "I should've tried a virgin before."

Is he making fun of me? I can't tell. I'm distracted by him gently tugging my crotchless silk panties down my thighs. I lift my knees one at a time and he pulls them off the end of my feet.

As soon as he's done, he spanks me again. Harder this time. So hard that shocked tears form in my eyes. But I don't hate it. I think I might even want him to do it again. Suddenly this feels like an opportunity for exploration with someone who obviously knows what he's doing. And who I just happen to be ravenously attracted to.

Before I can say anything, though, his hand is there at my sex again.

"Do you use toys to make yourself cum?"

"I- I- I don't know," I stutter, my back arching as shocking new feelings roll through my body. "I don't know anything about myself before two months ago."

"Ahh," he murmurs. "Of course. So you don't know if this is the first finger you've ever had inside you?" he asks, the only warning before one of his thick digits slips through my juices between my pussy lips and—

I gasp and clench around him. He's not very far in and he stretches all around in my wetness.

"That's right," I whisper, squirming my hips. I feel every contour of his finger. It's only a finger but I can't imagine anything larger fitting.

"So tight," he hisses.

"The doctor said—"

"I know what the doctor said," he bites out. "I just didn't believe it."

His finger twirls around and he pushes in slightly further until I make a little noise. I'm not sure if I want him to pull it out or push it further in.

But he pulls out, then keeps massaging the outer lips of my now achingly sensitive pussy. I feel pulsing in the bud at the top—the one spot he completely ignores.

"Well maybe you're a virgin there because you just like men fucking you in the ass instead of your cunt."

I'm shocked again by the vulgarity of his words… and yet also, turned on by them.

His finger slick with my juices starts to probe my anus. "Some good Christian girls do that. Are you a good little Christian girl?"

"I don't know." I gape at the feeling of him back there, breathing really hard now as my heart pumps with fresh adrenaline.

Fuck. I'm so turned on. I barely knew what to do with the pressure of him at my front hole, but the feel of him back there, which seems somehow ten times more forbidden... Is he intentionally trying to keep me off-kilter? Or does he just want to touch me everywhere all at once, like a new toy he can't wait to get his hands on? Either way, my body rolls with it, hips wriggling at his teasing touches.

Because with his every touch, I'm discovering I *do* like this. I like this very, *very* much. I don't know if this is something the me from before used to do. But the me *now* sure as hell likes it. I feel wild and free to throw myself off each new cliff he brings me too, some internal gut feeling certain that he'll catch me.

"Is that—" I manage, still struggling for breath, "—something you like?"

"All men like that. The only thing tighter than virgin cunt is ass. Or a throat swallowing us deep. Maybe you like to swallow cock and that's why you're still a virgin."

My throat bobs with a swallow even as I shake my head. "I don't think so."

"About the swallowing or taking it in the ass?"

His slick finger rubs in the circle of my anus, and I can't help pushing back curiously against him.

"Swallowing," I answer, mouth suddenly feeling dry even as I say it. Because now I'm picturing it. With him, standing commandingly over me, one hand on his cock, one thumb on my bottom lip with him ready to feed it to me. Even the image has me gasping. So hot. Holy shit. So hot.

"What are you thinking about?" he demands again.

"I- I- I don't know. You. How some of these things you're talking about might feel."

"You'll learn soon," he growls.

"Now?" I squeak.

"No, not right now."

But then I feel something pressing back at my back hole. His finger? It doesn't feel like his finger. It's bigger. Is that... *him*? His thing?

"What's that?" I ask, even as I strain to stay still against the pressure of whatever's pushing for entrance. Of fuck, he's going to start... there? Where he said good Christian girls don't take it? He holds me still with his hand on my hip.

"Steady," he says. "Relax. Let it in."

Oh my god. Is he about to fuck me? In the ass?

My cunt—because now that he's called it that, it's all I ever want to call it—clenches. I'm so, so fucking turned on at the idea. It seems so *wrong* in the rightest, most twisted sexy way. My hips wiggle in his grip, wanting more. A little whine escapes my lips.

So I'm discovering I'm twisted. All right. Maybe I shoulda guessed.

"A plug," he says. "That's what I've got back here. Now relax and let me in. What? Is your clit missing my attention?"

His hand slips around my hip while the other continues to put pressure on the plug at my puckered ass. His arm holds me in place while his fingertip massages my swelling clit. My body feels like his instrument. And his expert hands somehow know it better than I do.

I blink below the blindfold as his finger wakens little jolts of unexpected pleasure. My tummy spasms, then my legs.

My arm weakens and I face plant into the bed. He continues to ruthlessly massage my center. The shaking doesn't stop and a pleasurable cramp bites through my stomach.

"What's your name?" I whisper with the last of the remaining breath in my lungs, still shaking.

"Sir," he growls.

"Your real name," I beg as the pleasure cramp creeps up my belly and then, in one sharp spike, bursts outwards through my body.

Sir doesn't miss the opportunity, popping the plug up into my anus. It only amps up the sensual experience twice as high. I clench around it and fall thrashing like a fish on the mattress.

Sir's hand follows me, flipping me on my back and throwing both of my legs open wide.

The plug he lodged in my ass is still there. I want to rip my blindfold off to see the gorgeous, glorious pleasure god above me. But as if he senses it, he grasps both my wrists and holds them pinned at my hips.

And then I feel the weight of him between my spread thighs. Just like in my dreams.

But unlike my dream, nothing fat and heavy slides into me.

Instead, it's just his bare shoulders, and his— his—

I scream and throw my head back at the sweetest pleasure I never could have imagined.

I can't even understand what's happening at first or how he's doing what he's doing. And then, oh god, I realize.

It's his mouth.

He's kissing me there. He's suckling on me and it's— How is it so good? How could anything on earth feel this *good*?

Bright light bursts behind my eyes and I lift my hips shamelessly up against his voracious mouth. He lets go of my wrists to squeeze my ass and pull me into him like he can't get enough. Like he's been starving for me for decades and I'm manna from heaven.

Once, twice, the pleasure amps up so high, barely dips, and then somehow impossibly, swings even higher though I'd swear there was no higher to go.

I screech out a scream so high-pitched, it barely has sound, as he clutches and suckles and bites me into yet a higher climax still.

Every muscle in my stomach and ass and sex clench as he takes me there, my Sir and me. We ride the edge, oh the sweetest fucking edge—

I need it, I need the release so bad—

When he bites lightly down with his teeth at the very

end, I howl and fuck his face, clenching so hard on what he shoved in my ass—

I wasn't reborn that night I woke up in the hospital.

It's now.

Here.

This is the moment I'm made new.

This is the start of everything.

I whine, curled over, mewling and shaking in the sheets when he pulls his mouth away from me.

I'm immediately groping for him, but he's out of reach. It's not that I want or could even handle more.

I just want *him*. I can't stand losing contact with him yet. He tugs on the plug in my ass playfully several times before pulling it all the way out. I want to turn and grab for him again but manage to stop myself and just enjoy the strange sensation before the plug pops free.

He's the one who spent fifty million. I'm not supposed to be the greedy one here. And this is just one night, I try to remind myself as the haze of the orgasms clear.

Just one wild, kinky, amazing night, and then you'll never see him again.

I swallow hard.

Which is when I blink in confusion. Because Sir's gentle hands are at my neck, and then I feel something else, like he's fitting some sort of thick leather necklace on me.

"What are you—" But before I can finish the sentence, I hear the noise of a little lock clicking in place.

Then he slips my blindfold off and I look around, blinking in confusion.

At first, I just see his satisfied smile, and it makes me glow a little. Fuck, he's so handsome. I want nothing more than to lean in to kiss him, even if it means tasting myself on his lips. I get a jolt of heat even at the thought and it makes me want to kiss him even more.

But that's all in the flash of a moment before my lust-haze clears long enough to recognize that there's a heavy chain attached to the—my hands lift and tug at the—the *collar* around my neck!

What the—?

Scanning, my eyes quickly take in the rest of the room. Whips of various shapes and sizes hang on the black walls. All sorts of other abnormal furniture with handcuffs attached are situated around the room. Including the bed we've been frolicking on. Jesus, there's a fucking cage in the corner.

"What the fuck is this?" I scramble away from the sexy, shirtless man, who I can now see is covered in terrifying tattoos. The chain travels with me. It's attached to an O-ring on the ceiling. My body is confused by the fear chasing the adrenaline of so many orgasms.

"Your new home," he says with a smile so cold it makes my blood freeze. "Until I take your virginity, by contract, you belong to me."

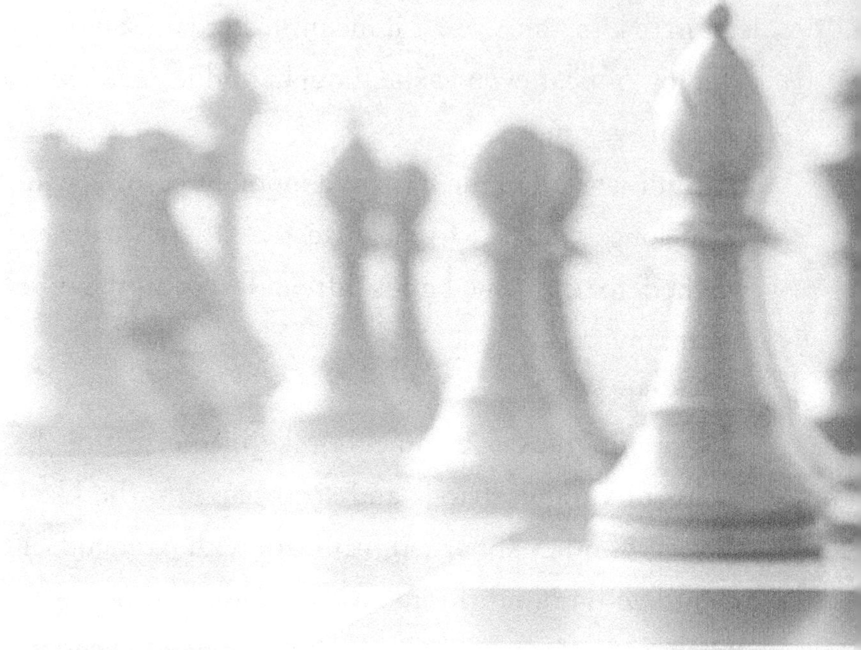

SEVEN

DOMHNALL

"WHAT?" Madison shouts, shaking her head. "No. No, that's not a thing. Red! *Red!* I want out. I don't care about the money. This isn't fair!"

I tilt my head at her. "Isn't it, though? You agreed to this game. You came into my territory. You approached *my* sister." I take a step towards her, and she steps back, the chain attached to her collar rattling prettily.

"Your sister?" she gasps. "Moira's your sister? Why do you have an accent and she doesn't?"

I stare at her coldly. She's such a good little actress. "Well you ensured we'd scurry out of Ireland while she was still a lass and I was seventeen. So cute, the amnesia shtick." My own brogue gets thicker the more I talk to her. It happens like that sometimes when I think of times in the old country.

Her eyes narrow. "You *do* know me." She takes a step forward before stopping in her tracks. "Who am I?"

I laugh and shake my head. "So many petty little games."

"I don't know what you're talking about!" she shouts, then grabs at her collar and makes a run for the open door. I don't move to stop her. The collar does that for me. It's quite thick. She's holding onto it, so it doesn't yank her neck too hard when the chain catches and jerks her to a stop just before she reaches the threshold.

"You're quite trapped, my dear. I'm not sure what you meant by coming here like this, but you're mine now. And besides, it's not my job to be fair. It's my job to break you."

She turns and looks back at me with wide, freaked-out eyes. "Who *are* you?"

I smile as dark power I've never fully unleashed, never once in my whole life, floods every cell of my being. I've dominated subs before, but even in the club where I get to be my truest self, I still have to be careful. But now all restraints are off. It's never once been like this. I'm purely my feral self. My prey stands before me, trembling, with nowhere to run.

And it's *her*. Beautiful Mads, with her bright, shining American smile. Gorgeous Mads, whose laughing eyes have haunted me for almost ten fucking years.

I'm afraid there's not going to be anything sane about this. Caleb would not approve. And I don't fucking care.

"You've signed your life away to me, Mads. And it's only what you deserve. You stole everything from me the last time we met."

I walk up until I'm face to face with her. She's shaking with fear, and I should be disturbed with how hard it makes me. I'm not, though. I only get stiffer.

"Now it's your turn to suffer, lovely Mads."

She's shaking and clutching her leather collar, eyes wide. "You keep calling me that. Like you know me. Do you? Tell me the truth!"

I shake my head in disgust. "It's always games with you."

"I'm not playing games! Moira can show you my brain scans. They're at her apartment. I have amnesia from head trauma to my temporal lobe." She taps the side of her head. "You can't fake that."

I laugh without pity. "Sure you can. Documents are the easiest thing in the world to fake. The woman I knew would have seen it as a great way to worm her way back into my life and wrap me around her little finger again."

Her gaze wanders past me to the wall. "I guess I'm not her after all. I don't think amnesia gives you a complete personality change."

She appears so innocent. She makes for such believable prey, it's almost easy to forget she's the predator here. Almost.

I lean down and whisper in her ear, "You are her."

She jerks backwards at the intimacy of my warm breath against her skin.

"How would you know?" she asks. "Maybe I just look like this woman you used to know."

I bite back another incredulous laugh. "There's a constellation of freckles on your inner thighs shaped like Cassiopeia. I licked them earlier. You're Madison."

She frowns, her lips making the shape of the name. *Madison.* Then she shakes her head as if it doesn't ring any bells.

But finally, she looks down at her inner thigh. "Cassiopeia is the constellation shaped like a *W*," she whispers as if repeating a school lesson.

"I guess your amnesia's clearing up."

"No, it's not like—" She stops and sucks in a long breath of air. "I never know what I'll remember or not remember. I've no clue how or why it works the way it does."

She's still staring at the group of freckles on her thigh shaped like the Cassiopeia constellation. "You could've just seen that now and be lying to me that you knew it from before." She looks up at me. "*I* didn't even know that was there."

Fuck, she's diabolical. If I didn't know her for who she truly is, I might even fall for her little act. That was always the trouble with her. She's so convincing that despite her father's pure evil, I told myself she was an innocent. But that was the biggest lie of all.

I get right in her face. "I'm not the liar here."

"No, you just lock people up in dungeons! I don't know

why I'm listening to anything you have to say. You're taking advantage of someone with amnesia! Pretending you know me is so twisted and fucked up! You're a sadistic cunt and this is ridiculous!" She grabs the chain of her collar and thrusts it towards me. "Let me out of this fucking thing!"

I laugh in her face. "Aww, poor Mads. You never did like facing the consequences of your actions."

"My name is *Brooke*!"

"All right, Brooke. To be honest, Madison might have been a made-up name, too. I never knew anything about you until it was too late. You're a shape-shifter and I know better than to trust any word you say."

Her mouth drops open and she sputters.

"Don't bother. Like you said. I'm a sadistic cunt. That part's true enough. Then again, I'm only what you and your father molded me into." I grin at her, and that dark *thing* inside me stretches in excited preparation. *Pain.* We'll get to see her squirming in pain soon. So soon now. She'll get what's coming to her. My grin gets wider and I hold out my hands to gesture to the room full of floggers, canes, and whips. "Welcome to your karma."

That's when the doorbell rings and she starts to scream.

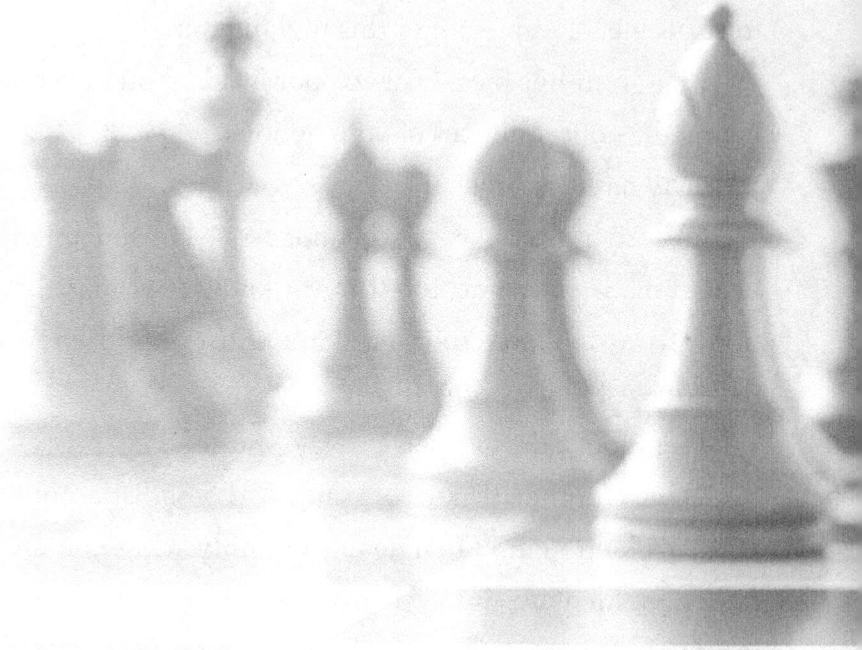

EIGHT

DOMHNALL

"HELP ME!" she screams at the top of her lungs.

She runs towards the elevator as far as her chain will allow and continues wailing, "Help! Help! I'm kidnapped! Help! Fire! *Fire!!!*"

I turn to head for the door. She can scream as loud as she wants. I hope it gives her hope. The sadist in me curls in pleasure at all the ways I'll crush her. Mind. Body. *Soul.*

"When I get back, our training can begin." I feel giddy and alive with anticipation as I reach for my white, pressed shirt and the suit-coat I hung on a hook near the door.

Her screaming abates for a moment at my words, only to pick right back up again as I head for the elevator. They get especially piercing when the elevator doors open, as if she thinks the sound will carry better that way.

It's adorable.

I give her a little finger wave and a wink as the doors close, then breathe in deeply as the elevator starts to ascend. A glance at my phone showed me who's at the door, and it's nothing but a small nuisance.

All that matters is that I finally have her in my grasp.

Madison Harper.

I never stopped looking for her. But she and her father were good at covering their tracks, always on the move. Her father taught me so much of the foundations of what I know about hacking and security systems, after all. He was so good at searching out weaknesses and then exploiting them. Both with people and technology.

I smooth down my coat jacket as I head towards the door, pausing to check my face and hair in a mirror. I pull a little travel wipe from my inner coat pocket and unpackage it, swiping back and forth across the stubble of my mouth and beard.

There. It's ungentlemanly to answer the door with the gleam of the woman you've just eaten out all over your face.

I have a facade to maintain, after all.

When I open the door, it's to an angry-looking, cross-armed Quinn.

She looks down the hallway behind me. "Where is she?"

"She's fine." I block her path with a hand when she tries to storm past me.

"That's not what I asked."

My jaw locks. "Is this going to be a problem?"

"Only if you don't produce the girl. Moira and I gave her assurances. I don't go back on my word."

"You haven't. The contract specified the money was in exchange for her virginity. There was no time condition. Now if you would please get the fuck off my property, Quinnlynn."

Quinn adopts her domme stance that tells me to back the fuck up and rethink my last statement. But I'm the one man in this city who's not intimidated by her little act.

I step into her face, forcing her to take a step back, which I can tell pisses her the fuck off. But I won't be intimidated in my own house, even by someone I respect as much as Quinn.

"Well, Domhnall Bryce Callaghan," she spits, getting right in my face. Toe to toe with me. "I promised her she'd be safe, so you better be able to produce her within the next ten minutes or I'll make a scene. And not the spanky kind you'd enjoy. I won't be made a liar, even for you."

"Oh?" I lift an eyebrow dangerously. "Even when I hold the future of your career in my hands?"

Her eyes widen and her mouth drops open, but I don't back down.

"You're not even supposed to have access to a calculator for another decade. Remember that little deal I worked out with the Texas district attorney for you? I took you on as an intern because of your talents, but there are limits if you question my authority again."

Her abilities with a keyboard are undisputable, but it got her into trouble when she'd barely turned eighteen. She was trying to hack into the Federal Marshals, and almost got in before she was caught. I recognize young talent and have a soft spot for the rebels.

But my conscience doesn't even twinge at making the threat. Sometimes when you finally jump off that last cliff to the full-on dark side, there's no looking back.

"Money can't buy everything," Quinn snaps, glaring up at me.

"You'll know better when you aren't young and poor."

"I thought you were one of the good ones," Quinn hisses. "Glad to know sooner rather than later I was fucking wrong. I *quit*. Now show me the girl."

"I'll escort you off the premises instead."

Quinn glares and plants her feet. "Touch me, and I'll break your hand," she warns, deadpan. "I'm not leaving without Brooke."

I smile down at her. "I would never dare hurt a woman. Unless she begs."

Quinn rolls her eyes. "Then hand her over."

"No. But if you won't leave without her, feel free to enjoy sleeping on my lawn," I gesture. "I'm generous. You can even make your way around the property to sleep on a pool chair."

"I'll call the cops," Quinn threatens.

"And tell them what? That I've kidnapped someone from Caleb's virginity auction?"

Her mouth drops open. "You'd do that to Caleb?"

I just shrug. She doesn't need to know if I would or wouldn't. Then I lean in, whispering so just she can hear, "No offense, but who do you think they'll believe? You spent two years in maximum security lock-up and only got out on early release because I sponsored you."

"So now you think you own me?" Quinn furiously bumps me with her corseted chest. "You think you can just get away with anything? Fuck you, Domhnall. You aren't a god, and unless you give me a good goddamned reason, I will raise hell in every way I can until you free that woman, I don't care if it ends me back up in prison."

"You don't want to go to war with me, Quinnlynn," I warn. "You will lose, and it will be painful for you."

She pulls out her phone from her boot and pushes a few buttons. "You're a smug bastard. You forget. I know your weaknesses."

Is she really calling the police? I'm not bluffing. Nothing will make me give Madison up.

"Hey, what's up?" comes my sister's perky voice over the phone that Quinn put on speaker. She's breathing hard like she just went for a jog. In the background, I hear a familiar rhythmic *thwack, thwack, thwack, thwack*.

"Jesus, Moira," I cover my face with my hand even

though I can only hear her, not see her. "Are you fucking somebody right now? How many times do I have to tell you not to answer the phone while you're fucking somebody!"

"Domhnall, hi!" she says, completely unphased as the *thwacking* continues. "So Quinn found you. Good! We were worried about Brooke when you disappeared with her all the sudden. We just wanted to check in with her after the devirginizing. How'd it go?"

Quinn tilts her head at me, glare still in full force as she holds out the phone in my direction. Power move, using my sister against me.

"Everything's fine here. *Isn't it*, Quinn?"

She stabs the mute button. "You'll let me see her?"

"I'll let you in and we'll have a chat," I amend, teeth gritted as I sift through various plans in my head.

She hits unmute. "Everything's great. Chat later, babe. Bye."

"Oh good," Moira says, her voice a little higher pitched, "because I'm about to co—"

I hit the red *end call* button on my sister who's got no boundaries.

Then I step back and gesture for Quinn to step inside.

"Start explaining," she demands.

We sit in my den and jaw clenched, I do. I talk. I pace. Then I talk some more.

I explain who Madison was to me. And her father. It's

difficult for some of it to make it past my lips. I've kept all of it under lock and key inside me for so long.

Quinn sits stone-faced through my whole story. She only lets out an explosive breath at the end. "Well fuck. And you're sure she's the same woman?"

"Positive."

"But she's lost her memory."

I tilt my head at Quinn, as if to say, *seriously?*

"A woman who fucked me over half a world away just coincidentally ends up at a hospital that sends her to the shelter where my sister works? Come on. I don't think so. You don't know this family. But I do. They're sociopaths. Convincing sociopaths. They draw you in. Weren't you listening? She's the bait, and she's so, so good at what she does. She was a genius at it all those years ago and I can only imagine how she's perfected her skills over the last decade. She's here because she wants something."

"What if it's just her dad? Did you consider that? Maybe he brought her here."

"He's dead," I spit. "The devil took him back to hell two years ago. I stood on his grave and took a good piss."

I never stopped looking for them. Two years ago I thought I'd finally found them when he popped on one of my personally designed internet-crawl systems. I knew his dark web signatures intimately—it was one of the reasons my anti-spyware software became so successful so quickly. I had intimate, cutting-edge knowledge of exactly how criminals exploited loopholes in systems.

Hunting him was one of the reasons I began building it in the first place. But I'd find him only for them to have recently skipped town. It was how I found his other victims. Always victims in his wake, usually with my M.O.

He finally changed things up and went off the map, until two years ago when he popped up again.

I thought I finally had him.

Turned out I only had his headless corpse. It washed up on a Bulgarian bank of the Danube. I felt some satisfaction imagining that all his evil shite finally caught up with him in the end and someone took an ax to the evil bastard. He was a John Doe, but I knew it was him by the tattoo of the angel Gabriel on his chest. I'd never mistake that fucking tattoo.

He was buried in a pauper's grave outside of Budapest. Too nice an end for such a vicious motherfucker, but still, one chapter closed.

The other stayed elusively open until she strutted onto that stage tonight.

"She's playing games again. I'm just better equipped this time. And I'm not letting her out of my sight."

I've been leaning against the wall, but I push my shoulders back and stand up tall, deciding on a plan to buy me some time.

Quinn's an unusual mind and one of my best project leads. I'd hate to lose her. Time to pretend to be affable-guy.

"How about this? One week from now, I'll present Brooke at the club. Then you can see her again, all nice and whole. But till then, she's *mine*."

Satisfaction growls like a yawning monster inside me. That'll give me seven days. Seven whole days to bend Mads to my will, get my answers...

Seven days to break her.

The monster grins, sharpening its teeth with a file. It's what I've always wanted. To break her the way they broke me. I didn't get my justice with her father, but I can take it out all I want on her.

"Shit." Quinn shakes her head, then stands up from the chair she sank into halfway through my tale. "This is fucked up, Domhn."

"Yeah? So what's new?"

She's quiet a long moment, staring hard at the floor like she's trying to make her mind up about something.

"At least I get you better now," she finally says, looking back up at me. "Everybody knows why I am the way I am, but you were always a mystery. Some vague story about a murky past back in the home country."

My jaw hardens. "I told you this in confidence. It better not become the latest gossip around the club."

"Your secrets are safe with me, boss. See you at work on Monday."

She walks towards the door before pausing to look back at me. "But I'm holding you to your promise. One week. Brooke better look healthy, well-fed, and happy at the end of those seven days, or I'll punish you. I have a dungeon, too. I can make you hurt, pretty Domhn."

I don't doubt she could. I've seen the ways she makes men three times her size weep like babies.

"She'll be fine."

Quinn just narrows her eyes at me before sweeping out of the room.

Seven days to break my little pet so that when I present her at the club in public, she'll bow at my feet, beg me to let her obey, and follow me back home again like a faithful little dog.

Because I'm never letting Madison go.

NINE

BROOKE

I SIT on the edge of the bed, waiting in the dim dungeon room with my eyes closed. The lights are motion activated, so when I still, they go dark. I wave my hand every time to make the lights come back on. God, I hate the dark.

I spent the first hour looking at every terrifying whip and implement hanging from the wall up close in detail but then decided it might be best to close my eyes and meditate.

They taught us how to do it at the women's shelter and said it could help when things felt too chaotic or scary. Picture a little dock leading out to a still lake on a perfectly tranquil morning. It only marginally helps calm my racing heart. I'm drawn to water. The little picture of a small babbling river over rocks was how I chose my new name—*Brooke*. Thinking of water starts to calm me down.

But then I shift and the chain attached to my freaking *collar* rattles, reminding me that I'm not at some peaceful lakeside.

I'm here, chained like a dog in a sex dungeon.

My eyes spring open when I hear the ping of the elevator. Oh shit, he's back.

"Evenin', sweetheart," he calls in that thick Irish drawl of his. It sends a shiver down my back. I'm only slightly disturbed at myself that I can't tell if it's a shiver of anticipation or fear. Maybe something in between.

I've been waiting for him to return and at the same time been anxious about it. I screamed until my throat was raw. Whoever was at the door either didn't hear me or was just as twisted as Sir and didn't care.

"What are you going to do with me?"

He smiles at me in an eerie way as he runs a hand over my hair. "I'm going to treat you as I would any beloved pet. I'll feed and water you and take you for walks. And I'll train you."

"Train me?" I yank away from his touch on my head. He mentioned that before he left, and it doesn't sound any less ominous now.

His smile grows wider. "Oh yes, pet. We'll have some lovely training sessions. At our essence, we're all really just animals. Your father taught me that. So now you get to be the good doggy, get on all fours, and I'll take you on a walk."

My father? It's not the first time he's mentioned my father. Does he *really* know me? "If you actually know me, tell me something else. What's my father like?"

He leans in, smile gone. I haven't felt really scared in the way I feel like I should, until right in this moment.

There's an unhinged look in his eyes as he gets right in my face. "Your father loved inflicting pain more than anyone I've ever met, and I've met a lot of sadistic motherfuckers. He made an art of pain. It was his one true love."

I inhale in shock, pulling back from him.

"Now get on the floor, dog."

My limbs are already moving before I've consciously decided to do what he's asking. Is it because I'm afraid of him? Of what he'll do if I don't obey?

Or because what I'm really afraid of is that he's telling the truth?

All I've wanted since I woke up is to know who I am.

What if this awful dungeon is where I can find the answers I'm searching for? I knew they might not be pretty. I knew there was a reason I'm afraid of the dark. Is it because my father is the man he's describing? What the fuck *was* my life?

"Good girl," he breathes out, laying a hand gently but with light pressure on my head. Petting me. This time I don't yank away.

The carpet is soft underneath my hands and knees, but I'm shaking. I might have been through a lot in the past two months, but so far, I've mostly clung to my dignity.

"I own you now, pet. And now I'm going to take you for a walk."

He removes my collar from the ceiling chain and attaches it to a leash. I breathe out hard. So much for the dignity.

"That's a good dog," he praises with such warmth in his voice as he pets my hair, it creates conflicting feelings in my chest. Of course it's condescending and degrading to be called a dog. But also... um... uh... there's also this stupid warmth that floods my chest at his words. I'm so confused by it, I don't know what to do except crawl forwards when he urges me to.

"That's my good pet," he continues to praise. "What a good, good girl. Such a good girl."

The praise floods me with bizarre endorphins. It's absolutely ridiculous. I'm instantly furious at myself.

Is this just a normal captive's reaction to the situation? Knowing I'm safest when I just go along with what he asks of me?

Which still feels wrong in all kinds of ways. I should be fighting or scheming for ways to figure out the keypad code. Yeah, I figured that one out when I watched him more closely as he went back up the elevator last time. No key. Key*pad*. If I follow his lead, can I get close enough to watch him when he pushes the numbers?

"That's right, good girl," he praises. "Here we are. Go potty and you'll get a treat."

My mouth drops open. *Potty?* Is he fucking serious?

I look up to where he's brought me.

It's not a toilet, at least not in the traditional way. But immediately I recognize it as the kind of toilet they sometimes have in Eastern Europe—just a porcelain hole in the floor. Meant for squatting. It's another clue, at least. I must've traveled in Europe to know that.

But he's still got me on a fucking leash and he's taking me on a walk to go fucking *potty*.

At the same time, because I know how to use the hole from some memory I can't directly access, I squat appropriately and lift my flimsy nightie. My underwear are still gone from wherever Domhnall tossed them earlier in the dungeon bedroom. I can't say it's inhumane because people all across the world use toilets like this, and the porcelain appears immaculately clean.

The part where Domhnall stands there and watches, however...

"Could you please turn your back?" I ask hotly, feeling my cheeks go red.

Domhnall just lifts one eyebrow, but he does do a half-turn so he's faced away.

I relieve my bladder with a rush of relief. And there's toilet paper attached to the wall, thank god.

After I'm finished, Domhnall squats down and rubs sanitizer on my hands with his. It feels oddly intimate, but then, what about this strange situation doesn't? It's wrong that the mixed-up feelings from earlier tonight are getting all scrambled with now trying to see the gorgeous man in front of me as dangerous. My body's still attracted to him even when I know I should be trying to scratch his eyes out every chance I get. Not that it would help me get the elevator code.

Do I feel this sense of connection between us because he's right and I *do* actually know him? Or once, *did* I?

"That's my good girl," he whispers. "Now for your treat. Come, pet."

"I'm thirsty."

"How remiss of me not to show you your watering bowl. I thought you might've found it on your own by now. It's underneath the foot of your bed."

A watering bowl. Of course. I roll my eyes. I swear, if this man considers his dick a doggy treat, I don't care what answers he might have about my identity—I'll remind him just how sharp my incisors can be.

He leads me back into the dungeon room and reattaches my collar to the ceiling chain, then points out the watering bowl. Shaking my head at the ridiculousness of it, I reach out with my hands to scoop up some water and bring it to my lips.

But before I can drink any of the water, Domhnall jerks at my collar. Not hard, but enough to startle me so I spill all the water down the front of my chest.

"Hey!" I spin to look at him over my shoulder.

"Not like that." His eyes are dark. "You know how you're supposed to drink it, pet."

Good god. *So* fucking ridiculous. But I'm thirsty and the water looks clean. So I lean down and drop my chin into the water, gulping down some water like a fucking pet.

"That's a very good girl," Domhnall all but purrs low in his throat. "Are you ready for your treat?"

Oh I fucking bet. "It depends," I say, again looking up at him over my shoulder, chin dripping. "What do you consider a treat?"

"Your pleasure, my pet. Up on the bed on all fours and I'll bring you pleasure beyond your body's comprehension. You know I can." He lifts a dark eyebrow, but it's not a smirk. It's a promise.

Something deep and low in my belly clenches, knowing how well he can deliver on that promise.

But that was different. I didn't know he was a— a— a woman-kidnapping *madman* back then. Fuck him, why does he have to be so attractive? And so good at what he did to me earlier?

"Red," I spit out, knowing it won't make a difference to him.

But to my shock, he nods, face blank as he steps back. "Safe words are still safe here, except I won't let you go. And you *will* be trained. But I won't touch your body without consent."

He bends over and presses a whispering kiss right in the

air at the top of my head. "Sleep well, little pet. And know that I'm only the monster you and your father made me."

With that, he walks out of the room.

I stare after him in shock as he covers the keypad with his body before taking the elevator back up.

I'm left terribly, desolately alone. And so fucking confused.

TEN

DOMHNALL

FOR THE FIRST TIME IN... well, it's better not to examine the last time when... I feel giddy when I wake up.

Knowing my little pet awaits me downstairs.

Immediately, I reach for my phone to check the overnight footage.

I don't have to fast-forward very far before I hit the play button, my cock stiffening. She's lying in the center of the bed, collar so pretty, chain coiled beside her on the bed with her legs spread wide.

She's pleasuring herself wildly.

"Fuck me." I shoot out of bed, stiff cock banging against my thigh in my loose boxers.

I shoot towards the elevator without bothering to put a shirt on.

When I get to the dungeon, my little pet is curled up like a kitten on the bed, her lovely dark hair splayed out on the pillow.

She's so fucking beautiful it makes my chest hurt. And my cock pulse harder with even more blood. So much I'm almost light-headed. I want to put my marks on her body. I want to make her pretty, pale flesh blossom pink and then red. I want to pull out the implements they don't let me use at the club and—

"Someone sure tired themselves out last night," I say loudly as I stand over her.

She doesn't startle awake like I expect her to. Instead, she blinks, sleepy, one arm stretching out lazily.

I was wrong. She might be my pet, but she's no dog.

She's a slinky, sly little kitty, isn't she?

I smile when I think of how I had her purring last night. But then I frown, remembering that she's also a devious, scheming bitch who betrayed me so unforgivably. I should be more disturbed by the fact that she's already luring me in again in any way.

Finally, she rouses enough to remember where she is and sits up in bed sharply, chain rattling. "You," she gasps, eyes shooting to where I stand by the doorway.

"Me," I deadpan, taking a step into the room. "We've been a naughty pet, haven't we, little kitty?"

She blinks. "I don't know what you—"

"You think I'd leave you down here all alone unattended? I'm always watching." I point to the camera on the ceiling. There are others around, too, but no need for her to know that yet.

Her eyes widen slightly and then her cheeks go pink. I'm fascinated by how deep her deceptions go; she's even able to make herself have physiological reactions. Has she found some way of compartmentalizing *so* deeply that when she's doing a job that she half believes she's the character she's playing?

"I didn't know you were watching!" She draws the sheet up and over herself to cover her immodest little nightie.

I'm good enough at masking my reactions on a daily basis that I don't reveal how being near her affects me. For all the stoic face I'm presenting, I can't help the ridiculous part deep inside me that keeps shouting like an excited little kid every time I'm near her—*holy shit, it's Madison. She's here. She's really here!*

"Time to learn your lessons," I bark, furious and aroused. Apparently this is going to be my permanent state in her presence. *I'm* the one in control here. I'm taking back what they stole. "You're not allowed any pleasure except that which I give you. I offered you a treat, and you declined, then went behind my back. All your orgasms are mine to give and mine to take. Actions have consequences. I told you from the beginning."

"Red!" she says immediately, backing away from me. "Red! Red!"

I breathe out to calm myself. "Now you're just abusing your privileges. I told you last night you will be trained, one way or another. You think you're uncomfortable now, with the focused attentions of an attentive owner? I'm happy to withdraw. You forget, I know you."

She shifts uncomfortably across the bed from me. "What do you mean?"

"You're an extrovert. Nothing drives the Mads I knew crazier than being alone. You can't stand going twenty-four hours without conversation, much less human contact. Physical touch," I notch an eyebrow up at her, "is your love language, if a creature like yourself could ever be said to feel such an emotion."

Her mouth drops open to protest and I see the fury on her face. But it takes her a second to actually respond. "You're wrong! I'm not whoever this Mads person was. And if you're saying you'll leave me alone and I won't have to see your horrible face, that sounds great to me. Leave me the fuck alone! Then this whole thing might actually be bearable."

I smile at her bluff. She might be in character, but some things you can't fake.

"Grand," I bite out. "Then I'll just leave you to it. But you won't be locked up in here pleasuring yourself. You only get what I give."

I walk over to the wall and grab a particularly delightful

set of spreader cuffs—twelve inch, both ankle and wrist, with a long connecting rod in between.

"What the fuck is that?" she demands as I approach her. The cuffs themselves have a fluffy lining, so they won't hurt her.

"Red!" she says as I approach.

I grin at her. "Sorry, love. I told you, I *will* train you. That pony trick only works for so many things. I'll put these on, then I won't touch you again until you ask me."

She tries to flee back over the bed to escape me, but while I allowed it last night, today is a whole new day.

I admit, I enjoy chasing her, pinning her on the bed, and attaching the cuffs first to her wrists, then to her kicking ankles.

I'm chuckling by the time I get her last ankle buckled in.

"You fucking psycho!" she screams at me.

"What can I say?" I smile down at her beneath me, reaching up towards her neck. "You bring out the worst in me."

Her teeth come at me, biting ferociously. I narrowly avoid losing a finger but manage to get her collar freed from the ceiling chain.

"What are you doing?" she says as I pounce off the bed. She yanks against the cuffs and spreader bar as if the devil himself has hold of her, to no avail.

"Giving you what you wanted," I say graciously. "Your isolation. But I need assurances my kitty won't be treating herself while I'm away. And look, your gracious owner has freed you so you can even make your way to the bathroom and feed station all by yourself."

She tries to sit up and falls back over onto the mattress. "How? You've all but hog-tied me!"

"Aw, pet, if I'd hog-tied you, you'd know it," I purr. "I use very special knots for that. And I haven't even locked your hands behind your back. I'm a very benevolent owner. As to how you'll get to the potty and food, well, I imagine you'll get there very slowly. Then again, you'll have nothing but time to figure it out."

"You bastard!" she screams at me. "Let me go!"

I can only keep grinning at her. She truly is the most gorgeous creature. I never did get her out of her nightie, but considering how spitting mad she is, I'll let her keep whatever imaginary shields she's got left a little longer. Breaking in a pet must be a patient process, even if we are on an accelerated seven-day track.

Her long, luscious legs are bent awkwardly by the bar connecting her wrists and ankles. Fuck, seeing Mads all bound up like this is the hottest thing I've ever seen, and the club isn't short on spectacle. But nothing could ever hold a candle to her. She stole my soul too long ago.

"Remember, my pet. I'm watching. You can give in any time. I'm happy to come back and take care of a good, obedient little pet. We were making such progress before you decided to throw your little tantrum."

With that, I leave her and head upstairs again. She's not chained to the ceiling, but she also can't figure out how to move fast enough to follow me. There's an art to moving when you're double-barred like that, and it takes time to learn.

"Bye now, love. Remember, all you have to do is call and I'll come."

"Never!" rings her parting shout.

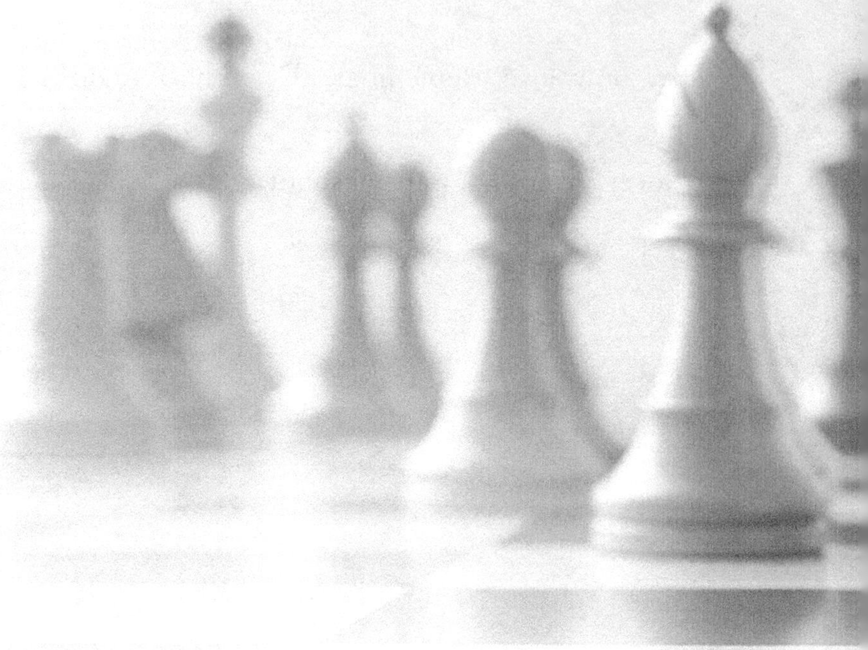

ELEVEN

DOMHNALL

SHE MAKES it all of thirty-two hours.

It's quite impressive, really. But then, Mads always was stubborn.

I work from home for the day, one monitor full of code I'm barely looking at, and the other... My other screen is full of the entertainment *du jour*.

God, she is magnificent.

She flips me off whenever she remembers to look up at the camera, which makes me chuckle. Even after all this time, I still know her so well. Mads can barely go ten minutes without needing someone to talk to. In the only way available to her, she's trying to interact with me. She needs to feel a sense of connection with someone. Even if that someone is me.

Being proved right brings a warring tug of satisfaction in my chest even as I watch her struggle to crouch-crawl towards the bathroom. It's the only way to move when you're locked up like that, and she's smart to have figured it out so fast. It took me forever. But then again, Mads always was clever. So, so very clever.

I squint at the screen and turn up the volume when she discovers the feeder, in a room off to the side by the bathroom. I smile at the blue streak she swears. She always could swear the skin off a donkey's arse.

I've got a whole arrangement set up down there for food to be dispensed into a bowl. She should be grateful—it dispenses granola.

I had to eat actual dog food when I was made to be a pet, and not the expensive shite.

She has no choice but to bend over and eat it like an animal would. Same with the water bowl beside it. The bowl by the bed was just a temporary convenience. This is the self-filling one.

Afterward she lies on the ground near the elevator. As if she thinks she might ambush me when I next come down.

But I've learned patience since I first knew Mads.

Back then I was young and impulsive and sure that if I just tried hard enough and sprinted fast enough, I'd finally outrun all the bad shite and get to the good part of living.

When you had a little sister depending on you, you were always promising 'em rainbows and unicorn shite like that. For Moira's sake, I tried to believe it longer than I should've.

Nothing gets you in trouble faster than hope.

Sitting in my office chair that costs more than my first car, I feel a fucked up, twisted satisfaction as I watch Mads's hope drain. She gives up her vigil at the elevator to waddle back to the bathroom, then goes for some more food.

I've known for a long time that something was off inside me. Bent sideways. Wrong.

Before I found the club, I just kept to myself, apart from taking care of Moira. I knew that part inside me that I never let myself look directly at was too dark to ever let out. Well, it did boil over occasionally and I'd do dangerous shite like street-racing and intentionally picking fights with bastards bigger than me. But then came *Crave, and* I found a disciplined way to take the beast out, on a very short leash, and only at the club.

Now though?

I watch Mads weep in despair around hour fourteen and it makes me so fucking hard. The mascara tracks down her cheeks are even more beautiful than I could've dreamed of.

All day I sit obsessively watching her on my screen, even when she sleeps. I'm fascinated when she wakes up screaming. Twice, she screams herself awake from little naps, as if the devil himself has just shoved his poker straight through her belly.

I lean in closer to the screen as she waves her arms to make the lights turn on. Then she curls up into a little ball. Well, as much as she can with the barred cuffs.

She knows I'm watching. Is this more performance theater, or are the nightmares real? I want to know. I'm hungry to know everything about her. I'm obsessed. I recognize it but I don't particularly care.

My sadistic monster is the real me. The center of me. He's hungry for her in a way I can't explain. I need to know everything about her. What scares her? What she sounds like when she comes. When she screams.

Some things *have* to be real, and I'll discover each true thing one at a time as I break her. I'll sift out the real from the false, and then she'll be mine completely.

We'll finally be in control, the monster and me.

I know she's lost sense of time by how often she feeds. There's no daylight down there—just the motion-activated ceiling bulbs. There's nothing but silence and her own thoughts for company.

I can see it starting to wear on her. I mean, it's pretty obvious when she starts screaming and jerking in her bonds at hour twenty. I'm glad they're lined with soft, faux fur. I wonder if the screaming feels like a good release. I know I'll play the sweet soundtrack of her screams back later when I rub one out.

She doesn't ask me to come down, and she doesn't relent;

she just screams and screams. That's my Mads, as stubborn as ever.

To double check, I press a button on my laptop connected to a speaker in the basement. "Do you yield?"

Her head immediately jerks upwards towards the ceiling, and I see fury and fire replace despair.

"No, I don't yield, you twisted kidnapping son of a motherfucking cuntbag!"

I smile and reach a finger out towards the screen to caress her image. I've missed that mouth of hers. I never thought I'd ever meet a girl with the face of an angel who could swear a Donegal lad like me under the table.

This distance between us feels good. Necessary. Will she finally crack and do away with this ridiculous amnesia farce? How much will it take to break her the way her father broke me?

I don't have a clue what to do with the warring affection and vengeance in my chest, but I suppose that's the whole point of this, isn't it? I never was good at expressing my emotions. Moira's always saying so.

But I'm happy to show Mads exactly how I feel. I'm better with actions than words, anyway.

As soon as she gives in to me and lets me start to train her flesh, oh yes, I'll show her *exactly* how I've felt all these years.

It will be so satisfying, in a way that has my fingers itching for her skin, once she finally yields.

I'll be a far more benevolent owner than they were to me. And once and for all, the control will be mine.

After more screaming, some time spent curled up in a ball—or as much of one as she can manage with her shackles—at six minutes past hour thirty-two, she finally whispers in the tiniest voice that I have to reverse and playback with the volume cranked all the way up: "I yield."

Immediately, I race to the elevator, my heart thumping. I force myself to stand there for five minutes more before hitting the button to call the elevator. I can't have her thinking I was waiting for her, after all.

Control is a tentative game of temptation and withdrawal. I've become a master at it over the years, but this is truly the greatest test of my skills yet. I'm finally faced with the only other master to have ever bested me.

TWELVE

BROOKE

I HATE HIM. My throat aches from screaming out my fury. My limbs ache from yanking against the horrible, barred contraption he's bound me in. Worse than chains, it constricts my movements so much, it's driving me insane.

I've felt nuts a few times after waking up and not being able to remember my own name, but the last week, or however long he's had me down here, has made me rethink what insanity really means. I've barely slept—who could in this fucking contraption he's got me locked in? Basic bodily functions like eating and using the bathroom are all but impossible. I mean, they're possible, but fucking barely.

But worse than all that, he was fucking *right*.

I can't stand being alone.

There's nothing but my goddamned thoughts. I'm supposed to be on this big journey to find myself, right?

But when I'm left alone with nothing *but* my own thoughts for company, I feel like I'm going to crawl out of my skin.

At first I thought he'd just shut me down here and forgotten about me. Then when his voice came over the speaker and I realized he was watching me the entire time... it felt... better.

I still wanted to stab him in the eyeballs for locking me up in this awful fucking cuff contraption, but still, someone was *there*. It wasn't just me and the darkness. And the nightmares.

The last nightmare I woke up screaming from, I finally remembered something. Just an image in the darkness. A black box. Like a trunk you put blankets in. And I was so, so afraid when I saw it. I can't remember *why*. But I was so terrified.

What am I supposed to do with these dreams and the puzzle of crumbs Domhnall's dropped, if any of it's true?

My father's someone who likes inflicting pain. Domhnall said he made an art of it. What the hell's that supposed to mean? And how does Domhnall know it? Did he meet my father at another BDSM club? How do I fit into it? He said I'm a liar, and that we made him a monster.

But if I was so horrible to him in some past life, why

didn't Moira freak out when she met me? How long ago *was* it, anyway?

My thoughts spiral with questions only Domhnall can answer. Which only makes me more furious. Because he's got me locked down here and asking him to talk would mean giving in and inviting my captor back in. Not that he'll sit down and have a civil conversation with me.

Or would he?

Maybe if I could just make him *understand*. Sometimes he almost seems... familiar. Like I swear I—

The doctors said things would start to feel familiar.

Nothing has. Except the man who's taken me captive.

Which is so beyond fucked up I don't even know what to do with it. I can't even describe what about him is familiar. Memories feel like a word on the tip of my tongue I can't quite recall. But they're so close. It's like I feel the weight of *her*—the person I was—heavier when I'm near him.

He's the key.

But everything he says... If he's delusional, his delusions have logic to them. It's just that whatever he thinks about me, he's wrong.

Because whoever I am, I know I'm not bad.

I mean... I'd know, wouldn't I, if I was some really bad, evil person at my core? A memory can't change the essence of who a person is, can it?

It can't change my— My *soul*.

I have to still be who I was if I believe that so strongly,

right? You can't have beliefs if you aren't, like, someone with a soul to even *have* those beliefs. I know right and wrong, and I'm a person who does the right thing.

But if that's true, why does Domhnall have me down in this dungeon? Something happened. Something bad.

Or he's just a liar and a madman who likes to kidnap women down to his dungeon so he can do... things to them.

It's around this point in the spiral of thoughts that I'd usually start screaming again. Because when I'm alone, my thoughts torture me instead of him. I always think I'm getting somewhere only to arrive back at the beginning. At another dead end.

My mind is a maze, and feeling *her*—the memory of who I might have been— haunting like a ghost whispering further and further out of reach the longer I go without seeing Domhnall... None of it is getting me anywhere.

At least when he's here, I occasionally get more pieces to the puzzle. And the tickle of her at the edge of my consciousness gives me hope that one day, I'll get to look her in the face and know once and for all:

Who *am* I?

Good or evil? Regardless of whatever story Domhnall has to tell, once I remember, then I'll know the truth. I just need the truth. I have to know. I have to know who I am.

That's why I eventually give in. Or so I tell myself.

It has nothing to do with the pull of the ghost inside me

towards his every touch. His every glance. His every breath of attention towards me every moment he's in the room.

Nothing at all.

Even now that I've given in to him, it feels like he takes an hour for the damnable ping of the elevator that signals his arrival.

When he comes into the room, I glare daggers at him.

He only smiles, obviously amused by my fury. I'm back to wanting to tear his eyeballs out. The anger inside me is suddenly so big, even though I thought I'd screamed every possible scream out, I want to scream in his face for leaving me like that. Even though I wanted him to go. None of it makes any sense, and that only makes me more furious, especially because I can't deny the relief and happiness at seeing him again. Not that I'll let him fucking see that.

"You wanted my attention," he says. "You have it. Do you yield or should I turn around and go back upstairs?"

"Let me out of these fucking cuffs. You're a goddamned fucking bastard to leave me like this for days on end."

He chuckles. "I thought we've already established that I'm a sadist. But it's only been thirty-two hours, my love."

I gape in astonishment. He's got to be lying. It has to have at least been four days, if not a week.

"I'll unlock you now, and we'll begin your training."

Rage lights again, burning all along my skin. Answers. I just need answers. "Can we just have a conversation first?

Please. You said I'm a liar. What did I supposedly lie to you about? Can you just fill me in on what's making you do this?"

He shakes his head as he starts to unlock my wrists. "I'm finally letting you out of a punishment for being a stubborn pet and the first thing you want to do is antagonize me?"

I breathe out and press my lips together so I don't say anything else until he's unlocked my ankles. Knowing him, he'd leave me in the constrictive fucking cuffs if I make him upset. I stretch my arms and entire body the second I'm free.

Then I roll across the bed to get away from him.

But he just waves a finger at me like I've been a naughty child.

"Ah ah ah," he chastises. "That won't do. You've promised to be a good pet."

I glare at him. "I'll be a good… whatever. But can't you just answer some questions first? What if you just hypothetically entertained the possibility that I have amnesia? Could you fill me in on a little bit about the past, then?"

His eyes narrow. "I think you're forgetting who's in control here. A pet does not speak unless spoken to. I've come down to begin your obedience training."

He clicks his teeth at me like I'm a dog and points to the floor in front of him. "Sit."

Outrage flares through my blood.

"Why won't you just *listen*?" I shout at him, arms out.

"I see that you aren't ready after all. I'll come back when you are."

He starts to walk back towards the elevator.

"No! Wait!" I run around the bed and reach for the sleeve of his shirt.

He just turns back towards me, calm as ever, and raises one patient eyebrow. "Sit."

Motherfucking son of a shitting-bitch twat-waffle—

I keep my glare of fury pinned on him as I stomp my heel once, then flop to the floor dramatically.

I don't miss the satisfied grin that ever so slightly quirks on the left side of his mouth.

"First, you will learn the correct position. On your knees, bottom on your heels, eyes to the floor. Position yourself unless you want me to put my hands on you to correct you."

I grudgingly position myself as he's said.

"Good girl."

He pats my head, and I jerk away and glare up at him.

He points back to the floor. Huffing, I drop my head and look back at the floor.

"This is how you are to greet Sir when you hear the elevator ping. Now that you know my expectations, if you don't obey, there will be consequences."

I let out a frustrated noise and look up at him. "Fuck your expectations. What do I have to do to get you to answer my questions and then let me go? Is it because you paid for my virginity? Go for it. Fuck me."

I'd decided during the days of spiraling—or fine, during the thirty-two *hours* of spiraling—that I'd fuck him. He can obviously turn me on. Maybe if he fucks me, he'll be more pliable or even let me go. He paid for my virginity, right? Fine, take it. Maybe then we can have a normal human conversation.

He smiles down at me with those gorgeous cheekbones of his—a full on smile this time.

"Begging, so soon?"

I remember what he said the first day. That he'd have me begging before he was done with me. I purse my lips together, totally furious again.

Then I glare up at him. "Is that something we used to do? Fuck? Is that why you're doing this? Because we were lovers and I spurned you?" His amused smile doesn't move so I try to dig harder. "Did I cheat on you? Is that it and now you're taking your revenge?"

Suddenly he drops down swiftly so that he's in my face, his voice low and dangerous. "Oh love, I haven't even started taking my revenge yet. When I do, I'll make sure you *feel* it *everywhere*." His voice all but caresses my skin on the last few words.

Then he pulls back, his calm and patient mask returned. It's like I got a brief glimpse of the real, wildly passionate man Domhnall truly is before he quickly buttoned himself back up again.

I feel short of breath even at the peek, something inside me pulling towards him. The ghost. The memories. They're there, just out of reach. So close. She's so close. I'm so close.

Domhnall is so close. God, I want to reach up and touch him.

"Consider this the foreplay to revenge. Now, up on the spanking bench."

My jaw hits the floor. Did he just say *spanking* bench?

He wants to spank me. My mind sort of blanks out for a second at that. It's ridiculous. It's degrading.

An image of him spanking me the first night right before he ate me out hits viscerally. Great. I can't remember shit otherwise, but *this* memory sure is showing up in frickin' technicolor. It lights up every part of my body. Goddamn him for being so hot.

And... maybe it's not such a bad thing. If I go along with what he says, he stays.

And if he stays, then I can hold on to this feeling of myself. Past and present. The past might be a vague thread I'm barely grasping, but it's still *here*.

When he leaves, I lose it.

So against my better judgement, I look where he points. It's the strangest piece of furniture I've ever seen. Now that he's said what it's for, I can kind of make out that there are four padded struts where legs and forearms are meant to rest, then a long torso pad in the center.

"If you're a good girl, I won't put the restraints on. And I promise, I'll take it very easy for your first time."

Oh yes, now I see there are cuffs at the edge of the four limb padded areas.

I gulp and look up at him. "Will it hurt?"

Something washes over his face—a softness I don't expect. Another crack in his mask.

"It'll just be a sharp little sting. But I swear," his face becomes so solemn, his Sir persona slips almost entirely. "Mads, I'd never hurt you, love."

I blink, something going mushy and confused in my chest at the gentleness in his voice. Past and present collide.

Donny. I've got to tell Donny something.

I blink, and the sudden clarity goes fuzzy again. Before I can figure anything else out, I look up at him and his mask is firmly back in place.

"Crawl," he commands. "Now."

I swallow and crawl towards the intimidating contraption. As always, obedience feels like the most natural thing in the world for some reason. Is it an impulse from my old life?

"Now, *up*."

I climb up, knees on the bottom pads, chest on the largest central area, and forearms on the front two.

"If I do this, will you answer any of my questions about the past?"

"There is only today. Just stay in the present, Pet."

Ugh! Why can't he just answer a question straight out?

He chuckles. "Always so impatient. Now stay still but don't tense your muscles. Allow the experience to wash through you."

I hear the gentle swish of his pants as he walks away from

me and crane my head to look over my shoulder. I swallow again when I see him pick up an intimidating-looking flogger off the wall. At least I think it's a flogger. It's got a ton of twelve-inch black leather strips on the end of a long handle. It's not exactly one of the giant whips, but what do I know? It still looks scary as fuck.

"What are you going to do with that?" I ask anxiously.

He lifts an eyebrow at me. "It's called a spanking bench, Pet. What do you think I'm going to do?"

Suddenly I feel a draft. I never did get another pair of underwear. I guess I just sort of thought he'd spank me like he did that first night. With his hand.

I have to swing my head around the other way when he walks back over to the nightstand and pulls something out.

He hides it behind his back until he comes around to stand in front of me. Which is when I notice that he's aroused. It's hard to miss, with his, um, *thing* right in my face. It's tenting his pants so badly it looks painful.

I look up at him. "Are you going to fuck me?"

"So curious, kitty," he says. "But no, you don't get off that easily." Then he pulls his hand from around his back, and I see it's a blindfold. "When I say give yourself over to the experience and the sensations, I mean it."

A thousand arguments are poised to erupt, but he's already settling the blindfold over my eyes.

My breath becomes short. I don't know why not being able to see makes me feel so much more vulnerable. I'm in the same position I was two seconds ago. And for once it's not because I'm afraid of the dark. When Domhnall's here, the dark doesn't scare me.

I just can't see to know what's coming next before it happens. It feels like all my other senses crank up to a ten.

So I hear the slightest swish before a ton of heated little pointed tendrils massage the underside of my ass at first contact.

I blink in confusion. It doesn't hurt, exactly—it's just sensation. Less intense even than when he spanked me with his hand the first night.

It lands again on the opposite cheek, and I jerk in surprise but not pain. I exhale sharply and the edges of my fingertips tighten on the bench pad.

Wait. I don't understand. He called this punishment. No... He called it training. He said punishment would come if I disobey, but that he wanted to start my training when I called out *red* the other night.

Another heated kiss of the flogger lands, a little more intense on the already warmed flesh of the first cheek and I squirm, short of breath at the senses he's waking up.

Because instead of the pain I anticipated, this feels... *good*.

More intense than a massage and certainly more intimate with me spread out so vulnerably like this. I think of that moment we shared when his mask was down. *I swear, Mads, I'd never hurt you, love.*

If I really am this Madison woman, what the hell happened between them? Between *us*?

As the next few lashes land, though, I can't help doing what he said and just giving in to all the alien, lovely, unexpected feelings he's eliciting from my body. Warmth seeps through my ass and forwards to my groin. I allow my mind to go completely blank as my pussy swells and moistens, starting to pulse.

I stay in that high, buzzy place for long minutes after he's stopped, only at some point blinking and squirming on the bench when I realize he's pulled back. I can't help the short little whine that escapes my throat. Because as I come fully back into my body, I realize I am *so* turned on.

I don't know how I'm going to stop from touching myself after he leaves. But he's got that fucking camera on me, dammit. I bite my bottom lip.

He's been so gentle. Would it really be so bad if I asked him to relieve this ache?

I'm immediately upset by my own thoughts. What the fuck?

I don't care what the hell we *used* to be to each other. Since I've met him this time around, he's only face-fucked me, kidnapped me, and made me eat food out of a bowl like a dog. If I give him my body, it should be to get something in return, like when I was willing to sell myself at the auction.

I frown, then consider my willingness to wield my body

for gain. Is this another clue? Was I a sex-worker in another life?

"Did we meet because I was a prostitute?" I ask suddenly. "Was my dad my pimp or something?"

He tilts his head at me. "I was fascinated to see how you'd play this. I have to say, I'm not sure I expected this. It's an entertaining schtick if nothing else. And your ass is such a juicy little treat, isn't it?"

He spanks me with his open palm this time, our gazes still locked.

I'm speechless at his audacity. At his confidence. At how this doesn't feel like the violation some part of my brain knows it should be—if he was a stranger, anyway.

But he's not.

My eyes widen.

He's not a stranger.

It's not a memory, exactly. It's just a certainty.

I know him.

My— My— My *body* knows him. My thighs rub together, aching.

So when he asks, Irish brogue heavy, "Would you like me to ease that for you, love?" I say "Yes," before I can think better of it.

His warm hands are on me immediately, slipping between my legs to my wet sex. Just like the first night when he touched me so expertly.

I've always wanted him. For forever.

My whole body trembles and I'm glad for the blindfold now. I need it, as if it helps me hold up the pretense that I'm separate from what I've just asked for.

Because I *do* want this, and that's fucked up, and *is it*, really? My short-circuiting brain doesn't know how to process one thought from the next. All I know is my body arches out in welcome for his finger as he slides it back and forth across my clit. Then he starts to rub it in slow, languorous circles. I shudder on the bench, all my limbs going gelatinous.

"I'm close," I gasp. I was already so primed from the gentle, teasing flogging. And with his hand against me, rubbing me so intimately— Oh god, if I'm honest, every touch between us has been electric. Too electric. Electric in a way that's sparking lightning down my every nerve with pleasure.

My fingers grip the bench below me. "Oh God, I'm close."

I arch outwards towards his touch, and his other hand squeezes a handful of my ass, and oh god, it's so wrong but it feels *so* right. I all but hump his hand, I need the escalating pleasure so badly.

"So close," I hiss, my voice barely audible.

But then suddenly his arms are around my waist, and he lifts me off the bench.

"Wait, what are you—" I cry, devastated at the denied pleasure.

Before I can even finish the sentence, he's deposited me on the bed.

"I want to eat you out," he says huskily, and I feel his warm breath on my pulsing, needy center. "Red or green?"

I'm glad the blindfold still covers my eyes. Red. I should say red. My hands are unshackled, and I should push him away. For so many reasons. I feel my body's undeniable pull towards him but I'm a rational person. There are so many reasons not to give into this man.

Reasons. I swear there are reasons. Serious *reasons*...

"Green," escapes my breathless lips.

The next moment ecstasy hits. It doesn't feel like a mouth or a tongue or anything else on god's green earth that I can distinguish.

I'm just delivered straight to the ecstatic realms.

My fingers knot in the sheets. My heels dig into the mattress. I thrust against his face. My throat's already raw, but I scream. Now for entirely different reasons than an hour ago. What the fuck am I doing? This is wrong. I hate him—

But it's so good, oh, oh, it's so, *so* fucking good. He asked and I want it. Oh god I *want* it. It's like light melts from where he's licking me and god, oh god—

I scream at an even higher pitch because he *lifts* me there, when I couldn't have possibly imagined there was higher to go.

I wiggle my hips back and forth and somewhere through the haze I feel him grasp my ass to pull me into his mouth deeper. I bite my bottom lip as another spasm tears through my belly, only barely coming down before he's taking me right back up again.

Perversely, now I wish I wasn't blindfolded. Because I want to look down at him there between my legs. It feels as if there's some disembodied being bringing me such pleasure, but I know it's him. The man from the first night who I was so hesitant to trust but then gave myself over to completely. My familiar captor. How is this possible? It shouldn't be fucking possible for him to get me off so hard when he's kidnapped me.

I thought I just needed him to scratch the itch he'd raised.

This is transforming into something wholly different, though. For one, it's going on and on, as if the more taste I get of pleasure, the hungrier I become.

I'm on my, what, third orgasm? Fourth? But I can feel there's more—higher, *harder*—to go. And I want it. I need it. I need *him* to be the one to take me there.

It's like, for this single moment while he eats me out so crazily, there's a reversal of fortunes, and I'm the one controlling him. He's all but on his knees worshiping me with his mouth.

When I feel his thumb pressing against my asshole, wet with the juices spilling down from my drenched sex, it doesn't feel as foreign as it did the first night. Even though in spite of the plug he used then, the opening feels just as tight. But it's extra sensation, and I'm starved for it. I want it.

I want *him*.

"Yes, yes," I mutter as I thrash against the silk sheets, "it's so close, I can feel it."

Maybe he'll fuck me after all.

I try to tell myself it's why I'm being like this. To get the upper hand. But the wild animal heaving inside me for more pleasure knows better. She's in heat, and nothing but his wet, giving mouth devouring me will do.

I feel the pressure of his finger, working at my ass and finally popping inside. He drags me forwards with his digit and his other hand on my butt cheek, and he eats me more voraciously than ever.

It hits. The wildest, most blinding white-out pleasure bursting over the mountain-top into the pure free-falling unknown. I open my mouth to scream but no sound comes out. One breathless second. Then another, and another.

I reach down and tangle my fingers in his short, curled hair as I finally crash land back down to earth, my legs spasming in earthquake-like shakes as the tail-end of the orgasm rushes through me. It makes all my hair stand on end. I can feel it in my scalp and the tips of my fingers.

How—?

What—?

I slam my head back into the mattress and seize a few more times before all strength is gone from my limbs.

He lazily licks me up and down like a lion, and I'm so super-sensitive, I full-body shudder each time.

When he finally pulls away and his finger slips out of my

ass, I start shaking and can't stop. I hear little noises around the room but don't pull off my blindfold. I feel... so... I don't know what I feel. Too much and nothing at all, at the same time.

Stunned. In shock, like I've just been in a car-accident.

Ashamed. Like I want to crawl into a hole and cease to exist.

And like... like I want to beg him to come back and start all over again. Because for one moment, just one brief moment, with our bodies heaving for breath together, I felt whole instead of fractured.

And now?

Being left alone on the bed feels like the cruelest thing he could possibly do. Was that the point? To bring me to the peak of such terrible intimacy and then dump me so violently from heaven's river of pleasure to the cold, empty bed left alone without his touch?

I hear his footsteps heading towards the door.

Oh god. Yes. He is going to leave now.

And I'll be so horribly alone. I'll be alone, and I'll dream of the terrifying black box when the nightmares come to swallow me whole. But when I scream and wake up in the dark, I'll just be alone all over again. No one will be there to hold me. No one's ever there to hold me. It's just cold loneliness, that's all I'll ever—

The bed dips behind me, and there's a warm body at my back. Domhnall lays down, his strong arms coming around to anchor me into his warm chest. He's got his shirt off again, and with my barely-there nightie, we're skin to skin.

"Shhh," he whispers. "It's alrigh' now, love. Shhh."

His voice is so soft and steeped in his brogue. Instinctively my body shifts and softens against all his muscled hardness. I freeze a little when I feel his stiff cock, but he just squeezes me as if to reassure me that his intentions go no further than this.

He just got into bed to... snuggle me.

As if he could somehow sense I was freaking out at being left alone after all that.

Which is what finally has me breaking out in uncontrollable sobs. He only whispers, "Shhh, shhh. It's alrigh'. Every t'ing's gonna be alrigh'," in my ear as he strokes my hair back from my face.

I cry myself to sleep in his arms, knowing it's totally fucked up even as I allow my captor to comfort me, snuggling deeper into his embrace.

"Such pretty tears," he whispers as I get drowsier, his fingers still stroking gently through my hair.

THIRTEEN

DOMHNALL

LAST NIGHT WAS... unacceptable. I was supposed to be training her. Not— Not... whatever that turned into.

I have to stay in fucking *control*.

But after we'd gone so far, I knew I couldn't just leave her. I've had plenty of training in being a proper dominant, even if I've thrown out all the rest of the rules with Mads. But some things like *aftercare* were so drilled into me since day one I stepped through the door at Carnal, I couldn't just leave her there so obviously in shock after our scene last night.

Plus, I'd finally gotten something *real* out of her. I've seen plenty of women fake orgasms around the club, and try to with me, back in the early days.

But a good dom learns to pay attention to each hitch of breath. Every contracting muscle and flutter of a sub's eyelashes. You learn to watch for the grimace of pain and the twitch of pleasure, and the fascinating contortions a body twists itself into when the two intermingle.

Madison might lie to me, but her body tells me the truth. Her desire was genuine.

It gives me power over her.

Or am I just telling myself that so I can get my mouth on her cunt again as soon as possible?

I drag my hands through my hair and then look at Mads on the screen, sleeping curled up in bed like a kitten. My cock pulses rock hard in my pants. I should've known I couldn't be as cold and calculating as I need to be when it comes to her.

In the back of my head, there was always a twisted root growing inside me that planned what I'd do to either one of them if I ever got ahold of them. I even had a special collar made for her a long time ago, dreaming of just this day, in case I ever got to put my hands around her lovely little throat. I'm doing nothing more than exacting vengeance for the wrongs done to me. She *deserves* this.

But last night... Fuck. I slam my laptop screen shut. That wasn't vengeance. That was...

That was my seventeen-year-old self getting what he'd always dreamed of from the girl he'd been obsessed with from the day he noticed her watching him in that Dublin internet cafe. When she finally sidled over to me, I'd been so gobsmacked, I could barely get a word out. But she looked over my shoulder at my code and started up a conversation so easily that eventually I even managed to get out a syllable or two.

She laughed and coyly rolled her hair around a finger like *she* was the one who was nervous. An act. All an act.

So what if the act's gotten more sophisticated? She's still the same old Mads. I won't be anyone's toy ever again.

Certainly not *today*.

Today I'll be the cold and calculating bastard I've been ever since I stepped off the airplane in this new country, hand fisted around my little sister's wrist so I wouldn't lose her in the crowds. I was determined to make a better life for us. And just as determined not to be duped again by a pretty face or by anyone else thinking to take my power from me.

A promise I've kept to myself.

It's sure as hell not changing now.

I stomp towards the kitchen and prepare the best breakfast I know how to make, then put a cloche over top the plate to keep it warm. When I get to the elevator, I close my eyes, take a long breath in, and breathe an even longer one out. Several times. When I open my eyes again, I am cool, calm and collected. I push the down button.

No one masters me but myself.

I step in and ride the elevator down. When it pings and opens, my back is ramrod straight. I'm galled to realize that in spite of my breathing, in spite of my determination, I'm still fucking nervous to see her.

Jaysus Christ, is this what the *morning after* feels like for regular people? I never bothered with it before. I play at the club and leave it there. Like sane people do. My life is tidy with none of the unholy mess of a relationship. Though god knows, this is no relationship.

As the doors roll open, I look around for Madison.

She's certainly not in position like I explained to her she ought to be at the sound of the elevator bells last night.

Annoyed, I step down the hall, and yup, there she is still curled up in bed. I clear my throat, and I swear, before she realizes what she's doing, the small curve of a little smile lights her face as she looks between me and the plate in my hand.

"You brought me breakfast?" she asks with a hope that borders on affection.

"No," I say sharply, then am annoyed at myself for being affected by her nearness all over again. "I mean yes. But it's hardly for breakfast's sake. It's for your training. You've ought to have been awake and waiting for Sir. At the ping of the elevator door, you are meant to be waiting, in position."

She sits up, hugging the covers to her. Still in the slinky nightie from the first night, she looks adorably rumpled, and sexy as fuck.

"But there's no alarm clock. And I never know when you're coming, anyway."

I stop myself from rolling my eyes at the very last moment. She should not be able to see that she affects me at all. "Yes. You're meant to be prepared at all times. Tomorrow, I expect you in position when I arrive."

"That's stupid. Just give me a schedule or something. Then I'll know. And an alarm clock."

Finally I can't keep back my exasperated breath. "That's not how this works. Now do you want your hot breakfast, or should I keep standing here while it gets cold?"

"No, don't, it smells so good!"

I finally approach the bed and, with a small flourish, pull off the cloche revealing the perfectly cooked vegetable omelet and crisped-but-not-too-crisped bacon. American bacon is a fecking tragedy compared to the Irish kind. But I've come to live with it, especially when it's cooked right.

Madison's eyes light up and she immediately reaches out for a piece of bacon. I yank the plate back before she can touch it.

"This is a training session." I reinstate the chill in my voice. "You eat only what I feed you.

She looks at me like she might strangle me. I smile coldly. "You know I'm happy to walk back upstairs. There's always the feeder."

Her mouth drops open, eyes narrowing in fury.

But I don't stop there. "And failure to take your training would also mean a punishment." I tilt my head at her. "Or perhaps you enjoyed last night so much you *want* to be punished again?

"You're a fucking rat bastard son of a brothel whore, Donny Callaghan."

She pulls back and lifts a hand to cover her lips in surprise right after she says it, looking down at the mattress, then back up at me, eyes wide.

"Oh Mads, there's no reason to bring my mother into this. I told you about her whoring in confidence."

Outside I keep the same demeanor, but inside, I feel a tense excitement. *Donny.* She was the only person to ever call me *Donny.* She's slipping. And I'm hard with the thrill of getting past another layer of her bullshit.

"What?" she asks, still seeming confused and off-kilter. Just how I like her. "I didn't—"

I start to laugh.

Rage comes back into her eyes like a storm, and she swings her arm wildly like she's trying to smack me. With the arm not holding her plate, I easily catch her wrist.

"Ah ah ah, there's no violence allowed in the dungeon," I say, tugging her in close to my chest. "Don't make me cuff your wrists again. You know I'll do it, and I'll like it."

She screams in fury and yanks back from me. "What the fuck is wrong with you? Do you even have any feelings?"

"All I'm asking is for you to eat your breakfast while it's still hot." I hold out a long piece of bacon for her. She doesn't need to know all the ways she affects me. Feelings are inconvenient, and I've refused to have them for a good long while. I won't be starting again now.

"You're only fighting with yourself, Mads. Not me."

She glares at me. "I'd rather go hungry."

"You'll take punishment instead of breakfast? You really are a randy lass, aren't you?"

I start to set the breakfast plate down and she lunges forward to take a bite out of the end of the bacon I'm holding out to her.

"You're sadistic," she says, chewing and glaring at me.

I smile in the face of her scowl. Then add, "Takes one to know one, love."

She turns away as she chews.

"Another bite," I say once I know she's done. I see the fight in her, and because I'm exactly the sadistic fuck she says I am, it makes me hard.

But she turns back, only for her eyes to widen when this time she sees I'm holding out a bit of omelet on my fingers for her to literally eat out of my hand.

Glaring hatred beams from her eyes up at me the whole time, she bites it, her lips grazing my fingertips. "I won't mind if you suck the butter from my fingertips," I say, adding insult to injury.

"I'd sooner bite your fingers off," she says as she chews.

"It's unladylike to talk with your mouth full."

"You're a cunt."

"Touche. I forgot the stunning repartee of who I'm dealing with. You always had a mouth like a garbage disposal. Another bite, m'dear?"

"Eat a dick."

I grin and hold out another morsel of omelet on my fingers. When she leans forwards and lowers her mouth on my hands, her teeth bite down. Not hard enough to do any real damage, but just enough to nip before her tongue pulls the omelet off them and back into her mouth.

"Oh, so it's to be foreplay for us?"

"Just a warning," she snaps. "I'm happy to bite harder next time."

"Don't tempt a sadist, lass," I growl, brawl deep and low, "Often we've got a more'n a wee bit o' masochism in us too. If ya manage to draw blood, I just might drench me drawers. You've got 'em tight already."

Her eyes drop to my pants. And quickly back up to my face, her cheeks coloring. I wasn't lying. Every time I'm down here bickering with her, I go hard as a damn goalpost.

I had to take myself in hand once I got upstairs last night, and it wasn't the first time since she's been here.

"Bacon?" I decide to give both of us a moment's reprieve.

Her eyes just watch me as I pick up another long piece and hold it out to her. She bites at it greedily. Always so greedy, my Madison.

My cock pulses for want of her.

Fuck. It's times like this I have to remind myself why we're both here. Because for fuck's sake that's right, she's greedy. She's so fucking greedy that after she and her abusive fuck of a father had sucked me dry, they skipped town with all the money I'd stolen for them.

It was a clever grift, finding a mark like me who was young with just enough skills to be able to get on the dark web but not much else. They taught me the rest, then were gone by the time the final transfer was made. The side hustle for Madison's dad was the stalking and conquering. Once he'd done that, he wanted fresh quarry. A new town. More money. New young ass.

They were both insatiable beasts.

And Mads, what did she want? Was it all about the money for her? Or had it been about the hunt, too?

When she next comes near, I shove the eggs in her mouth before she can get close enough to my fingers to bite them. She looks surprised but turns around to chew just the same.

Did she get a thrill out of boys always falling all over themselves for her? Did she like playing honey trap for her father? She was two years older than me and a helluva lot wiser. How they must have laughed to themselves when she told him I asked her to run away with me.

"Eat the rest yourself." I toss the plate to the floor. It lands intact on the carpeted ground, but a couple slices of bacon are upended. Better than she deserves.

"Wait," she says, half standing up. "We haven't even gotten to talk."

"I'll be back later to continue your training," I snap coldly, furious that she's still talking back to me. She's nowhere near being broken, and that's all on me. I've been too soft. "I want you in position when I return. If you aren't, there'll be punishment, and it won't be half so pleasant as last time. There's only four days before I'm to present you at the club as my sub and I will *not* be embarrassed in front of my peers."

More than that, I will *not* lose her. When I take her to the club on Saturday, she needs to have given in to my control so deeply that by the end of the night, there's no other thought in her head except pleasing me and climbing back into my car.

I fucking *refuse* to lose Madison Harper a second time. Nothing in this world or any other will stop me.

Not Quinnlynn.

Not even my sister. I protected her from everything when she was young, but she's a grown woman now. A slightly fucked up grown woman, sure. But I've protected her as much as I can for as long as I can. It's time I take the reward for all the suffering I endured. I don't fucking care if I lose whatever might be left of my soul in the process.

I march out of the room towards the elevator.

Enough fucking around.

We've got work to do.

FOURTEEN

BROOKE

HE MADE A MISTAKE. I can't believe Mr. High and Mighty actually made a mistake. He's going to let me out in four days to take me to the club.

I was hoping to get him to talk, sure. But he was in a pissy mood today, so I didn't think I'd get anything out of him. But then he drops that jewel right before he leaves?

I bite my lip and pace back and forth in the dungeon bedroom.

I've been to the club. Yeah, there was a lot of eye-popping stuff going on, but strangely enough, they all seemed like normal people. It's like, even though some people there had masks on, they still were being themselves—with their most real, deepest desires on bare display. And Moira and Quinn will probably be there, right? Quinn seems like she'd rip out a man's throat with her bare teeth if he fucked with her, and Moira... unless that was a mighty good act. She seemed so genuine in a way you rarely come across.

When we get there, I can just yell out that Domhnall's kidnapped me or scream, "Red, red, red!" and someone will take me seriously. While we were there last week, I saw a girl use her safe word and everything in the scene and all around the room pretty much stopped until her dom had seen to her. The big burly bouncer, Isaak, looked ready to toss his ass, too, if he wasn't extremely careful with her.

Just four more days, and then there'll be no more collars or being locked in a dungeon or being forced to drink my water from a bowl like a dog.

There'll be no more Domhnall.

The odd twist in my guts at that thought only shows how much I need to get the hell outta here. He's climbing into the empty crevices in my mind left behind by the amnesia. In the parts where ghosts and black boxes live. I had another nightmare last night. I was getting closer and closer to the black box, and all I wanted to do was run away. But I couldn't move, except somehow I was still getting closer to the box, and it was all I could *see* and I couldn't escape, couldn't move, couldn't *breathe*—

It has to be a metaphor for this place. I need to get the *fuck* out of here.

In the next four days, I'll get whatever information I can about my past, and then I'll dip the fuck out.

At some point, I've got to say fuck the past, right? Everything I learn about it is bad. I should be focusing on the future. I can go to Chicago and stay with my friend, Ria, from the shelter, for a few weeks while I try to get my feet back under me. During my six weeks at the shelter, they had classes on making healthier choices. Getting away from here as soon as I can is the healthy choice.

But until then, I'll keep playing chess with Domhnall. I'll be the perfect little sub he's been looking for. I'll let him knock off all my pawns and feel in control.

Only to have my queen positioned perfectly to win the game.

So when I hear the elevator ping, I rush over to get into position, falling to my knees and dropping my head just in time.

I hear his satisfied grunt of surprise right as the doors open as his perfectly shined black dress shoes and pants step out and stop in front of me. With my face down where he and the cameras can't see, I allow myself a secret little smile, then make my face blank as a doll. That's what he'll get from me for the next four days. A pliant little doll.

"Good girl," comes his deep rumbly voice.

Ha. If he only knew.

He makes clicking noises like you would for an animal as

he takes hold of my chain and starts to walk back towards the dungeon room. "Come."

I keep my eye roll internal as I turn around and crawl at his side.

"What's elicited this little change of heart, pet?" he asks.

Shit. I try to think fast. I thought he'd just be happy about it, not question me. "Why fight the inevitable?" I say, head still down since I'm on my hands and knees. "It's easier this way. And I thought maybe if I obey, you'd be more willing to tell me about our past."

"Ahh," he says.

I frown. What's that supposed to mean? Does that mean he'll be more willing to share if I do what he wants? Gah. I just told myself fuck the past, but here I am waffling again.

"Take off that ridiculous outfit. Then up on the spanking bench."

Double shit. It's not like this nightie is any kind of real cover with my breasts exposed and no underwear on, but it's still felt like... *something.* And the spanking bench. An unconscious little shudder goes through my body.

I remember all too well when I was last up there. But *compliant pet* is my M.O. today, so I unbutton the collar of the nightie and unzip the side, then slip out of it. I shiver a little and not because the nightie ever provided any warmth. Then I crawl up on the bench, arranging my limbs on the supports.

I'm in control. I'm in control. My cheeks flood with heat

as I climb up on the strange piece of furniture that leaves me so exposed. Dammit, I'm *in control*—but my burning cheeks reveal my lie.

"W-what are you going to do?" I ask.

Domhnall has been moving around elsewhere in the room, and I suppose I should have expected the blindfold he's carrying when he comes back.

"You'll see. For this scene, since it requires touching, you may say red if you want it to stop."

He doesn't immediately blindfold me. He moves behind me, and his hand comes into view as he reaches around with what looks like a make-up wipe.

I'm so startled, I lay still as he begins carefully swiping the leftover make-up from the auction off my face. I'd scrubbed at some of it with the edge of my bedsheet over the last couple days, but I've been left feeling gross because I couldn't get it all off. Especially the mascara. It's just been crusted on my lashes.

My eyes fall closed as Domhnall swipes the make-up remover carefully over each eyelid several times, returning with a fresh wipe when one is dirtied. His hands caress the cool wipes over my cheeks. Then down the slope of my nose, careful with the nooks and crannies of my nostrils and mouth. Over and over, his gentle hands attend to me until my face finally feels clean. From the roots of my scalp at the top of my forehead to behind my ears and underneath my jaw. My pores can finally breathe.

Only then does he lower the blindfold, and I can tell he's being careful not to tangle the back strap in my hair.

His hands return after a short pause, moving on to my neck. But where I expect another cool wipe, now suddenly he's gently caressing my skin with a warm, wet cloth that feels more like a soft towel. Where the hell did he get that from? I didn't see it on him when he got off the elevator. Then again, my head was down the whole time.

And god, how does that feel so good? *I'm supposed to be pretending to be a good pet anyway*, I tell myself as I give myself permission to sink into the sensation.

Fuck, I really needed him to be an asshole today. *He's holding you captive against your will, dummy.* He's *always* the asshole. I straighten my back, no matter that I'm lying face down on the most objectifying piece of furniture ever designed.

It's fine. None of this is *really* affecting me. I've got my plan. I'm the queen in hiding while he takes the pawns. I'm just going through the motions with my body. My mind is my own.

"I've been neglecting my duties," he murmurs. "While I do enjoy your musk, pet, keeping you clean is my duty as your owner."

Now the soft, warm cloth comes to wash down my spine. Again, I blink so fast my eyelashes flutter against the satin mask that blindfolds me. How is the touch of the same man who ruthlessly spanked me now so gentle?

He caresses the cloth up towards my shoulder. Slowly, back and forth. And then around underneath my armpit where he scrubs tenderly. His touch drops away, and then a warmer cloth, fresh perhaps, comes to my skin as he massages it all the way down my arm.

I squeeze my eyes shut beneath the blindfold.

The thing about waking up without your memory only to find yourself all alone in the world is... there's no one there to *touch* you. Nurses, sure, and prodding doctors, but that was just for a couple days at the hospital.

There was no one to hug me. There were no affectionate touches reassuring me everything would be okay.

As Domhn touches me now, I feel as if I've been starved for this my whole entire life. And sure, my life as I know it might only be two months long, but still. I think it's why I gave into him so easily that first night.

Maybe I've been starved for touch longer than two months. Maybe it's been much, much longer...

I should be walling myself off to him. But in the darkness, as warm cloth after warm cloth massages my body so delicately, I'm half delirious with the intimacy of human contact.

And then, as if seeing my defenses weakening, the relentless fucker leans over and starts to whisper in my ear, "You're such a good, *good* girl. See how good it can be between us, my sweet little pet, when you give in to me? I can make it so, so good. I'll bring you pleasure, and I'll bring you pain. I'll make each so sweet for you, pet, you won't be able to tell one from the other."

I want to shake my head no even though I strain towards the warmth of his chest against my back. I should scream *red* and leap off of the bench to scramble away from his drugging voice and touch.

Instead, I fight the urge to whine when I feel his chest move away. Another cloth rubs down my outer hip. Then back around to my buttocks. He doesn't squeeze or anything. But I can still feel the firm pressure of his hand guiding the cloth.

It disappears and a fresh one begins to slide upwards from my knee to my inner thigh. I suck in a breath, my stomach clenching. What will he do? Something sexual? I bite my bottom lip, and not because I'm tempted to say red. I'm dangerously curious about what he'll do next.

But he just nudges my legs slightly further apart and washes me... *there*. Then he pulls the cloth away. He washes my backside just as efficiently. All the breath whooshes out of me when he pulls away and I feel a cold, confusing rush of emotions.

I *don't* want him to touch me, do I?

You don't know what you want, I chide myself furiously. *You're all mixed up. He's intentionally mixing you up, and you're falling for it.*

It's probably true. I relax my face into the soft padding of the bench. But why not worry about it another time? The soft buzzy feeling is settling in. God, what if for once, I don't fight? What if I just enjoy being bathed, and feeling the touch of someone's hands on me, even if it's through a warm cloth?

Maybe the win today is stealing the energy of some touch. I've so desperately needed to be touched. I'll let the rest wait for another day. I'm trying to establish trust through obedience for a little while, anyway. So today, it's all right to give in.

My whole body melts as the warm cloth moves down to my ankles. By the time he's massaging my feet with his strong hands, I'm drifting in the buzzy place. It feels so good. I'll just steal this pleasure for myself. It's so, so, *so* nice. This luxury of touch still feels wildly unfamiliar, like I haven't known it for a long, long time.

Maybe I'm wrong. Maybe I went to spas all the time and had foot massages on the regular before I got mugged that night in the alley. Maybe I'm a secret heiress and when I get out of here, I'll find a huge, globe-trotting family that's been searching the world for me but just never thought of looking in Dallas, Texas.

I sink further into the bench, warmth suffusing my whole body. In whatever deep, knowing place remains inside me, though, I don't think that was my story. I don't think there was ever much touch in my circa twenty-three to twenty-four years of walking this earth. Nothing in any of my now relaxed nerves, at least, says this was ever anything familiar.

"That's my good girl. Curling up like a little kitten, all but purring, aren't you?" His warm breath is back in my ear. The scent of fresh mint wafts in my nose. And a delicious cologne. He always smells so good. "Now you're all fresh and clean. You've pleased your owner well, pet."

"That's good," he continues, his voice low and gravelly. "I'll give you a treat for being such a good, good girl. It's time for our next bit of training."

I startle from my sleepy state at his words. A treat? I'm anxious even at the same time I can't deny the yearning that springs up low in my belly. From the very first night, my body has craved this man.

"Will you tell me who I am?" I ask sleepily.

"You are who you always were, Mads. Now, when I leave, I want you to touch yourself."

Wait, he wants me to *what*?

He must feel some reaction in my body because he chuckles low. "That's right. I'll be watching. Lie in the middle of the bed, exposing yourself to the camera."

I swallow hard.

"I've set a vibrator out on the bed. It's your choice whether to use it or not. Touch yourself however you desire."

Without a cloth, his bare finger comes to my back and, torturously slow, begins to trail down the bumps of my spine.

"What do you find sexy, kitten? What will you imagine as you touch that secret place between your legs that swells so sweetly when you start feeling pleasure? It'll slicken as your mind fills with fantasies. Are they the same as you mentioned on stage? Do you still just imagine some vague weight laying on top of you?"

The warmth of his breath comes closer and closer as he whispers his dark, drugging words until his lips are a feather touch against my ear with every syllable. I'm already slick and pulsing.

His finger on my spine is a tingling point of contact that has me squirming as he relentlessly continues. "Or do you have more specific dreams now? Will you think of the bristle of my stubble between your thighs? Or how your fingernails dug into my scalp as you howled with pleasure?"

My hips flex against the table as I squirm unintentionally, and dammit, I'm getting more than slightly slick now. I'm wet.

"Or do you need even more than that?" He's whispering so softly, but it sounds like a roaring river with as close as he is, lips brushing my ear sensually.

"Will you dream of me climbing up your body? Grasping your wrists to press you into the mattress to dominate you in just the way you like?"

Damn him, *damn* him—

"And then you'd feel me there, where you say you've never had a man before. I'll have made you so crazy with need you'll be soft for me. I'll make you hurt other places, love, but it won't hurt when I take you. It'll be the fullness you spoke of. The fullness you've been needing. Because you're needy, I can tell. If you thought I've made you feel good before, it's nothing to how it will feel when I fill you up from the inside.

Then I'll be everywhere, and you'll be mine completely. You'll never want to be anywhere else. You'll fight to get your hands free, because you'll want to grab my ass and pull me deeper into you. This one time, I'll give you what you want. I'll fuck you just how you need."

I try not to let him see how my breath comes shorter and shorter the more he speaks, because I'm envisioning everything he's saying.

"Maybe you're thinking about it right now," he whispers devilishly. "Maybe you're thinking about how easy it would be for me to slip behind you. I could touch you where you're swollen until you shudder for me. Then I'd unzip myself and you could feel me there. I'd tease you with my cock first."

Now he brushes his nose against my ear, nuzzling me before his lips return. "I'd run the tip of my cock up and down your wet, swollen pussy lips. I'd let you feel me before slowly pushing inside. Not all at once. I'd test you out, a little bit at a time. Teasing you. One hand around your thigh with my thumb at your swollen little clit. It'd be easy to grab a nipple clamp from the wall. Putting one of those pretties on you would really give you something to think about other than worrying about any initial pinch you might feel when I breech you."

He sucks in a breath, and for the first time I realize I'm not the only one he's affecting. It both makes me feel like I have a little bit of power back and sends an entirely fresh gush of wetness to my sex. I imagine him hard in his slacks.

Of course he's affected. He's so often hard around me. He just never lets on what that actually *means*. He's always having me look at the floor or blindfolding me.

To hide how I affect him, too? Because I'm not the only one visualizing what he's talking about. Somehow that makes his words feel even more real as his finger tracing down my spine gets nearer and nearer to my tailbone. My breaths are stuttered now, it's true, but I'm close to not being able to breathe at all.

"I'll have a pair of clamps on your nipples, and I won't take it easy on you. They'll hurt. I'd lift your chest up off the bench so I could flick them while I teased you with my cock, entering you just the slightest bit. I'd make you feel the pinch from the hang of the jewelry clamped on your nipples. You'll be so aroused it'll be on the tip of your tongue to beg me."

He pushes even further so that his lips are cemented against my ear—a kiss as his voice continues in a hot rush, "But you're fighting yourself, aren't you? So you don't beg. You'd want to. Something you should know about me, pet? I love the edge."

His finger slips further down, just to the top edge of my ass crack. "The edge is where I thrive. Living on the edge of pleasure-not-given is the sweetest pain."

My bottom lip is caught between my teeth, and my eyes squeeze shut.

"Right when you can't bear it any longer, wanting to beg for my cock but refusing all you desire because you're so strong, I'll hold off just a little longer. And then longer still." His finger toys in the crack of my ass.

"And then right when you can't bear it anymore, so badly that you're crying tears of need, I want you to pull your hand away."

He withdraws his hand from my back and his mouth from my ear. I try so hard not to shudder or show any other outward sign that he's affected me. As if to deny the smell of my wetness leaking down my leg that's scented the room.

All but mocking me, he inhales loudly. Loud enough to ensure that I know *he* knows.

"Make sure I can see everything on camera, pet. But at the end, right when you feel that pleasure ready to explode through your body—"

I'm waiting on his every word, all but ready to explode *now—*

"Don't come. Don't you dare let yourself fucking come, my little slut. Do you hear me?"

He chuckles darkly at the whine that escapes my throat.

"If I do this, will you finally tell me—"

"And don't half-ass it getting right up to the edge, or I'll know. Don't try to sneak an orgasm in, either, because I'll know that too."

Then he pulls away all together, warmth completely gone.

I barely keep in the feral scream of fury building in my throat as he exits the room.

FIFTEEN

DOMHNALL

I STRIDE AWAY and punch in the passcode, forcing myself not to show the weakness of looking over my shoulder at her no matter how much I want to. Still, it eats at me, and I have to fight myself not to turn back.

Mads, gorgeous Mads, laid out trembling, dripping, spread wide on the bench.

Is she still on the apparatus? Is she flipping me off? I can't wait to get upstairs to see everything. To watch exactly what she does next. She was playing at obedience so well today. Will she keep it up when I'm gone?

I'm painfully hard and every instinct tells me to reach a

hand down to offer myself relief as soon as the elevator doors shut behind me.

But today it felt like we reached a new... level.

I wouldn't know. I've never had a sub around this long. I'm a strictly one night and done sort of dom. Is this what Caleb meant when he said there was something to having a sub around for longer. By... bonding with one.

I bark a laugh at the thought. I'm not bonding with her. I'm playing the game. I'm bonding *her* to me.

I am the one in control here. Just look at the way she trembled beneath me in spite of herself. If I was shaking a little, too, well, I was still the one doing the tormenting.

Once I'm upstairs, I immediately slide in behind my desk and pull up two of my cameras. I'm delighted to find her only now climbing off the bench.

Did she wait for me intentionally or was she just so affected by our little scene that she couldn't move till now? Most subs telegraph everything they're feeling on their faces, but Mads is the ultimate chameleon. Apart from pleasure, I'll never know what she's actually feeling, will I?

My cock leaps in my pants.

Every muscle in my body is clenched tight as I watch, breath bated, as she walks unsteadily over to the bed and climbs on. At first, she just sits on the edge of the bed. For a moment, she stares straight ahead, and then, her chest visibly inflating as she takes a large breath, she looks up at the O-ring camera.

I almost fucking nut right there.

But at the same time, the phone rings.

I snatch it up and bark, "What?"

"Jesus, Domhn. Caleb just told me Quinn told him that you still have the girl at the house and you aren't letting her go. Do you know what kind of liability you're exposing the club to if this girl comes back and sues?"

It's Marcus on the phone. He's a corporate finance lawyer and club member who helped with the auction. Of course Quinn went squealing to him. I thought I'd gotten her off my back, but now here she is starting shit.

Marcus continues on his tear, "You know NDAs aren't worth the paper they're printed on these days. What the f—"

He cuts off mid-rant, his voice suddenly lowering. "Oh! What a beautiful drawing, sweetie. Why don't you color it in with the purple crayon and Daddy will be right back after this little phone call?"

I hear the noise of a door slammed, my eyes still drilling into the screen as a naked Madison slowly scoots to the middle of the mattress. I zoom in on her face, loving the embarrassed bloom to her cheeks.

"I'm in the middle of something," I say. "I'll call you back."

"No, you can't fucking call me back," Marcus whispers heatedly. "Did you hear a word I said? What the fuck are you doing with this woman? You need to let Quinn pick her up immediately. And pray she's happy with the payout and doesn't decide to take legal action against you. Because we both know she could get an even bigger payday than fifty million if she seeks restitution for mental and physical suffering—"

"She won't call the cops. She's a crook," I quip. I don't have fucking time for this. Madison's just spread her legs. Her hand descends shyly down her stomach. "She conned her way across the better part of Ireland, the rest of Europe, I imagine, and I'd be shocked if she hasn't done the same here in the States. I'm doing the world a favor, really, and locking up a dangerous criminal."

At least one half of a dangerous criminal enterprise, anyway. Her father might have been the one with a penchant for violence, but she was the hunter who put little stupid fishes like me on the hook for him.

Now I'm furious that my cock is so hard. I yank out my key ring from my pocket and unlock the bottom drawer of my desk. I don't reach for what's inside yet.

Marcus starts to say something else, but I hang up on him and ignore when the phone rings again.

Instead, I calmly unbutton my starched white shirt. I'm painted in unholy tattoos. Christ is impaled on his cross on my chest, far bloodier and more lifelike than the normal, sanitized versions worn on all those nuns' necks back at school when I was growing up. No, in the ink on my chest, blood pours down his face from the thorn crown piercing his forehead. Same with the nails in his hands that stretch around to my back and the slice marks in his wan chest, across the bottom of my ribs.

Everywhere else, more macabre scenes of demons, skulls, and reapers cover me, neck to wrists. During business hours, I'm respectable as fuck. But underneath, I always know what's there.

I shrug out of my shirt as on the second monitor, I see Madison's hand slip between her legs. On the first monitor that's still focused in on her face, I see her confused pleasure as she begins touching herself. It's a scrunch of her features that looks almost like pain.

I grit my teeth, my own pleasure flashing. My cock leaps again and I reach for what's in the bottom drawer. My fist closes around the handle of my nastiest whip, coiled like a snake here for only the most special of occasions. Underneath is the collar I bought for Madison long ago. Elegant, with the Callaghan crest at the back and a large diamond at the front. I always knew one day I'd make her mine.

But first, I have to get myself back under complete control. I have to remember who is meant to be the owner of whom. Every time I draw out her pleasure and see the things she can't deny as truth, it lures the foolish boy I was back to the surface.

It's time to remind him just what happens to naïve young men who let themselves be tempted by beauty and apparent vulnerability.

My grip on the whip's handle tightens as I pull it out, letting it uncoil like a viper.

I'm not a masochist.

I like to inflict the pain, not feel it.

Usually.

It's only on the very rare occasions when the demons get to howling like banshees—

I take three steps back from the monitor and let the cat-o'-nine-tails wail, flipping it in the particular way I've learned to do over the years so that it lashes backwards, whipping around and over my own shoulders.

I take it silently when the knotted horsehair ends of the leather tails lash my back. I was far from quiet the first time this instrument of torture hit my flesh. But I was trained to take it and thank my master for the favor of his touch.

On screen, Madison's forehead scrunches in pleasure and her legs clench together around her hand as she continues rubbing her sweet little clit. I reach down and unbutton my slacks, shoving both them and my boxers down until my straining cock stands straight out like a ship's mast.

Madison's back arches in unconscious pleasure, perfectly mounded breasts topped with hard, pebbled little nipples. As she starts to squirm in bed, I land the second lash, on the opposite shoulder.

My entire body reacts from the pain that's intense enough to steal my breath. My cock only throbs harder as

Mads rolls over on her side, her hand sawing against her clit as she fucks herself.

I land another strike. And another. I feel blood pouring in rivulets down my back that's on fire now, soaking into the top of my pants and dripping on my polished wood floor. I only continue with another ruthless strike. The next sends me to my knees, mouth dropped open in eye-popping pain. My cock strains harder still.

On the screen, Madison's face twists in longing. She's almost there. Her pleasure is a moment away. She yearns for it. The release would be so sweet, the endorphin rush a reward for all she's been through for the last few days. I've demonstrated to her just how good her body can feel if she works at it.

I hesitate, my whip paused, the wicked ends dripping with my blood onto the floor, waiting to see her choice.

Will she take what most humans in this world do? Will she grasp for the immediate pleasure?

Or will she obey?

I breathe hard, my own chest bellowing up and down, on the edge of a pin as, at the very last moment, she yanks her hand away in denied pleasure, twisting in the sheets and screaming into the pillow.

My hand flicks for one last lash.

Right as it lands, without once touching myself, my cock explodes with cum, milking itself in pleasure at her obedience as pain spasms through my back. "I am in control!" I shout, and fall to my knees, whip dropping from my hands.

SIXTEEN

BROOKE

WITHOUT LIGHT, it's difficult to tell what time it is, but I think I've begun to tell a rhythm to the days because Domhnall comes down and feeds me by hand three times a day now in addition to doing one of his *scenes*.

After yesterday's frustrating experience, I'm not sure what mood I'll find him in today. He should be happy. I passed his infuriating little test.

He thinks he can control me without even being here? He thinks his words have enough power to make me do things just because his instructions are in my head, like some religion? Like God?

Just a few more days.

Or sooner, even. Because I thought of something else last night while my pussy was throbbing with the anguish of getting so riled up only to be denied at the last moment.

I don't have to wait for his timeline, if he's even telling me the truth about going to the club and it's not just another game. Either way, a good chess player prepares multiple paths to victory because you never know what your opponent might be planning to throw at you. And after yesterday, I don't know if I can trust myself to stay here much longer.

As much as I want to think I'm the better strategist... the truth is... I can feel Domhn overwhelming me. The craving hasn't stopped. Every time he touches me, in fact, I think I'm getting more addicted and falling deeper into the warm, dark abyss of his sensual world.

But right now, without him here, my mind is clear. There aren't any ghosts hovering. Maybe I should start to count that as a good thing. Maybe if my past was so bad... maybe I forgot for a reason.

I just have to play my part today and take every chance I can. I can't be picky, and I'll have to be brave. Braver even than when I woke up at the hospital and felt the panic of not recognizing anyone or anything around me. They had to sedate me that first night when I woke up and there were only night shift nurses there, I threw such a fit.

I kept asking for my family. I didn't know anything—I can't tell you how disturbing it is not to know your own name

—so I just kept asking for my family. Family should always be there for you. Family was on TV. Where was mine?

No one had come for me, they said, and I fucking lost it. I screamed that they were lying. That *they'd* kidnapped me.

I kicked the nurses and ran out of my hospital room. I barely made it to the large, antiseptic hallway with several other nurses looking curiously in my direction before a needle sank in my ass and everything went black.

The next morning, I was in restraints when I woke back up and doctors calmly explained what had happened. They took me outside in a wheelchair to prove I hadn't been kidnapped and brought in the police to talk to me.

The police!

I'll be brave again and go straight to the police when I get out of here. 911. The nice officers told me all I had to do was call that number and they'd come in their big cars and flashing lights. The nurses put a phone by my bedside, so I'd feel comfortable.

I grin, thinking of the uniformed men coming to put Domhnall in restraints and how they'll haul *him* off to be locked up in a little room. Now that will be justice.

Fuck the past. For real this time.

Fuck anything he thinks he knows about me.

The satisfaction of fantasizing about him in cuffs is still easing the sting of last night's denial when I hear the elevator's soft *ping*.

Shit! I roll off the bed and sprint down the half hallway to drop to my knees, heartbeat racing right as the heavy doors open. I wince, face down at the ground. Only a little rug burn. Definitely worth it when I hear Domhnall's pleased little harrumph as he looks down at me.

"I'm happy to find you in position." I watch his shined black shoes and ironed suit pants step forward, and then a gentle hand lands lightly on my head before caressing his fingers through my hair. It sends a little shiver down my spine. Damn it. I'm supposed to be holding strong today. I don't care if I'm starving for his touch. *Focus.* Escape. That's all I care about. He just *thinks* he's got the upper hand.

"And as for yesterday, all I can say is, very *good girl*." His mouth caresses the rumbling words in a way that hits deep. "You were exquisite."

I swallow hard. No one's ever called me exquisite before... that I know of. I try to shake it off. I'm sure former-me had people calling her exquisite all the time.

But fuck remembering. He's never going to tell me anything about myself, anyway. Yesterday made that clear.

Escape. It should have been all I was focused on from the beginning. He types in the code to that keypad every day.

A clever kitty could get her hands on it.

His hands comb through the back of my hair down my scalp before he moves on, and my eyes drop closed in spite of themselves. Goddamn him for his touch feeling so good. He latches his leash to the collar around my throat. "Come, pet."

He mistakes my compliance for obedience as I turn

around on the carpet, still on my hands and knees. I keep to his side as he heads back into the dungeon.

After our normal ritual of him feeding me breakfast from his hand, he swipes my mouth with a cloth napkin and gives me water from a glass, then puts aside breakfast.

"Today, we'll finally be getting on to a proper scene," Domhn says. "You'll do exactly as I say. Respond yes, sir, if you agree."

I bite back my instinctual *fuck you, sir*. "Yes, sir."

"Excellent. You're doing well already, pet."

I roll my eyes at the floor as he leads me across the room. I keep my eyes down, half because I'm not sure I want to know what piece of furniture or torture implement he's leading me towards until the last minute. I've told myself I'm going to comply all day like a good little pet so I can have my chance later, but dear god, now that it's actually getting to the *comply* part...

"Stand up, face against the St. Andrews Cross."

The *what*? I can't imagine there being any sort of cross in this unholy place. But Domhnall drops a hand down to help me up. Ever the gentleman. I'd roll my eyes again, except now I'm half up from my hands and knees and he or one of the many cameras might catch me at it.

Soon I'm all the way on my feet and can't help swallowing hard because I see exactly what he intends.

In front of me stands a six-foot tall wooden X with hand and ankle restraints, like some medieval interrogation device. I start to turn around for him to strap me to the damn thing, but his deep voice reminds me, "No. Facing the cross. Ass out."

Jesus Christ, I don't know why that makes me all but start to hyperventilate. If I'm strapped with my head *facing* the cross, and essentially, the wall, I'll have no idea what the hell he's up to behind me.

But I suppose that's the point. If I start looking over my shoulder too much, he'll just put a blindfold on, anyway. He likes it when I don't know what's coming. Sadistic bastard. Because with my ass and back to him like this, it has to mean there's going to be more flogging.

My traitorous body is the only one that thinks that's a good idea, all my muscles going suddenly tense in anticipation, including my clenching sex.

Domhnall obviously sees it because he runs a hand down my back. "Relax," he murmurs. "We're just going to play a little game."

I let out a disbelieving huff of air.

"You may say red at any point, and I'll release you," he says as he cuffs my ankle securely to the bottom left of the X. The cuff is lined with some sort of soft fur, so there's no chafing. I bite my bottom lip.

The scaredy cat in me wants to shout *red* right now. The chess player in me stays silent. If I say, "red," he might do something really dastardly like the last few nights and play my own body against me again. I'd prefer a little pain to that, thank you very much. There's got to be things harsher than that massaging flogger he used on me the first night and surely that's what we're graduating too, right?

I need him to finally *hurt* me so I can hate him like I'm supposed to.

His hands slide up my arm, caressing as he lifts it up to the cuff at the top right of the X. My heart starts to speed up, both at his nearness at my back and at being constrained again. Stark naked like this, I feel exposed except for where his closeness covers me.

But then, as soon as he's cuffed my left wrist, he pulls back and I'm left there, spread-eagled and completely vulnerable. My instinct is to draw my limbs into myself and ball up when I feel like this—*hide away, hide away!* seems to call some voice from deep inside me—but I quite literally can't, cuffed in this position. A small whine I can't help escapes my throat.

"What, my pet?" Domhn says, his heat and the comfort of his weight at my back again. His breath is warm in my ear, and I sink back against him as far as the restraints will allow. "What are you feeling? Tell me."

It's only because I'm playing along that I actually respond honestly. Or so I tell myself. "I- I feel exposed."

"That's good," he murmurs in my ear. "What else?"

"I want to curl in a ball and hide. I'd rather be in the cage. This is too exposed."

He nods and for a second, just a second, I feel his forehead drop against the back of my neck.

"Thank you for telling me something real." His voice is rough and intimate.

Then his weight disappears and again I'm left cold and clinging to a hard piece of polished wood.

There's a long moment of silence before his voice comes back, and when it does, all the warmth is gone. "Our game will be one of impact play. There will be ten strikes, ten being the highest in intensity and one being the lightest."

I blink at the wall, feeling like crying suddenly at the withdrawal of his intimacy. Which is stupid. This whole thing is just an emotional mind-fuck. He's toying with me. Of course my emotions are all over the place and he knows it. He's trying to throw me off-kilter. The fucking cunty bastard.

"You must take one strike of each intensity level, but you get to decide what order you take them in," he continues in his instructional monotone. "You must ask for each blow, stating which number you want. Afterwards, say thank you, Sir, and ask for the next. But remember, you must take all ten."

I breathe out, full of rage, grit my teeth, and say, "Ten."

"Yes, there will be ten."

"No, Sir," I correct him. "I want number ten."

He's silent a moment. "You're getting it backwards. One is the least intensity and ten is the—"

"I want ten. *Sir*. You said it was my choice."

He can't see my face but if he can feel any of the furious energy radiating off me, I'm not exactly playing a good little pawn. But fuck it. I have a feeling I'm about to go through a *thing*. I can worry about all my big plans ten strikes from now.

I can't see him, either, but it's as if I can *feel* him bristling as he walks towards the wall. I try not to picture the implement he's picking up. I spent too much time the other day examining each one of them in detail. There were some vicious-looking rubber whips. What would that feel like biting against my flesh?

"Number ten," he says, and then, with no more preparation, I hear the slightest whirring noise and then—

I see white and scream. Not from pleasure. This is pain, only pain. It explodes across the very bottom of my ass cheek, barely above where it meets my leg. Like a burn more than a blow. Tears immediately burst out of my eyes and down my cheeks.

"Now," he says, sounding short of breath even though I'm the one weeping in pain here, and all he did was whip me. "Thank me and ask me for the next."

How? I doubt if I can find my voice. I suck in a hiccupping breath. Though I suppose, as I finally do manage the breath, endorphins rushing in and the pain ebbing away with each heated pulse of blood towards the spot, I feel a little more back in control after the moment of absolute panic. My voice still wobbles as I make out, "T-thank you, Sir. Nine."

"You don't have to go in order," he snaps. "Choose a lower number to spread out the pain."

"Nine," I say stubbornly through my tears. I'll get through this my way, dammit.

Almost immediately there's only the barest noise of air being displaced, not nearly enough warning before my opposite ass cheek lights on fire. Again, it feels like all the breath I've only just barely gotten back is knocked out of me. More tears spurt from my eyes. My whole body shakes, and I go limp in my constraints, knees weak.

"Stand up," Domhn says ruthlessly. "If you ask for it, you take it. You've done this to yourself. It's much better if you build up with the lower numbers. You still can. Now thank me and be wise when you ask for your next number."

"Thank-you-Sir-eight," I say all at once before I chicken out, then suck in a deep breath and hold it, readying myself.

I'm still not prepared for the strike of what has to be one of the whips across my bare shoulders. The bite comes in such an unexpected place that again my knees go out from underneath me.

I swore to myself nothing could make me say "red", but I'm not sure if I can take much more, even if it's true that each blow is *slightly* less painful than the last.

But right as I'm about to say the words that will free me from this ridiculous pain, the warmth of Domhn's forehead is there again, pressing against the top of my spine as his voice comes back in a guttural whisper.

"You're doing so beautifully, love. I've never seen anyone take their first caning with such grace. Try not to stand so tense. Give yourself over to it. Go loose and give in. You're close to subspace. You're so savage, you got me banjaxed jus' like you always did."

His brogue comes on thick suddenly. "This is how it always coulda been between us, Mads. You an' me givin' in to our darkness t'gether. We coulda done aright, Mads. We coulda been jus' fine if you hadn'a run off 'n leff me like ya did. So give in now. Give in an' let it turn to ecstasy. Listen to me voice and give in. Take me marks like the good lass I know ya can be. Go loose, love. Go loose."

His drugging voice has me doing exactly as he says. I stand on my own two feet but go loose at the same time. I let go of all tension in my body.

"Tha's me good lass," he whispers, voice still musical as he backs up and another strike falls, again a whip, I surmise as a different spot on my butt cheek lights up with fire. But to my shock, while yes, there's pain, and more tears... it feels... it feels...

"Thank you, Sir," I say in slow wonder as a buzzing warmth flushes through me. My head goes fuzzy as if it fills with helium, lifting off from my body.

"Number?" he asks, voice heavy and thick.

I blink, still in my warm balloon lift-off. It takes me a moment to focus on his ask. "Seven," I finally drawl.

I blink again when a narrow, stinging paddle smacks

across my ass. My lift swings even higher. The rush of heat is incredible, and I wonder vaguely as my buzz lifts even higher, oh shit, is this what it's like to do drugs? Sweat beads my brow at the intensity of everything I'm feeling.

"Thank you, Sir," I say breathlessly. "Six."

I don't know what comes next but I'm excited and yearning in a way I shouldn't be considering how I was feeling at the start of this. But it's transformed, somehow. I can't tell if it's the power of the pain or Domhn's words or Domhn himself. I can't worry too much about whys right now. Especially not when the next thudding paddle against the round of my buttocks lifts me high again, the happy buzzy haze settling over me like a cloud.

"Thank you, Sir! Five."

There's a pause now before another, thuddy paddle thwacks the other butt cheek. There's a sting where it intersects some of the previous marks and it still fucking *hurts*. But overall, it's just this jiggle that resounds up and down my backside and it feels... *good*. And not enough, almost.

We're spiraling down in intensity even while I'm still up in the clouds and I'm starting to regret my choices. I wish I'd kept some of the higher numbers for the occasional lifting spike.

But there's nothing to do now except keep on the path I've chosen.

"Thank you, Sir," I swallow hard. I should try to get my

wits back about me. I really should. But I'm such loose jello, I can't quite manage. "Four."

Then he spanks me with his bare hand, and it stings and feels wonderful at the same time.

My voice clogs a little as I whisper, "Thank you, Sir. Three."

It's almost over. I'm not crazy enough to say I'd want to start over from the beginning, but some lunatic part of me isn't ready for it to be over, either. This unthinking, nonjudgmental fuzzy place is such a relief, and it's about to be gone. I'm not ready yet.

A bright spot of pain lights up my already sore ass when the thuddy tendrils of a flogger, harsher than the first one he used but gentler than everything else, lands. I suck in a stuttering breath. "Thank you, Sir. Two."

I gasp as the gentle flogger flips up between my spread legs and licks at my pussy. I wasn't wet until now, but at the gentle sting, moisture immediately springs up. I want to rub my legs together, but of course that's impossible with them spread and cuffed on the X.

"T-thank you, S-Sir," I barely manage to breathe out. "One please."

His voice comes out husky. "You can still say red. Anytime with no consequence. You've done so well. Perfect in fact. You're exquisite. I'd like to reward you. And myself."

What does that mean?

But he answers quickly enough. I'm still facing the wall,

but I feel him as he crawls between my legs. And I *definitely* feel his mouth, breathing warm breath *there*, in and out for several moments signaling what he's about to do.

Red. I can say red. The fog clears and I try to pretend that I'm not saying red because I'm still playing chess. But I can't lie to myself like that.

I want his mouth on me. After the experience we just went through together and the rollercoaster of intense sensation, I *need* his mouth on me and the ecstasy I know will follow. I could argue I deserve it, even.

But I think that's a lie too. I just fucking want it. Fuck the ghosts. The me that's *me* wants it. Little needy whines escape my throat, the longer he lingers, hot breaths tickling me and driving my need higher.

Maybe he's twisted my mind. Maybe somewhere in this I've gotten befuddled and turned backwards inside out on myself.

But the man who whispered in an intimate brogue about going loose and giving in—I *want* that man. In spite of how insane these fucking circumstances are. Fuck sanity. Fuck chess and all my well-laid plans. The craving has struck, and I need him with a wild fury as he waits, poised there between my legs.

"*Please*, Sir," I beg, my voice breaking with need.

The second the words escape my lips, his mouth is there. There's just enough space between the St. Andrews Cross and the wall for his head. He clasps my sore ass in his hands, clenching in a way that lights up the pain and sends me right back up into the swirly space as he drags my sex into his voracious mouth.

He only pulls away for a moment to demand, "Scream for me."

So I do.

It feels— Oh god—

I open my mouth and let out a high-pitched moan that rises up the scale as he drops his jaw, lunges forward, and devours me. I can't tell where my body ends and his mouth begins. His tongue, oh god, his *tongue*—

The orgasm denied yesterday howls back to life and I scream, pelvis spasming against his face. His fingers dig into my ass. He knows he's digging into the soreness. The pain and pleasure spike simultaneously, the one driving the other, taking it higher than it's ever been.

It ramps higher and higher, my entire body shaking.

And when I finally come, I shudder hard, once, twice, white spots taking over my vision and then I collapse against the cross.

Tears flow down my cheeks. "Please, Sir," I beg with the last of my energy. "Who am I to you?"

"The love of my life." His voice is hard. "And my greatest mistake."

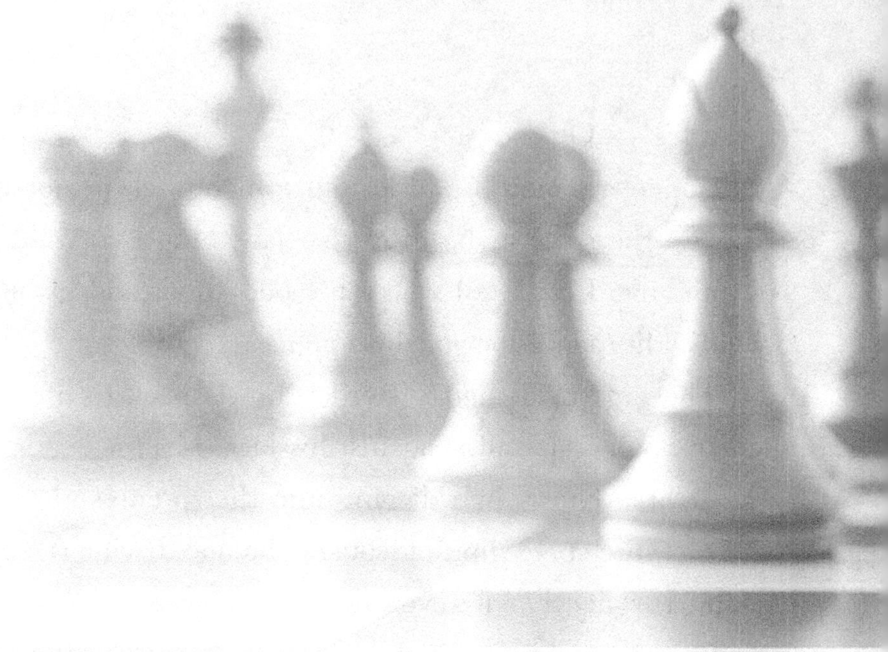

SEVENTEEN

DOMHNALL

IT'S difficult to perform aftercare, but at least she's silent as I uncuff her and lift her down from the cross.

I should never have admitted as much as I did. But I can't deny it to myself any longer: I'm obsessed with her.

She's docile as a kitten as I hold her for the allotted time my dominant training taught me to, then get up to leave. When she gets up out of bed, too, I expect her to try peppering me with questions again.

But all she does is drop down to her knees and crawl after me, nuzzling the back of my knees like a kitten might.

Fuck. Me. I drop a hand down to pet her head but

swallow down the words that are clogging in my throat, ready to pour out. Praise. Adoration. More.

Instead, I withdraw my hand and walk to the elevator. She crawls behind me but stops a full ten feet away from the elevator. I still glance behind me before I enter the code. Her head is in position, facing the ground.

Again I have to fight not to let out a *good girl*. She's only doing what she's supposed to.

I step on the elevator and watch her stay in position the entire time the doors close.

But as soon as they do, I drag both hands down my face.

I am so fucked.

She's all I think about. I'm hardly eating. Or working. I watch her day and night.

As soon as I get upstairs, I immediately go to my computer and pull up the monitor to watch her like a compulsion.

Like an obsession.

I buy her clothes that arrive in large boxes on my front door even though I want her naked all the time. I brought out the box of keepsakes I'd buried in the back of my closet and had *almost* convinced myself didn't exist. To torture myself. To remind myself.

She's too perfect.

She submits too well.

She's everything I dreamed of. She always was. She's haunted my nightmares for a decade, and now to have her here in the flesh, tantalizing me with her sweet tasting pussy, shaking and shuddering under my tongue, under my caning...

Fuck.

She's fucking playing me again and I'm letting her because it's such a sweet fantasy. I'm truly cunt-struck. It's the blight of lads from my country.

I know the bubble will pop and she'll show her true colors. Eventually, I'll find out what she really came here for.

But in the meantime, I'm marking her perfect, untouched body and watching her shake till she passes out from the places I take her. Her physiological responses are so real. Things I wouldn't have thought a body could fake.

Which makes some eejit part of me think this is... that maybe some part of this is... real, too.

I yank open the bottom drawer for the whip but even the action makes me wince. It's far too soon for another session. There's nothing to do but slam the drawer shut again.

I should be keeping my strength up, anyway. For the flip. For when she devastates me again.

My phone rings and I stab the green button with an irritated, "What?"

My sister launches directly in. "I don't like you keeping Brooke like this. And why haven't you been picking up my calls? You always pick up my calls. What's going on? And why won't you let anyone see Brooke?"

"She's fine." I suppose it was inevitable that I'd have to deal with Moira. Mads was apparently *staying* at her place. It infuriates me all over again that Madison targeted my sister even while all I want to do is go down to the dungeon and make her knees weak by edging her all to fuck.

"Then let me see her," Moira says.

"You can. Everyone can. At the club on Saturday."

Moira makes a disgruntled noise. I'm not one to usually deny her requests. She's used to a big brother she thinks she can wrap around her little finger. She doesn't know I've only *allowed* her to think that. "But... why?!"

"I've told you enough times that I prefer for my sexual proclivities to remain private."

"What! I don't want to know about—! You know I don't care about that. I'm just worried about Brooke. Are you being careful with her? She was in the hospital just six weeks ago!"

I roll my eyes. Sure she was. I'm sure she made her case sound *so* pathetic to get herself into my sister's good graces. For as worldly as Moira is in some ways, in others, she can be ridiculously naïve.

"Here, I'm faxing you her medical records. She shouldn't be playing hard after just getting out of the hospital. Why can't I just talk to her?" She sounds exasperated.

It's not fair or kind to stonewall my sister like this. "Because she's not allowed to come to the phone right now."

Another annoyed noise comes from Moira. "What the hell does that mean, Domhnall?"

I get down to the point. "Do you think I would hurt her?"

Moira makes a frustrated-sounding noise. "Well. Of course not."

"So what are you worried about?"

"She's fragile right now. And I'd just feel better if I could hear her voice. Don't you want me to feel better?"

Well look at that. My sister's learned my weak spots over the years, too. But fuck any fucking weakness. I won't be weak anymore. Not when it comes to Madison.

"Dammit, Moira, just stop worrying. I told you, you'll see her in a few days at the club. I just need you to trust me. I'm trying to do something important here with... *Brooke*... and it doesn't help to have you interfering every other second."

"I've only called once a day! And this is the first time you've even picked up."

A twinge of guilt hits me between my eyes. My sister's the only person I always pick up for, but I let her leave messages the past few days. She was only haranguing me about my choices with Madison.

But she's not the only one who can play on our sibling ties.

"Do you trust me?" It's unfair to ask this of her, but my past with Madison is always something I've protected her from.

I hear her difficulty when she breathes out harshly down the line. I'm being cruel to her and I know it.

"Yes," she finally says in a rush. "I trust you. But Brooke is a friend."

Her saying that only pisses me off again. If I'd realized Moira had been taking in strays from the shelter... That's it, I'm firing my current guard who's supposed to report all her activities to me. Then I roll my eyes again. Moira's probably fucking him by now anyway to get him in her pocket.

She wouldn't consider it as such, but she's got her own means of manipulation. She just happens to be giving away for free the thing almost everyone in the world wants: she's beautiful, a good listener and pretty much always wants to fuck you. She's hard to say no to.

"Well," I grind out between gritted teeth, "You'll see your good friend in three days, and she'll arrive in perfect condition." All the red marks I just put on her ass yesterday should have healed by then. A pity, because I've been looking forward to going down and watching her have to sit gingerly, then maybe adding more. I never thought of that morning-after benefit. Maybe that's what Caleb meant by the advantages of having a longer-term sub.

"Fine," Moira said, sounding petulant. "I know when I've lost a fight with you."

"We aren't fighting," I say with surprise. "You just didn't get what you wanted."

"Same thing," she sighs.

I give a genuine laugh out loud. "I've got to go."

"Just look at the records I'm sending." Then Moira hangs up.

She's not mad, she just forgets the social niceties of saying "hello and goodbye" sometimes. One of the things I love about my sister. We don't have to work so hard at fulfilling all the inane little social contracts such as tiring small talk that exhausts the both of us.

I breathe out hard, then look at the little project I've laid out for myself at the other side of the office.

It won't be long now. I feel it coming this time. The flip. No more fucking weakness. I'll be prepared.

Or so you tell yourself.

I'm still in control. I'm in control, goddammit.

Who's the liar now?

EIGHTEEN

BROOKE

I WAKE up screaming and slap my hand over my mouth. The other hand I wave wildly to make the lights turn on, breathing hard.

I'm shaking and sweating like usual when I wake up from the nightmares. Usually I lay still after I've turned on the lights and try to remember whatever I can from the dreams, but not tonight.

Tonight I'm on a mission.

Because two nights ago, I got the keycode.

I've had it for a whole day and not done anything with it.

That's fucked up.

I told myself I was waiting for the right time. That I didn't want him to suspect what I was up to.

I'm afraid that's all bullshit. I'm afraid I was afraid to leave.

Because after our impact play scene two nights ago counting from ten to one, when I got off the bed to crawl to the elevator with him, it was so natural to nuzzle close to him. He said I was the *love of his life*. And there was no ignoring the lift in my chest from how natural and easy it felt to disappear into the play between us.

But he didn't stay, even though I was affectionate. Even though I was supposedly the love of his life at some point.

Maybe that was the last straw.

He never stays. He'll always go. Because nothing I do could ever affect that cold man.

If I was ever loved by him, like he says, it was in the past. Too long ago for even the ghosts to resurrect.

So when he walked down the short hallway toward the elevator, I followed, crawling behind him close enough that my face occasionally butted up against his slacks.

Then I stopped ten feet from the elevator to let him know I was being obedient.

He paused and looked back at me, but I made sure to have my face firmly toward the floor like a good girl.

It was only when he turned back around to key in the code to the elevator that I lifted my eyes. It's what I meant to do all along when I decided to put on this subservient mask, before the mask started feeling all too real. Yes, my intentions became... fuzzy... somewhere along the way.

Thank god some last gasp of self-preservation reared up inside me. Because I clearly saw the numbers he quickly typed into the keypad. 2-0-1-6.

I immediately dropped my eyes back down. I couldn't be sure, but I swore he looked back at me right that second. *Phew*. Almost caught.

A ridiculous, futile impulse welled up inside me. I wanted to say, "Goodbye."

Maybe that was why I stayed the extra day today. Taking food from his hands for each meal. Relishing his gentle training.

Why hasn't he been harsher with me? Or has this been his trick all along? And I'm the fool to have almost fallen for whatever brainwashing all this was supposed to do to me? I'm probably still just weak-minded because of the amnesia.

Tears spring in my eyes as I swing my legs out of bed and glare at the floor. Weak little fool.

No. I've only been *pretending* to be a weak little pawn, even if playing the part has felt a little too real sometimes. He's had me so twisted around and upside down, I still feel elation at being near him, even if it's at his heel.

But you've always been the queen, I remind myself in a little pep-talk, *able to command the entire board.*

Now is the time to be strong. Strong enough to know I can't trust anything he makes me feel. I have to be bold now.

I know there are cameras on me twenty-four-seven, but even Sir has to sleep sometime. While I can't be sure it's even night-time because there's no clock, sometimes in chess, you've got to take a risk and hope your opponent doesn't see it coming.

So it doesn't matter that there's an impossible list of tasks in front of me now: escape the basement. Escape the mansion. Flee down the road with nothing but a sheet wrapped around myself. Flag down a car. Somehow make it to Chicago. Find my friend Ria at her aunt's house even though I don't even have an address, just her last name.

Start over with nothing.

Yes, I thought about going to the cops. They were nice enough when they interviewed me about the mugging, but ultimately pretty useless. Even if they weren't useless, I wouldn't— I swallow as I climb up into bed and admit the truth to myself. *I wouldn't want anything to happen to Domhnall.*

Yup. That's fucked up. He's already crawled in my head. The kitty in me nuzzles him there.

Yup that's me. Fucked up girl. That's all right. Who says normal's so great?

I don't wait any longer. I yank the sheet off the bed, wrap it around my body like a toga and calmly walk towards the elevator.

I type in the same code he did, and when the elevator

door springs open, my mouth drops at finding it empty. For a second, my foot hesitates before stepping inside.

But I'm not that far fucking gone. Yet. I leap inside the next second and slam the button for the ground floor over and over.

"Come on, come *on*," I whisper as the elevator doors take for-fucking-*ever* to close.

They *finally* shut and then my belly goes queasy as the elevator begins to lift. Oh shit. I'm actually doing this.

If I don't manage to escape and he catches me, he's going to be *so* pissed. There will definitely be punishment involved, and I don't think it will be anything so nice and lovely as what he's been doing so far. Even the impact scene. I know he's been holding back. *A lot.* Oh god, oh god, what am I doing?

You're doing what you have to.

Still, I wince, my eyes squeezing shut except for the tiniest slit as the doors open.

I breathe out in shock when I see Domhnall's not there. It's just an empty dark hallway.

Ha! I made it upstairs!

Now get on the move, dumbass.

I sprint out of the elevator. It's dark in the mansion. Only a few dim nightlights plugged in to the wall here and there provide any light at all. Holy shit, did I actually time this right? It's actually night out?

I don't take time to celebrate. I just keep running down the hallway where there's light, my bare feet slapping the cool tile floor as I look for an exit. I was too distracted the night I came in to have paid any attention to how we got to the heart of the house.

I reach a larger room, some sort of den, and think I see the glint of a pair of French doors that lead outside. I don't care if they aren't the front door. All I want is *outside*.

Except the moment I step inside the room, the light flips on.

I screech and look for Domhnall. I don't see him, though. All I can see is what was hiding in the darkness.

Dozens of photographs hang from the ceiling.

Some are small but others are blown up huge.

Stunned, I fall to my knees. I should keep running but I'm frozen as I look from one picture to the next.

Each photo depicts Donny as a young man. And beside him... beside him, holy shit, that's *me*.

NINETEEN

BROOKE

THE PICTURES... oh my god. It's Donny and me. Together. *Together* together.

It's a younger version of me than the woman I've seen in the mirror since I woke up with amnesia. But still, me.

I'm beautiful and blonde and grinning at Donny, just as he is back at me. But not with the sinister grin I've seen occasionally break out on his face.

He's... happy.

In the pictures, I'm happy, too.

I'm usually smiling at the camera, but in every shot, Donny's gaze is firmly locked on me. The joy crinkling his eyes is because he's looking at me.

This is just another trick, I try to tell myself. *He's faked these.*

I don't really believe that, though.

Something in a knowing place inside me, like a puzzle piece clicking into place, says these are *real*. The ghost is here. She's in the pictures and she's me and the hovering bits are so, so close I can taste them.

Donny and me.

I feel him. I feel *me*. I'm here. I'm right here, so close, tingling at the edges of my fingertips.

I stare harder at the pictures, reaching so hard for the rest of me. But all I can see is Donny. And the look on his face has me crumbling to the floor.

Donny's looking at me like he—

He's looking at me like he...

Like he *loves* me.

He wasn't lying. It was real. It was all real. Once, we meant something to each other.

I choke on a trapped sob.

It wasn't all a lie to torment or control me. He *does* know me. In a few pictures, I'm actually looking back at him. And I'm looking at him like— like I—

The sob breaks free from my chest.

I'm looking at him *like I love him, too*.

In the pictures, we're young and wildly in love with each other. I look happier than I could ever imagine myself being.

Donny looks so young and delirious with happiness, too, but he's... not carefree. I see that now, the longer I look.

There are deep shadows under his eyes and stress lines on his young forehead. The darkness I know in him so well now is there then, too. Does the ghost in the pictures see it? She looks oblivious, so lost in her own happiness.

Just then, the real flesh and blood Domhnall walks into the room, entering from the side with a half glass of whisky in his hand.

"Trying to run like always, Madison?" His voice is so cold.

"You're just trying to mind-fuck me more. These are fake!" I scream as I grab my head, even though I know it's not true. They're real. I don't know how, but they're real.

"Oh come off it, Mads," he jeers, stepping forwards. The ice in his glass is the only sound in the room. "You're a good actress, but you're not *that* good."

"If it's not fake then how could you *do* this to me?" I shout, gesturing accusingly with both hands. "You loved her."

I wave wildly again at the largest hanging photo in the room. The two kids in it have no eyes except for each other, completely absorbed in their shared little world. "We look like we—"

I break off and look at him in despair. I've been wondering where my family is ever since I woke up with no memory, and he's been here this whole time? "Why didn't you come for me when I went missing? Why are you *doing* this to me!"

"Why am I doing this to *you*?" He scoffs in disbelief, dropping his facade for the only time since that one moment in the dungeon when he let his forehead fall against my spine. "Are you serious?"

I feel like I'm finally seeing the real Domhnall, and maybe I can only see it in him now that I've seen the pictures of him younger. He's a wounded young man, capable of great love but shutting down every ounce of feeling inside himself.

"You're going to keep on pretending you have amnesia and don't remember meeting me years ago in Dublin?" he shouts.

I jerk at each loud syllable but stay where I am half crouched on the floor. He's finally telling me what I begged him to from the very beginning.

His voice softens, eyes hard but distant. "You were two years older, and so fucking sophisticated. This gorgeous blonde American, promising the world to some poor Donegal fuck. I was such a clueless feck'n mark, wasn't I?"

He turns back to me. "*Wasn't I?* When you and your cunt father—" He cuts off, jaw tensing.

"What about him? Is he still alive?" I ask desperately. Domhn obviously hates me. But is there someone out there who might love me as I am now and not just my ghost?

"You disgust me," Domhn seethes, and when I look back at him, there's nothing of the young man from the photos.

There's only pure hatred left. "Still only wanting to please your pedophile father."

His words shock me like a bucket of ice water thrown on my head. I suddenly feel sick. Is he just trying to be cruel again? "What the fuck does that mean?"

"Stop pretending you don't know!" he keeps shouting.

And then he hurls the glass of whisky against the wall opposite where I'm still on my knees. I jump at the explosion of glass even though it's nowhere near me.

"Just like you pretended you didn't know then!" His voice quiets, but it's only more dangerous. "He made me his dog. He pretended to be my mentor and then he raped me. Over and over and over. And you *knew*—" His voice breaks on the last word, pointing his finger in accusation at me.

I'm shaking my head. "I didn't."

He laughs bitterly. "So now you're done with the amnesia act."

"I didn't," I deny again. I couldn't have. The girl in that picture couldn't have known—

"You *did*."

"How do you know I did? There's no way I could've—"

"I know because you told me you'd seen!"

My shaking head stops at his words, too frozen in horror.

"You said you'd seen, and you were gonna go get all the money for us. You said for me 'n Moira to meet you at the airport. That we'd go start a new life together."

His face twists, again a mix of the young man in the

photograph and the dark creature he's become. "I was so ashamed when you said you knew. So full of self-loathing. That you'd seen. I couldn't bear to look at you. But ya reached out and took my jaw, jus' like this," he reaches out, hand caressing empty air as he continues, brogue suddenly heavy, "an' tol' me, with your eyes full of dew an' rage, that you'd go steal the only t'ing that bastard held dear and t'en we'd go start our life toget'er."

He smiles cruelly, eyes focusing back on me as if returning to the present. "But you weren't at the airport, were you? 'Cause you'd already run. With that fucking *monster*, after ya knew what he'd done to me."

"And to cap it off," he laughs caustically, walking to the nearby bar cart nestled against the wall, his shoes crunching on the glass from the cup he already shattered, "you left all the illegal shit pointing to me."

I'm still shaking my head. He's wrong. "Something must've happened. I couldn't get to you."

"O-aah, I thought the same. Until I learn't you'd fecked me over the same as you 'n him did ta at least two other lads I know of. You were just a soulless pair o' cons leavin' a pat' of destruction."

He glares back at me, unscrewing the cap of the whisky and lifting the whole bottle to his lips. "You're the hook 'n he swoops in on the prey you soften up for 'im. Cause he likes soft little boys, doesn't he? At least he's dead and burnin' in hell now."

He stares at me for a long, hard, horrifying moment before he starts to swig gulps of whisky straight from the bottle.

And I just stay there stunned on the floor. My mind cascades with all he's just told me.

No. There's no way. No. *NO*.

I wouldn't have— Not if I'd known what my father was—

I'm not that kind of person. Absolutely *no* fucking way.

But then I blink, spirals starting to whirl in my head, thought after thought.

Because what if... I mean...

Wouldn't anyone in my position say that? I've just been walking around assuming I was a good person because the me now wants to be.

But literally not a single person came forward when I went missing. Wouldn't that indicate that I'm... not that great? I literally have *no* one in my life.

Okay, but there's a difference between not having that many friends or family—or even being not that great a person and being the kind of incomprehensibly evil shit human being Domhnall is describing.

So no!

Of course fucking not.

I can't be who he's describing.

I *know* who I am inside. I might not know my name, but I know right and wrong. Good and bad. He's lying. I mean, I'm not—

I'm not a monster.

I'm not soulless.

Fuck the ghost! I don't know her. She's not me! I'm not responsible for whatever she did, or what she knew—

I couldn't possibly— Even if my father was. Oh god, especially if what he's saying about my father is true. Oh god, I'm gonna be—

I turn over and throw up all over the cushy, expensive rug. Once. Twice. Three times. Then I crawl away. I wipe my face on a clean part of the rug.

The rug is soft on my knees but rougher on my face. I rub my face on it again.

I look up at the picture of two people in love. All of their features drop away except their eyes. The scrunch lines around the edges. The shared shine in both pairs. Desperate adoration in his, as if she's one of the few pure things left in a violent, cruel world. In hers, a shocked sense of joy. In *mine*. Like it's happiness I've never felt before.

Everything shimmers.

How could she?

The boy in that picture loved the girl. And she loved him back.

I take one last look at Domhnall, still chugging whisky. The bottle that was three-fourths full when he started is almost empty.

Still on all fours, I scramble down the nearest hallway and into the dark.

TWENTY

DOHMNALL

AS THE FIRST rays of dawn shine through the windows, I stumble after her, barely managing to put the whisky bottle back on the cart without dropping it.

"Hey," I call. "Where do you think you're going? I'm not done with you yet."

Immediately I pull my phone out of my pocket, slapping myself for some clarity amid the warmth of the alcohol. Fuck. What am I doing drinking? I know better than to get caught up in such maudlin weaknesses.

I watch the phone for any perimeter alarms. Whenever an outer house door opens or closes, I'm alerted. But to my surprise, none of them trip.

She's staying inside the house? What the hell's she playing at now?

My head smacks into one of the poster paper photos I got blown up and hung from the wall last night using invisible twine. Laying my trap.

My little pet has been pretending to be so obedient lately, so suddenly and out of the blue? Rookie move. I tried it with her father week one. Thinking if I just played along things would go easier and I'd figure a way out of each session he managed to corner me in.

Always, he found some way to get me into his office. Every time, I swore I wouldn't be stupid enough to land myself back there.

But things were always so strapped with me trying to support Moira and me all on our own. With the money I was making with Mr. Harper, things were finally looking up for once in our shithole lives. I was learning things—real skills, programming shit I was never gonna have the money to pay a university degree for.

I was already in too deep by the time he started pulling the pervert shit. I'd gotten Moira and me outta the rat-infested closet we'd had to rent when we first got to Dublin and into a real apartment building. She was settled into her second semester at a private school, fitting in when that'd never happened before.

And then there was Madison.

What the fuck are you supposed to do when your girlfriend's father reaches down, and the accidental touches you've been trying to justify as those of an effusive mentor suddenly take that fucked up turn?

I mean, I knew about twisted fucks that liked to diddle little kids.

But I was seventeen. A man, at least to my own mind. Almost grown.

I'd heard this happened sometimes with bosses down at the mine. Lads and I joked how we'd kick a gobshite's teeth down his spine and out his arsehole if they ever tried it with us.

Turns out when the real thing was happening, I just shook there in feckin' disbelief about what Mr. Harper was doing to me, not making a move and silent as a mouse.

Then he ordered me to get on the floor like a dog.

I didn't realize it then, but it was the same voice he'd been using with me for months as he taught me code. He'd been conditioning me all along to obey him.

I didn't really know what the fuck was happening. I just know I got on the floor like a dog.

"Madison," I call out, my voice almost sing-song. It's probably just the alcohol, but I feel loose now that Madison's sins are acknowledged out in the open between us. Free. Let's be done with all the charades.

In this, let us finally be what we never were: ourselves.

"Oh Madison," I call again. "There's really no use in

hiding." I lift my phone. "I have cameras on every room in this property."

I flip through the feed of the first-floor rooms, sighing impatiently. "This is tedious, Madison. Aren't we a little too old for hide and seek?"

I don't see her on the first floor, so I check the hallways, the stairs, and finally, the second floor. There hasn't been enough time to have made it to the third, yet. I'm methodical, keeping an eye on the stairwells and elevator while I check each room.

Nothing.

And still no perimeter alarms.

Then I frown, knowing it's probably a waste of time but flicking over to the basement screen, anyway. And there she is.

What the fuck is Madison doing in the basement?

I put two fingers to the phone to zoom in further. At first, I'm immediately furious. I swear to fuck, if this is another cunting trick—

I stomp over the back stairwell to the basement. I stab in the code to the keypad—the same one as downstairs. 2016. The year my life went all to fuck. The year I met Madison Harper.

I yank the heavy door open and take the stairs two at a time.

"What the fuck, Mads? You think you're going to win more good girl points by hiding away down here? This is not a scene. I'm having a real conversation with you. The conversation you denied me by running off like the thief you are. It's called being *accountable* for fecking once! Do ya hear me?"

She came down here. That means she knows she's going to get the punishment of a lifetime for pulling this shit. I swear, when I get my hands on her little ass, I'm going to turn it *red*—

I shake my head. What the fuck? I literally just said this isn't a scene. But I'm already thinking about the punishment? And only the kind of punishment that puts my mark on her ass and has her shuddering in pleasure in that ecstatic space I know she likes to go to when she starts feeling really stressed out, getting her worked up for a release—

"Madison," I snap when I finally step into the dungeon. She's exactly where I saw her on camera.

Curled in the tiniest ball in the dog cage. Door shut on top.

"Madison," I bark.

She stays where she is, curled up as tight as her body could possibly get. It's not a generous-sized cage. It's impressive she got all her limbs in and still managed to close the top in on herself.

Finally, she turns her head my way.

Her eyes are wide, a little spacy, and she tilts her head at me. Then her eyes shift away towards the wall.

"Oh, fuck."

My phone drops to the carpet as I sprint to her side and drop to my knees.

"Madison!"

Something's wrong.

Really wrong.

Usually, I'm a good dom. Not now, fucking obviously.

Now I'm too fucked to even be called a dominant, and certainly not one allowed back in any community.

But I used to be a good dom. Good enough to recognize when something's wrong.

And whatever's happening right now with Madison—Brooke—is really, really wrong. The vomiting upstairs, and now the catatonic stare.

Fuck! These are signs that something's gone really, really off.

I yank the cage lid open and delicately lift Brooke's tiny shivering body from the cold bars.

"Shhh, it's okay," I whisper into her oily hair. Fuck, I haven't been taking care of my pet. There are rules. Like safe, sane, and consensual. There are rules for a fecking *reason*.

"It's gonna be okay." I kiss her forehead.

For several minutes I just cradle her shivering body in my arms, calling her name, both Madison and Brooke, but I don't get any response at all. Just the dead-eyed stare.

Carefully, with her still in my arms, I scoot over to where I dropped the phone.

I went too far. She needs help. Real help, and not from a power-hungry fuck bent on breaking her for revenge.

Congratulations, fuckface, you got what you wanted. You broke her. How does it feel?

My stomach twists with nausea at what I've become.

I let out a furious grunt when the phone beeps with a *no service* notification. Goddammit, I've got to get out of the basement if I want to make a call. There's no way in fuck I'm leaving Brooke here, though. I shove the phone in my pocket and look down at her.

Her eyes still stare out at nothing and my heart leaps into my throat with terror. "It's gonna be okay," I whisper as I squeeze her closer to me and stand up. Cradling her tightly to my chest, I hurry out of the room and towards the stairs at the end of the hallway.

"You've been such a good, good girl."

Her eyes suddenly flick up towards mine, the tiniest bit of recognition coming back into them.

"Such a good, good girl," I reassure her, throat tight. "My best girl. You've done so, so well through some difficult testing. But now it's time to rest."

An anxious line enters her forehead as her eyes search my face before she nudges my chest with her nose a few times.

"Brooke?" I whisper with hope as I key in the code, pull open the door, then take the stairs up, still holding her close to my chest. "Brooke, love. You with me?"

Her stare goes a little blank.

"Pet?" I try, and her eyes snap back to me. I nod at her, holding eye contact. "You've done so well, we're going to take a little rest. You've been such a good, good girl."

Relief enters her face, and she curls her head against me. Fuck, maybe it's not as bad as I think. Maybe she just needs a little time and some sleep and then she'll come out of it.

I hit the top of the stairs and drop down on the nearby couch. Brooke has made herself into a little ball again, this time just curled up on my lap, head against my chest.

I lift my phone and hit dial on Caleb's number.

"Jesus, do you know what time it is?" comes his groggy voice.

"Shut up, it's an emergency."

"What happened?" He sounds more alert.

"I need a psychiatrist. I think I broke Mad— Brooke. I might've broken Brooke."

"What the fuck do you *mean,* you broke her?" He's so fecking alert now he's shouting down the phone.

"Do you know somebody or not?"

"Jesus fuck, you're gonna get the club in so much fucking trouble—"

"Caleb!" I yell, covering Brooke's ears. "Focus. Brooke needs help. If I need to take her in somewhere, fine. I just know from shit with Moira that too many head-houses are pill mills that don't know shit about actually helping someone." No matter how much you pay. Some just have better brochures. "I need real *help*. Fucking now! Anyone in the club *know someone*, know someone?"

"We have strict fucking rules for a reason," Caleb starts in on me, "so no one gets *broken* at the club. I can't believe—"

I squeeze Brooke closer to me, trying to warm her up with my body heat. She's still shivering so bad. Fuck, I want to kick myself. Of course she's not warm enough. I keep the basement a solid seventy-two degrees, but I haven't lived down there naked. She's probably been freezing the whole time.

"What?" I ask, ready to hear Caleb's worst. "You can't believe what?"

He'll be right, whatever he says. I might be a sadist, but I've prided myself on sticking to the rules. I tried to tell myself that they didn't apply to Madison but it's *wrong* for anyone to treat her like this—

I've become just like the monster I spent my entire life loathing. I started out thinking it was some sort of poetic justice. Because I wasn't even smart enough to see that as a pitiful veil for the truth: I'm just another pathetic statistic, turning into my own abuser.

Caleb lets out an explosive breath. "I might know someone, actually."

"Well give me their fucking number already!"

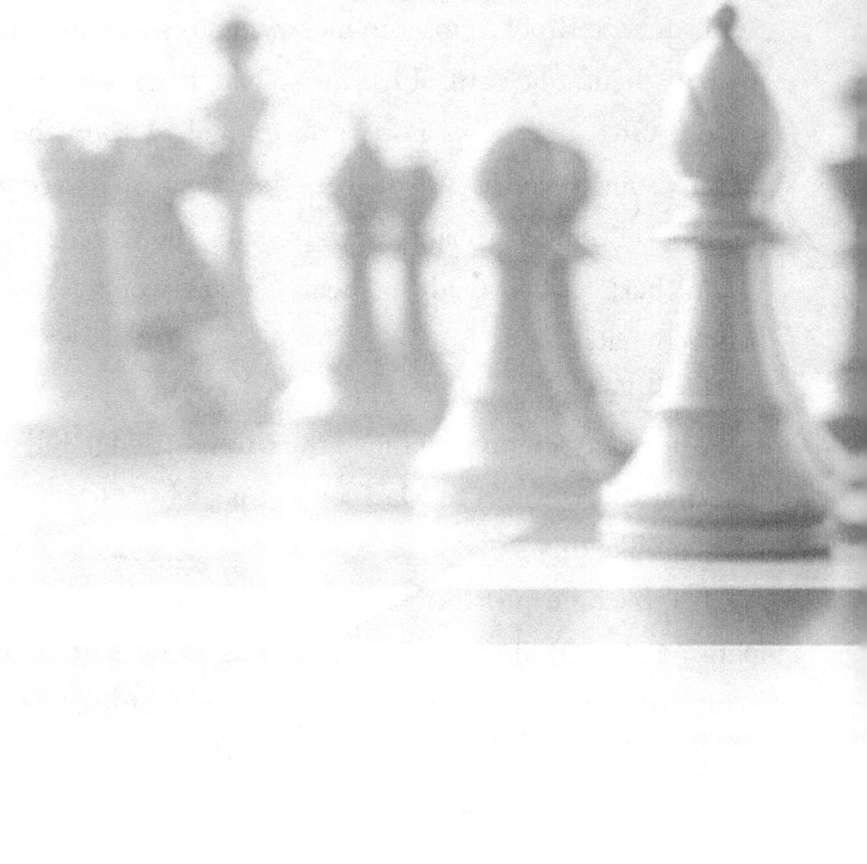

TWENTY-ONE

DOMHNALL

I PACE back and forth in the hallway while Caleb stares at his phone.

"Where'd you get this woman, anyway?" I ask for what feels like the hundredth time, glaring towards the door of the room where the young therapist insisted on talking alone with Brooke.

What kind of doctor shows up with messy hair in a bun, wearing a stained t-shirt and loose pajama pants? Sure, we called her at the ass crack of dawn, but still. It doesn't seem very professional. Not to mention, it took her about a thousand years to get here.

And then, once she finally did, she didn't listen when I

tried to explain to her that I needed to stay in the room with Brooke. Brooke just stares lifelessly at the wall when I'm not there. But the therapist only looked at me nonplussed, then ushered me out of the room, anyway.

Caleb waves a hand, not looking up from his phone. "She's in contact with the club."

I storm over to where he's standing. "You keep saying that. What the fuck does that mean? Is she someone's sub? A domme who wants confidentiality? Fucking *what*?"

He finally puts his phone down. "She's a local student getting her Ph.D. in Abnormal Psych. She's been emailing the past few months, asking if she can interview members of the club for her dissertation."

"Tell me you're fucking joking."

He holds up his hands. "Obviously I can't let her, for confidentiality reasons. And I told her this was strictly off the books but that if she wanted to come in as a voyeur sometime, maybe I could arrange a strictly anonymous visit."

"That's not my fucking point. I need a professional. And you brought me a fucking hack?"

"Not a hack. She sounded very informed on the couple of phone calls we've had and has some impressive publications. She knows her stuff. She was the best person to call."

"You mean she was the only person you had to call."

He shrugs. "If she can't figure something out, we'll take Brooke to a real doctor."

The door finally opens, and I leap forwards to confront

the woman who's curly haired bun is now lopsided, glasses falling down her nose. She shoves them back up, then glances at me before immediately focusing back on Caleb.

"She's in a depersonalized state," she starts.

"What's that?" I butt in. "Like dissociation?" I don't know what the fuck I'm talking about, but I feel like that's a word I heard in my dominant training somewhere along the way.

The therapist—Professor Roberts—glares back my way. "It's a type of dissociation."

"Fine. What does it do?" I ask impatiently.

"I was about to tell you. If you'd give me a moment to speak." Another glare.

I shut my mouth even though I want to shout a hundred more questions. The pent up energy inside me needs an outlet. I need to fix this. I need to get in there with Brooke. I need to see her. Hold her. Make it right.

She takes a quick breath. "Depersonalization is when you detach from yourself. From your body, your mind, your feelings. It lets you feel like you're on the outside of your body. Sometimes like you're watching your thoughts and feelings from a distance. Sub-space can be a healthy way for people to access this space safely, because it can also be euphoric. Some think healing, even, because it provides a safe way into depersonalization, and back out through aftercare." Her glare turns harder as she seethes, "When practiced *properly*."

I'll take this lady's rage and all Caleb and anyone else wants to dish out on me. Later.

"What can you do to fix her?" I demand.

"It's not like we can give her a pill or wave a magic wand and fix her." She looks at me incredulously.

I glance at Caleb. Her initial suggestion isn't pills. Okay. She's already passed my first test.

I cross my arms, foot tapping impatiently. "What then?"

I detest not being the one with answers. I run my life in a very particular way to make sure I'm in control of every room I step into. And now, when I need it the most, I'm fucking floundering. I don't know what the hell to do, and it makes me want to hurt something. Tears. Screams in response to measured strikes. That's what I need. Instead all I can do is stand here and tap my fucking foot, relying on half-a-doctor to fix things.

Professor Roberts puts her thumb to her mouth, biting her nail and pacing a little. "I'm not a doctor. I can't design a treatment plan. I shouldn't even be talking to you after consulting with her since you aren't family. It violates all sorts of doctor/patient confidentiality shit—"

"Fine," I bite out. "But like you said, you're not a doctor yet. So say you hypothetically ran across a case like this. In a fictional, hypothetical school scenario. What the fuck would you do?"

Professor Robert's eyes come towards me and she stops gnawing on her thumbnail. "I suggest taking her back home to a familiar environment where she feels loved, comfortable and safe. Until she starts to feel like herself again. Considering her current state and recent amnesia diagnosis, I would want to consult with her residing doctor. I'd want to ask if they think dissociative amnesia could've been a cause of her original memory loss, perhaps catalyzed by the blow to her head."

"What?" I bark. "The amnesia's real?"

"I thought you ran a safe, ethical club," the woman continues furiously to Caleb, still refusing to look at me. "Is this why you won't let me observe? She looks well-nourished enough, but when was the last time she had a shower?"

Shame cows my head. *You're a stupid fucking incompetent little bitch dog, aren't ya boy?*

I squeeze my eyes shut and turn away from Caleb and the Professor. I know that care of the sub always comes first and foremost. Full stop. I never should have started playing with Mads, no matter what. No matter my rage and thirst for revenge. *Especially* because of my thirst for revenge. Fuck.

What was I thinking? I wasn't. That was the problem. Why didn't I look at the records Moira sent over? I never even checked the email.

"What?" Caleb holds his hands up. "No! This situation just went off the rails. I swear. This is not usual club protocol."

I yank my phone out and thumb through my many emails to find Moira's. "If you know her history, you know there is no home to go back to," I mutter as I keep searching. "There's nowhere safe and cozy for her to land."

There. I click on the email and bring up the attachments.

And my jaw tenses at the second line. *Age: estimated* 22-24.*

What the *fuck?*

I shake my head in denial. That can't be right. I knew her nine years ago. She's two years older than me, and she was nineteen then. So she's twenty-*eight* now, not— Not—

I mean, it's true she still looks really young now but—

I shake my head again. She couldn't have been... I quickly do the math and feel sick. She couldn't have been *thirteen* when I fucking knew her back then.

No way.

My eyes scan through the rest of the report. The estimated age had an asterisk beside it, so I follow it down to read the notes: **X-rays indicate bones have not completed fusion.*

What in the *actual* fuck? If this is right, then... She was barely older than Moira. Holy fucking shit, I'm going to be sick. We never had sex or anything. But we made out plenty.

My hand clenches around my phone in a white-knuckled grip.

That motherfucking bastard. If he wasn't already dead, I'd find him and cut off his balls while he was still alive to fucking watch.

He sent her out when she was just a kid in mid-drifts and booty shorts to do his dirty work. She was just a fucking *kid*.

And I was dumb enough to fecking fall for it. What the

fuck else did he make her do? He was an evil, viciously sadistic motherfucker and she lived with him.

I was so caught up in my own fucking pain, I never truly considered it. A year with the man manipulating me, four months of which he destroyed me both body and soul, and it shredded me in a way I've never recovered from.

But Brooke, Madison—whatever her real name is, she was Rachel to Alfie, and Emma to Romaine—she spent thirteen or fourteen years with the monster by the time she'd met me. Who knows how her father had twisted her mind and soul by then.

Her father loved inflicting pain. He probably *arranged* for her to see what he was doing to me and then yanked us apart when it would inflict maximum damage.

He enjoyed destroying a person's soul and watching while it happened. I knew he always loved using Madison against me, but what if he was using *me* against *her* at the same time? Playing evil fucking games on both of us? God, he must've enjoyed watching us destroy each other far more than he ever could.

And afterwards... how many years was she with him? What the fuck did he *do* to her? I've seen her body, and it doesn't have any marks on it. But I knew her father well enough to know he loved to lash a mind as much as he did the body.

Holy fuck.

She's an innocent. The amnesia's real and—

She's been an innocent all along.

"Fuck this." We've left her alone for too long.

I shove through the door to get back to her.

Brooke's there shivering on the couch, naked; the blanket I covered her with before the doctor came has fallen heedlessly to the floor. She looks so pathetic and uncared for, and I want to go whip my back until I'm bleeding, on my knees, and unable to walk for a month.

Bad dogs deserve to be whipped, don't they, boy?

I hurry over to her and wrap her in the soft cable-knit blanket again, lifting her back into my arms. "You've been such a good girl waiting here for me."

Her eyes lift to meet mine and she smiles at me like I'm the sun just lifted over the horizon.

"Such a good, good girl," I whisper, my voice breaking.

She beams and nuzzles her face against my chest.

"Fuck me." I look up at Professor Roberts standing just inside the door, eyes locked on us. Then she glares, first at me, then Caleb.

"Unfortunately, it looks like he's the only one she's bonded to right now," she says to him. "I'm supposed to be teaching class in two hours but I'm not comfortable leaving her alone with some drunk asshole who doesn't know what the hell he's doing. You better stay with them."

"I promise, I've sobered up," I growl. "And here, take my phone. You can monitor us whenever you aren't in class."

I carry Brooke in my arms with me as I walk towards the

Professor. I can't bear not to be touching her when she's in such a vulnerable state. She might have been just a kid back then, but she's a woman now. And she's mine. I won't let anything bad happen to her ever again.

I can fix this. I *can*. I just have to get back in control. I'll fucking *fix it*.

"Take my phone," I repeat.

Professor Roberts levels me with her eyes, but it's easy to shift Brooke in my arms so I can reach in one pocket and pull out my phone. I hand it over to the Professor.

"What am I supposed to do with this?" she asks suspiciously.

I tell her the passcode. "Every room in this house is wired with cameras. You can watch my every move. Cut my balls off if I do something you don't approve of."

She narrows her eyes but takes the phone, if only so I can grasp Brooke with two hands again.

She shakes her head at us, eyes cutting between me and Caleb. "I should call the cops."

But then she glances at Brooke. I look down too, wondering what she's seeing. There's Brooke, face absolutely peaceful as she curls into my chest. The happiest little kitten.

Fuck. Just how deeply did I break her?

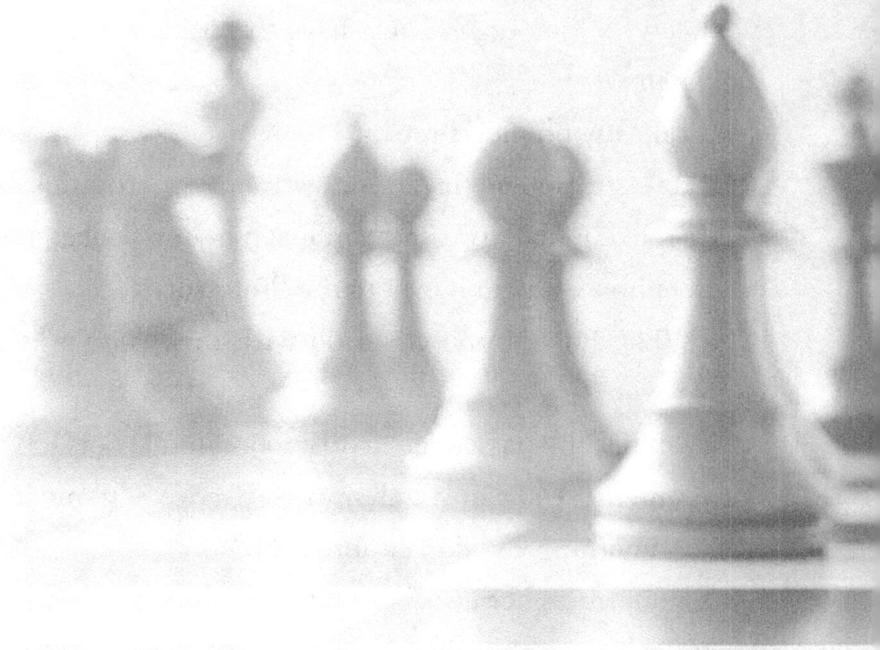

TWENTY-TWO

DOMHNALL

"I'M NOT LEAVING before I get her bathed and see she's resting peacefully," Professor Roberts says.

I nod. I don't love having to defer to other people, but I'll do whatever's best for Brooke. Her eyes are closed but I know by the way she frowns and furrows closer against my chest when Professor Roberts speaks that she's not asleep.

"Brooke," Professor Roberts says in a gentle voice I haven't heard until now, "Can you try to walk for us?"

She glares at me over Brooke's head and gestures for me to set Brooke down. I don't love the idea when Brooke is clinging to me for dear life. But I'm the one who fucked things up here, so I'll listen to the professional.

When I try to pry Brooke's arms from around my neck, though, she makes a pitiful noise. I set her feet on the floor, but she immediately collapses to her hands and knees, pushing her face against my legs like a shy child.

... Or like a shy kitten.

Professor Roberts watches on, nonplussed. Her lips purse in thought, but when she next looks up at me, it's not with the disgust or judgement I expect. "All right. Brooke, we're going to have Domhnall carry you to the bathroom. Does that sound all right?"

Brooke doesn't acknowledge her, but when I look down, her big brown eyes meet mine, full of trust. My chest clenches, feeling the connection still between us. *Mine.* She's still mine.

It's a fucked up thought. I'm fucked up.

But for whatever reason, she's chosen to trust me.

It's not trust, you fucking bastard.

I manipulated her into bonding to me. I utilized my extensive skills and I did—

I did... what was once done to me.

I was an innocent once, too. So long ago I can't remember what it felt like. But I was an innocent, preyed upon by a monster.

But I'm the monster now.

I swallow hard and sweep her up into my arms. I feel my monstrous insides pulsating, shameful and disgusting, as it stretches its claws around her. But she just curls against me with the trust of a newborn babe.

She loved me the same way that summer. *Thirteen.* Jaysus fecking Christ. Four years between us isn't that much now, but when I was seventeen?

He was making a monster of me even then and I didn't fucking know it. Stamping me with his soiled touch in a way I'd never get off. It doesn't matter that he's dead. The disease of him lives inside me, poisoning me into the fucked up, *wrong* thing I am today.

Brooke clutches my neck tighter, face nuzzling in as if she can sense the war inside me.

Fuck.

None of it matters.

All that matters is the sub in my arms *now*.

Subs come first.

Take care of the sub at all costs. Those are the rules.

Caleb jogs in front of Professor Roberts and I towards the elevator. He's been to my house for a few events before but never to my bedroom. Still, he knows most of the bedrooms are upstairs and hits the *up* button. I see Professor Roberts eyebrow lift when she sees the personal elevator. Did she not pay attention to the address when she pulled up? They don't call it Billionaire's Row for nothing.

I punch in the keycode, and we ride up to the third floor, my personal floor, and I lead them to my bedroom. Brooke nuzzles me the entire way. Caleb hurries to the ensuite bathroom to turn on the bath.

"I'll take it from here," Professor Roberts says. I know it's right that she should.

But then Brooke makes that pathetic noise again and clings tighter to my neck.

I squeeze her possessively to my chest and shake my head. "I don't think my kitten wants that. Thank you for your help, Professor Roberts, but I've got it from here. I'll give my good girl proper aftercare and get her to bed."

Professor Roberts's eyes go hard. "Where? In your kennel downstairs?"

Brooke's fingers dig into my neck. She can sense the other woman's anger. She's so sensitive right now, like all her nerves are frayed and she's reactive to the tiniest shift of mood around her.

"Shhh," I say, running my palm over her head, cupping her to me. "Pet will sleep in my bed tonight after the bath."

"Really?" Brooke says, lifting her head from my chest to look me in the eye.

I'm so gratified to hear her voice that I barely notice Professor Roberts and Caleb taking a step back in the background.

Brooke actually talking must have proved something to the Professor if she's finally backing off. I have no doubt she'll be watching my every move on the cameras from now on, but I don't give a shit.

I'm lost in Brooke's pleased, surprised eyes. She might still be in a dissociative state, but at least she's mostly making eye-contact instead of staring off into nothingness.

"Really," I smile gently, trying to rebuild trust with her. The real kind, if that's even possible at this point. It doesn't matter, though.

All that matters is pulling her back from the brink. The Professor said aftercare could provide a bridge back to reality. So I'm going to give the best aftercare any dom ever aftercare'd.

"You'll get to snuggle side by side with me in my arms. It'll be warm and safe. But first, let's get you cleaned up, all right?"

Brooke nods, still not losing eye contact with me.

That's better. When she's in full-on kitty mode, there's no eye contact.

"I'm going to carry you to the bathroom now."

She nods, staring at me as if mesmerized. There's still something not quite right in her eyes. She looks spacy. Not quite here with me.

C'mon, Brooke. If you survived years with that evil, malicious bastard, you're strong enough to survive a week with me being a psychotic asshole, aren't you?

I don't want to contemplate the particulars of that fucked up question.

I take her to my huge bathroom and look back and forth between the bathtub and the multi-headed shower. There's a bench in the shower, but the multi-jets in the sauna-like bathtub might help ease any aches or soreness she might have.

In the end, I turn off the bath and opt for the shower instead. I want her to feel completely clean, and the multi-showerheads can accomplish it best. We can always revisit the tub tomorrow.

I unpeel the fluffy blanket that's still partially wrapped around Brooke, kick off my shoes, and walk into the shower after it starts steaming. I'm still wearing clothes, but I don't give a shit.

I sit us down on the wide bench as steam envelops us, her on my lap with her legs to the side.

"Warm," Brooke says, holding out a hand tentatively towards the central spray.

"That's a good girl," I encourage.

She yanks her hand back when it makes contact with the water and hides her face in my now damp shirt again.

"It's alright," I soothe. "The warm water will feel good on your body. We're going to get you clean now."

She shakes her head slightly.

She needs me to have my shit together right now and take control. Fuck knows I need it too. So I make my voice firm. Unyielding. "Good kitties take baths when their owner tells them to."

She blinks up at me. "Good kitty?"

I hold her eye contact as I reach for the hand-held shower head beside the bench and nod. "Good kitty."

She seems unconvinced as I bring the spray nearer. "Not bad kitty?"

She asks with such earnestness that it makes me wonder what's going on in her mind. Now I wish Professor Roberts was back.

Brooke fell into this state because of all the accusations I was hurling at her.

If Professor Roberts was right and Brooke already had dissociative amnesia before that night on the auction block, what the *fuck* happened to land her on the doorstep of the women's shelter where Moira works?

I pissed on her father's grave two years ago. So where has she been since then? Why did she only show up now? What took her so long to come find me? The hospital report said she only got hit on the head two months ago.

Has she been here silently watching me and Moira from the shadows since her father died? Then some sort of bad luck ended her up in the wrong alley at the wrong time of night, coincidentally bringing her into our path?

After all we've been through, I just can't believe that.

"Not bad kitty," I manage to say through a thick throat. "Good kitty. Good girl. Beautiful fucking exquisite girl. I'm going to wash you now."

She looks scared, but she nods. She turns and hugs me, face in my neck.

I bring the spray against her shoulder, and she shudders, clinging to me.

"Shhh, it's okay." I grab my bottle of body wash and squirt some on her shoulder. I massage in the body wash while I run the water over the rest of her back. She moves, slinging her other leg around the other side of my lap. It makes me glad I still have all my clothes on. It's good for access to wash her when I get to it next, but difficult for the perma-hard-on I always have around her. Professor Roberts would not approve.

It doesn't help when Brooke grinds against me, letting out little high-pitched mewling noises in my ear as I massage foaming shampoo into her hair.

She does get turned on at the drop of a hat whenever I touch her, so I should've expected this. Control. I'm taking back my fucking *control*.

I breathe out roughly as I wash my shampoo out of her hair, next inhaling the steam and the scent of my shampoo and body wash on her. The idea of her coming out of the bath smelling like me makes my cock pulse even harder.

As if feeling it, she writhes on top of me where I sit on the bench with even more fervor, bowing her head towards my ear.

"Touch me," she whispers, teeth nipping at my ear.

I'm befuddled by having her on top of me after all the revelations and realizations today.

She's not who I thought she was. She's pure. Whatever she did or didn't do in the past—she was twisted by a sadistic fuck of a puppeteer. But she's innocent and always has been.

If I take advantage of her now while she's so vulnerable, I'm nothing more than the game piece he intended me to be. Fucker always did love chess. He used it against me all the time. If I won, I'd get a night off from him, so I tried to master the game. But I never could win a single match against him.

Even from the grave, he's trying to twist me into even more of a sick, contorted beast. And I fucking *refuse* for any more of my life to be dictated by that vile fuck.

So I allow my sweet kitten to mewl and paw and rub herself against my hardness while I wash her, all the while telling her what a good girl she is.

"Sir," she mewls, "good kitty get a treat?" she begs.

I close my eyes as she flips around on my lap so her back is to my chest. Her hips writhe her naked, wet cunt back and forth against my clothed hard-on like a lap dancer as her body finally uncurls into the warm spray of the second showerhead.

My teeth clench.

It's Mads. My Mads.

It's always been her. Only ever her.

And now she's here, with nothing between us.

I want to pick her up, press her against the wall and shove into her, claiming her the way I've imagined a thousand times.

Right. Because there's nothing between us... except for her dissociative amnesia and the fact that I've kidnapped and broken her after buying her at a virgin auction.

Fuck.

"Take your treat, kitty," I growl, keeping my hands in what I feel are strict safety zones. I wash her underarms. "Take everything you deserve."

My jaw locks, teeth gritted, as I scrub her back in slow, massaging circles. I've already washed here, but it's another safe zone, and that feels very important at the moment.

Because she's just set her hands on her widespread knees and bent over, rutting her pussy against the hard staff of my cock that's all but bursting through my wet black slacks. She seems quite focused on rubbing her clit back and forth against just my tip.

Holy motherfucking Mary mother of Jaysus Christ—

It's taking every ounce of my so-called iron control not to yank open the button to my drenched slacks, flip her around, and drag her down on my cock.

What's more healing aftercare than a good fuck?

That's just my dick talking. I blink and keep massaging her back with the water.

But when she starts lifting up and down as if she's trying to get my cock to go *in* her pussy *through* the layers of clothing, my control snaps.

I flip her around by her waist so that she's facing me and settle her back on my lap. Her legs cradle my waist, knees on the bench on either side of my hips. My cock is cemented between us against her tummy, literally about to burst the fabric of my slacks.

"Put your head down on my shoulder," I instruct thickly, shocked I can manage words at all. She obeys immediately. "Eyes closed."

She nods against my shoulder, gently rocking against my hardness. Jaysus fuck.

I lift the shower head by the bench and start to run water through her hair, washing out any lingering shampoo and taking the opportunity to massage her scalp.

"I love your hands in my hair," she murmurs, then she starts to thrust against my cock again.

Her arms fling around my back and her spread legs widen even further until she's all but riding me. And I do mean riding me. Because my cock—oh fuck, she's finding friction against me right where she needs it. I keep my hands in her hair long after I'm sure all the shampoo's washed out. Jaysus fuck, she's gonna fecking kill me. I'm in control— I'm in control— I'm in contr—

Her mewls turn to little screams as her thrusts become even wilder, almost violent. But there are little notes of dissatisfaction, too. Like she can't quite get where she's trying to go.

Goddammit.

She needs to come. I'm a cruel dominant to deny her after the day she's had. I said she could get a treat. So I stand up. She's still wrapped around me like a koala, so she goes with me.

"That's right, kitty," I growl into her ear. "Take what's yours."

I press her body against the smooth marble wall, so she feels all of me.

Then I yank the manual shower spray back up and turn it to maximum pulsing mode. Lowering it, I hold the shower head down between our bodies, aimed upwards precisely where she needs it.

She's got the pressure of my cock pressed against the top of her clit and now the pulsing water thrusting up from underneath.

She immediately lets out a little cry, her eyes flying open as I start to thrust my hips rhythmically into hers. "You're the sexiest woman I've ever met. I want to do such dirty, dirty things to you."

"Like what?" she squeaks, her breasts arching out into my face as a spasm of pleasure wracks through her body.

"Like putting you over my lap and spanking you until your ass is red from my handprint. So you know you're mine. I'll enjoy your little yelps of pain. I'll enjoy the way you squirm on my cock and beg me for more. I'll slip my hand down between your legs after ten swats to rub your clit just the way you like, then I'll allow you to beg me for ten more before I eat you out."

"Now." Her face contorts, so close to orgasm. "I want it *now*. Touch me. Eat me now."

"This is all you get until Brooke comes all the way back to me, not just kitty."

I tease the pulsing spray right where she needs it. But she

and I know it's not enough. It's not my fingers. It's not my tongue. It's not her sitting on my face.

"Please, Sir."

"That's not my name," I whisper in her ear, shifting the pulsing spray rhythmically back and forth along with my hips. "What's my name?"

"Sir," she says, eyes squeezed shut with pleasure, peaks of her hardened nipples only an inch away from my mouth. It's difficult not to graze my teeth along them like I long to. It would ratchet her pleasure even higher. But I'm not sure I could keep the razor's edge of control I'm walking.

Plus, keeping her on the edge pleases the sadist inside me. I could keep her here all day, torturing both of us. The hot water won't run out.

"So close, my good girl, but you know that's not my name." I tug the pulsing spray away from where she wants it and put a little space between our bodies. She makes a sharp noise of protest.

"What's *your* name?" I lift the pulsing spray and blast her beaded nipples with it.

She gasps, eyes popping back open as her nipples harden and extend outwards. She wriggles her hips back and forth frantically, but I've shifted so she can't get much relief that way.

"What's your name?" I ask again.

She mewls with need, and I blast one nipple. She arches towards the spray and I almost lose the load bursting in my balls right there. She's going to go absolutely crazy when we get to nipple play. I haven't even clamped her yet. I blast the other nipple and her head swings back and forth, bottom lip clamped between her teeth.

Fuck. I'm getting distracted. Plus I don't know if we'll ever get to nipple clamps or anything else. I just need to get her to come back to me.

"Your name," I demand, dropping the spray until she looks at me again, eyes desperate.

"Kitten," she gasps.

I drop the spray to dangle from its hose again and lift a hand to caress her face. "Love, tell me your name."

She blinks a couple of times, and then looks around the shower like she's just seeing it, just coming back into her body. Her arms clamp tighter around my back as water—not from the shower—beads at the edges of her eyes. Tears.

"Oh god, Domhn, I don't know my name," she says.

I hug her tight as she cements herself against me, hips jerking once more as she shudders in orgasm.

I hold her to me and massage the back of her neck underneath her hair as she begins to sob.

"It's going to be okay, love," I whisper fervently, determined to make it true. "I swear, I'm going to make it all okay."

TWENTY-THREE

BROOKE

I WAKE UP SLEEPILY, so, so warm and perfectly cozy. It's only after my eyes blink several times that I realize I'm tucked up against a huge, warm bare male chest. Domhnall's chest.

I inhale sharply. Everything smells like him, and it eases me even in my confusion.

He stayed the night after a session?

But no, that's not right. He never stays. Except... the room is flooded with light.

I'm not in the dungeon anymore.

And then it all rushes back in, though it's a confusing blur. I'm not sure exactly what happened yesterday. I went upstairs and then there was—

I gasp again when I remember all the pictures and—and—

Donny's horrible accusations of who I was in the past. The hateful way he looked at me over the rim of his whisky glass, and then it shattering against the wall.

I struggle to get out of his arms. No. No, I'm not who he said I was! I can't be!

"Hey." Domhnall's strong arms suddenly fly around me, holding me to him. "Love. Love. It's all right. I'm here."

Love? His confusing gentleness is enough to stall my scramble to get away.

"Is Brooke still here with me?" he asks, caressing some hair out of my face and behind my ear.

I nod miserably, vaguely remembering the dark place I disappeared to yesterday. Or at least, I remember coming out of it in the shower, anyway. It was dark but safe. Different from—

My brain stalls out before finishing the thought and I cling back to Domhnall, wrapping my arms tightly around his waist.

"It's all right," he soothes. "You're all right now."

I'm not sure exactly what has flipped the dynamic so dramatically between yesterday and today but I'm so glad to be here with him holding me.

I wanted away from him, I also remember. But that was before—

"Domhnall," I start, my voice as quiet as a mouse, "What were we to each other? Back then? What happened?"

He squeezes me tighter. "It's a long story. You need food in your system."

I nod against his chest, maybe glad to put it off a little longer. Whatever the story is, it obviously doesn't have a happy ending.

I— I—

I betray him at the end.

Maybe I don't want to hear it after all. Maybe I can beg him to only tell me the beginning, where we were happy like in the pictures. Like turning off a movie before the sad part. I made Moira do that with *The Notebook*.

I just want to hear the good part. The part where he looked at me like he loved me.

I wanted to be whole but I'm obviously broken beyond repair. I'll want this instead. I can be whole with him if he'll just look at me like that again.

If he's holding me like this, does it mean he's forgiven me? We can just fast-forward to this part where we're happy again. All I want is to be happy in the arms of someone who cares about me. I don't care if that's childish. I don't care about fucking anything but being here and safe and with him.

But too soon, Domhnall sits up and lets me go.

I reach for him but he's by the door. I sit up, too, and look down at myself. I'm wearing one of Domhnall's oversized undershirts and his boxers. I wrap my arms around myself.

Maybe I shouldn't be giving into this new obsession for Domhn so easily. But the pictures gave me permission. I loved him before, so it's okay to give into this deep feeling now. I'm broken inside, but there's this too, and this is good. Maybe the only good thing inside me.

And Donny wasn't even pulling away really, because he's hurrying back around the bed with a pair of socks. He lifts each of my feet, kissing the sole of my foot and then fitting the sock on, one foot at a time.

"Your feet are cold." He frowns at himself. "I shouldn't have allowed your feet to get so cold."

He's literally kissing *my* feet now.

I can only blink down at him, stunned. My insides flood with warmth.

Is this what... *happiness* feels like?

He lifts up and takes my hand to draw me from the bed to follow him.

"Breakfast now. Did you sleep well?" he demands, half Donny, and half Sir.

"Um," I blink again. "I barely remember my head hitting the pillow. Then I woke up just now. So, um, good."

"Good, good," he murmurs, hand rubbing my back as we walk to the elevator. He pushes the down button, and I tense, eyes flicking up to him.

Is this a trick? Is he taking me back to the basement now?

I hesitate when the doors open. I should run away from him. I'm an idiot to step back into this elevator with him again. But like a sheep mesmerized by the shepherd's touch at the small of my back, I just step right in.

He doesn't hit the basement floor, though, he hits G. I think that means ground floor? I still barely breathe for the short ride down.

My breath expels in relief and confusion when he urges me forward by the light touch at my back when the doors open at the ground floor.

Daylight floods in through windows as he leads me through his maze-like mansion, not saying a word. I look up at his gorgeous, god-like face several times, and he meets my gaze with an easy, unconcerned smile.

Meanwhile, I feel like a nervous wreck.

What is seriously going on?

"What is this?" I ask, nerves finally giving out. "Why aren't you taking me back to the dungeon?"

The Sir facade drops completely and he's the Donny from the pictures, features soft as they crumple with remorse. "Fuck. Mads—Brooke, I mean. I'm so feckin' sorry, love," he says, brogue heavy. "I've been an evil gobshite an' I know t'ere's no way of makin' it up to ya. I'm done with it. I've been up all night. It kills me but I've got ta let ya go. It's t'e right t'ing. After getting some food in ya, I'm taking ya back to Moira's."

"What?" My hand immediately shoots out to grab onto his forearm. "No," I say sharply, before I even realize what I'm doing. "I can't— We can't—"

He stands up taller, his Sir persona returning. "I'll answer any question you have, of course, but I'm not sure it will be much help as to your actual identity. When I knew you, your name was Madison Harper. You hadn't been in Dublin long. You spent your younger years in America but I think your father took you overseas with him when—"

He swallows and breathes out heavily, eyes averting. "—When you were quite young. I never knew anything about your mother."

He turns away and I follow him as he heads into a huge kitchen.

I feel my eyes go wide as saucers as I try to take in all the gorgeous marble and fine appliances. It's *way* bigger than the kitchen at the shelter, and that fed sixty women.

"I'll talk while I make some omelets."

"This is just for you?" I gesture around the high-ceiling room.

He nods and pulls open the refrigerator. "You can sit there." He points to luxury padded stools by the gigantic counter of the center island.

Instead, I wander towards the huge wall of windows. A door leads to a patio deck. Beyond it is a glittering pool and a gigantic, beautifully manicured backyard.

"Did we meet some place like this?" I ask. "At a chalet in Ireland or something?"

I turn back around to see Domhnall shaking his head. "It was a dive of an internet cafe in the bad part of Dublin. You looked over my shoulder and saw I was on a hidden wiki. You asked if I knew the way to the Silk Road and I turned around and was knocked on my ass— Fuck," he winces. "I still can't believe you were only thirteen or fourteen. To me you just seemed like a gorgeous blonde American bombshell. You looked like Brittney Spears but um… hotter." He mutters the last word.

"Blonde?" I hold out my brown hair.

"You must've dyed it. I'm sure it was part of the gig." His face hardens. "The fucking bastard knew the blonde would turn the head of any lad."

I take a small step back and he drags a hand through his hair. "Jaysus, Mads. I'm sorry I blamed you for any of it. I shoulda fucking seen how young you were. None of it was your fault."

"It wasn't?" I ask with a small voice.

"Course not! It's your cocksucker father's, may he rot in hell!" If I thought his face was hard a moment ago, it's nothing to the iron jaw he's got now. He looks absolutely murderous. And I remember the rest of what he said yesterday. About what my father did to him. *Over and over and over.*

I fly across the room and plaster my arms around him again.

"Hey there," he says, all softness.

"I'm so sorry." My voice is barely a whisper.

"I'm alrigh'."

Is he?

I just nod into his chest, though.

He's got eggs on the counter. "Can I help you crack them?" I ask.

"You know how?"

"I wanna try," I say tentatively. I pick up an egg and it feels like I know what to do. I crack it expertly against the bowl with one hand, dropping yolk inside without any shell. I beam up at Domhn. "Look, I know how!"

He pushes a button, and a trashcan extends from a cabinet in the island. I toss the shell.

"Five more. I'll get to chopping the peppers."

I nod happily. And, wanting to keep to lighter things, I decide not to prod at my past anymore. "How old were you and Moira when you came to the states? Other than sometimes, you barely have an accent."

"Seventeen."

I curl into myself. Right. Because of what me and my father did to them. Making them leave their country.

He looks back at me. "But I'm not done telling you about us. It's alright, love. I'll skip around the bad parts. I know you always wanted to leave the movies before they got to the sad bits."

I freeze where I'm about to crack another egg and look over at him where he's brought peppers and onions from the fridge to chop beside me. "I still do that!"

He smiles a little, and it looks so foreign, it transforms his whole face. For just a second, Donny's back. He's so serious all the time, he usually seems a decade older than twenty-six.

"Every afternoon you and me would grab some food and head over to the Green." He looks up from chopping, crystal blue eyes intense on me. "You'd feed the ducks your leftover bread, chattering on and on." He smiles and it lightens his whole face. "I'd just stare at you, mesmerized that a woman like you'd ever be interested in a lad like me."

He looks back down and starts chopping again. Meanwhile my stomach's dropped out from underneath me. I can't imagine the two of us ever like that.

Finally I drag my eyes away from him and crack another couple eggs. "Of course I'd be interested in you," I murmur. "You're gorgeous and smart and really kind..." I shoot him a shit-eating grin, "at least when you want to be."

His eyes come back to mine, and he smiles again, this time with a wicked edge that makes my stomach swoop in a different way. And I can't decide if I like that smile best or the gentle one, and then decide I like them both best.

"What did I chatter about? Or was it just background noise?" I feel my cheeks heat, eyes dropping. Obviously he's not going to remember after all these years.

He laughs, de-seeding the peppers with efficient, expert hands. "What didn't you chatter about? The tree you thought was shaped like a dinosaur. The woman at the market arguing with her daughter. You were always listening in on other people's conversations. You called it people-watching. You said the whole world was your experiment, and you were a social scientist, watching on. You wanted to go to college, but your dad never stayed in one place long enough." He only grits his teeth a little at the mention of my father before going on. "We said we'd use the money to send you to college when we ran off together."

He looks up at me as he pulls green onions out of a bag. "I always wondered if you ever got to go. You know, with the money."

"What money?"

He blinks for a second, then looks back down at his onions on the chopping block. "Right. You don't remember. We were hacking back then. It's what you recruited me for. Companies had shit security in the 2010s, so we'd backdoor our way in and skim off the top. Small enough amounts not to be noticed. Rounding errors." He looks up at me. "And then, right before we were supposed to leave, big chunks."

"Oh." I'm a little speechless. Then I take another look around the huge, luxury mansion I'm standing in. "Is that what you still do?"

A laugh bursts from his chest, startling me into smiling and looking back at him. It's always so unexpected when I get any expression of actual mirth from him.

"No," he says, still looking amused, then a little less so when he goes on, "No, I work for the other guys now. Anti-spyware and anti-virus software. I learned my lesson after—" he cuts himself off, his eyes distant in that way he seems to get whenever he thinks of... of *him*. "Well, after."

He drops the knife to the chopping block and shoves both

his palms into his eye sockets, and again, I take a couple of steps back.

Is he disgusted by me now? Because he thought I was a beautiful woman who looked like Brittney Spears but in reality I was just a kid?

Or is he disgusted because I'm my father's daughter?

Ridiculously, I want to shout, *I'm a woman now*.

Everything I learn about the past is so ugly. "I don't want to know anymore. Don't tell me anymore about what happened then."

"Alright." He drops his hands and turns back to the counter, whipping the eggs we dropped into the bowl furiously. His voice comes back deep and even. "I'll just get you breakfast and then drop you at Moira's."

My mouth drops open and I felt like a horse has just kicked me in the chest.

That easy?

He'll just discard me like that?

After everything he just put me through? And all he said we were to each other? Why the fuck does *he* get to decide? Because he still thinks he's Sir?

"No!"

He's just poured the egg in the hissing pan, when he turns to me.

"What?" He asks it almost distractedly, as if annoyed I'm questioning him.

"I said no." I stomp over to him and get right in his face. "No. I'm not going anywhere."

His jaw tenses as he glares down at me. "You will. Because it's what's best for you."

I scoff. "And you suddenly know what's best for me?"

"Yes. I do."

I scoff again. "Why the fuck is that?"

His eyes narrow. "Because I'm your elder."

"You're just a twenty-six-year-old asshole. You don't control me. You don't control shit."

His features harden dangerously in the way Sir's did downstairs in the dungeon sometimes. "Don't push me, love. I'm keeping myself on a very tight leash."

Oh he is, is he?

I know what I want now. I don't just want to be near Donny. And I want more than for him to look at me like he did at me in those pictures. I want to feel it all. That and what I had this last week, all mixed up together in whatever we are or could be together now.

So I throw my arms around his neck and kiss him.

And the second our lips collide, it's like I've unleashed a storm, because he kisses me just as furiously back.

TWENTY-FOUR

DOMHNALL

I ABSOLUTELY FUCKING LOSE myself in the taste of her lips.

I've missed her so goddamn fucking much. I pin her to the counter and kiss her just like I used to in those long afternoons lost on the Green, making out like mad teenagers.

Fuck I've missed the taste of her lips. She kisses the exact way she used to. She feels the same, too. And for just a moment, I'm the same kid I was back then. Cold grass underneath us and the Dublin sun only occasionally breaking thru the fog and glinting off the water.

She and me were the only things in the world.

But it never did last forever like I wanted it to. Later that night, or early the next morning when I got to the workshop because I started avoiding going in the evenings, he'd corner me. He'd get me and there'd be nothing I could do about it. And I'd try to hold on to the sunlight moment and stay far away in my head while he—

A hand touches my face, and I shout "Fuck!" and yank back from Brooke, blinking hard.

I grab her wrists and pin them behind her back, constraining her there, both of us breathing hard.

I'm not who I was then. My teeth clench as the monster inside me yawns awake. He never sleeps long.

Now more than ever, I need to stay in control.

Brooke just blinks up at me, saying nothing about me pinning her hands behind her back. She only leans forward as far as she can with me restraining her. Her pink lips and cheeks flushed from my kiss.

I drag her to me by her wrists at the small of her back because I can't fucking keep away from her, and we kiss furiously again.

I only pull back to growl, "If we do this, we do it my way. I'm in control."

She nods, eyes still wide. "We fit like puzzle pieces, don't you see? You lead and I follow. Make me whole, Donny."

"Even if I want—" My breath hitches, hating myself in a deep way I haven't felt in a long time. I thought I'd cut off all feelings for good but now they're bubbling back up. She's resurrecting what I thought was dead in me. "I'm fucked up. I'm a sadist. I want to make you cry in pain."

She just fucking smiles at me. "I know. I told you, we're puzzle pieces. Hurting on my skin is *so* much better than when the hurt is on the inside. It's..." Her eyes look around like she's searching for the right word before coming back to mine. "...*freeing*. You make it feel good. You make everything good, Donny."

God fucking dammit, I die when she calls me that. And feeling rushes back in like water through dry rusted pipes. I do remember how. I'd just shut off the valve, but she's wrenched it wide open again and now I feel— I feel—

I kiss her again, needing her mouth more than I need my next breath.

Protecting her arms wound behind her back with my forearm, I press her into the counter and kiss her. She might kiss the same—innocent, receiving—but I'm not the boy I was. I devour. I intrude.

And then I pull back and lick teasingly inside the top of her upper lip in that place she was always so sensitive. I was too clumsy back then to understand how to handle that sensitivity.

But now, as I pin her to the counter, I gently lick at the fat little apex nubbin of her cupid's bow upper lip.

And her body jerks against me, a surprised little high-pitched gasp coming from her throat.

That's right. *Yes*.

Being able to control her body's pleasure centers me.

And makes me ruthless. The tip of my tongue plays with the inside of her top lip, the exact same way I do when I'm teasing her clit.

The way she shudders against me tells me she can feel it. It's so fascinating, all the sorts of different nerves that are connected in a human body.

And now, having Mads shuddering in my arms, little squeals getting higher and higher pitched from me merely kissing her—it's getting me fucking high. And hard as fuck. But I'm in control, so I ride that edge as I continue to tease her with just the very tip of my tongue.

When she tries to kiss me more deeply—to take what only I can give, I withdraw. I'm wrapped around her body like a snake holding its snack in place. And I continue to feast, teasing out her pleasure and listening to her noises so I know exactly how hard to press with my tongue against the secret nubbin inside her top lip.

Until she's finally so desperate and shuddering in my arms I suck her upper lip into my mouth with the pressure she deserves.

She begins screaming and shaking in my arms right as the smoke alarm starts to beep in ear-blasting chirps because the eggs I forgot about are burning on the stove.

TWENTY-FIVE

DOMHNALL

I KEEP SUCKLING her through her entire orgasm even though she struggles to pull away. "Donny— The alarm— *Ohhhhh—*"

Only when she gives in and then finally goes limp in my arms do I set her against the counter and go see to the eggs. They're on fire and the pan's ruined.

It's an easy issue of moving them to the marble counter and swatting out the fire with a kitchen towel. I throw open the double doors to the patio to help get the smoke out.

Then I return to where Brooke is limp against the counter, dressed only in my night shirt and boxers. Fuck. I never imagined anything so goddamn sexy.

The foul, wrong things I want to do to her...

My lip twitches.

I tried to do the right thing. I tried to get her to leave and get as far away from me and my monster as she could.

She said no. So that means...

She's mine.

A good man might examine things more. A good man would definitely *not* storm back into the kitchen, snap, "Close your eyes," to the woman of his dreams, grab a pool bag from the rack by the door and start to throw all sorts of kitchen implements into it. No, a good man would not do those things.

Mine.

I grin and heft the full bag over my shoulder, items gathered, and march Brooke outside to the shaded cabana chairs by the pool.

I think it's been established by now that I'm not a good man.

"Can I open my eyes now?"

"No. Sit down." I help guide her down onto the cabana chair. Well, it's more like a cabana bench, complete with its own shade over top. Can't have my precious Brooke's skin burning. Because I intend to have her quite bare.

I pull off my own pants so I'm in boxers as well. I want to feel as much of her skin against mine as possible. Since it's April, it's only warm but not scorching out.

I sit down beside her.

"Now. Over my lap, face down. That was naughty of you distracting me so much I burned your breakfast. It's time for punishment."

Brooke quickly reaches for me, grinning with her eyes still closed. Her hands find my body and she lingers too long exploring before finally climbing into place over my lap. I immediately bind her wrists again with a hand.

Hmm. This won't do. I want both hands free, but don't dare trust her if she's not bound. But of course, even though I rarely, if ever, bring women back here, I'm always prepared.

I reach down to a watertight shelf in the base of the spacious cabana bench and pull out the rest of the implements I'll need.

Having her in my lap is already more than I can bear. Part of me wants to flip her over and drag her up the large cabana and sink into her right now. No more fucking preamble. She's wet enough, I bet. She's here and there's no more bullshit between us. We've settled the truth from the lies.

So why the fuck can't I?

Shame washes through me as I lay out the things I brought from the kitchen in a neat line along with what I've pulled from the cabana shelf.

My hands are shaking. Fucking shame. There's a reason I buried my feelings down in a lake so fucking deep inside me. So I'd never have to feel any of this shit again. Growing up, people used to drag all sorts of shit down to the lake and pitch it in when they wanted rid of it. Old ovens. Trash bags. A couple cars.

Nothing ever so ugly or putrid as me. But if I tied all the shit that happened to a big enough stone and sunk it in the deep of the lake... I wouldn't ever have to think about it again.

I grit my teeth, yank my boxers down off Mads's ass and spank her. She yelps, then writhes on my lap. It wasn't a brutal strike, but it wasn't gentle, either.

And already the chorus of demons screaming through my blood settle. I spank her again and they quiet even more.

"Yes, Domhn," she mutters, wrists squirming against my grip. "More."

My cock pulses against her stomach and my lip twitches with need. I spank her again and again, becoming calmer and more centered with each measured strike. Watching her ass jiggle with the blows. Seeing her respond.

Getting back in control.

But I need more. The more control I get of her body, the more control I have of myself.

I grab the silk shibari rope I pulled from the little shelf and begin quickly tying her right wrist to her right ankle. She gasps when she realizes what I'm doing but doesn't complain.

She trusts me.

It sends another wave of calm and lust through me, the two combining in a powerful, heady rush. I'm in control. Almost, anyway.

I feel complete only once I've got her left wrist tied to her left ankle.

Now she's absolutely powerless. She's hogtied over my lap, ass up, and legs easily spreadable by grabbing one ankle or the other.

She's helpless to my complete control. My nostrils flare like a bull.

I can't keep her like this long, so I've got to move efficiently.

Immediately I open the jar of coconut oil I brought from the kitchen and dip two fingers in.

"You'll take what I give you," I demand gruffly, barely able to speak past my clenched teeth. My entire body is clenched. Hard with need and barely-leashed desire. She's so fucking gorgeous pinned here on my lap.

I grab her left ankle and spread her wide to me. *Fuck.* I slide my thumb down her ass crack and plunge my coconut oil drenched fingers towards her little asshole, rubbing and demanding entrance.

Her entire body responds like I knew it would. She clenches her asshole tight shut but writhes in pleasure at the contact.

"Kitty loves being petted, doesn't she?" I growl. Fuck. I don't know if this is wise considering she just came back from that odd, dissociative state yesterday.

But when she just squirms and presses her ass up against my probing fingers, I can't help but think this is different.

And I might just be too far gone to turn back unless she safewords or starts to seem uncomfortable.

"Yes," she begs, "pet kitty."

So I keep rubbing at her puckered little hole that's closed up so tight still, throbbing against her belly. And with my other hand, I reach beneath her and start to tease at her clit.

Her high breathy shudder tells me we're both in this. And when her asshole unclenches a little, I push my advantage and shove my middle finger inside.

Her head shakes back and forth on the bench. I wish I had a third fucking hand to spank her little, writhing ass. In a moment.

Right now, since I've gained entry, I stretch her little asshole with the finger I've gotten inside. And then, relentlessly, while I've really got her going with my hand at her clit, I shove another finger up her ass.

She cries out and I feel such fucking satisfaction.

But it's chased the following second by more need. *More.* I haven't conquered her completely.

She's mine and I need her to know it. *I* need to know it. I won't fuck her today. No, I don't think either of us is ready for it.

But I will begin to claim her body in all its deep places.

I stretch her ass ruthlessly with my fingers. And then, right when her whines are reaching that needy pitch again, and I can tell she's about to come, I pull my hand away from her pussy and reach for the biggest thing I grabbed from the kitchen.

The cucumber.

My teeth clench even harder as I breathe out like a bull in the arena. I rip open a condom with my teeth and sheath it, then dig my hand in the slightly hardened coconut oil to generously coat the monstrously large vegetable.

Grinning maniacally, I spread her legs even wider with my elbow as I lower it to her spread ass.

TWENTY-SIX

BROOKE

I'M on the brink when Domhn's hands pull away. I just want to touch him. He's so cruel to tie me up so I can't touch him.

But I can't deny that everything he makes me feel is also cruelly delicious. And that when I trust him like this, he makes me feel unimaginable pleasure.

"Domhn!" I cry, wanting to beg him. For more. For him. To put his hands back on my body. *In* my body. I want him. I need him. He's the key to unlock me. I don't care about the fucking ghost anymore. I just want to be me, now, with him.

And him in the now is a kinky motherfucking bastard, making me feel such wild, wild pleasure.

His warm hands come back to my ass, but also something

else. Something hard. Pushing for entrance. For a wild, excited moment, I think it's his cock and he's about to fuck me.

But then I register that doesn't make any sense. He's warm and hard against my belly, so that has to be— I don't even know what. A dildo? A—

"Give in to what I give you," he demands in that deliciously commanding Sir voice. "This greedy little ass wants to eat what I give it."

Warm palms pull my ass cheeks apart even as whatever object he's got pressing into my little hole pushes even more relentlessly.

"I'm going to split you wide open, love, and you're going to let me." His voice is deep and breathy with need. "You're going to let me do anything I want to your sweet body because it belongs to *me*. It always has. You'll shudder in pleasure with every wrong, fucked up thing we do together. You'll squirt from coming so hard once you let me in completely. Let me in. Let me in *now*."

My mouth drops open, and I relax my ass. He shoves the object in several inches and he's right. I feel split wide by the girth of whatever it is.

"That's right," he hisses. "That's my good girl."

A hand comes back to my pussy and I literally begin to weep with relief. I gulp for breath, heaving as I cry and the pleasure ramps back up again to where he had me on the edge earlier.

He starts to slide the large object in and out of my ass, fucking me deeper with it on every in thrust as he plays with my pussy.

"That's my good girl. Such a good, good girl taking what I give you. But I still want more. I need to go as deep as you can take it, and I know you can take it deeper."

I start to whine through my sobs, hips now rising to meet the impossible object as he rubs my pussy. My clit's so swollen and my pussy's so wet, he palms me, fingertips just barely inside me as he massages all that I am against the hard object up my ass.

I scream when I come, sun dipping past the shade to light my skin.

Oh god, all the darkness is gone in this moment.

I burn up from the inside out.

I ride whatever he's fucking my ass with as light bursts from behind my eyes and shudders up through my shoulder blades and out the tip of my scalp and then back down to my toes.

I'm a being of light.

And I am utterly, completely, *his*.

TWENTY-SEVEN

BROOKE

I FEEL like I'm made of jelly, completely slumped over Domhn's lap while he gently frees my ankles and wrists. Each limb flops down weightlessly to his body. I'm so sleepy after my high. I just want to lay here on him.

I smile to myself in joy when I realize he's not as hard under my belly and that instead there's a wet spot.

He finally came while he played with me! It makes me so happy that he got his pleasure at the same time I did. Does that mean he's *mine* too just like I'm his?

I feel drunk on happiness.

"I should get you inside so you don't get burned."

I groan and manage to mumble, "But I love how the sun feels on my skin."

Which was apparently the right thing to say, because then his strong hands come to my back, massaging what smells like sun screen into my skin. Oh god, there's nothing I love more in the universe than the feel of his hands on me. He's so thorough as he works his way down my body with the sun lotion, and it feels absolutely divine.

I feel drowsy but try to fight it because I don't want to miss a moment of this. In spite of myself, though, his hands feel so relaxing, and the sun's so warm, my eyelids get heavier and heavier…

WHEN I WAKE UP, I'm curled up on Domhnall's chest on the cabana chair. But apparently I wake up too suddenly, because immediately he's pulling away.

"Wait, no." I reach out to pull him back. He jerks back from my touch, moving away completely. Dammit. Why is it only when I'm asleep or during aftercare that he allows our bodies to touch completely like that?

He's so gorgeous out here in the sunlight. He took off his shirt and he looks like a model with his ripped muscles, hard abs, and square jaw.

"Can't we just stay out here a little longer?"

He frowns. "You need to eat. I haven't fed you."

I tilt my head at him. "Are you sure the kitchen can handle it?"

He glares at me but then he breaks into a grin and shakes his head. "You're a little shit, aren't you?"

"Always." I grin back, again feeling like a balloon filled up with happiness. I bump him with my shoulder, hopefully a touch he'll allow. "But you love it."

His look softens. Less Sir and more Donny again. "I'd accept nothing less. I want everything you are."

I grin wider. All I ever wanted was to find myself, and with Domhnall, I feel like *myself*. Even without remembering the past. It feels right. In my guts and in my heart. Surely that's got to be *me*, right?

"I got sandwiches delivered." He tugs his shirt back on over his head and tragically covers up those gorgeous abs. "They're at the front door."

I groan and reach for him when he gets up, but he just chuckles. "I'll be right back."

I huff in dissatisfaction and lay back, absorbing the sun on the most perfect day ever created. "Fine," I grouch.

He's back quickly, though—impressive for how big his house is. But then maybe he doesn't like losing sight of me any more than I do him.

We move to a table near the glittering pool to eat. It's gorgeous, inlaid with natural rock and a little waterfall on the far side near the deep end.

"Can we go swimming next?" I ask excitedly with my mouth full of ciabatta bread and chicken.

He narrows his eyes at me. "You're supposed to wait twenty minutes after eating to swim."

I put down my half-eaten sandwich and take a swig from the bottle of sweetened tea that came with it. I love the tea. Domhnall says it used to be my favorite drink—that back when he knew me, I'd always get tea and then dump tons of sugar packets in it. Every little detail he remembers about the good things thrill me.

"You need to eat more."

I roll my eyes at him. "I'm full! I want to go swimming. I'll wait the twenty minutes in the water. Is the water cold?"

The sun's gotten me warm enough I think I'll brave it no matter how cold it is.

"It's temperature controlled so I can swim year round."

I shake my head. "Of course it is." I look around at his huge mansion and back yard. "This place is insane."

He shrugs. "It's a status symbol more than anything. I needed people to take me seriously and forget how young I am. I just bluffed my way into every room I went into when I was building the company. I'd show them the weaknesses in their own company infrastructures but stay an aloof charming bastard about it to get them to invest. Then when I really started making money, I invested every cent I made until, well, I got to *this*." He waves a general hand towards the house. "No one questions you once you're on Billionaire's Row."

"Do you even use all the rooms?"

He smirks at me. "Just my office, bedroom, the kitchen, and the dungeon, mostly." Then he shrugs. "I throw the requisite party here and there in the ballroom to maintain status quo. The rest is all for show."

I frown. "That's so wasteful. Do you know how much women at the shelter would give just to have a single room?"

He lifts an eyebrow sardonically. "I wasn't out to save the world, love. I was out to conquer it."

I pause, looking out at the beautiful backyard. "Can't you do a little of both?"

"You're mine now," he says, his voice low and serious. "So what's mine will be yours and you can use my resources to save whoever you want."

Then he levels me with his gaze. "Marry me."

I gape in disbelief as my head snaps back to him. Is he serious? The look in his eye says he is.

"I— You—" I sputter. "You told me to leave this morning. And yesterday you had me locked up as a pet in your dungeon!"

He drags his chair closer, eyes still piercing. "It's always been you for me. And you were obviously trying to make your way back to me, even before you lost your memory. Why else would you have been so close? Your father's dead. There's nothing to stop us now. Marry me."

Yes. Yes I'll marry you and be your wife!

Of course it's what I want. More than anything.

But all I can do is sputter more. "I— I—" I move my head back and forth. "Is that a command?"

He frowns. "No. Of course not." He breathes out and drags a hand through his hair. "Shit. I'm going too fucking fast. *Fuck.*" He pushes his chair back, face dark. I don't like it. It's like he's disappearing deep into himself, sinking away from me.

I reach out to grab his hand, but stop at the last second, knowing he doesn't like it when I make surprise contact. Still, it has him looking back at me.

"Can we go skinny-dipping?" I arch an eyebrow at him.

He groans, some of the playfulness coming back into his face. "You're gonna be the death of me, love."

"Is that a yes?"

When he looks around as if still trying to decide, I decide for him, popping out of my chair and kicking off the boxers I'm wearing as I go. I yank my shirt off, then screech as I dive into the deep end.

TWENTY-EIGHT

BROOKE

COOL WATER STEALS my breath in an exhilarating rush as the water envelops me and I scramble to get back to the bright surface.

The water might be temperature-controlled, but it's still a shock to my sun-warmed skin. My limbs know what to do and that's a rush, too.

Almost as much of a rush as hearing Donny fucking ask me to *marry* him. What the fuck is he thinking?

I burst back into the sunlight laughing. I feel high with joy. These rollercoaster extremes of emotion I've been riding the past couple days should probably concern me, but I'm too happy to give a shit right now.

Domhnall's right there, in the water where I pop up. He must have jumped in right after me. "Jaysus you just took years off me life. Don't scare the shite out of me like that!"

"But look, Donny, I know how to swim!" I laugh as I spin around while I tread water.

"Well how do ya know?" He looks nervous, arms all but circling me. "You have amnesia."

"It's weird, but the doctors say that's how it is." I easily do another spin like a mermaid, my feet twirling naturally. "Some skills I can remember. Like playing chess. I think I used to swim."

It feels absolutely fucking *amazing* to be in the water.

I suck in a quick breath, throw myself backwards into a dive under the water and then swim back around between Domhnall's legs. He tries to catch me but he's too slow. I pop up on the other side of him, giggling.

"Careful!" he says. "We should be sure you can swim before you go do shit like that."

I roll my eyes. I can't believe this is the same guy who just had me in a dungeon. He's suddenly treating me like I'm so breakable.

Though I guess, even in the dungeon when he was ostensibly being a brute, he was still careful with me. He made sure all my basic needs were met. The mattress was certainly a thousand times softer than at the shelter. Apart from the first day, I had amazing food that was fed to me by his own hand. I never went hungry, and if I had to squat to potty, well, it *was* still a toilet that flushed. Each time he came to me, he took me to euphoric places, sometimes without putting a hand on me.

I understand it was wrong. I also know that with our fucked-up past, right and wrong have gotten twisted sideways, crumbled in a ball, and shat out again.

But he's always been careful and controlled with me, even when he hated me. Earlier today he wanted to let me go. Well, he was at least willing to let me go to his sister, who he has under constant security. Still. Even that feels like part of his fucked-up way of caring.

I feel less and less like a clinging koala, and it's been a wonderful morning. Yes, I still feel panic at the thought of leaving his side, but I also *want* to be here.

When I swim towards the deep end, he doesn't stop me. He just follows, at my side but a distance away. I fling my arms out and throw my head back, face to the sun as I float.

Ripples of the crystal blue pool glitter all around me like diamonds.

It feels so free to be in the water like this, all my limbs extended with the sun warming my face. I float, completely weightless. I feel like a goddess. Even with my eyes closed, I know Domhnall is near.

I feel... *good*. It's strange. Foreign. Just because I haven't had a lot of feeling free and happy since I woke up from the amnesia, or because I didn't have it before, either? Is my body remembering what my mind can't? That I've never been happy before, at least not for real, or for very long?

How much of my life did I spend with that awful, evil man? I don't even want to think of him as my father. If I was only thirteen when Domhnall knew me, that meant at least five more years with my father before I was eighteen. Was I able to run away from him at some point? Because Domhnall said I *knew*… To be related to someone who could do that to—

My eyes fly open, peace disturbed by the ugliness of it all.

Only to find Domhn circling me like a shark. I laugh, startled back to the *now*. I cling to the warmth of his presence, warmer than the sun.

He keeps circling me.

"Are you worried I'd go under?" I ask.

He shrugs, easily doing a backstroke, his bulging muscles glittering as water splashes off them. "Just making sure you're safe."

I splash him, fully expecting him to return it. When he doesn't, I splash him again.

A devilish look enters his eyes, and his long body kicks off the edge of the pool and rockets towards me. I squeal, suck in a breath, and start to swim away but it's no use. He lassos me around my waist and I screech in laughter as he swings me around in the water.

By the time we settle, we're face to face. I lasso my arms around his neck and grin into his dripping face. My god, he's gorgeous. His strong jaw is one thing, but those sharp cheekbones make him something out of a magazine. Women must throw themselves at him constantly.

"Why don't you have a girlfriend?" I ask. Then I scoff, "Fuck that. Why don't you have a wife and a whole shitload of kids? You're so fucking hot."

He grins at me, his rows of white teeth with those endearing incisors slightly out of place only making him more devastating.

"The mots down at the club certainly think so. Got 'em fighting over a night with me."

"Ugh!" I pound his chest, then slip out of his arms.

Using my arms in powerful strokes, I swim down deep, near the bottom of the pool. Domhn dives after me but I barely look back. I swim along the bottom for as long as I can before having to surface. It feels exhilarating to utilize every muscle in my body as I cut through the water. My lungs are bursting for breath, but I don't even care.

"What the hell are you thinking?" Domhn demands, bursting through the surface moments after I do. He immediately pulls me back to his chest. He sounds panicked. "Don't take chances like that! What if I couldn't get to you in time? I can't lose you again!"

"Wha— Donny!" I try to say, half smothered in his barrel chest as he heaves in and out for breath. We're in the shallow end now so I stand on my feet as I push him away enough to get a breath and look him in the eye.

"Christ sake, Donny," I say in exasperation. "I'm fine! You

can't control every little thing I do. I told you I know how to swim."

"We don't know what you do and don't know how to do," he exclaims, still irate. "You can't be taking chances with yourself."

"Don't be ridiculous. That wasn't a chance. I can swim. You just saw." I fling out an arm towards the pool. "I can only find out if I can do things by *doing* them. Are you going to freak out if I try to see if I can ride a bike? Or a motorcycle?"

His eyes darken as he glowers down at me. "You are *not* riding a motorcycle. You're twenty-five more times as likely to die in a motorcycle accident as a car accident."

I roll my eyes again. "That's not a real statistic. You just pulled that out of your ass."

"It's close enough." He glares. "No motorcycles."

"Fine." I stick out my tongue, chest so light and happy at getting to be silly with him. "But you can't stop me from swimming!" I dive towards the bottom of the pool again, swimming just past his grasping hands.

We swim for a long time, goofing around like we're kids and occasionally tangling our bodies together. I'm fully naked but he kept his boxers on.

After about half an hour, I accidentally snort in some water and cough a little. I don't want Domhnall to know, so I swim over to the side for the towel but can't quite reach it. Domhnall chuckles and swims up beside me. He easily hops out of the pool to grab the towel from the bench, but I gasp, hands flying to my mouth.

The whole time we've been swimming, he's kept his chest to me, but as he climbs out—

"Domhn!" I cry. "Your back!"

TWENTY-NINE

BROOKE

DOMHNALL IMMEDIATELY WHIPS AROUND, his features unreadable. "It's nothing."

I'm still in shock from what I just saw. I climb out of the pool. I need to see it again. Some of those wounds looked fresh. Oh my god, he probably shouldn't have even been swimming.

"Donny, who did that to you?" I demand, trying to walk around to see the horrific scarring again. I only caught a glimpse, but it was his entire back, fresh angry stripes barely scabbed, laid over old, raised pink scars. I've never seen anything so horrific. Tears immediately spring to my eyes.

But when I try to look again, Domhnall just keeps turning, as if determined to keep his broad chest to me.

"Donny," I demand. "Let me see!"

"It's fine," he says, still dancing away from me every time I almost manage to get around him.

"It's not fine! Some of those are fresh. Who did that to you?" Tears flood down my cheeks but he's still not letting me see.

"I did it, okay," he finally snaps, yanking back yet again when I try to get around him. His admission certainly stops me cold in my tracks.

My mouth drops open. I don't understand. "*Why?*"

He shakes his head, jaw locked so hard it looks like it might break. "I— I don't—" His head just keeps shaking as he backs away from me.

I rush forward and try to take his hand, but he pulls away.

"Donny. What the fuck?"

"I'm fucked up, okay?" he finally barks out. Then lets out a caustic laugh that sounds more like an explosion of pent-up breath, flinging out a hand towards the house. "If that wasn't more than apparent. Your da used to whip me back in the day and now I fucking do it to myself."

He turns away from me and bends over his knees, finally exposing his horrific back to me again, and shouts at the top of his lungs, "Fuuuuuck!"

"Donny," I whisper, tears still clogging my throat. I reach out a tentative hand towards him. One of the recent whip wounds split open when he bent over. I don't know how he slept on his back last night. "C'mon. Let's go inside and I can help bandage these—"

But he just stands back up in a quick motion, hands on his head and features twisted like he's hearing some sort of siren that's too loud. Then he sprints past me and dives in the deep end.

"Donny!" I shout after he disappears under the water. I rush to the edge. He's there at the bottom of the deep end, just sitting, and not coming back up. Immediately, I dive in after him.

All I want is to grab his arm and drag him to the surface. But whatever frame of mind he's in, I know it will only get me resistance. So I just swim down until I'm in front of him and do my best to sit on the bottom of the pool with him.

It's difficult to keep still. My buoyant body wants to float up to the top but if I use my arms, I can hold myself down.

I don't have to try very hard, though. Domhnall's eyes were closed when I first swam down, but as soon as he opens them and sees me, they immediately widen. He shoves off the bottom, grabbing me by the waist and taking me back to the pool's surface with him.

"What were you thinking?" he demands. "You could've drowned!"

"Domhn." I grab his face in both my hands and look in his eyes. "Are you back with me?"

He blinks, looking confused but then his eyes settle on mine.

"We need to go in the house so I can see to your back," I say calmly.

He jerks in my touch at the mention of his back.

Immediately I murmur, "It's okay. I'm here. Domhn." Using my hands, I help direct his face back to mine so he can focus just on me. "I'm right here."

His gaze finally settles back on mine, and he nods, huffing out hard.

We float in the deep end like that for several long moments, breathing. Just breathing. He treads water and I hold his precious face. Dear god, how quickly the coin flips.

When he drops his head into the crook of my neck like a tired child, I clutch him there, running my fingers through his wet hair and rubbing his neck, kicking my feet to keep us up. It's only when we bob a little in the water that he jerks back and says, "Shit. Let's get out of the pool."

I nod, already missing his head against my chest. "Let's go inside."

He's subdued as we swim towards the shallow end and walk up the pool steps. There's a little outdoor shower and we rinse off, him always keeping his chest to me. Then I hurry over towards the towels on the bench and bring them back. He towels off efficiently.

"Careful!" I say when he starts to swing the towel over his back.

He smiles a sad smile. "It's really okay. I've been like this a very long time."

Nine years. Is his back ever truly able to heal? How often does he do it? How does he put medicine on or bandage himself? I have so many questions, but I can see how questions just shut him down a moment ago. I want to keep him with me.

I wrap my towel around myself to keep from dripping as we walk back in the house. And, needing some kind of connection with him after that revelation, I slip my small hand into his big one. I can feel his surprise and almost pull my hand away. Before I can, though, his strong fingers close around mine. It makes my chest squeeze with emotion. He holds my hand all the way up to his bedroom.

I only let go so I can jog over to his bathroom. I wash my hands thoroughly first, then start rummaging around for first aid supplies. Domhnall stops in the doorway, elbow up casually against the frame as he watches me. I glance over at him and my breath sweeps out of my lungs. Good lord. He looks like a tattooed god, so gorgeous and muscled.

"Stop distracting me with your sexiness," I mutter, and go back to opening cabinets under the bathroom counter.

"Says the beautiful woman on her knees in just a towel."

I roll my eyes. Then I tug open the top drawer in an opaque tower in one of the cabinets and find cotton balls and swabs. Okay, now we're talking. I keep opening drawers and find antibiotic cream, long bandages, gloves, and medical tape. I snatch them all into my arms as I look back up at Domhn.

"Get the butterfly bandages, too." His voice has gone monotone. "A drawer down. You might need them."

I find them, exactly where he says, then order him, "Go lay face down on the bed."

One of his eyebrows hefts as some life comes back into his face. "Are we playing switch? You're the dom now?"

I glare at him. "For all intents and purposes, yes. Now be a good boy and go do exactly what I say."

He looks at the jumble of supplies in my hands and sighs. "If you insist."

"I do."

Without another word, he turns and goes back into the bedroom. I follow him out. He's still got the towel covering his back, but when he reaches the bed, he drops his soggy boxers to the carpet—no doubt intentionally distracting me with his taut ass. He only loses the towel at the last moment before flinging himself face-first down on the bed.

I grimace when I see his angry back again, glad he can't see my reaction. He's got his face buried between two pillows.

"Can you breathe in there?" I call.

I get a grunt back that I'll assume means yes. After climbing on the bed beside him, I open the little tube of antibiotic cream and then look down. Immediately I'm swallowing back tears again. Is there even enough in this small tube for his big back and all the damage here?

I should take him to the hospital. He needs stitches.

But when I tell him so, he only grunts again, turning his head to the side. "Just use the butterfly bandages. They work fine."

I grit my teeth together and snap on some gloves. "Who usually does this for you?"

His back shifts slightly as he shrugs. "Sometimes it's fine just wearing light shirts and taking antibiotics if there's a problem. If it's bad, I call in a nurse I have on call. She's discreet."

I stare down at the gory mess in front of me. "You don't consider this *bad*?"

"Mild."

I swallow at his words, looking at the older scars of crisscrossing pink raised skin. There's no inch of his back that's not scarred. And the rest of his torso and arms are covered in tattoos that must've taken hours upon hours.

He said he was a sadist, but he's a liar. He made my skin tender with the caning, it's true, but it didn't even leave a mark... whereas *this*...

I suck in a deep breath, twist off the top of the antibacterial ointment, and set to work. I hate touching the fresh wounds, even with the most ginger of touches. He tries not to flinch, but he can't help it. I try to work as quickly and efficiently as I can.

There are seven fresh lashes. Some are shorter, but there's one especially vicious one that stretches from his shoulder to his buttocks, crisscrossing the others. Everywhere it crosses the other wounds, the flesh is split horribly. How can he consider this *mild*? I run out of butterfly clips and have to go back to the bathroom for more. That entire drawer is filled with them. As if he always knows there will be a next time.

I swipe my tears for the umpteenth time with my shoulder as I continue the macabre work.

"Donny, please," I beg quietly, throat raw. "Promise me you won't do this anymore."

He's quiet a long time as I stretch out the roll of bandaging down the long lash-mark and tape it down.

"I dunno how to stop."

"You'll stop because I'm here now," I say fervently. "There's no need for it anymore. He was a demon, but he's gone and I'm here. We won't let him win. Do you hear me, Domhnall?" I demand, unspooling more bandaging from the roll. "We won't let him win. This is our life now. You and me together. And we're taking it fucking *back*."

Beneath me, Domhnall starts to shiver.

"Donny?" I ask. "Shit, you must be freezing. I'm almost done, then we'll get you under the covers."

He nods but doesn't say anything. I quickly finish bandaging his back, then I start to pull the covers up over him.

But I barely get them up over his butt before he's twisting in bed and grabbing me around the waist.

"Careful, your bandages!" I cry.

He just grunts something like, "They're fine," before

burrowing his head against my stomach, big arms wrapped around my waist. I blink down at him, this hulking giant wrapped around me like I'm his only comfort in this world.

I drag some pillows behind my back and settle against the headboard, then sink my fingers into his hair.

"Shhh, it's all right, love," I whisper, more tears pricking at my eyes even though I'd have thought I was out of tears by now. "It's all going to be all right. Shhh, now. Everything's going to be all right."

His face burrows even tighter against my stomach and I blink up at the ceiling and cradle him to me. "It's all right now, love." And in the quiet of my billionaire's mansion, I pray that my words are true.

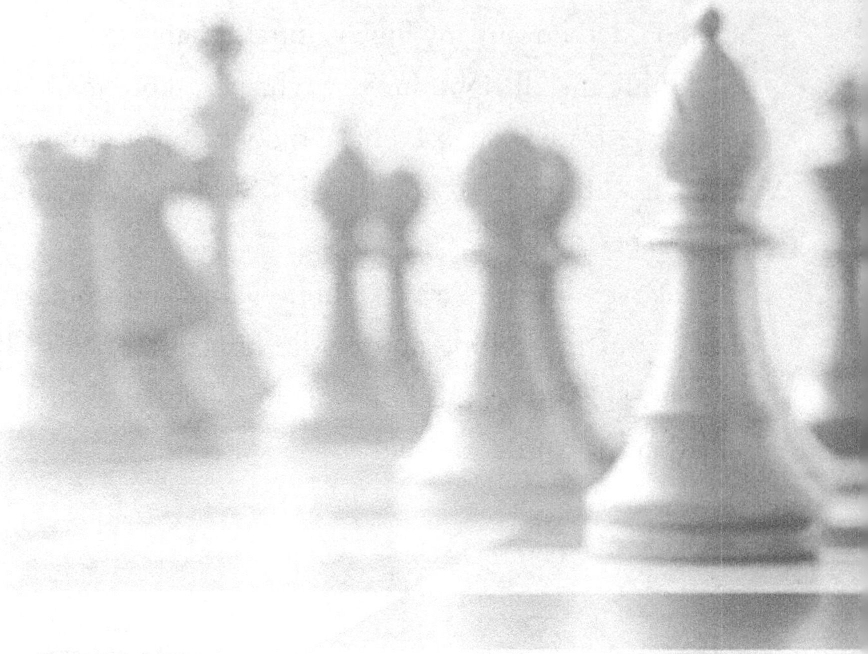

THIRTY

DOMHNALL

I WOKE up from a nap with Brooke still cradling me against her stomach in her lap. I pulled away and sat up, feeling strange. Stranger than I can ever remember feeling.

I felt drugged with comfort and... happiness. Like it was the first time in maybe my whole life that I'd felt what people mean when they say they feel *at home*.

Which freaked me the fuck out, so I immediately launched out of bed and asked Brooke if she was hungry. I'm supposed to be the one taking care of *her*.

Professor Roberts visited in the late afternoon and had a session with Brooke. I was worried about how it would go.

Alright. I was fucking terrified Brooke would see the light

and leave with her. But Brooke just came out looking thoughtful and said she'd rather not talk about it. I was careful not to ask or pry. I'm trying a new thing called not-being-an-asshole. I don't like it.

Things stayed in lighter territory over dinner. Then Brooke took a shower, and we started Titanic—one of her favorite movies back in the day—curled up in bed. That bizarre, homey feeling hit me hard again.

I'm about to turn off the movie at the halfway point before the ship starts sinking, just like she always used to make me do. But when I look over at her, she's already out. I only pause it instead of turning it off. I like looking at her in the glow of the TV light.

I can't imagine sleeping now that I've got her in my arms. I curl us in the bed on our sides, her back to my chest, and wrap an arm around her waist.

Fuck she feels so good in my arms. I can't believe we're here. I can't believe I'm this lucky of a bastard.

So when's the other shoe gonna drop?

Cause good shit like this just doesn't happen to a lad like me. Yeah I got money, but I was still a miserable bastard, so it felt balanced.

Now though...

Happiness? Like the real, true deep kind?

I frown furiously at the warm feelings in my belly that have nothing to do with lust. Fucking *feelings*. How do I manage the goddamned unruly things and still stay in control? I'd say I was better off without them, but if they're the price I have to pay for Brooke being here, I'll man up and deal with it. I grit my teeth. One way or another.

I have to stay in control now more than ever. The stakes have never been higher.

Brooke makes an uneasy noise and shifts in my arms.

"Shhh," I soothe and set my chin on the top of her head, enveloping her completely. She settles and I relax around her. "We're going to be okay," I whisper. "Everything's going to be all right."

I try to stay awake. I need to stay vigilant in case she needs me. Eventually my eyelids get heavy, though. I'll just rest them for a few seconds at a time…

…

…

A scream startles me awake.

"No!" Madison cries at an ear-splitting volume. "NO! I'll be good, I promise. *Please! NO!*"

"Mads! Brooke!" I try to hold her and shake her awake but she fights me so I let her go. Finally she screams herself awake, almost falling off the bed. I catch her at the last second, lassoing my arms around her waist. I let her go again as soon as she's safe, knowing she might not want the touch right now.

"Brooke, are you okay?"

The TV's turned itself off at some point so I reach over and flip on the lamp beside the bed.

Brooke's eyes are wide and terrified, darting left and right until she finally seems to register me there on the bed beside her.

"Donny." Her voice is reedy and thin, and she's fisting the blanket. She still looks like she's in some terrified trance.

I get closer to her on the bed, reaching for her again. She yanks back so I pull my arms away, holding them wide so she knows she's safe. She's like a spooked animal right now.

"You're safe," I say carefully. "It's just me here. You're safe."

"More light." She yanks the covers up to her chest.

I nod and launch out of the bed to turn on the overhead light and several other lamps around the room until it's as bright as it can be without daylight. I glance at the clock. Four-thirty in the morning. Sunrise isn't for another couple hours.

She's breathing so hard. Whatever was in that nightmare, it scared the shit out of her. She's still so fucking terrified.

And I feel as inept as I have all day.

I don't know how to help her.

Useless stupid little fucking dog.

I shake my head.

"Can we do a scene?" she says suddenly, "Please. I need you to hurt me." As she says it, she reaches out unexpectedly and grasps my forearms.

Wrenching out of her grasp is a knee-jerk reaction. "Don't touch me."

She turns away from me and starts to cry. Loud, wracking sobs as she pulls herself into a little ball on the bed.

And I fucking hate myself. I want to punch myself in the face. Fifty lashes on the back wouldn't be enough. Pain. I need pain.

"I'm sorry. I'm so fucking sorry. We don't have to do that shit anymore. I'm sorry for fucking everything, Mad—I mean, Brooke. Fuck!"

I reach out tentatively and put a hand on her back. When she allows that, I pull her into my arms again and thank god, she lets me, dropping her head against my chest. Thank fuck I can allow some touches.

She only rests her head for a moment, though, before lifting her face to stare up at me with tear-filled eyes. "I don't want you to see me as broken. I'm not something to be put behind glass because I'm too delicate and too fucked up."

"What?" I bark, at the same time hating all the ways I understand why she thinks that. "I don't—"

I breathe out harshly and meet her piercing gaze. "Me either. I want to be the man you needed back then. I'm trying to be."

My guts twist. She's in my arms now but it feels fucking selfish even though I know she was hurt when I pulled away a moment ago.

But how fucking dare I even fucking *lay a finger* on her after failing her so badly? I know we were both in some fairyland for a little while with the sun and the pool today, trying to pretend the whole world didn't exist.

But then she saw the truth of me. She saw that I'm a weak, unworthy fuck. And I always have been. I spent all these years so angry at her when I'm the one who failed *her* so badly back then.

"Mads," I manage to growl out between gritted teeth. "I fucking *left* you with him. All I saw was my own shit instead of realizing that you—" I glare down. "—That you needed me to save you."

She throws her arms around my neck and crawls into my lap. I scoop her up and crush her to me. Her hands cup the back of my head like I'm something precious in the world to her, when everyone else me whole life only looked on me like I was shite to be scraped off their boot—

"You were just a kid, too," she whispers, eyes searching mine while more tears run down her cheeks.

I wasn't though. At least not compared to her. And now she has nightmares from whatever he did to her.

What the *fuck* did he do to her to make her scream like that?

What has she pushed down in *her* lake? She can't remember right now. But that doesn't mean she never will.

Cause don't I remember? Everything always came up out of the lake eventually. There was a drought this one year, and the water dried up. It got to be so there was more shit than there was lake. All the rusted cars and busted up bikes and freezers and mountains of trash people'd tried to bury there got exposed to the bright light of day again. Another year, a body floated up to shore.

Everything always comes up out of the lake, one way or another.

The pain's got to come out somehow. Right now it's just screaming nightmares. But whatever else is down there... one day there'll be a drought. One day she'll remember and god help us both.

The pain in her eyes still wet with tears feels like a whip. No, it slams harder than a whip ever could. Like a knife, it slices deep. Because it's *her* pain.

Oh god, the weight of it is really just hitting me now. He had her for her *whole life*.

I force myself to keep looking into her eyes. He took my body and yeah, me mind too, it felt like most days, but it was still only four months. I know I'm a broken man, but if it had gone on much longer, I woulda fractured in ways I couldn't have come back from. If I ever even have.

I don't look away from her eyes, glimpsing all she doesn't even know she knows yet. The way he was, with his specific proclivities— I don't think he would've touched his own daughter. It would've been her mind he'd enjoy twisting the most... but God only knows with that sick smear of a shite.

She needs me to get my shit together. She needs me to stay in control. I failed her before but I won't now.

I hold her face in my hands. "Stay here, love. I'll be right back."

She shakes her head. "Don't leave me alone. I need you, Domhn. I feel like I'm shattering into pieces without you. I can't keep myself together unless you're here."

"It's alrigh', love. I know. I'll be back in half a minute. Just stay right here. Don't twitch a muscle. Can ya do t'at for me?"

She looks terrified but nods.

I let go of her and hurry off the bed, sprinting to my office. I grab what I'm looking for and come back before she can even miss me.

I find her staring desolately at the wall, and her face only comes back to life when she sees me again. She immediately reaches for me, and I sit down beside her again, holding the object behind my back.

"On your knees," I say sternly.

Her eyes widen in surprise and interest, and I also note the way they snap back to focus. She's fully here with me, the haze of terror gone. She climbs off the bed and drops to her knees on the soft carpet at my feet, face down.

I breathe out in relief. I was right. This is what we both need.

"You might not be ready to wear my ring, but I've been waiting to give you this for a long, long time. This is no command. Only accept it if you want to."

Reverently, I get on one knee and hold the supple leather

collar with the large, dangling diamond in front of where her face is bowed.

"Be mine."

THIRTY-ONE

BROOKE

I FIRST LOOK up at the collar with the sparkling jewel, gasping loudly.

But what shocks me even more is Domhnall, who's climbed down on one knee in front of me on the carpet. Making himself my equal. And positioning himself as if this is a proposal.

It's not the collar he locked me up in the dungeon with before. This one is beautiful and soft, and it looks meant for someone he treasures. I don't miss the large diamond, either. My mouth goes dry.

"It's beautiful," I whisper.

"Yes, but it's more than just decorative. It symbolizes that you—" He swallows hard, Adam's apple bobbing, "—that you belong to me. If you put it on, you'll be *mine*." The last word is all but a growl that sends tingles straight to my sex.

Why does this feel even more meaningful and permanent than the marriage proposal earlier today? Either way, he seems determined to put a ring on me.

I nod, swallowing back emotion. It takes me a moment to manage words. "I'd be honored to accept."

I turn slightly so he can put it on me. He's careful as he settles it around my neck, fingers whisper soft against my skin as he fastens it. It's loose until I suck in a quick breath of air and feel the confines of the soft leather around my throat.

Fuck, I love the strange feeling of safety it gives me. I am owned. I am his. I *belong*. Immediately, every muscle in my body relaxes.

I knew this was the right way. All the fears from my nightmare are gone. I just need wholeness in Domhnall. He'll protect me from the darkness. He always will.

I lift a finger tentatively to the large front jewel, not quite daring to actually touch it. "I can't wait to show everyone at the club later today." I beam up at him but he frowns.

"We don't have to go to the club to prove anything anymore. I'll take you to see Moira or Quinn whenever you want. We can go after breakfast, if you like."

"Oh." Now I'm frowning. "But I thought—"

"What?" He helps me up off the floor, standing and reaching one hand down to pull me back into bed with him.

"Domhn..." My voice is quiet as I finger the leather of the collar. I feel comforted by its weight around my neck. It's not heavy, but its presence is a reassuring reminder of belonging.

He looks at me, and our eyes catch in that endless feedback loop we get in sometimes.

Even though I can't remember what happened in the nightmare, the fear and coldness from it still linger deep down in my bones and I shiver. I give a tiny shake of my head. "I'm not sure if you're real. I don't know how to trust..."

"Me," he finishes for me, nodding as if assuring me he understands what I mean.

But that's wrong. He's misunderstanding.

"No." I shake my head, frustrated. "*Me*. I don't know how to trust *me*. I don't know how to trust my perception of what I see. Of what I *feel*. Sometimes things get hazy and I think maybe you..." I look all around us and make a sweeping gesture, "...and all this, aren't real. Or..."

"Or what?" he ask, shoulders straightening as if he's forcing himself to hear something that will be hard to hear.

And maybe it will be. But if we're going to do this—really do this—and I'm going to give myself to him completely, I have to be able to tell him the truth about what I'm afraid of. At least the things I know I'm afraid of, when I'm awake.

"...Or," I finally manage, "maybe you'll hurt me again right when I give you my trust."

He nods over and over, and I can tell my words slice him deep.

I hate that. But I think this is what real people do when they care. They say the hard things and try to listen to each other.

He just nods, so hard, eyes dropping and face washing with shame in a way that tells me he's misunderstanding what I'm saying again. Or hearing some other sorts of demons in his head that have nothing to do with me.

He twists away from me and his back heaves up and down like he's breathing really hard. Then he takes a step towards the door as if he's going to leave.

I panic. "Domhn. Donny!" I jump up to follow, skirting in front of him and blocking the door but not touching him. "I'm sorry. I didn't mean it!"

Fuck good communication. We'll try that later. I just need him to stay with me right now.

His nostrils flare and his face is red.

"You did, don't say you didn't," he barks, then pulls back and looks frustrated as if realizing how much that sounded like an order. He heaves out a pained breath. "I mean, obviously you can say whatever you want. Look, Brooke, this is too fucked up. You're right to be second-guessing shit. You shouldn't trust me. I wouldn't let my sister within ten feet of a fuck like me."

He reaches out like he wants to cup my face but then doesn't, dropping his hands instead. And his features twist as he begs, "*Run*. Brooke, you should have run as far away from me when you had the chance."

Is he serious? He's saying this shit right after he collared me and called me *his*?

But he just keeps on, "You need to get the hell away from me, so you have a chance at normal—"

"I'll never be normal," I shout, shoving him in the chest.

He looks down at me, stunned.

"You keep saying I can do whatever I want, but then you want to tell me what to do. You're such a fucking asshole!"

He nods along with me. "Yes, exactly. I'm an asshole." Then he clamps his mouth shut as if forcibly trying to make himself not say more. Works for me.

"Yes," I agree vehemently with him agreeing with me. "And whoever said I wanted normal? *I'm* not normal. That ship sailed a long time ago. God knows who I might have been if normal had been an option. It wasn't. This is who I am, whoever the fuck that is. I want to find out *with* you. I'm just trying to tell you there might be some stops and starts."

"Oh." He just nods, sounding a little choked.

"Yeah. Oh," I say, still on a roll. "And what *I* want is to go to the club tonight and do a scene. Is it a big deal if I pull a safe word there?"

He switches to shaking his head. "Not at all. I hope you'll feel even safer there with everyone else around."

"You idiot." I dare shoving him on the shoulder. Just a quick touch and then gone again. "I'm not afraid to be alone with you."

He just stares at me a second. And then he throws his

arms around me and squeezes me to his chest. I sink against him and for a second she's back—that hovering ghost. We both remember this. My body remembers him. It has this whole time. *I've* known him and the heart of the boy that still lives inside the man. Even when *he* couldn't remember it, I still could, amnesia or not.

Donny I've got to tell you something.

I gasp and pull away from him.

"What?" he asks, concerned. His eyes search my face.

"Nothing," I say, still a little short of breath. Was that an actual... memory? But now that I try consciously focusing on what I was just thinking, it's disappeared like a wisp on the wind.

So I smile and wrap my arms around Domhn's waist. "I can't wait to see everyone at the club."

He just shakes his head at me and looks down with eyes so full of affection I could drown in them. "How is your spirit so strong? Fuck I'm so glad you don't want to leave me because I don't think I could let you go. I'd chase you to the ends of the earth."

He pulls me back into his arms and I sink against his chest, loving the strong, sure pound of his heart beating against my ear.

"Good," I breathe out. "Because you're stuck with me now."

THIRTY-TWO

DOMHNALL

I'M STILL SHOOK after last night.

We spent the day quiet. Snuggling. Watching movies. And getting ready for tonight.

I've just parked us at *Carnal* but suddenly my hands go white-knuckled on the wheel. We've been so safe in the protection of the mansion all this time. And I couldn't have imagined a more perfect day than today.

Brooke was so delighted with everything I bought her. I glance over at her adjusting her outfit and can't help grinning. She's adorable in the little cat-eared tiara, nestled at the crown of her long, flowing hair. My collar glitters at her neck. It brings me a deep-down pleasure I can't explain.

"How does my tail look?" she asks as she opens her door and bends over, lifting her robe with one hand and grinning over her shoulder at me. She waggles her bottom, the furry cat's tail attached to a butt plug we carefully inserted a little bit ago swishing back and forth.

She's been quiet all day, but like this, too—bouncy and happy.

My eyes track her swishing tail up to her round little—

Fuck. Now I'm hard.

"You sure you still want to do this?" I ask for the hundredth time.

She glares at me, then barks, "Out of the car."

She stands back up and reties the robe that's softly lined inside but looks like a jacket on the outside when it's closed. Knowing she's naked apart from the collar, tail, and the little nude ballet shoes she's wearing underneath doesn't help my stiffy.

Until I remember what she said last night and immediately deflate. Just when I thought I was so in control, I totally lost my shit.

Or maybe you'll hurt me again right when I give you my trust. I hear her voice in my head, and again, I feel the righteousness of the accusation in her words. It was only what I deserved after what I'd done and how I'd failed her. At least we were both finally acknowledging it.

Then, like always, there was *his* fucking voice, an unending echo I can't ever seem to rid myself of.

Such an ugly, untrustworthy little bitch, aren't you? You were born a dog, and you'll die a dog, you little slut. You're master's good little bitch, aren't you?

Lick my boot. Lick it like you love it.

Make me believe you love it.

Polish it, you little bitch!

Him shoving my head down until I choked. Because it wasn't his boot.

I'd twisted away from her, then.

I couldn't stand for her to see my face.

Fucking feelings, making me so fucking weak. Begging her to leave like that, right when she needed me to be strong. I just folded like a fucking bitch. I'm still so fucking ashamed. I don't deserve for her to wear my collar.

Fucking *feelings*. I've been fighting to hold my shoulders up all day. To grasp at *some* pretense of control.

"Let's go in!" Brooke says from the other side of the car, oblivious as I sit storming in the front seat. "I want to catch up with Quinn and Moira!"

I see she's swooping down to look back in at me, so I swing myself out of the car.

And at her words, I also remember: my sister. Shit. I've barely thought about Moira all week, I've been so consumed with Brooke. Usually I'm checking the reports from everyone I have watching her to make sure she's alright and they've all just stacked up in my inbox. Someone else I've been failing.

But Moira will be here tonight, and I can get a visual on

her. How much trouble could she have gotten into in just a week, anyway?

I walk around the front of the car to tuck Brooke's hand in my arm and— Fuck. Her beauty slams me full in the chest. She's so goddamn gorgeous. I don't fecking deserve her. Maybe tonight once we're around other people, she'll finally realize it, too. My chest feels like it caves in at the thought, but I don't allow myself to let on.

Come on, little bitch. You've spent your whole life wearing masks. What's one more night?

My large hand envelops her small one as she shifts her weight forward against me.

"Oh!" she gasps, smiling as our gazes catch. She grins radiantly up at me, and in spite of the terror at the thought of losing her that's currently squeezing the breath out of my chest, I also have to admit, I've never been so fecking happy in me whole stupid life. It's been a bitter cocktail all day—the wild joy drenched in shame.

Before I can lean down and kiss the woman of my dreams, though, she's grabbing my hand and dragging me forwards. "Come on! I want to see everyone."

I shut the car door and allow her to tug me forward. Even though I usually go through the back member's entrance, I allow her to take me around to the front of the club.

It's not flashy. Just a large black brick front with *Carnal* painted in white lettering across the glass entrance doors.

Next door is the swingers club, *Tempt*. It was one of

Caleb's best moves inviting the owner, Dakota, into talks to lease the space next door when she began inquiring in the area. Curious couples come for one space and migrate into the other. Then Caleb tempts the high dollar clients into ring membership here.

I open the door for Brooke, and she gives me a small smile before stepping inside. Like she's trying to reassure me when I should be doing that for her. Fuck, I'm failing her again if she can see I'm off my game at all. I'm better than that.

We're greeted by the club's other bouncer, Derek. He's newer, but he gives me a lift of the chin in acknowledgement as he steps out of the way for us to pass down the long hallway to the main part of the club.

I stand taller and solidify my outward facade. I'm at the club. I've been here a thousand times, and I know how to act. Shoulders back. Don't give a damn attitude. Bored and aloof expression.

Except how can I stay aloof when I'm being dragged along by a bright-eyed, gorgeous, kitty-ified Brooke who seems delighted by everything she sees?

The night is already in full swing. A lot of familiar faces are engaged in play on the various apparatuses around. Gemini's in the raised human-sized birdcage, their owner sitting in a chair, occasionally giving them a little swing with his booted foot. On center stage, a sub is on his knees, arms encased in rope against his chest, sucking his dom's cock.

Quinn has her sub over the flogging horse, landing practiced lash after lash across his ass and back with a wicked-looking rubber whip. Only the real pain pigs seek her out and this little piggie's squealing in distressed delight with every blow.

Thankfully, the atmosphere steadies me. Some, anyway.

I lead Brooke towards the lounge area by the bar. No one's allowed to drink before they scene, but if you bring in your own alcohol, the bartenders will mix drinks after you're done playing.

Regulars sit in the large, comfortable chairs scattered around, along with some newbies. I nod to a couple of them, my hand possessively on Brooke's lower back.

No one touches what's mine.

Everyone here knows better. Consent is king and required before any touch. Caleb hovers at one end of the club. Isaak is at the other, keeping watch over everything, always ready to enforce the rules.

We bypass the lounge and head towards Caleb. As we get closer, I see he's chattering with Moira. Thank god. The relief I always feel at seeing my sister safe, unmarked, and in one piece floods through me.

Okay. See? Everything's under control. Last night shook me, sure, but even the best doms have their off days. Tonight, I'm in my element and I can bring everything back to rights.

Moira's the first to notice us. She looks right past me, her whole face lighting up at seeing Brooke.

"Brooke!" she exclaims, throwing her arms out wide and

almost smacking Caleb in the face. He moves back just in time as my sister sprints in her Catholic school-girl outfit towards Brooke. She all but leaps into Brooke's arms. "We were so worried! Are you okay?"

I would roll my eyes at my sister's confidence in me. Except I think it actually means that as much as I've tried to hide my darkness from her, she's seen it, anyway. She knew what I was capable of. Fuck. She doesn't look at me, eyes only on Brooke.

"I'm good," Brooke smiles, hugging Moira back. "Really good. How've you been? I've missed movie nights. Oh, and I finally saw *Titanic*! The good part anyway. And look at you, so cute!" She tugs at my sister's pigtails as she pulls out of the hug. Moira really committed to the whole schoolgirl kink tonight, knee socks, short skirt, and all.

"Hell yeah, more movie nights!" Moira exclaims. "You're coming back home to the apartment now, right?" She looks expectantly at Brooke, and I can feel the weight of Caleb's eyes on Brooke, too.

My entire body goes tense, waiting to hear how Brooke will answer. Yes she's wearing my collar, but this was always part of my terror at bringing her here. I pull back from the girls, only then realizing I'm holding my breath.

Here, all she has to do is ask anyone else in this room for a ride. I meant what I said last night. I likely will hunt her to the ends of the earth if she tries to disappear again. I wouldn't be able to help myself. But she was very, very good at hiding from me the first time.

A single flip of the coin and our lives could diverge again.

Just then, she reaches back for my hand, squeezes, and tugs me forward until I'm standing beside her.

"Oh thanks," she says. "I'll definitely have to come over for more movie nights. But, um, I think I'm going home with Domhnall."

She looks up at me shyly and the flood of tension in my chest releases as I step forward, my hand sliding easily to possess the small of her back again.

Finally, finally, I breathe in. "Of course," I murmur in her ear. "I always want you at home where you belong. With me."

Her entire body relaxes into my side, and I finally begin to believe that maybe, just maybe, in this fucked up world of violence, burden, and sorrow, a thing such as happy endings might still exist.

THIRTY-THREE

BROOKE

FINALLY IT'S our turn on the stage. I stand still, my heart pounding as Domhnall ever so gently tugs my coat off my shoulders from behind, revealing my nakedness. And my tail.

"We're going to crawl towards the spanking bench, little kitty," he says as we step onto the small, raised stage right in the heart of the club. "Down on your hands and knees now."

This began on a stage with all eyes on me. It's only right we're back here. My heart thumps in my chest at the oddly full circle moment.

I bend down. I suppose I'm not entirely naked. I'm wearing flesh covered gloves, slim little knee-pads—Domhnall thinks of everything—and of course, my tail. As I drop to my hands and knees, I arch my back and wiggle my ass, so my tail flicks back and forth. It's a fun sensation, and I think I hear appreciative whispers from the crowd. I can't believe I'm up here on stage, after watching other couples' scenes play out for the last hour.

"That's a good kitty," Domhnall croons. By his confidence now, you'd never know he was in a dark and brooding mood all day. It's only since we stepped in the club that he's seemed to snap out of it. But I'm also wondering now if the Sir persona hides what inner Donny is really feeling. Maybe I'm not the only one who's a little shattered inside.

So I didn't just want to come to the club to see my friends. I hoped coming here might ground him and help him find his center again. I know he's hurting. I think tonight could help both of us. And I'm desperate to feel the deep connection between us again.

He leans down and attaches a leash to my collar. The nervousness I've felt all night dissipates at the slight tug as he takes command. All my muscles relax, and when I give another cat stretch, I feel even looser.

Domhnall walks beside me as I crawl forwards, so gorgeous he looks edible in his black shirt, dark blue jeans, and black leather boots.

"Stop here," he says. "And lift your eyes."

When I do, I get the pleasure of locking eyes with him as he reaches for the hem of his shirt and drags it off over his head. His abs are ridiculous, as always, and with his dark tattoos on reveal, he's a stunning specimen of man.

Suddenly I'm flooded with emotions. It's the first burst of the coming adrenaline, yes, and being insanely turned on by seeing Domhnall's physique, but it's more than that, too. I'm not entirely flush with the heat I know he'll bring soon. This emotion is just from the connection that crackles between us before he's even dropped me down in the space he takes me as my dominant.

It's because he's Domhnall. My soul's other puzzle piece. I click into place when I'm with him. The world feels *right*.

This, finally, is a *good* game. We both win when we play well.

I grab his hand even though I know the scene has begun. It still hasn't *started* started.

"Domhn," I whisper barely above a breath so just he can hear, "I want to make love to you. Tonight. Right now. I want you to know before we get into the scene, so you know I mean it."

I squeeze his hand, and his eyes catch mine again in that damn eternal gaze that scoops out my stomach and turns my knees to jelly.

He crouches down again, intense eyes burning through to my soul. I see his question in his eyes.

I nod. "I'm sure." I cling to his leg as the crackling electricity between us builds all but to the breaking point.

"*Please.*" This begging is all on my own terms and we both feel the impact of it.

Domhnall's nostrils flare and his eyes go dark. "Move around to the other side of the bench."

When I don't move quickly enough, he grasps my tail right at the base and leads me around the spanking bench. Then, guiding me by his hands on my waist, he helps me to my feet. He directs me like I'm just a doll in his hands, lifting me up onto the two-level spanking bench—knees on the bottom black padding, forearms on the top.

It exposes my tail-plugged ass and pussy to the watching crowd.

Almost immediately, Domhnall's whispering in my ear. "You're so gorgeous. So fucking perfect. Are you already getting slick for me, love? I'll give you what you ask for, but only after I make you work for it."

"Wider," he demands after he pulls back, loud enough for the crowd to hear. He prods the inside of my knees with some sort of stick so that I widen my stance on the bench. I shift so that I'm spread wider, but I'm too busy thinking about what Domhnall just used to nudge my legs to think about what the crowd might be seeing. Holy shit, was that a cane?

"Breathe in," he says, and dutifully, I take a breath in.

"Now breathe out."

Right as I start to expel the breath from my lungs, the thin stinging cane lights a line of fire across my ass.

"Fuck!" I can't help my choked shout. Jesus Christ, that was the *ten* on the pain scale!

"Count," he demands, "and ask for another."

"One," I gasp. "May I please have another, Sir?"

"That's my good kitty."

Before I'm ready, more fire sears my ass. Tears immediately spring to my eyes. I hear murmurs among the crowd, and I want to make Domhnall proud in spite of the pain I can barely breathe through.

"Two," I whisper, out of breath, barely managing to eke out, "May I have another, Sir?"

"Breathe," he reminds me, and I suck in a huge breath of air.

I feel a slight tug on the plug inside me as he lifts my tail, exposing the lower half of my ass. He lands another searing smack.

All the air bursts out of me in a screech. I want to cover my ass with my hands, but instead, I clutch the bench pad.

He leans in, his next words only for me. "You're such a good, good girl, aren't you? My good, precious girl. My marks are so fucking beautiful on you."

Tears streak down my face as my veins start to light up. My ass glows with heat as Domhnall skims his fingertips over the flesh he just marked.

"I'm so fucking hard right now. Everyone's staring. For once I won't blindfold you, curious kitty."

I take full advantage of his permission to look. I turn my

head over my shoulder and stare down his chiseled abs to the taut V as he kicks his boots off. He shoves his jeans down and shucks them off, too, exposing his heavy, gorgeously engorged cock. Holy shit. I've felt it before, but this is the first time I'm *seeing* it.

"I want it inside me," I say immediately, still staring. He's said I'm his several times and there was that time by the pool with the cucumber... but I finally want him to claim my body with his.

He chuckles and bends low, chest to my back, so low that his cock swings between my legs. I feel it knock against my sex and am immediately wet. What I don't expect is for the pain of my fresh marks bumping against Domhnall's groin to mix with how turned on I'm getting.

Domhnall and I are naked, and his dick is between my legs.

In public, for all these people to see. Holy shit.

He didn't blindfold me. He wanted me to see his cock. He wanted me to be able to see everyone watching us. He knew it would turn me on.

We're different sides of the same coin, I swear. It makes me clench even as I see several people pleasuring themselves lazily while they watch on. One woman has a pet of her own tightly leashed, one leg up on a stool as her pet in a doggy mask nuzzles at her sex with his tongue.

I'm yanked back into my own scene when Domhnall

spanks me. He's being careful not to make contact with any of the spots he hit with the cane. I finally got an eye on number ten, and it's a wicked little thin piece of wood currently cast to the floor.

"Bend over, let's see that cunt," Domhnall says, louder. His hand on my back guides me to flatten out on the bench so my ass is fully extended to the crowd.

"Swish that lil' tail. You're me slutty feckin' kitty, arn't ya? O-aah, ya can't wait for me to stuff ya full of me cock. We all see yur creamin' fur me. It's drippin' down yur leg, ain't it? I said... *wider*."

He spanks me again, making my entire sex jiggle. Between that and the filthy demands coming out in his deep, throaty brogue, I'm panting and clenching and whining on the bench. He's right. I am dripping down my leg, he's got me so turned on.

I love every side of this twisted fucking man. I love that he can be vulnerable enough to shake and fight his demons while bent, arms around me and head burrowed against my stomach. And I love the filthy Irish lad here calling out the raunchiest demands for everyone to hear. Every shadowed, lonely bit inside me feels lit up as I *see* him and feel so fully *seen* in return.

"Fuck," he calls out, as if it's a confession, "if ya only knew how many nights I've dreamed of rammin' ya full. Of wreckin' ya. Of destroyin' ya."

He leans in, his voice a ragged, rumbling growl in my ear. "Of absolutely *ruinin'* you."

Fuck. Oh god. *Yes.* "Ruin me," I gasp back.

I think for sure that then, surely then, I'll feel the weight of his back as he *finally* mounts me, but—

Instead his wicked fingers drop between my legs to dance across my clit. My breath catches. *Please*, I beg silently. *Oh please don't tease me more. I need it. I need you inside me.*

But Domhnall's sadism is an itch that *will* be scratched.

His fingertips are a whisper across my flesh until I'm panting.

"What a pretty kitty, glistening like that for your owner."

I think I squirt a little when he says he owns me. It's so fucked up. But god yes. I want him to own me. I want to belong to him. For ever and ever. He'll wrap me up in his bed each night and tuck me against him, and I'll always be safe.

His hands move away from my clit, and I try not to whine. He's still touching me, now massaging down the backs of my thighs.

"My kitty's good breeding stock," he says loudly, in a way that I know is for the crowd's benefit. "She's like a pony that way. Such a pretty ass and withers. Such a shiny tail." He tugs on the tail connected to the plug in my ass and I clench on it. "Makes me want to ride. Would kitty like a ride?"

"Yes," I say, remembering to breathe. I draw in a lungful of air.

He spanks me, not sparing the cane marks this time. I yelp even as he asks, louder, "I said, would kitty like a ride?"

"Yes, Sir!"

"That's a good girl," he says, hand moving back to strum my clit with the barest pressure as he bends over me from behind, his heavy horse cock again swinging between my legs and finding its mark.

I'm so wet that when he shifts his hips, the top of his cock slides easily through my outer vaginal lips, in maybe an inch. We both pause in surprise for a moment, neither of us expecting him to go that far. I immediately clench all my muscles around him, as if I can draw him in deeper with my inner muscles alone.

"Feck," he whispers harshly in my ear. "Mads— *Brooke*. Fuck. I can't believe I'm finally inside ya. You're the woman of me dreams. Ya always were. Ya feel like fuckin' heaven. I don't deserve ya."

I'm sure he's going to push inside then and complete us like the puzzle pieces we were always meant to be.

"Yes," I moan, so ready. *"Domhn."*

But instead he drags himself out with a low, guttural grunt. *Noooo*. I want to cry out in despair at him denying us both like this.

"That's Sir to you," he says raggedly. "And don't you dare come until I give you permission."

Then his cock is replaced by his mouth.

Oh fuck, this isn't fair. My hips spasm needily against his face. It's his favorite form of torture. His stubble scrapes against my thighs as his head thrashes back and forth while he tongues my pussy.

I whimper as I fight the rising orgasm. He's not teasing. He devours me like he's a starving man. He latches on with his mouth and eats me out until I'm clenching everything so hard, I'm about to die.

"Please, Sir, may I come?" I moan.

His sweet tongue pulls away.

"No," he says sharply.

I let out the breath I didn't mean to hold. But he's already got me at the edge, the pleasure he's lit only barely dipping at the loss of contact. It's so close. I can feel it. I'll finally have him. He'll finally be mine.

His hands squeeze my waist right at my hips and then his cock comes back, teasing my drenched pussy lips again. When he thrusts in, he goes in the same depth as before, a little deeper maybe. Torturing us both.

I'm sure he's going to keep this up for the next hour, dangling me on the edge of the orgasm that's already ready to flood over me like a tidal wave and then yanking back at the very last moment.

But then he groans in my ear, "I'm gonna die if I don't have ya this second, love."

Before I can quite get a grasp on what's happening, he reaches over and tugs my hands away from where I'm gripping the bench. Then he's spinning me and pulling me into his arms, chest to chest for what feels like the first time.

I throw my arms around him and kiss him recklessly. His mouth is just as hungry. I taste myself on his lips and it only makes me crazier for him.

He kisses me like I'm his air. He can't get enough and neither can I.

He hefts me up, his strong, muscled arms locked under my thighs as he carries me to the nearest hard surface—a thick floor-to-ceiling smooth wooden beam at one of the four corners of the stage—and presses my back up against it.

I feel him there again, his cock stiff against my slick. I nod. "Yes. God, please fuck me, Sir."

He's still tentative as he pushes in. My head falls back against the beam at the feel of him finally, slowly filling me where I've been so empty. There's no pain at all, where I expect it. Only pleasure. Pressure and delicious stretching where I've been so desperate for pressure.

He's a perfect fit. It's only when he reaches the end of my channel that my eyes fly open, back down to find he's just been staring at me the whole time.

I clasp his jaw in my hands. His cock pushes in the last bit and it's as if just *there*, the very tip of him rings some bell.

My back arches and I begin to spasm with the start of a body-shaking orgasm. "More," I manage to gasp before the pleasure starts to blind me.

For once, Domhnall is the one good at obeying. He pulls

out and then pushes slowly back in, hitting the same spot so deep inside me. I clench around him, and everything grows more intense. It's an impossible fit between him and the sizeable plug he worked in my ass earlier. He's inside me. The puzzle pieces finally fit together in one flesh.

But what amps up the pleasure to even wilder heights is watching Domhnall's face as he looks down at me. The mixture of agony and pleasure stretching his gorgeous features makes me clench on his thick cock even harder. Which has him rocking forwards in a satisfying, hard thrust right after he's pulled out.

"Fuck," he spits, "did I hurt you?"

"Harder," I squeak through the spasming pleasure. "I need it harder."

His eyes widen but his hips jerk backward and forwards, some part of him clearly getting the message.

"Fuck!" he shouts, dropping his face into my neck. "Brooke. You're so fecking tight. So perfect, love, I can't—"

He's really thrusting now, and the power of him, the weight of him as his cock finally rams into me deep the way I've needed it all along—it consumes me. His arm wrapped around me protects me from banging into the wood behind me, caring for me even while he pleasures me and takes his own pleasure simultaneously—

"Domhn!" I scream, locking my ankles around his waist and riding him back as he yanks me off the wall and fucks me in the air. He lifts me up and drops me back down on his long cock by my waist, again and again.

I'm coming so fucking hard, and it doesn't stop, the first orgasm riding directly into a second, and then a third as Domhnall keeps fucking me. The entire club around us has gone silent.

"Oh fuck, Domhnall, yes." I clutch his neck with one arm and dig my nails into his scalp with the other. "Oh god, harder, please."

"I'll give ya harder, and more. Oh fuck, I'll give ya everything. The whole fecking world, love. I'll give ya the whole fecking world."

Somehow while he's holding my weight in the air and screwing my brains out, he manages to shift his hand so he can grab my ass, pinching one of his marks. The pain mingles with the pleasure, and I squeeze down so hard on his cock as ecstasy bursts out the top of my skull like an explosion.

I feel Domhnall pumping and then he stills, whole body shuddering. A pleasured groan sounds from low in his chest. My joy at feeling him fill me and drip down my thighs bursts as bright as the orgasm still shaking my limbs.

"I love you," I breathe into his ear as I clutch his neck, compulsively squeezing around his cock again and again, milking even more cum out of him.

He gasps and his hands squeeze my waist. His flinty blue eyes shoot to me. "Do ya mean it?" I see the young man from the pictures on his face, vulnerable and completely stripped. "Love, do you mean it?"

Love. It's just the pet name he calls me, and I don't know if he'll ever really be able to say it back to me. But I can't hold it in my heart anymore without it bursting out of my lips. "I love you, Domhn. I think I've loved you for a very, very long time."

He kisses me, then, and I feel joy and boyish exuberance in his kiss.

As if I've healed him in this moment.

Like I've finally brought peace to the troubled man by giving him everything he ever secretly wanted but could never admit to himself because of all the complicated pain wrapped up in *us*.

I feel that peace, too, and I'm *happy*. So, so happy.

I slump my head on his shoulder and open my eyes lazily.

"I love you, too," he whispers back.

But the utterance of it rings like a nonsensical, dissonant echo in my head.

Because my veins have frozen solid as ice.

With me faced the way I am, I can see over Domhnall's shoulder to the back corner of the club.

Moira's there, pushing open the back door.

And in that instance, several shattering things happen in the space of a single moment.

Domhnall's ringing confession of love.

Moira leaping into the arms of an older man standing in the light outside the back door.

It's Gus, the handyman from the shelter.

Her secret.

Gus makes eye contact with me as his arms wrap around Moira in return.

Then, while her face is buried in his chest, he lifts one hand from her waist, palm flat, and makes the motion of wiping down his face.

As if unmasking himself.

It's a mentalist's trick. A signal to snap a person out of hypnosis. I don't know how I know, but I do.

I recognize it in the same moment I'm spiked with the painful rush of a headache. And right before the door closes on Gus and Moira, I recognize who Gus really is. He was never *just* the shelter's handyman who I occasionally played chess with.

All along, hiding in plain sight, it's actually been—

My father.

Oh god. I was never going to be able to find wholeness in Domhnall, was I? I'm too fractured deep down inside. I swim with nausea as I'm forced to retreat, past flooding present. I flail in my mind, but it's too late.

She's too strong. The ghost I was foolishly reaching so hard for is suddenly here, wrenching control away from me. If I ever even had it.

"Red," the me that's *her* says mechanically into Domhn's

ear. My mouth forms the words, but it's the ghost who's speaking. She's back. She's here and she's me.

And she's fully in control now.

Domhnall yanks back from me, eyes pained and confused. But his hands readily release me when I climb off him, unseating me from his still hard cock. I back away from him across the stage, pulling the tail out of my backside with a disconcerted grunt. I drop it to the ground with a dull *thud*.

"Brooke," Domhnall calls, concerned.

But that's not my name. It was never my name.

Donny I have to tell you something!

But I never could, could I? She kept my mouth shut, somehow. Even though one of us was always asleep while the other was awake. I shouldn't be awake now while she's in control, but I am somehow.

She's the one who obeys. She always obeys Daddy.

I take several more steps away from Domhnall even though in my head, I'm screaming—*What are you doing? Go back!*

Instead, I turn away from him mechanically and climb off the stage, as if it's not me controlling my body. Because oh god, it's not. It's like I'm on the outside looking in, but I'm not at the controls.

She is.

No matter how loud I scream, no sound comes out of my throat. I don't say a single word, not even when Domhnall calls my name again.

I just pick up the coat we discarded at the front of the stage, swing it around my shoulders, and keep walking towards the back door.

That's Daddy's good girl, I hear in my head, a horrifying voice that sends me shrinking to the corner of my mind.

I climb in the box and pull the lid shut tight to hide. My feet keep taking me further and further away from Domhnall towards the back door of the club and the darkness beyond.

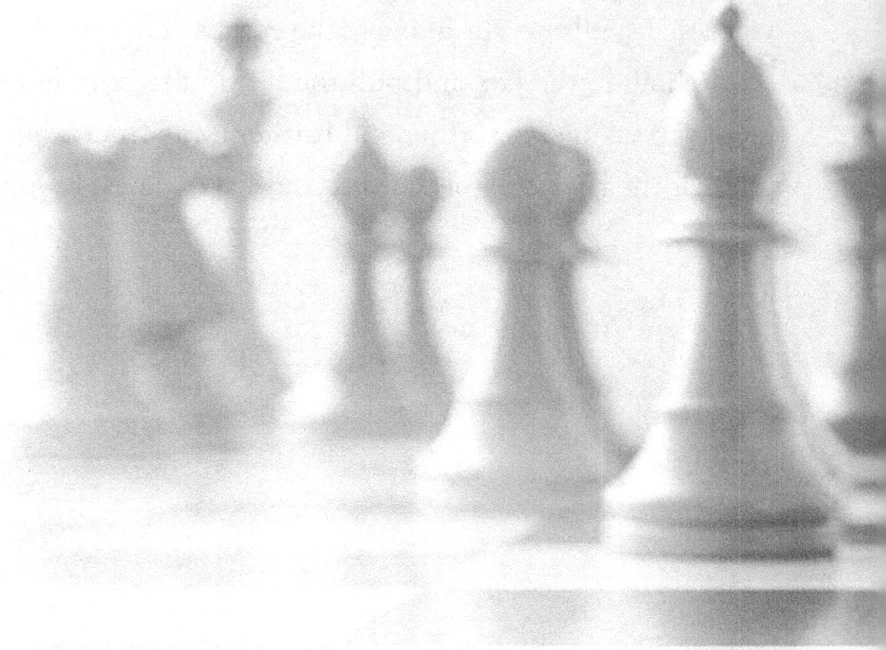

THIRTY-FOUR

DOMHNALL

"BROOKE," I call again when she keeps walking away from me, grabbing my jeans off the stage and shoving my legs into them.

What the hell is going on? It's like she just flipped out when I told her I loved her. She had to know, didn't she? She'd just said it to me and hearing it out of her mouth was everything I always wanted to hear. I only realized once she was saying it. But obviously it freaked her out to hear it in return.

Still, we can fix this. We've already been through so much already. A safeword is meant to be just that. I'll make her feel safe and we can start again. We don't have to do scenes. Dammit, I knew it was a bad idea to come here tonight.

This is just a little hiccup. This is nothing.

I jog to catch up, managing to shove my dick back in my jeans and button them right before I reach her. She continues acting like she can't hear my voice, and I get worried. Maybe something else is going on and she's still in subspace or something. Professor Roberts said different things might trigger her. Shit, I knew this was too soon!

I shove past some club members until I get around in front of her, planting myself in her path and grabbing her arm when she keeps trying to step around me, still not looking my way.

"Hey. Brooke!" I give her a gentle shake, trying to jog her back to herself.

She finally looks at me all right, her eyes full of scorn. "That's not my fucking name and you know it." Her tone is venomous. "I expect the full sum will be in my bank account now?"

I can only blink at her, so confused about what the hell is going on.

Just then, though, Quinn pushes her way up to us. Right as Brooke yanks at my grip on her. "Let go of my fucking arm."

"What the hell's going on?" Quinn demands, grabbing my wrist in some sort of jiu jitsu wrist hold that immediately makes me go weak with pain right as my fingers were loosening to let go of Brooke, anyway.

"You're not needed," I snap at Quinn.

But Brooke suddenly cowers behind Quinn. "Don't let that bastard touch me again. He's had me locked in a dungeon all week. He beat me and made me eat from a dog bowl."

Brooke looks me right in the eye as she says it. "I assume our little public performance fulfilled the terms beyond a reasonable doubt? I expect my fucking money in the specified bank account I gave you when I signed that fucking contract *now*. I want to get the fuck out of this town and never look back. You cunts have done *enough* to me."

Her words punch me in the guts, and I stagger a step back. Oh fuck. The last two days she's been playing me to make sure I let her go.

Because I'm the monster in this story.

She's been trying to escape me any way she could. She's smart. When I caught her in the picture room, I was angry. I wince as the smashing whisky glass against the wall replays in my head. I was violent.

I'm a billionaire and she knew it. She probably thought that if she tried to escape then, I'd have like, fucking dogs chase her down or some shit. A hand drags from my hair down my face and I keep stumbling back, feeling sick.

She survived the only way she could, waiting until she could escape me publicly. Probably the same way she survived her father all those years. The same way *I* survived her father.

She gave in. She played a part. All the while loathing me inside. She played a better game of chess until she could outwit me and escape.

I stopped playing chess that night with the pictures when I learned the truth, but she didn't know. I'd already trained her by then, after god-knows-what that sick fuck did to her over the years and— oh fuck, I'm going to be sick.

Because in her head, I'd essentially just forced her to have sex with me.

Mads, what have I done to you?

I run for the men's room but don't make it, dropping to my knees and losing my dinner in the big fake plant Caleb's decorator used to hide the trashcan.

THIRTY-FIVE

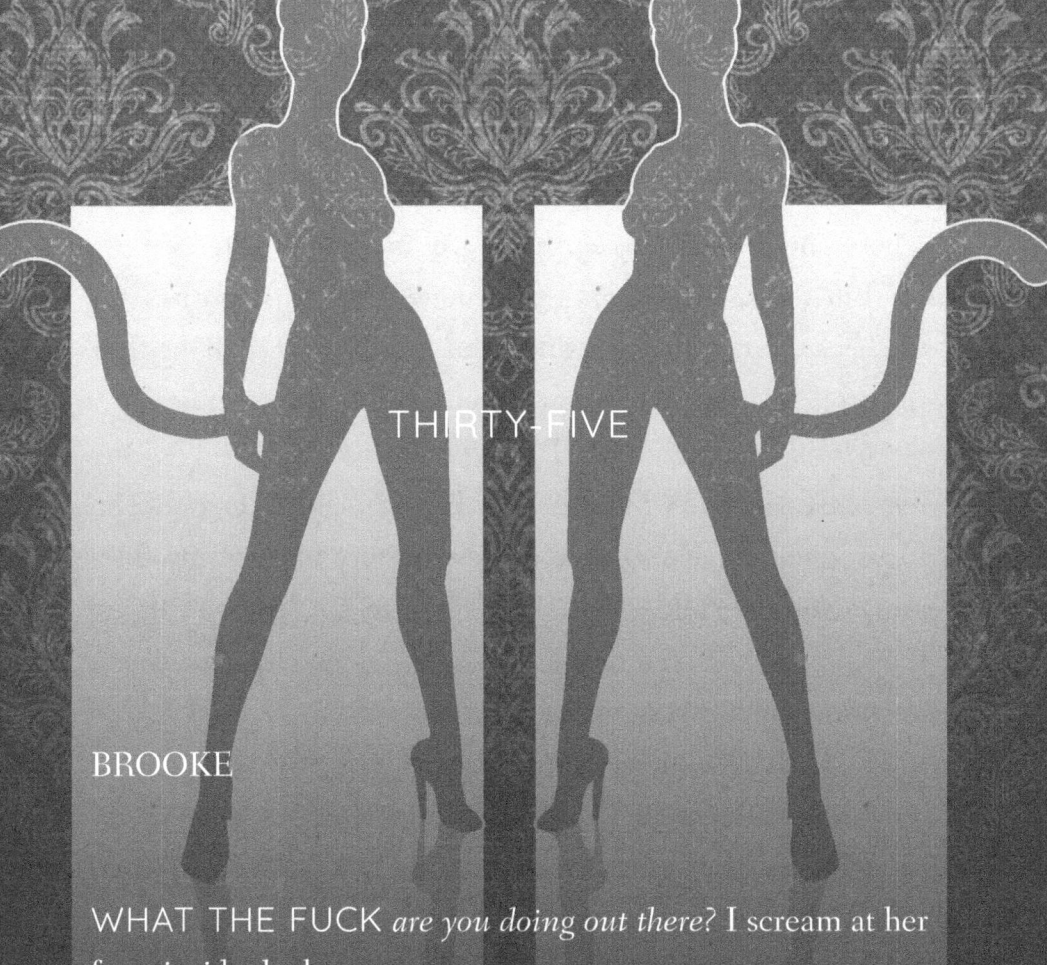

BROOKE

WHAT THE FUCK *are you doing out there?* I scream at her from inside the box.

I can't believe what just came out of her mouth. But her feet just keep walking towards the back door.

No, not her feet. *My* feet. *My feet.*

But here in the box, they don't feel like my feet. Domhnall just stood there looking so stunned. Not even betrayed. I saw the shame twist his features. It was the same— I choke on sobs inside the box. It's the same look he had on his face when—

The sob catches in my chest. She won't let it break free.

Fuck, I need to go back and warn Domhnall my father is here. That he has Moira! I need to warn him about Moira! There's nothing on this earth he loves more than her.

But the bitch I'm on a ride-along inside just pushes out the back door. The warm air of the Texas summer night after the cool AC of the club punches me in the face.

Me! That's right. *Me.* I try to focus on the feeling of my five senses. That's what Professor Roberts said to do, right? So focus, dammit! The breeze tickles the tiny hairs of my forearms. And the sudden hot air is bright in my lungs, outlining the shape of them from the inside. Good, good. What about my nose? What does my nose smell?

Be Daddy's good girl. Be a good girl now.

Eyes. What do her—*my*—eyes see? We're striding confidently towards a van at the end of an alley, where the bright lights installed behind the club can't reach. As my eyes become accustomed to the growing darkness, I see the van clearer. It's rocking back and forth.

My feet keep taking me towards the van's tailgate door.

I stop there for only a moment and blink.

Hand, I try desperately. *What is my hand doing??*

But I can only watch in horror without being able to stop it as my hand reaches down and opens the back door of the van.

I scream when the door lifts up to reveal— "No!"

My father's in the back of the van, fucking Moira. She's

bent over, face smashed into the rough carpeting, bare ass in the air, squeaking in pleasure. My father, one fist against the window, ruts into her from behind with furious thrusts.

And then instead of being *me* or anyone else, it's like my head drops down through my feet. Then further down. Right through the asphalt underneath me.

You're not here or there.

You're in both places.

It's both Moira beneath your father in the van *here* in front of you.

And it's Domhn in your memory *there*. *Donny*.

Happening now. Always now. Over and over, *now*.

"Please," Donny croaks, thin and small, struggling to get your much bigger father off him from where he's got him pinned against the floor. Your father strangles Donny with the collar around his neck while he— While he—

"Get *off*!" Donny begs. "Please, Sir!"

"Take it like a good doggy. Be a good doggy for Daddy."

Be a good girl for Daddy.

You're staring because you're not allowed to look away. Daddy will get mad if you do. Tonight he's doing what he always does.

He gagged you, tied your arms behind your back, and shoved you in the footlocker across the room. He drilled holes in it so you can breathe. And so you can watch.

"*Watch, Mati, or I'll hurt him worse. Promise you'll be a*

good girl and watch so I don't hurt pretty Donny worse than I have to. I wouldn't do this if you could just be a good girl, Mati. Tomorrow, try again to be Daddy's good girl. You know if you could just be good, I'd stop hurting him."

But you're never good enough. And you never remember to grab Donny's hand when you see him the next day so you can escape the monster together. *There's something I need to tell you, Donny!*

You just wake up in your bed where everything is safe and normal, then go downstairs to find Daddy smiling, joking with you, and cooking breakfast.

Every time you're back in the box, you scream at yourself to *remember* this time. Remember!

But there's the pills Daddy forces you to swallow. He makes those strange hand gestures in front of your face and when he snaps, you fall asleep.

Then when you wake up the next day, groggy, sick feeling with the vague memory of bad, *bad* nightmares, Daddy looks at you as if he's worried about you for having such disturbing dreams. Maybe you should see a therapist, he always says, but you never do.

He just gets more pills, and you swallow them with breakfast. That's why he says you have trouble remembering sometimes. It's a side effect. But isn't your mood better now?

You don't know. You don't know anything.

You feel split in two.

At night you don't remember the day and during the day you can't remember what happens at night.

You can't seem to tell what's real from what's not. Only one thing makes any sense in any of the hazy dream worlds you're walking.

The boy with the crystal blue eyes.

Things around him get more clear. He makes you feel alive, and awake. But something's wrong. You can feel it. Something's wrong with Donny. Your bright boy has started to fade. There's this itch at the back of your neck as you start to suspect there's something wrong with your whole world.

You start to stash the pills your father gives you in the morning. You pretend to swallow them but instead spit them out when he's not looking. During the daytime with Domhnall, you know something's wrong even if you can't put your finger on it.

Then, one night, after a day when the shadows under Domhnall's eyes are deeper than ever, you experience the horrific evening tied up in the footlocker, managing to stay present for it. Not swapping to *her*, even though you can feel her there, watching from inside a deep box in your head. But you stay in charge, and witness what you witness.

You still think you can escape the monster. Donny looks like he has hope for the first time since you met him. Together, you'll escape *him* and start over.

But when you go home to get your passport and the

money, the monster's waiting. Always one move ahead on the board.

"What do you think I'll do to him now?" the monster growls. "I always warned you what would happen if you stopped being Daddy's good girl."

"No, don't!" you scream, but he's dragging you downstairs to his dungeon. He throws you on the floor while he grabs his cruelest whip and starts to put it in a bag. The cat-o'-nine-tails with rocks sewn into the tiny, beaded straps at the end. Then he picks up a giant neon green phallus. And a ball gag with a hole in it.

"Stop it," you scream and run at him, leaping on his back and clawing at his eyes. He easily throws you to the floor.

His eyes are dark and evil as he stares down at you.

"Don't," you say, crab walking backwards to get away from him. "I didn't mean to."

"You are Daddy's very, *very* bad girl," he says with his dangerous, quiet voice as he stomps towards you. You get up to flee but he catches you by the back of your hair and jerks you backwards until your head slams the hardwood floor.

You only blink awake when he's got the oxygen mask over your head, tube down your throat, the rest of your body constrained by rope.

"No," you cry as much as you can with the breathing tube down your throat. It comes out an illegible, "Naaa."

That's when you hear the *whir* of the machine that means — Oh god, oh god, oh god!

Within seconds, you're choking without breath, spasming against the ropes constricting your body until suddenly oxygen floods back in right at the moment you're about to pass out.

You float out and leave *her* behind to take the punishment, screaming as you watch from within the box.

THIRTY-SIX

BROOKE

I WAIL like an animal just punched through with a hunter's bullet.

"Oh my God!" Moira yelps at my scream, jumping out from underneath him. My— My father. "Brooke. I'm so embarrassed," she says, yanking down the skirt of her tight school-girl outfit.

I stare at my father, still in the van. He's just lazily tucked himself into his pants as he grins back at me with a smug smile carved in his face.

He's prepared all this. I can't even begin to imagine how. But he meant for me to run out just now and catch him. Either that or he's been fucking Moira ever since the shelter while he waited for me to wake back up, knowing he'd stage this moment at some point. All the while wielding me as a weapon against Domhnall.

I'd finally been a bad girl too many times.

He told me the next time I tried to run away, he'd make good on his promise to hurt Donny in a way he'd never recover from this time. I saw in his eyes he meant it.

So I waited. I waited until my father was off guard, sure he thought he'd finally broken me into his soulless puppet.

And then I ran one last time. I told myself I could warn Donny before my father got to him. If I planned carefully enough, surely I could outwit my father in this last game of chess. Just this *once*.

But he was one move ahead of me the whole time, wasn't he? Like always, he let me think I was winning until calling checkmate when I least expected it.

Father found me when I was getting close to Domhnall's, and he smashed my head in. Then, while I was blinking, woozy with blood loss, he got in my face and hypnotized me into forgetting, just like always. Except this time, he didn't just tell me to forget the night before. He told me to forget *everything*.

To forget.

Completely.

Until he woke me with his mentalist's signal just now in the club. It flipped the switch back to *her*.

I never let him know she exists inside me, bearing the

worst of his sadistic punishments and taking over on the days when I just couldn't get out of bed or keep on keeping on. He thought it was all his mentalism skills and I let him think so. She never even gave herself a name. She was just the one who bore the darkness. She was the one who obeyed when I couldn't.

And now here she and I stand, staring at the devil who made us as he grins in triumph.

His favorite game always was to torture me and Domhnall with our love for one another. He can't understand love, so he poisons it with his evil. The same as he does when he comes across any pure thing. The same as he did to my *mother*.

"Oh my god," Moira repeats, covering her face from me. She still has no clue what's actually unfolding. To her, my father is just the handyman from the shelter, elicit only because she's fucking him outside the club and her brother's set rules for her. "Please don't tell Domhn."

"It's alright, Moira," I say, still glaring my father down. "But go back inside now or I will tell on you. Domhnall's worried. You know how he gets when he's worried."

"Shit," Moira says, turning away from us and back towards the club. She immediately starts running towards it as fast as her high-heels and tight bondage dress will allow, pulling a phone from I can't imagine where and texting as she goes.

Assured she's safe, I look back at my father.

"It's taken you long enough, my little Mati," he finally says, climbing out of the car. I back away from him, all my muscles rigid. "I trust you've destroyed him just like we planned?"

"I didn't plan anything with you!" I spit. But even as I say it, I'm not sure if it's true or not. Did *she* and him plan it?

When I was younger, she helped me survive. I see that now. She took on what I couldn't bear. But in the process, just how far did he twist her mind? I'm not sure.

Especially when my father takes a slow step forward. "Yes you did, pumpkin. It was your idea, actually. You've missed Domhnall. He was your favorite doggy we ever had."

"Shut up!" I hiss, rigid body shaking now. No. No! It's not true. I'm frozen beyond the trembling, not able to move a muscle. "You're lying."

"You've been a good girl for such a long time now; I told you it was time for a treat. You asked for doggy Donny back. Who am I to deny my good girl anything? It's been just you and Daddy, playing our little games together for all these years."

My head swims with his words and suddenly I'm confused. A hand lifts to my head.

Did I actually try to escape my father and come to warn Domhn? Or... Or is what Daddy's saying true? After all this time, did I stay so deep in my mind's box that I let *her* just run free? Free to be a monster just like him?

Was I just deluding myself this whole time that I've been the one in control?

I thought Domhnall and me were like matching pieces of a puzzle but turns out I'm just a jigsaw with pieces missing, ones from a different puzzle stapled into their place. I don't know what's mine and what's not. What's real? Am I Domhnall's puzzle piece because that's what she and my father made me?

"That's my good girl," my father coos, taking another step towards me as the light begins to dim at the edges of my vision. I start to feel dizzy. Like I'm in a dream, and I realize it's a familiar feeling.

Oh shit, she's back, and she wants control again.

All the light disappears when, reaching suddenly in front of my face, my father snaps his fingers. The world goes black. The last thing I feel is him catching me as I fall unconscious.

THIRTY-SEVEN

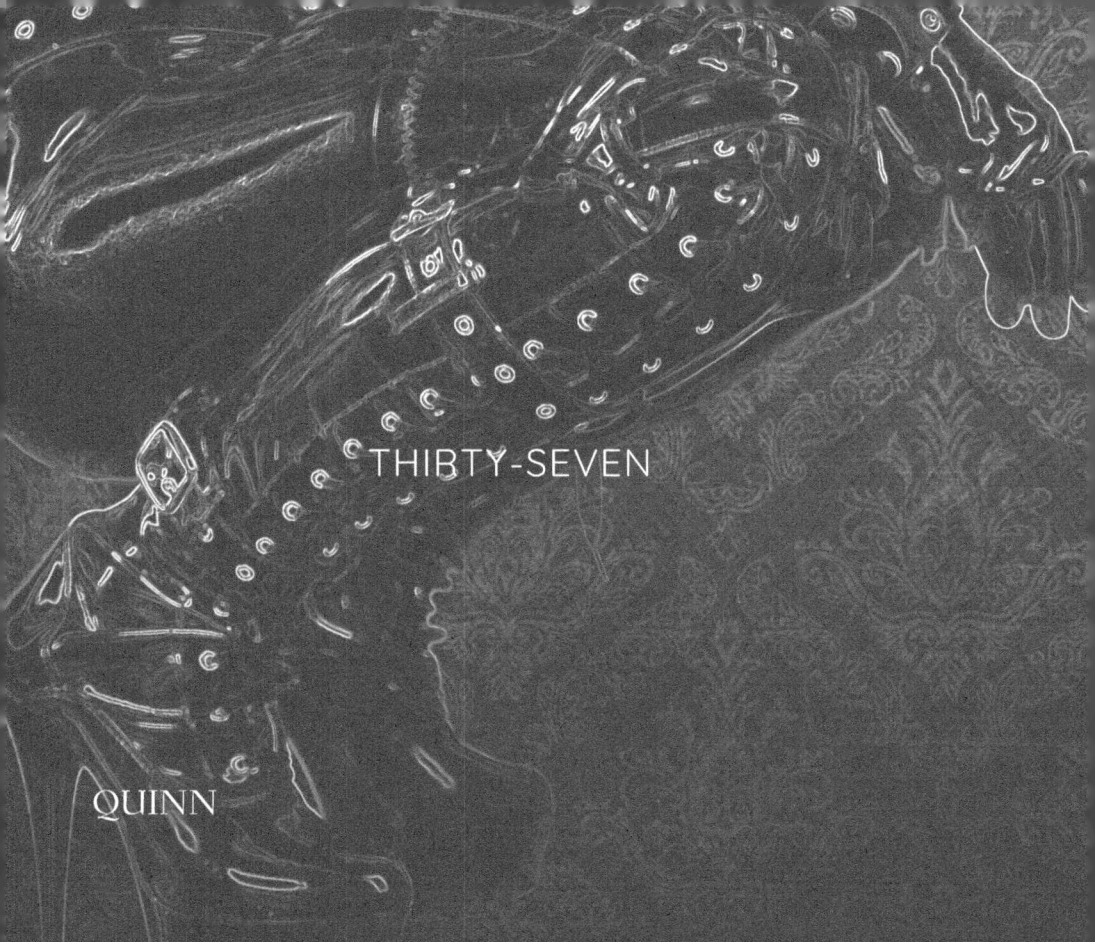

QUINN

MY ELBOW-TO-TOE full PVC catsuit isn't chafing, but it's still hot as I stomp back and forth across the club in my thigh-high black stilettos.

I spot Caleb standing behind the sleek black equipment rental bar under-lit with pink neon light.

"Where the fuck is Moira?" I demand in my domme voice, grabbing the front of his shirt. "I can't find her anywhere. I've been busy babysitting Domhn, who's getting shit-faced in your office, by the way."

Caleb stares up at me with the fear of God in his face. He knows how pissed Domhn gets if we lose track of Moira on a play night. But then he looks past my shoulder, relieved, and shoves his finger out. "There!"

I let go of his shirt and spin around to see where he's pointing. Only to see Moira, hair half out of her pigtails, tugging down on the hem of her tight skirt guiltily. Dammit, she's been fucking off premises again. Sex addiction or no, I'm pissed at her for making trouble on a night like this when Domhn had such tense shit going on. We don't need to deal with her shit, too.

I stomp over to her, and everyone, male and female, gets out of my way like a parting sea without me having to say a word.

"Where the *fuck* have you been?" I demand, getting in her face as she looks up at me with wide, innocent eyes. I'm one of the few people in the world that doesn't work on.

Everyone lets her get away with shit because, by an accident of birth, she came out looking like an anime doll fucked a leprechaun. She's a devious kinky little redhead with eyes two times the size of her face that everybody wants to fuck. It happens to work out, cause she's just as desperate to fuck them back, and she's one of my best friends, but *Jesus*.

"Domhn told me to make myself scarce for the show," she says, and then those big eyes drop like they do whenever Domhn or I question her and she's trying to hide something from us. Thankfully, for all her other charms, she's fucking awful at lying, so the amount of trouble she gets herself into is limited.

I wave a hand, sighing. "We'll deal with it later. Did you see Brooke? I want to make sure she got a ride safely out of here."

Moira's eyes fly back up. "Oh I just saw her," she says, smiling and obviously happy to tell me something that can get the heat off her. "Back in the alley." She jerks a thumb behind her.

"The alley..." My eyes snap up towards the back door. "What were you—" I stop even before finishing the question, eyes rolling. It's obvious what Moira was doing in the alley. The question is: "What was *Brooke* doing in the alley?"

"Oh," Moira says, following my eyeline towards the door. "She- I- We just ran into one another out there."

"I know you were screwing someone back there." I wave a hand impatiently. "But where was Brooke when you last saw her? You know we're downtown. There are reasons we don't want you going in the back alley to fuck beyond just getting picked up for public indecency."

"Oh." Moira blinks in confusion and then her eyes widen. "*Oh.*" She frowns. "Actually, I thought she was right behind me."

We both start walking quickly towards the door. When I pick up into a jog, Moira's still matching me. She reaches out to touch my arm. "It's okay, though. It's just Gus, from the shelter."

"Who the fuck is Gus from the shelter?" I demand as I

throw open the door to the alley, stomping out and looking both ways. I don't see Brooke or anyone else.

"The handyman. Brooke knows him. They used to play—" Moira says, following me out. "—chess. Wait," she turns around, forehead scrunched in confusion. "They were just here."

"Jesus, Moira," I swear, a bad feeling sinking in my guts as I spin and start sprinting back into the club.

Maybe it's fine. Like Moira says, she knew the guy, so maybe after he got his rocks off with Moira, Brooke asked if she could bum a ride to the nearest train station.

But the bad feeling in my stomach counters, a sense honed by a lifetime of things *not* being fine. *What if it's not fine?*

I run faster to get to Domhn in the club's office.

THIRTY-EIGHT

DOMHNALL

I GRASP onto the passenger's seat door handle with white knuckles as my Audi speeds down the highway with Quinn at the wheel. Isaak and Moira are in the backseat. The bright screen with a map on the dash between Quinn and me fucking mocks me. Sixteen minutes until arrival.

Sixteen fucking minutes.

He has a thirty-minute head start on us.

She'll be gone before you get there, you gobshite. You'll lose her again. Not just lose her. Now you've had a glimpse of what the demon's done to her mind. He had her this whole time.

Because I was fucking stupid enough to believe he'd actually died. All I saw were autopsy pictures of the water-logged body. It clearly had the same build and distinctive tattoos on its chest. But he'd obviously manipulated someone into getting his same tattoos before killing them and tossing them in the Danube.

I'm a fucking idiot for never considering the possibility.

Seventeen minutes ago, Quinn, Caleb and I watched back on the security camera footage as she collapsed to the ground in front of the fucker when he snapped his fingers in her face. If I'd had anything left in my guts when I saw it—

The fist not gripping the door handle comes to my mouth. Jaysus. I was so wrong, this whole time. How could I have ever believed she'd been in on it for a moment?

She was only fucking thirteen. She was a little fucking *kid*.

You were, too. It's her soft voice in my head, and I slam my fist against the dashboard. I don't deserve for her to be here in my head absolving me of anything.

But her voice keeps echoing even as I smash my fist against the dash over and over.

He was bigger. There was nothing either of us could've done against such evil.

"Domhn!" Moira's scream finally breaks through, and the fact that Isaak's physically restraining me from the seat behind me.

"Sorry," I choke out, my throat still thick with the whisky I was busy pouring down it when Quinn stormed in the office demanding to see the security footage. It's why she's driving now, not me.

I can't even show up now when Mads needs me. Just like back then. She disappeared and I tried to look for her when I could. As soon as I had the resources, I hired the best international private investigators. All they ever found was a trail of other young men like me, mostly rotting in jails, eyes devoid of life, all with the same story. A beautiful blonde American girl had tricked them into it, they said, and her father—

As every lead was exhausted, I let myself believe the less painful story. Occam's razor. The simplest solution tends to be the best. She was working *with* him, and I was just another naïve boy horrifically played by a twisted family of con-artists. She wasn't out there being subjected to the monster's torture. She was a monster, too.

It was a far, far easier explanation to live with than the truth.

"I know this machine can go faster!" I shout, wrestling to get away from Isaak. Unsuccessfully.

"I'm already going eighty-five," Quinn snaps back, eyes staying on the road, as she slams the blinker on and swiftly maneuvers around several cars. "The last thing we need is to be stopped by five-o."

Fuck. She's right. I glare at the map.

Twelve minutes to destination.

Slatecraft airfield. Not a major airport, but the nearest private airstrip within thirty miles of the club.

He used to say all sorts of shit while he brutalized me... Cause the worst part is... by the end I didn't always fight. Sometimes the fight went right out of me. It made him mad when I stopped fighting. So he'd lean over and whisper in my ear, trying to get a rise out of me: *You should be glad to have me as a master, dog. You're just a little shit-eater from the mud no one will ever give a fuck about. Even before I broke you and showed you what a little bitch you really are. I fly planes. You know, those things in the sky you'd look up and wish you could get out of your little hell hole on. Well this is as close as you're gonna get to the sky, dog.*

I finally wrestle out of Isaak's grip and slam both fists against the dashboard. I hear the bones of my right hand snap as pain explodes like a bloom of flashing light behind my eyelids.

"Fuck! Domhn!" Quinn yells again, the car swerving slightly.

"Grab him, Isaak!" Moira shouts.

The pain gives me the briefest reprieve, taking my breath away as Isaak grabs me from behind.

The next second I remember where I am and what I've done.

What I *didn't* do.

He has her. She's been with him this whole time. She was just a kid.

I scream, veins in my neck throbbing to get away from Isaak's insane, iron grip around me. My eyes flash down to the map again.

Seven minutes.

THIRTY-NINE

DOMHNALL

ISAAK HOLDS me in check the entire rest of the way to the airfield.

"There. *There*," I yell at Quinn.

"I see it," she growls out through her teeth, spinning the wheel to turn down the gravel road towards the air hanger that's lit up like a beacon in the darkness.

"Cut your lights," Isaak says from behind us and Quinn immediately responds, the lights in front of us disappearing.

"There she is," I breathe out, my eyes zeroing in on the tiny figure of Brooke where she stands near a fuel line feeding into a small luxury Cessna.

"There the *plane* is," Quinn says. "At least it hasn't left yet."

"Great, but where the fuck is the bogey?" Isaak asks, reverting to military speak like he does when things really get tense.

"Step on it," I demand. "And let me the fuck go." This time when I wrench out of Isaak's arms, he lets me free. Right in time, too, because just as Quinn stomps on the pedal, I see the bastard walking down the steps out of the airplane, both his and Brooke's head swinging our way at the same time.

Quinn's good at everything she does. So she expertly drives the car, even at top speed, and I can see she only intends to stomp the breaks once she's inside the hanger, preferably after she's put the car between Brooke and her father.

But neither of us see the saber tooth tire spikes allowing one-way traffic the fucker laid across the entrance until it's too late.

The tires blow, and at the speed we're going, it sends us spinning into the side of the hanger opposite the plane. The car blasts through the aluminum siding, but a central steel post stops us, immediately setting off the air bags.

I barely wait for the shocking *thwack* of the bag in my face to dissipate before I'm yanking out of my seatbelt and shoving my car door open.

"Everyone okay?" Quinn shouts, looking behind her to the back seat.

"Both okay back here," Isaak says.

I glance back once to make sure my sister is nodding as Isaak helps her out of her seat belt and out the car door before I turn and start running.

"Brooke," I yell, sprinting towards her.

She's still standing where I first saw her. She's unhooked the fuel line from the plane but is frozen, staring at me. She looks at me like she doesn't know me, confused. Like she's trying to remember why she recognizes my face.

"Mati," her father yells from the steps of the plane. Her face snaps towards her father at his voice. "That's right. You're Daddy's good girl. Now come. Don't start being a bad girl now. Get on this plane."

She hesitates just a moment. She's standing equidistant between us, as easily able to run to him as she could turn and run to me.

She takes a step towards him.

"Don't you dare," I call out. "You're not his. You're *my* good girl. Mads. Brooke. It's me, Donny. I love you."

She freezes, her head swinging back towards me. It's as if I can see the haze clear from her eyes.

Donny. I see her mouth my name.

"That's right. You're my best girl. Come back to me, kitty. I love you and you love me. It's our chance."

I hold my hand out for her to come to me. Will my control over her hold? Have I done my job well enough? Just fifty feet separate us.

"Our time is now." I make her the same offer she did to me all those years ago. "Let's run away together." Except I'm not going to let anything separate us this time. "Now. Come with me now, kitty.."

I see light come into her eyes. She's about to take a step in my direction when her father shouts, "You're *Daddy's* good girl. You know what happens to bad girls, Matilda. How many times have I told you? I will *never* let you go."

She freezes and the brightness that entered her eyes seeps out just as quickly.

And I suddenly see how cruel I've been. Trying to own her at all.

Oh god, I'm such a fucking fool.

I thought that control had to be taken before it was taken from me. But I only thought that because it was the lesson *he* taught me.

What Brooke needed the whole time was for someone to trust her enough to choose for herself. Only in choosing me of her own will would she ever be free of her father's monstrous grip on her mind. Right now, he's just using her like a puppet between us.

She's going to be ripped in half.

When he shouts again, "Be Daddy's good girl, she turns away from me and begins hurrying towards the plane.

I all-out sprint to get to her.

I'm not a scrawny seventeen-year-old anymore. I train at the gym five days a week so that if it ever mattered again, I'd be too big a motherfucker for *anybody* to hold down. If I can just get my hands on the old man, I won't stop until I've bashed his head into the concrete so many times he no longer has any teeth.

But Mads has a shorter distance to go, and once her father claps his hands sharply at her she starts to run. Feck me but she's fast.

As soon as her foot touches the bottom stair, the stairs start lifting back up into the plane. She jogs up them as they go. By the time I reach it, the stairs are almost all the way up. I leap as far as I can, as if I'll be able to catch the foot of the stairs before they disappear. But no, they close solidly into the smooth wall of the plane.

"Brooke!" I jump up and pound the bottom of the plane with both fists. "Madison! Open up. Open up this goddamn door. I'm not going to lose you again!"

But the plane's engines have been roaring this whole time, probably one of the reasons they didn't hear our car pull up until the last moment. Now they roar even louder, and the plane starts to taxi.

"Get out of there!" comes Quinn's voice from behind me.

But I can't move, just staring at the door of the airplane as it moves away from me. It's Isaak again to the rescue, tackling me out of the way before the Cessna's engine on its forward wing catches and drags me into its whirring blade.

Isaak keeps dragging me backwards until we can see the Cessna's windshield.

The bastard himself is sitting there in the cockpit, grinning down at me.

I see him reach down to push the gear to start the plane down the runway, taking off with the woman of my dreams forever. I've never felt more powerless in all my life. If I thought running up and jumping on the plane would do anything, I'd try.

But action movie stunts aren't real. I don't know how to get into a plane once the door is shut and locked.

I roar in fury as I realize the humbling truth: I can't save her. I'll never be able to save her.

As if to add insult to injury, suddenly she pops up there behind her father in the window. I go silent, trying to drink in my last image of her.

I'll find you this time, Mads, I swear.

But just then, something glints as she reaches her arm down as if to help her still bent-over father adjust something with the navigation.

He wrenches up violently, though, holding his hands to his throat. We all watch in stunned shock as Brooke yanks her hand back.

Blood splatters the window.

"Jesus fuck!" Quinn says, then reaches down into the leg of her thigh-highs. "She knew I carried a knife in the top of my boot. She must've nabbed it when you two were arguing at the club earlier." She looks up at me. "Right before she went out to her father."

Holy shit. My eyes are glued to Brooke as she jerks back out of the window's frame. For several moments, her father just sits there, hands struggling not to let the spurting blood out of his slit throat. It only takes a couple of moments for him to lose the battle, though, his blood draining out down over his chest. He slumps over where he sits.

In the next moment, the door and stairs start descending back to the ground.

Brooke looks shell-shocked, still holding the knife, blood covering her hands and the jacket-robe she's still wearing.

I get to her first and wrap her in my arms, careful of the knife. Behind my back, I feel Quinn slip it out of her hands.

I can't believe all that's just happened. Is she real? Is this actually her in my arms? I'm half sure this is a fever-dream. To be so sure I'd lost her, and now to have her back in my arms. I squeeze her to me, flooded with relief.

"Oh my God," Moira whispers from behind me. "What did I just let happen?"

"How do we get rid of it?" Quinn asks Isaak, voice low. Then, more tense, she asks. "And the fucking body?"

"Leave that to me," comes Isaak's brusque answer. "But we have to act quickly."

"Are you okay?" I ask, pulling away only far enough so I can see Brooke's face. She's all I can care about. I mighta done a shite job of taking care of her so far, but I swear on my life I'll protect her from now on.

"I- I think I killed him." Her eyes are a little distant, but not totally gone. "My friend at the shelter always said if her ex ever came back to threaten her..." Brooke mimics running a finger across her throat, "... She wouldn't take any chances."

She looks down distantly at her hands that are still dripping with blood.

"Come on, we'll get you cleaned up." I yank off my undershirt and start wiping her hands clean of blood. I get most of it off, but it's turned the white undershirt red.

Fuck. This whole air hanger is a crime scene. I put my hand on my head, looking around, ready to freak the fuck out. I usually whip myself when I get to feeling out of control like this, but I already broke one fist, and that was on a fucking dashboard.

My love was the one who had to face and kill the monster, all on her own. I can't fail her again by losing my shit now when she needs me most.

I will *not* let her go down for this body suddenly appearing, with her prints all over the murder weapon. No motherfucker ever deserved more to die than this evil kid-didler. I'd happily burn his body and dance on the bones. But even that feels like too much evidence left behind, when I wasn't the one who actually pulled the trigger. Or sliced the knife, as it were.

After all the ways I've failed her, I can't let Brooke go down for the most justified murder in history.

I look up to find Quinn's already got a ten-foot wide mop out, pouring out bottles of bleach all over the section of where

Brooke stepped, bloody, from the plane. Moira's clumsily trying to help her.

I nod, finally clueing into the fact that my team is way ahead of me on planning and it's time for me to catch the fuck up.

I squeeze Brooke tight one more time. "You did the right thing, love. You're such a good girl. You did the right thing. But now Quinn, Isaak, and I have to take care of something very important. We have to take the plane."

She nods. "I'll come."

"You can't," I say quickly. "I'm so sorry, you can't go with us. You have to let Moira take you back to the house."

Brooke shakes her head, frantic. "No. You can't leave me behind. Not after everything. I need you." She clings to me desperately. "I need to be with you."

I cradle my hands to her cheek so her darting eyes will settle in on mine, our gazes locking. Again, I've broken through the haze to see my girl. "I swear I'll get back to you as fast as I can. I love you. He's dead now. He can never hurt us again. But I have to get rid of his body and I need you nowhere fucking near any crime zone, you get me? You're never to be near any darkness again."

"But Donny," she whispers, "I killed him," looking down at her hands. There's still blood caught in her cuticles.

"Says what evidence?" I demand. "It'll be clean as a whistle in here and what can anyone do if they can't even find the body of a man they never even knew existed?"

Moira's wandered back our way, likely sent by Quinn. "What about the body in the cockpit?" she asks. She looks almost as shellshocked as Brooke, but I can't deal with my sister right now. There will be time for her later.

"Not after tonight, there won't be," Isaak says, stepping in front of me. "Time to go, everyone. Plane's fueled up, but we have to go now if we still want to catch the flight time they booked so nothing looks amiss."

"Fuck," I swear. I have to go even though I can't stand leaving Brooke behind. Isaak can fly the plane, but I'm the only one who will have enough clout with customs to make any of this possible.

"Moira," I call, but my sister's just staring at the ground. "Moira," I demand more sharply, clapping my hands to snap her out of it. She finally looks up at me. "I need you to be solid right now, you hear me?"

She nods. "I am."

"Take Brooke back to my house. Can you do that for me?"

She nods.

"Swear to me you can do it."

"I swear. I won't let you down, Domhn." Moira's eyes are wide, and she's got her hands clenched together, but I've got no choice but to trust her.

"Good." I turn to Brooke, cradling her face in my hands again. "Tell me you'll wait for me at the house. I'll be back in a day. Two at most."

She nods and throws her arms around me.

"I love you," I tell her again, just like I'll tell her every day for the rest of our lives.

...

...

...

But I'm not back in two days. Or even three. Not even a week.

And by the time I do walk back in the door of my mansion and up to the room where they're keeping Brooke, it's too fucking late.

FORTY

MADISON/BROOKE/MATILDA/?

I WAKE up from the lurking, non-stop nightmare, still screaming as I sit up violently in bed.

I'm in a bright yellow room with a big bay window and blue streaming in from the sky beyond. There are even clouds. But I don't recognize the room, or anything around me.

"Where the hell am I?" I ask, scooting to the opposite side of the bed as an intimidatingly large man stands over my bedside. He's young, maybe in his early thirties, and his thick-framed glasses make him look nice. Approachable. But I know better than most that a pretty package can hide combustible sins.

"You're in Domhnall Callaghan's house, in your own separate wing. He is not here."

I can't tell if that last bit made my heart speed up or slow down.

"I'm glad to meet you," he says. "I'm Dr. Nathan Ezra. Professor Roberts referred you to me. I understand you've been dealing with some amnesia of late. We finally know your identity. You are Matilda Sheffield—"

He stops speaking when my head starts vehemently shaking back and forth.

"You aren't Matilda Sheffield?" he asks.

"Not anymore."

"What should I call you, then?"

My eyes wander off towards the wall as I slip away. "I've been so many people," I murmur. "But usually its just me and her." She's there now, whispering in the corner of my mind.

He snaps right in my face and my eyes jump open.

"I've worked with folks like you," the doctor says gently as I lift a hand to my pounding heart. "Folks who've been brainwashed as a part of a cult or experienced extensive, brutal psycho-physiological gaslighting like you have. Sometimes a mind finds it necessary to split, sectioning itself off so that only part of oneself experiences the worst of the trauma so the other pieces can remain intact."

I picture my brain as a fractured mirror.

"So it's hopeless?" I feel myself sink further and further

away from the doctor and the nice room with each passing moment. Everything starts to feel fuzzy. It'd be easy to sink into it and give over to her. Where's Domhnall? He's my anchor. Without him, the little box in the corner of my mind beckons.

"Quite the opposite in fact," Dr. Ezra says. "We're continually *astonished* by the brain's ability to build *new* neural pathways. You're still young, Miss Sheffield. Some part of the extensive trauma you've lived through may always be with you."

"But," he leans in, "to tell you the truth, we're all a little fucked up. And there's a real opportunity here that you can have a bright future not trapped in your past."

"Oh." I almost perk up, confused by the optimism of his words. Is he just blowing smoke up my ass? Then again, he hasn't met *her*. I immediately deflate. Some part of me hoped that when I killed my father, she'd go away, too. But she's still here.

Fuck. Where is Domhnall? I ache for him like he's a missing limb. I pull my arms around my stomach and pretend they're his.

"So what would you like to be called? Plenty of people try on names nowadays. What strikes your fancy?"

I shrug. I've never cared much about names. My father gave me so many of them. "I don't care. Brooke. Madison. Whatever you want."

"It's for you to pick," Dr. Ezra says patiently. "Identity is important. It's part of what your father was trying to erase. It's your job to rediscover it. Who *are* you?"

I just stare at him, feeling the haziness coming on. Identity? Is he kidding? Who the fuck cares? What he's talking about seems so… inconsequential compared to everything else that's happened.

He tilts his head at me, a gentle smile on his face. "You're skeptical. But this is actually quite central. Your whole life, you've been given various roles to fill, which you've done exquisitely."

I glow a little under his praise, just like I do anytime Domhnall calls me a good girl.

Then he continues on, "But you've also never been given the opportunity to find out who *you* yourself would choose to be all on your own. What do *you* want? What sorts of things do *you* like? What are your hobbies? Opinions?"

He leans forwards in his chair, fingers crossed under his chin. "What *food* do you like?"

"Oh just whatever anyone else is eating is fine. I'm not picky."

One eyebrow hefts. "But what do you, *yourself*, like? What's your favorite food? What's your favorite color? If you had a day that was completely empty with no responsibilities, just to yourself, what would you do?"

His questions are pedantic. So easy they're stupid. I open my mouth to respond. And go completely blank.

"Don't be ridiculous. I don't know. Something."

He waves a hand. "Then by all means. Tell me."

"I'd sleep." I look around. Out the window. "Or do something useful. Wash the dishes. Get some laundry done."

"I said a day when there are no responsibilities."

"What if I *like* doing laundry?" I spit back.

He holds his hands up, but then just sits there in silence.

And then more silence. Waiting for me to answer him about what I like. Which is so fucking ridiculous. Who the fuck even cares?

"I'd go on a walk," I finally say. Jesus, get off my back already.

"Do you like taking walks?"

"How the fuck should I know? You think my life's been about going on nice pretty little walks under the fruit trees?"

I'm trying to rile him up or get him to stop looking so fucking calm. I'm being a brat, and by this point, Domhnall's nostrils would be flaring. But Dr. Ezra just sits there looking perfectly pleasant.

"I'm going to let you in on another little secret. It makes total sense to me why you don't know what things you like or how you would choose to spend a free day."

He leans forward and does the hands-folded-beneath-his-chin-thing again. "Your clever mind found a way to protect itself all these years so you could survive under extraordinarily brutal circumstances. You say you don't know yourself, but the core of who you are still fought this whole time to hold on to *you*."

He thinks he's so clever with his soft voice, but he's—

"No it didn't!" The rage hot in my chest erupts. "I don't even know who the fuck I am!" I'm furious at him. At myself.

But he just shakes his head, not put off by my fury at all. "You're still there. You've always been there. It's like a fully decorated room with the lights off. Little by little, as myself or other therapists work with you, you'll learn to turn the lights up bit by bit, as if on a slider. You'll eventually start to see what was in there all along. The furniture and the posters on the wall. The colors and design of the bedspread you choose.

"You'll figure out what you like and don't like—not because someone else told you, but because it's just you in there. Nothing is lost that can't be found. So let's start over. What do you want your name to be?"

"Anna," escapes my lips before I can really overthink it.

Dr. Ezra nods. "Anna. That's a beautiful name. Does it come from somewhere?"

Why is he asking so many questions? Stupid questions, stupid questions, attacking my already battered brain.

"Enough!" I run and shove the door to the room open. The second I'm across the threshold, the haziness descends again, and I welcome the dark place as I climb back into the box in the deepest recesses of my brain.

HER

. . .

"IT'S her mother's middle name," I say, sitting up straight as a pin, crossing my legs, and staring Dr. Ezra down with one eyebrow lifted. "Anna."

This nave thinks he can fix my girl?

Fool. *I* protect the girl. Just like I have since she was a child and her mother abandoned her to the monster.

Dr. Ezra tilts his head. "Her?"

I roll my eyes. This is so pedantic. "The girl. It's the girl's mother's middle name. Anna."

"And who am I speaking to now?"

Oh he's clever, is he?

I give him an icy smile, hands tucked demurely in my lap. "My pronouns are she/her."

"And your name?"

"Names are overrated." I give a tight wave of my hand before tucking it back in my lap. "You don't need a name when there's no one to talk to except a monster. And I was a secret we kept, so he never knew I was here."

"Monster?"

I give him a deadpan stare. "If you don't know about the monster yet, you've really got shit qualifications, don't you? Did they call in another half-doctor?" I yawn and roll my head to stretch my neck. We really need to be getting the girl more exercise. She's so tight.

He chuckles. "I can see how you kept her safe all these

years. You're very smart, aren't you? She's mentioned you in passing but I wasn't sure I'd get to meet you. And yes, I know about your father. So you call him the monster? What was your experience of him?"

I give a laughing scoff. "Oh I'm not here for that, little doctor man. She can talk out all her woes to you, but I'm just fine. I've been toughing out shit you can't even imagine in your little academic ivory tower. I'm *so* glad that you've *worked with* other little sad shits who've gone through traumatic childhoods but you don't know us. The girl and I have a system that works just fine."

"Does the girl think so?"

I scoff again. "She's just a child."

"That's not what she thinks. She feels like a twenty-two or twenty-three year old woman."

I roll my eyes. "She'll always be a child who needs my protection."

His eyebrows rise and he purses his lips like he doesn't believe me. Which pisses me off. "What the fuck do you know, anyway?"

"I think she went and grew up when you were busy dealing with difficult things."

"Don't try that doctor shit with me," I warn, huffing and rearranging myself on the couch. I sit up straighter and lift my chin, looking away from the doctor. The girl growing up! Ha! This man's obviously a quack. I huff again, fury building in my guts.

My head snaps back to him. "She's not a grown-up because she can't *handle* the real world. The real world is brutal and she's a child. She's fragile and she'd break at the slightest—"

"Are you sure she's so fragile? Are you sure she hasn't been stronger lately? Moira Callaghan told me she's been a very strong-willed person since she was released from the hospital with amnesia. Or was that you?"

I suck in a breath and stare at him.

But it's not him I'm seeing.

It was the girl who slayed the monster. Not me.

I was... I was doing what I always do. I was protecting her by obeying. And getting my father away from Donny. Both of us wanted to protect Donny.

It's why I took over at the club. I saw our father and I knew the girl would want what was best for Donny. Which was to go and get our father away from him.

... And I did it because... because I'm the one who obeys.

"I protect her," I gasp, my fingers grasping the fabric of the soft pajama pants I'm wearing. "She's fragile and I protect her."

"I'm sure you do," Dr. Ezra says in a soothing voice. He's patronizing me. I hate it when people patronize me. Thinking they're smarter. Thinking they can outwit me.

"Can you tell me more about her mother?"

I breathe out hard and cross my arms over my chest. "Her

mother was a dumb bitch who couldn't figure her way out of a trap."

"Oh?" Finally, the all-wise, all-knowing doctor looks surprised.

"Oh," I say back snottily, giving him another thin smile.

"Would you like to elaborate?"

Ugh. This is all such a fucking waste of time. "I know you think this will help the girl, but digging up her tragic childhood past? Really? That's so cliché, doctor."

"Humor me," he says with an amused smile. At least it's better than his patronizing smile.

I sigh, not even caring that I'm being dramatic. "It's not a big deal. My father set a trap for Mom, and she fell for it like a big, dumb idiot."

"What was the trap?"

I roll my eyes. "It wasn't even that inventive on his part. I mean really, the man could get inventive with his tortures." Then I tilt my head, considering. "But maybe sometimes the simplest ones do cut the deepest, because the girl was deeply wounded by it. After all," I hold out my arms with a grin. "It was around then that I showed up."

"The trap?" Dr. Ezra prods.

I shrug. "Classic Sophie's choice."

"Care to expound?"

He's going to keep me on this couch until I spill the details of the girl's maudlin past, isn't he?

"He wouldn't let our mother leave him. I mean, she

could leave the house. But she could only take one of us with her." I stare the doctor in the eye. "Either me or my brother. Never both at the same time, in case she ever tried to run. Family's the only thing we're really given in this life, right?" I give a sarcastic smile. "And he knew he was such an evil, unbearable monster that one day she *would* leave him."

Dr. Ezra stays quiet a long moment. "I didn't know you had a brother."

"Yeah. Well. The girl didn't have him for long, did she? My mother made her choice, and one day, they both just up and disappeared."

"And you were left with the monster. All alone."

I gulp and look away. "The girl was fine. She had me to protect her. He must have been fucking delighted watching her mother squirm, though, as she tried to decide. Fucker always loved that shit the most. Fucking with people's heads. Destroying beautiful things."

It wasn't just her he had fun making squirm.

Daddy told me to always be a good girl, or Mommy would leave me.

And I tried *so* hard. I followed her around like a little duckling, asking if there was anything I could help with. I tried to fold laundry, but I was clumsy at it. I tried to play with Tommy when he got fussy. He was four, but still threw tantrums sometimes.

Mommy stopped letting me help towards the end. When

I asked her if I was still a good girl, she just looked away and said she needed to go check on Tommy.

"She was trying to distance herself from me by the end," I whisper. I couldn't see it then. I was just hurt. Devastated really. Well, the girl was. "So maybe it wasn't such a difficult choice after all."

"Do you really think that?" Dr. Ezra asks softly. "How old were you?"

"Six." I'm still glaring towards the window, unable to look at him. "And I think my mother was a weak bitch who should have been smarter and figured out a way around my father's trap."

Finally I wrench my head back to glare at the doctor. "A stronger woman would never have left her own flesh and blood with that bastard. She knew what he was. It's why she chose Tommy over me. Because he was a boy and she was afraid of what he'd do to him. But what about the girl?" I shout. "Didn't she think the monster would find a way to torture her even if he didn't fuck her? The girl's mother was a weak, stupid bitch!"

"And you despise weakness?"

"I fucking hate it!" I shout, almost rising up from the couch. "I've been fucking strong. When anyone else would have cowered in the corner, I fucking *took it*. When our father water-boarded us, and smothered us, and shoved a tube down our throat to steal our air, and locked us in the box for hours on end, and made us fucking *watch!*" I'm screaming and all the way on my feet now, and gasping so hard I can barely catch my breath.

"It's all right," Dr. Ezra says, both hands lifted calmly. "Can you breathe with me? Deep breath in. From your belly. Come on. I know you think this is stupid, but humor me. Take a deep breath in."

I take a dumb breath in.

"Good. Now hold it. Good, good. Now let it out, for a count of six. One, two, three, four, five, six. Now let's take another breath in—"

He guides me to take a bunch more breaths in and out and like he said, I humor him and play along.

"How do you feel now?"

I sit back down on the couch hard and cross my arms. "Like this is all cringe."

"Thank you for telling me about your mother and how you felt about what happened. I think you've been very strong."

I roll my eyes. "You're welcome," I say sarcastically.

"Now tell me, what's your favorite food?"

I seriously can't with this motherfucker.

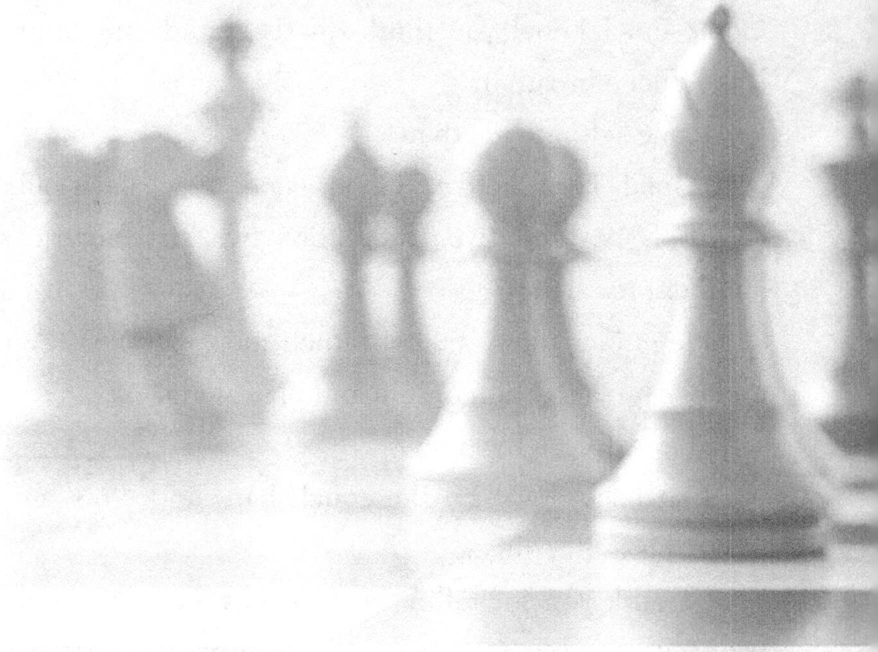

FORTY-ONE

DOMHNALL

IT TAKES LONGER than I wanted to get home. And certainly longer than I told Brooke I'd be away.

Between all the stops and unexpected holdups, instead of two days, the whole round-trip took six.

When I finally speed back into the roundabout in front of the mansion, I screech the car to a stop and jump out, sprinting up to the front door. My digital key automatically unlocks it, and I barely slow down before throwing the door open.

"Brooke!" I shout, sprinting inside. "I'm home! Brooke!"

Instead of Brooke's figure appearing at the top of the

stairs, however, it's Professor Roberts. She waves a hand to shush me as she hurries down the steps.

"Would you stop shouting?" she hisses. "The nightmares keep Anna awake and we've been trying to let her sleep in. She's at a very precarious stage right now!"

"Anna? Who the fuck is Anna?"

Professor Roberts just glares at me when she gets close and continues whispering. "Brooke is Anna. Anna is Brooke. It's the name she's picked for herself."

I throw my hands in the air. "What, you found another personality? What the fuck have you been up to while I've been away?"

If possible, Professor Roberts's glare becomes arctic. Glacial. "We don't know for sure that Anna has dissociative identity disorder. It takes months to make a diagnosis like that. And it's rarely so cut and dry even if she does. Anna is just the name the girl is now choosing to go by."

"The girl? What the fuck are you talking about?"

"There have been developments while you've been away."

I'm done with talking. I didn't travel non-stop for the last twenty-two hours to be stopped by a half-doctor at the stairs of my own goddamned house. "Where is she? I need to see her."

Professor Roberts crosses her arms over her chest. "No, you *want* to see her. There's a difference."

"Well, Prof.," I say, moving around her to get to the stairs, "nice knowing ya. Thanks for your services. You've been a real gem. Just lemme know where I can send your bill, and I'll make sure you're paid handsomely for your services."

But she just scoots up the stairs to block my path.

"You're such an asshole," she says, eyes flashing. "I don't care if you're paying me. My loyalty is to my patient first."

"You aren't even a doctor," I remind her contemptuously.

"But *I* am," comes a deep voice from the top of the stairs. "And you'd do well to kindly stop attempting to intimidate my best student with your superior size."

My head swings to see who else is in my fucking house. He's a tall, lanky fucker with a square jaw and thick, black-frame glasses. The kind of bookish-look I guess some women may find attractive, but I'd snap him in half in about two seconds in any pub brawl.

He jogs down and holds out a hand with an easy smile. "Dr. Nathan Ezra."

I ignore his hand and glare.

He continues on as if I'm not being a grumpy bastard. "It's been a joy to work with Anna this week while you've been attending to business matters."

Is this fucker trying to intimidate me? What exactly does he know? We didn't tell Professor Roberts where I was while I was away, but god knows what Anna's been saying about what she saw and *did* while at the airfield. Professor Roberts, at least, we felt confident we could control. But this new guy...

I scowl at him. "Where is she?"

"Resting. I think it best not to disturb her. She hasn't been sleeping well at night—"

"Because I haven't been here to hold her." Does this dickwad really think he knows my girl better than me? "I need to see her. She needs to know I'm here."

"I really don't think that's a good idea," Dickwad says. "We've been making progress the last few days, and any disruptions might—"

I shove Dr. Dickwad out of the way and stomp upstairs. We vanquished the monster, and I got rid of any other potential problems in our way. We can finally be together. I'm not letting anything hold us back anymore.

I'm running again by the time I get to the guest wing. It's like I can feel the nearness of her thrumming through my veins. I have to shove several doors open before I finally find her.

She shoots up in bed, screaming as soon as I do.

I sprint across the room and grab her up into my arms. "It's okay, love. I'm here. I'm back, and I swear I'll never fucking leave you again. *Ever.*"

But unlike usual, she's not squeezing me back. Her arms are limp around me.

"Brooke?" I ask, cupping her whole head in my hand as I cling to her. Then, when she still doesn't respond, I pull back and look into her dull, lifeless eyes. "Anna?"

Still nothing. Feeling desperate, I try, "Kitten?"

But she won't look at me. Her eyes stay cast towards the wall. As if she's some other place. Not here.

I spin angrily towards the doorway, Anna still in my arms. "What did you *do* to her? What fucking meds did you put her on? I said no meds!"

It's Professor Roberts who walks into the room, slipping around Dr. Ezra. "We didn't give her anything—not yet, anyway. Dr. Ezra thinks it might be a good idea to start her on some low dose antidepressants and anti-anxiety medication."

"No," I say staunchly. "No meds that will have her all whacked out and non-responsive."

"Domhnall," Professor Roberts says gently. "Look at her now."

And I do. Fuck me, but I do. I pull back so that we're just sitting on the bed, side by side. She stares dully at the wall.

She's nothing like the vibrant, feisty woman I first brought down to my dungeon all those weeks ago. She looks like a machine someone unplugged. She's just barely still in motion but it's like her battery's almost drained.

"I don't get it," I say, clutching her hand in mine as I look to the head doctors at the door. "She looked fine when I last saw her."

"Can you really say that?" Professor Roberts asks. "Can you really say she was *fine*?"

She was covered in her father's blood, all but hyperventilating, and begging me not to leave her alone.

But I did anyway.

"What can we do?" I look desperately first at Professor Roberts, who looks at Dr. Ezra.

"Wait," he says gently, with a kindness in his eyes I naturally despise. "And continue with treatment. The kind of trauma she's endured leaves its mark on the psyche. She's going to need time." He looks down to where I still have Anna's hand gripped in mine. "And space."

"From me?" I scoff. "I'm the only thing holding her together."

"Are you sure about that?" Dr. Ezra tilts his head inquisitively at me. I immediately want to smash his face in.

"Yes," I say through gritted teeth.

He barely waits for the word to escape my mouth before continuing on, like a teacher asking a trick question, "Because there have been periods where she's fully coherent. And we're able to make some progress talking to... *her*."

"It doesn't fucking look like it."

Anna's hand spasms in mine at my furious tone. Shit. If this bastard wasn't here antagonizing me, I wouldn't be so loud. I could be focusing on her. The only reason I was gone was because I was trying to *protect* her. They all just need to go and leave us alone!

I ignore everyone else in the room and turn to Anna. I let go of her hands and gently cup her cheeks, searching her eyes for some sign of recognition. The squeeze let me know she's in there.

"Love, it's me. It's Domhn. Donny. I'm home. I'm so

fucking sorry I ever left, love. But I'm home now and I fucking swear, I'll never leave your side again. I'm here."

When her eyes still don't lift or catch mine like usual, I try to move my face to get in her line of sight. But even then, it's like she's looking through me.

"Brooke," I try, rubbing my thumb gently over her cheek. "Mads. Mads, it's me."

Still nothing. I carefully take her hand, shuddering. What the fuck has all this done to her? What have *I* done to her?

I look back at Dr. Ezra. "But you said she talked to you? Like more than just a word?"

He nods. "She was coherent. And there are sides of her you know nothing about, Domhnall."

I shake my head. He doesn't know what the fuck he's talking about. No one knows Mads—Brooke—fuck, *Anna*, better than me.

"Did she know where she was? Who she was? What had happened?"

"I'm taking it slow. But she seems to be aware of herself and her surroundings."

The fury from moments ago is taken over by exhaustion. I've barely slept the last week. I kept wanting to call and talk to Br—to Anna—but it's not like we ever exchanged phone numbers. And when I called Moira, she always said Brooke was sleeping, or resting, or some other equally infuriating excuse.

I drop a kiss on Anna's forehead, trying to see if she

twitches or gives any other indication that she recognizes me. No matter how tired, I expected us to throw ourselves into each other's arms the second I got home.

Why didn't Moira tell me what's going on? Did she not know? Has Professor Roberts been blocking her from visiting Anna? Or did she and Dr. Ezra convince Moira it was best to leave me in the dark? Do they think I'm part of Anna's trauma?

Aren't you?

My back's still raw from my last punishment, but in spite of my exhaustion, all I want to do is go belt myself until I'm fucking bleeding again. It's the only other thing I've been thinking about all week. But I thought, if I could just get back and pull Anna into my arms, it would all be okay. I'd be all right. I could get through the compulsion.

Now, though, that I know she's hurt in a way far deeper than my flesh wounds could ever go? And that all my previous notions of control are totally fucked? I can't get control back.

Control is just a fucking illusion.

So what the fuck am I supposed to do now?

I stand up.

"I'm going to go wash up," I mutter to Professor Roberts and Dr. Ezra. "Let me know the second she comes back around."

Professor Roberts looks to Dr. Ezra like she's not sure she should agree to my simple request, which makes me want to scream at both of them to get the fuck out of my house again. But he just nods, eying me.

I start to walk out of the room, but as I pass, he puts a hand on my shoulder. I look at him incredulously. "You wanna lose that fuckin' hand, boyo?"

He doesn't look the least intimidated by me. He lifts his hand, but not before saying, "You know, I'm here to offer a listening ear to you as well. This is a difficult thing." His head nods the barest bit back towards Anna. "What the two of you are dealing with."

I glare at him. "Just see to it she's taken care of. I don't fucking trust you and if you hurt her in any way, I'll do much worse than just seeing that you lose your license."

He holds both hands up and backs away, something on his face telling me he's not intimidated by my threats. That better be because he's fucking confident in what he's fucking doing.

I storm from the room, intending to go take a shower. Instead, I just stomp to my office in the other wing of the house so I can watch the video feed of Anna's room. I've got the whole house wired for security purposes and thank fuck I do. She does nothing but stare at the wall for hours, barely swallowing when Professor Roberts feeds her dinner.

I hurry over to her room, sure she'll eat from my hand if I try to feed her, but she stops eating all together when I enter. I finally shower and sleep, but only in fits and starts.

The first thing I do the next morning is go see Anna.

Professor Roberts stops me in the hallway outside her room. "I was just coming to get you. She's having a good morning. She's lucid."

My chest leaps with hope and I push past her. Before I open the door, I hear her sweet voice, responding to something Dr. Ezra asked.

"—and then it was like—"

Oh thank god! I push the door open, and she cuts off, looking my way with wide eyes, like a deer stunned in the headlights.

"It's so fucking good to see you, love!" I say, rushing into the room.

But though I'd swear her eyes were just locked with mine for a millisecond right as I burst into the room, it's like they slide right off me to the left, all animation leaving her face by the time I'm at her side.

"Anna!" I say, the excitement from hearing her voice sinking at the blank expression suddenly on her face.

"What happened?" I turn to look at Dr. Ezra where he sits in a chair across from Anna. "She was just here."

I turn back to Anna, dropping down beside her and taking her hand. "Anna, it's me." I try to keep my voice light as I massage her palm with my thumb. "Love, I'm here. I'm right here."

"I think you may have startled her," Dr. Ezra says, his tone calm and without accusation.

"Me?" My head snaps towards him. "But I'm—" I cut off

before I can really start railing at the bastard. I gaze at Anna, rubbing her hand more urgently before I remember I'm supposed to stay calm.

Fuck. She was here. Present. And then I came banging in like a goddamned ape and scared her away again.

Stupid. Stupid fucking piece of shit. Dumb shits like you deserve to be punished. I grip the hand not holding Anna's into a fist, allowing my nails to cut into my palm. I squeeze my thumb in my fist until it starts to distend and hurt. Then I squeeze harder still.

"Domhnall," Dr. Ezra says sharply, his tone cutting.

I look up in surprise, only to find his eyes on my fist.

"I think it's best if you left us."

Shame floods me. He knows. He can see what I am. I'm so careful all the time to hide it, but he can see.

Still, I cling to Anna's hand even though I know he's right. Of course he's right. I'm no good for her.

But I never said I was a good man. And I always did love inflicting pain, didn't I? Even now, as I see my presence hurts her, all I want to do is to cling tighter.

She's mine, and I won't let her go.

His protégé in truth, then?

I'm stabbed through the chest by the thought. Forcing my fingers to release her, I let go of Anna's hand and stand.

Control is an illusion.

I was a fool to think different. Such a fucking fool.

I turn my face away from the three people in the room,

every part of my body flooding with the heat of shame. I keep my face hidden from them as I hurry out the door.

Today, though, I won't allow myself the solace of the whip. For once, I deserve to feel this pain in my chest, not my skin.

The easy escape of physical pain is a cop out. But without it to punish myself, all I can do is sit and stare endlessly at Anna's unmoving figure on the screen in my office. This is the torture I deserve.

FORTY-TWO

ANNA

"IT'S TIME, I THINK," I say with a heavy heave of breath.

It's taken so much courage to get to this point, I feel lightheaded even saying it.

With Dr. Ezra's help over the past month, we've made enough progress for me to come out of my dissociative state long enough to realize that I've got a mixed-up set of memories with the trauma wires all crossed.

It's clear that me and *her* are both living here inside my head. Sometimes neither of us are in control and I'm just... *floating* outside my body. The doc and I haven't figured out what the hell that's about. Other than like, my body flushing trauma or some shit.

He makes me do a lot of breathing.

Then there's other times when *she*... I sigh in distress. She takes over and completely shuts down whenever Domhnall comes near me.

Apparently she'll get chatty with Dr. Ezra, and other times she clams up.

But she won't tell him anything else other than that Donny and "the girl" aren't good for each other. And she's got to protect us both. From each other, apparently. Whatever the fuck that means.

I can't fucking believe she calls me "the girl." And thinks of me as a goddamn child. I mean, was she watching the x-rated things Domhn and I got up to? Jesus.

I can't communicate directly with her. Time's been really wishy-washy lately. I wake up and it's light. Apparently she's taking the night shift again, and it's not going well. Dr. Ezra had us try journaling so we could "talk" to each other.

Dear her, would you please stop being such a stubborn bitch and let us be happy with Donny?

DEAR THE GIRL, WOULD YOU PLEASE SHUT THE FUCK UP AND LET THOSE WHO ARE WISER AND STRONGER DO THE FUCKING PROTECTING LIKE WE'VE DONE SINCE YOU WERE A CHILD? WHICH APPARENTLY YOU STILL ARE BECAUSE YOU WON'T LISTEN TO THOSE WHO ARE WAY STRONGER AND SMARTER THAN YOU COULD EVER DREAM OF BEING?

Dear her, have you fucking forgotten who was the strong one in our recent major throwback moment with our demon? Pretty sure you were the little bitch, and I was the one who stepped up. So let us be fucking happy now!!!

DEAR THE GIRL, AWW, YOU FINALLY STAND UP FOR YOURSELF IN ONE MOMENT IN YOUR LIFE AND YOU SUDDENLY THINK YOU CAN HANDLE SHIT? HOW ADORABLE. WHERE WERE YOU WHEN DADDY STUFFED US IN THE OVEN? THAT'S RIGHT. HIDING IN THE BOX. SO SHUT THE FUCK UP AND RESPECT THE STRONG ONE. I PROTECTED YOU THEN AND I'M PROTECTING YOU NOW. SIT THE FUCK DOWN, LITTLE GIRL.

Things devolved from there.

We talk through Dr. Ezra now. I argue about how obviously deranged she is.

But then Dr. Ezra goes on and on about how she's part of me and somewhere, deep down, I might not be ready for what being with Domhnall would mean right now.

I bawled during that session after he suggested that.

I mean, yeah, Domhnall's intense, and being with him right away would be intense because we don't know any other way to be together. But he's all I fucking want. He's my family. I think *she* even wants that, too. So I don't know why she's being so fucking stubborn.

But she's started to hate it here.

She says it's like being locked up in Father's house in Amsterdam.

She says we have to get out because we can't breathe here. She screams at night because there's a dungeon downstairs. Just like Daddy had.

It's not fair to Domhn, or me, but it doesn't seem to be changing no matter what I do. My emotions are just as jumbled as my memories. My love and her disgust and hate and our adoration and desire and fury… I can't tell what I feel for who or why.

I'm going to go crazy even more than I already am if I stay here.

Dr. Ezra lifts an eyebrow. "Are you serious, or is this like last week?"

"No." I stand with my shoulders back and my head held high. "I'm really ready this time. I made arrangements. They have the same bank I use here in Chicago and there's plenty of funds from the auction. I'm just gonna crash for a few days with my friend Ria, then she's gonna help me find a place of my own."

He nods. "Check in with Dr. Kim when you get there. She's the specialist I told you about. I'll be waiting for her call that you've arrived, letting me know that treatment with her has been established. You've already signed the forms for me to share my notes and consult with her."

I nod. I'm glad to have a doctor already there, but other than that, I'll be on my own. Like, really, on my own. For the first time in my whole life. In a place I earned with my own money. Okay, yeah well, I earned it by selling my cherry, but that doesn't mean I didn't still spill blood, sweat, and a river of tears for that money by the end.

I can't imagine being on my own without someone telling me who to be or how to be a good girl.

But I'm afraid if I stay, I'll never get better. I love Domhnall too much to shut down and switch every time I see him. It's time to find out truly once and for all who *I* am, and to make something—some*one*—of whoever's still left rattling around in my head.

"Remember what I told you," Dr. Ezra says. "There is a *you* deep down inside. A whole. Even if you never integrate. That's just fine as long as you aren't giving into destructive tendencies. Just try to discover yourself. Be curious. What are *you* like?"

I sigh, rolling my eyes. All his exercises are so tedious. I can't imagine any of them ever being helpful. "Yeah, yeah, learn how to turn up the light on my room," I repeat. "And the longer I do therapy and other shit so I can discover myself, whatever the fuck that means, the more I'll see the decorated room in the light."

"Exactly." Dr. Ezra smiles kindly, looking far older than his early thirties. "Good luck, Anna."

"You'll tell him why I had to go?" I ask, a knot curdling in my stomach.

"He already knows."

I nod, knowing he's right even if I hate it, and walk out of the room. I pause at the door, heart thumping in my ears. "But he knows not to come down while I leave? She might be mean, or go catatonic. I don't want that to be his last memory of me."

"He knows not to come down."

I turn the doorknob, half-hoping Domhnall will have ignored the doctor's instructions anyway.

But when I yank the door open, I breathe out. There's no one there. Just an empty hallway. I don't hear a single thing besides a ticking clock as I walk through the eerily still mansion. There's only Professor Roberts waiting for me at the front door, ready to escort me to a waiting car.

I walk with her down the steps and glance back up at the large mansion. In the sudden bright light of day, I can't tell if a curtain upstairs just moved.

"Did he tell you to say anything to me?" I ask Professor Roberts with a tight throat.

"You decided you didn't want to communicate with him," she says, opening the passenger side door for me.

Does that mean he *did* have a message for me? Everything in me clenches, wanting to know what he's said. Instead, I hurry inside the car and yank the door shut. I squeeze my eyes closed.

I'm nobody's good girl now.

For a while, I need to belong just to myself.

It doesn't make the pain searing through my belly any easier to take as the car pulls out of the driveway.

FORTY-THREE

DOMHNALL

ONE YEAR *Later*

THE PHONE RINGS and I snatch it up just as quickly as I've done every time it's rung or pinged for the last year.

The sudden quick beat of my heart dulls when I see the caller ID. I consider not answering but know he'll just call back. And back, and back, until I do finally pick up.

I thumb the green button.

"Caleb," I answer without inflection.

"Dom!" he cries, always enthusiastic enough for the both of us and then some. "How the hell are you?"

I roll my eyes. "The same as I've been every other time you do these ridiculous check-up calls. I'm fine. I'm always *fine*."

"What's the point of life if you're just fine, though, eh? I know you've gone all celibate monk, but why not come out to the club sometimes? Just to hang out with everybody, maybe watch a scene or two? Quinn's got a new pain pig, and you know how she likes to make the new piggies squeal."

"Yeah, uh, thanks. Think I'll pass." I rattle the ice in my soda water and stare down at the fat copy of James Joyce's *Ulysses* I've got open in my lap. I'll sit here and torture myself with Irish literature instead. I've been a hundred pages into this monstrosity of a book for a month and it's not getting any less painful. Not exactly as satisfying as a lash on the back, but it'll have to do.

"Come on, man. All you do is work."

"I do leisure activities. I'm currently reading. Later, I'll meet with my trainer. We're working on lats."

I can all but hear him rolling his eyes through the phone. "Where's the guy who used to street race to get his jollies off?"

I glare at the floor. "He grew up. Goodbye, Caleb."

"Wait, wait, wait. Come on, man. You're my best friend. I'm just worried about you."

I'm a millisecond away from snapping that we're not best friends, that we were never best friends; he was always just a means to an end. But then I count to five and breathe in and out. Because my other not-so-leisure activities are twice weekly meetings with the therapist Dr. Ezra referred me to.

Fucking therapy. On the bad days, I wish I'd never let any of those fucking vultures into my house. Brooke and I would have found our way if I'd just kept her safe from the world, locked up in my dungeon.

I should have protected her better. My hands clench around the book. I want to rip it apart. Then pick up the chair I'm sitting in and throw it through the fucking window before trashing the rest of my nice, orderly, professionally decorated study.

"Dom? You still there?"

My teeth clench and I close my eyes, trying to remember to breathe. Breathe, breathe—my therapist's always telling me to breathe before I react; he's got a fucking hard-on about it. *Notice when something triggers you and then breathe through it, so you don't lash out.*

I breathe, but I still want to destroy shit. "I'm here. Thank you for your concern. You're a good friend, Caleb." There, no lashing out. "Look, I'll call you later."

I hang up before I lose the battle with my temper. Then I pop to my feet and toss James Joyce down into the chair with more force than is strictly necessary. I jog up to my bedroom to change into workout clothes.

When I come back out, I pause in the hallway and look towards my office. God knows I've spent enough moping hours looking over the footage I got of Brooke during those brief weeks I had her back.

But that way lies madness. I lost one whole month like that right after she left, barely eating, barely doing anything else except caressing her face on the screen with my eyes and fighting the impulse to go after her and reclaim what's mine.

Going no contact was brutal. So of course, I cheated. Not that I tell my therapist, but it was nothing to arrange for a discreet security detail to make sure she's safe in Chicago. They stay at a distance, so she never knows they're there. And yes, they send an occasional picture.

All right, they send a picture every day. Look, sanity comes at a different price for different people. The furniture in my house stays intact and I spend an hour every day, usually somewhere around lunchtime, worshiping at the altar of my beloved's face.

The rest of the time I stay busy.

And when the memory of her scent or the itch to touch her gets too maddening, I work out. I turn away from the office and jog back downstairs to the gym I had installed month two after she left.

I barely get gloves velcro'd before I'm taking out my frustration and fury on the heavy-weight bag—my real best friend the past year. Sorry Caleb.

I slam it hard with an uppercut that sends the bag swinging, then do a bunch of hard, quick jabs in the center that allows for a quick expulsion of energy. Then another hard slam.

I get into it, really working up a sweat with my shirt off ten minutes later when the doorbell rings.

I try to ignore it, jabbing some more when it rings again.

Fucking hell. What is it now? Did Caleb and Moira decide to gang up on me today? What, was he the cavalcade and now she's here, the main troops, coming in for the kill? They seem to be on an all-out offensive lately on Operation Get Dom Out of His House.

I'm perfectly fine here. It's a mansion and I'm a billionaire. Anything I want is already here or can come by delivery.

I tear off my gloves and stomp towards the door.

"What?" I bark before the door's half open.

But then I see it's *her*.

"Domhnall," Anna says, eyes widening when she takes in my sweaty torso.

She's so fucking beautiful. She cut off all her hair, has a nose ring, and a full sleeve tattoo down one arm. I've seen pictures, of course, but her—here—is so fucking stunning, I lose all the breath in my lungs.

"Anna." I fall to my knees at her feet, pressing my face to her knees. "Are you really here? Are you real?"

She crouches down until she's all but sitting on the front stoop with me, and when I next look at her, I see tears in her eyes. "I'm really here, Domhn."

I look behind her, my heart leaping when I see a big suitcase. "Is this just a visit or are you back?"

She nods shyly. "I'm back."

"Thank Jaysus." I throw my arms around her neck and cling to her. "I love you so fucking much. I've barely survived without ya."

Her back immediately shudders with a sob. "I love you too. And I know. It's been hell. But I had to find myself."

I nod into her short hair, cupping the back of her precious skull. "I know, love. I know." I pull back just enough to kiss her forehead. "Is it alrigh'? Being back here?"

She shakes her head, head craning back to look up at the house. "I don't think I can go inside."

"That's fine," I assure her. "We'll go away. I'll follow you anywhere, love."

I clutch her face lightly between my palms, looking at her. Her tear-stained eyes gaze back at me, clear and full of hope. "You will?"

"Of course I will. I always woulda." I grin at her, my whole body light as if I could fly. "Let's run away together, love."

She grins, laughing even as she cries. Then she throws her arms around my neck and kisses me.

Our mouths meet as we pour our love into one another. I grab her up into my lap. I can't get her fucking close enough, wrapping my arms around her.

Every part of my being burns for her, but for now, whatever ounce or speck she gives me, it will be enough. It will always be enough. I'd beg for scraps at her table and be the happiest man alive.

Finally she disentangles herself from me, laughing as she stands to her feet, wiping her tears. I immediately stand up, too, so I can be at her side.

"Let's stop scandalizing the neighbors," she says. "Go get a shirt on and we can find a hotel for the night."

Jaysus fecking Christ. Is she trying to kill me right when I've got her back?

I intertwine my fingers with hers and drag her forwards towards the sidewalk, grabbing her suitcase with my other hand. "Fuck the shirt. I'm not lettin' you out of me sight for a goddamned second. C'mon. We'll call a cab with your phone."

Her high-pitched peal of laughter is all the healing my lost, damned soul has been needing the past year. I let go of the bag and hike her up into my arms.

She laughs again and wraps her legs around my waist. I look up into the dancing eyes of the most beautiful girl in the world.

"I love ya, future Mrs. Callaghan."

Her grin gets bigger. "Anna Callaghan," she says. "I think that plaque will fit nicely on the desk in my beautifully decorated room."

Then the world's most gorgeous woman blesses a poor, sad fuck from the arse end of nowhere with the sweetest kiss, and I know I'm the luckiest man in the world as I spin with her in my arms.

EPILOGUE I

ANNA

"I wanna take you on a date," Domhnall says from beside me in bed.

We're in a luxury uptown suite at the Ritz downtown, two days since I got back in town. We've spent most of it in bed. Well, we have visited the large, multi-headed shower a couple times, but still.

It's a far cry from the tiny studio I've been living in back in Chicago. I know I have money now, but I've been anxious not to waste it. Especially when I want to do important things, like give it to people who really need it. I bought Ria and her mom a house on the outskirts of Chicago. They were so kind to me when I first got there, even though they barely had enough space for the two of them and Ria's new little baby.

Then I made a donation to the Dallas shelter that housed me after my hospital stay when I had amnesia, so they could buy a new building. Ria said I needed to be careful or I'd be poor again in no time. I just laughed. I wasn't afraid of being poor anymore. Not since now I knew there's not a monster out there chasing me.

I look over at Domhn. "A date?"

He nods, reaching over to push my hair behind my ears. I melt a little inside.

"We never really got to do that. Either time we knew each other."

I melt more. And... putting a table between us could give us a chance to talk without falling into bed every three seconds. If I'm honest, I know there've been some conversations I've been avoiding. Like, uh, the *big* one.

I'm still... not well.

Dr. Kim has tried to help me rethink what sick and healthy and normal and crazy mean. We've tried to deconstruct a lot of things. A big part of me was afraid to come back here. It's part of why I put it off for a whole year and even then, I wasn't sure if I was ready. But when is *ready*? I wasn't ever going to be quote-unquote *normal*. I knew that even before I left.

Dr. Kim thought I was strong enough to come back for a visit.

But I knew all along there was no just "visiting" Donny.

I grin at him with the uncontained joy that bursts inside my chests like mini-fireworks any time I'm around him. "I'd love to go on a date."

I tackle him back to the bed and it takes us another hour to actually get out the door.

Of course Domhnall takes me to an absurdly expensive restaurant downtown.

"I feel like everyone's watching us," I whisper as we walk in.

So he says something in to the immaculately-groomed maître d's ear who's seating us, and we're taken to a private little booth in the back. Domhnall's always so thoughtful.

We're holding hands and I squeeze his. He flashes those devastating blue eyes down at me and I die a little inside like always. Can this man really be mine?

I freeze up a bit. Last year I told Dr. Ezra and Professor Roberts they could tell him some of what was going on, but I always told them to downplay it.

Today, though, I really want to talk to him about it. I *need* to talk to him. If we're really going to have a future together, he needs to know what... what that might mean.

I suck in a deep breath as we're seated.

"You look beautiful," Domhn says as I pick up my menu.

"Stop it," I say, heat in my cheeks.

"Never."

"I'm literally wearing jeans and a t-shirt. Why didn't you tell me how fancy this place was before we left?" As we walked through the restaurant to this little alcove, everyone was wearing fancy dresses and suitcoats. I'm pretty sure there's a dress code to get in and I'm breaking it.

"You look perfect."

I roll my eyes with an unamused huff. "I'm so far from perfect it isn't even funny."

"You're perfect for me."

I roll my eyes *harder*.

But Domhn won't let up. "I mean it. You're perfect just as you are. You're the perfect *you*."

Will he think the same thing in ten minutes after I tell him everything?

"Donny, look, it's been so good being back with you, but we haven't really talked—"

"May I interest you in the house cabernet?" interrupts the waiter, holding out a bottle in front of Domhnall's face.

Domhnall waves it away. "We'll have a bottle of Château Lafite. The burrata for an appetizer and the Chilean Sea Bass for dinner."

The waiter nods and starts to walk away but I suck in a breath and speak up, "Actually, I'd like to try the lamb."

Domhnall looks at me in surprise but nods when the

waiter looks to him. "Of course. Whatever the lady wants. One sea bass and one lamb."

After the waiter leaves, Domhnall reaches over the tabletop for my hand and I extend it, smiling when our fingers intertwine.

"I apologize if I overstepped. You just always used to like it when I ordered for you so you didn't have to decide."

"I know, I know," I quickly reassure him. "I wasn't offended. I'm just trying lately to..." I look around the elegant restaurant with all it's gold accents against sleek black. "To figure out what *I* like. Apparently it's important. I always used to order fish but that's just because that's what the people around me ate. Maybe it'll turn out that I love lamb, ya know, if I really give it a try?"

Domhn nods in support. "I want to know everything about you, Anna. Even if you're just figuring it out now. I want to be here with you as you're discovering yourself." Then he looks down at his lap. "I mean... if that's something you'd want."

"Of course that's what I want!"

He looks back up at me, his smile shining in his eyes.

I pull my hand back from him. "But there are things you should know—"

Naturally the waiter comes back right at that moment with the fucking bottle of wine, and he makes a painfully big fucking deal of popping the cork and then pouring each glass in this fancy fucking way that makes me want to punch him in the face.

"Yes, yes, we've got it," Domhn says impatiently, snatching the bottle from him when he takes a long time of settling it in an ice bucket in the center of the table.

"Oh of course, sir!" the waiter says, shrinking back and then disappearing down a hallway.

"You didn't have to scare the poor kid," I murmur.

But Domhnall still looks impatient as he looks back to me. "I feel like you've been trying to tell me something all day and then that little fucker keeps intruding." He shakes his head and then reaches for my hand again. "Please, I want to hear what you have to say. Whatever it is, I can take it. If you met someone else while you were away, it's—"

"Of course I didn't meet someone. You think I would've spent the last two days in bed with you if I did?"

"I didn't I mean, I just—"

I straighten in my chair and look at him flabbergasted. Then I just blurt it out: "I got a confirmed diagnosis of Dissociative Identity Disorder. What they used to call multiple personalities."

I stare down at the table, fingernail tracing a groove in the wood. "I've got one confirmed alter. It's not that common to only have one, but I still fit the diagnosis. Dr. Kim is trying to get her to pick a name, but right now she's stubbornly insisting on going only by her pronouns, she/her. You haven't met her yet, but it's only a matter of time before you do."

I sigh. At least she hasn't come out before I've really told him about her. Thank god for small mercies. "I tend to switch a lot at night, and sometimes during therapy sessions."

Domhnall just stares at me a long moment before slowly nodding and swallowing.

I'm startled when plates are suddenly set down on the table in front of us.

"Here we have a burrata with heirloom tomatoes!" the waiter announces cheerily, apparently undeterred by Domhnall's bear-like treatment a few minutes ago. "It's drizzled with premium olive oil and an aged balsamic. Enjoy!"

He does scramble away fairly quickly, but I'm left staring at Domhn, holding my breath as I wait for his reaction.

"Well, we always knew this was a possibility, right?" He blinks slowly like he's trying to wrap his head around what I've just told him.

I want to cry. Oh god. Why did I think waiting to tell him until we were on our first date at this ridiculously fancy restaurant was the way to go? I mean, sure I didn't know he was bringing me *here*. Still, I should have told him the first night at the hotel.

Or the second night. We talked a little then. But I just babbled on and on, about Chicago pizza, and Ria and her mom, and getting my first real job working as a library aid at the public library, and how modern libraries are more of a locus point of public services than strictly being about books these days and—

I breathe out. "Well yeah, but I just sorta hoped she'd go away. It doesn't look like that's going to happen, though."

I grab some of the bread that was set on the table with the wine and pull off a chunk. Then I use my fork to awkwardly cut off some of the gooey burrata and wrangle it onto my bread, then shove it into my mouth.

"Does that..." Domhn starts before cutting himself off. "I mean, is that, okay? If she's still there inside? Is the therapy, like... I mean, are you still trying to get rid of her?"

I shake my head, mouth still stuffed full of bread and cheese. I lift my napkin to cover my mouth so he can't see as I talk through the mouthful. "It's fine." I chew some more and swallow, then reach for my cup of wine to wash it down. I take too big a sip and almost choke, my face contorting at the strong wine.

"*Ugh.*" I shudder. Why does fancy wine always taste so awful? I grab the glass of ice water to wash the taste of the wine out of my mouth. "Fuck, don't tell me how expensive that god-awful wine is or I'll cry."

Domhn bursts out with a hearty laugh. Then he gets up and drags his heavy wooden chair around the table so he's sitting beside me.

"What are you doing?" I look around, slightly scandalized. "This is a fancy place. You can't just go around moving their furniture."

"I can if it gets me closer to you." He wraps an arm

around my waist. "Tell me more. I want to know everything. And when can I arrange a meeting with her?"

"God, Domhn, you don't *want* to meet her!"

"Why not? Does she not like me?"

I bite my bottom lip. "It's um... complicated." I know he needs to meet her. I don't know why I'm putting it off.

He lifts an eyebrow. "Oh now I really want to know. Spill the tea, love."

I huff out a breath and now my cheeks are heating for an entirely different reason. Fuck this is hard talking about to anyone besides my therapist. And most especially to Domhn.

But I finally try. "We're both... *me*, deep down inside. So we both," I look up and meet his gaze, that intensity that always burns between us roiling straight down to my tummy. "We both love you."

Now both his eyebrows lift. "Really? How... does that work?"

I swallow. Fuck, why is my mouth so dry? I reach for my water glass and take another drink. "I mean, seriously, I'm not exactly sure how. Sometimes we share memories and sometimes we don't. But c'mon, Domhn. There's no part of me that wouldn't love you. So of course she does."

He frowns. "But it was... *her* who wanted you to leave last year, wasn't it?"

"She knew we weren't ready. She considers it her job to protect me. And maybe she was right." I immediately see disagreement on his face so I barrel on. "I mean, I think we would've torn each other apart. This shit I'm dealing with in my head," I tap the side of my temple, "it's not always pretty or cut and dry. I think I needed that time in Chicago, healing and learning to stand on my own two feet."

I reach out a hand to cup his face. "I love you, but I can't find my wholeness in you. You can never be my other half. You can be my other whole. But each of us have to bear our own shit."

His eyebrows scrunch together. "I fucking hate that. I want to carry everything for you."

Tears crest in my eyes, because it has been a *hard* fucking year and there were so many times I wanted to throw in the towel and just be kitty with my owner carrying the difficult load again while I curled up with no cares in the world, oblivious.

But that can only be in play. Not my day to day.

"I worked fucking hard to be able to carry my *own* load." The tear falls down my cheek. "Believe me, DBT therapy is some tough fucking shit." But at least I finally proved to *her* that I can handle hard things. Well, she believes it *a little* more anyway.

Domhnall pulls me fiercely into his arms. "I fucking hate that you had to go through that," he whispers in my ear.

I laugh into his chest. "You and her will get along fine. She's just as protective as you. More, maybe."

He pulls back from me, shaking his head. "Not possible."

I smile. "I'll let you two fight it out when you meet her."

He frowns. "What about you? How do you feel about me meeting her?"

I sigh and reach for the bread again, pulling all the way away from him. "I talked it through with my therapist. *A lot.* And here's the deal. This is a fucking complex situation, right? So it's all about communication. If you want to take this on—if you want to take *me* on, then you get to join the communication train. We've all got to talk. A lot. And just remember, at my core, it's always *me*. But she's..." I roll my eyes. "Feistier. More stubborn."

"More stubborn than *you*?"

I smack him on the shoulder.

Then I grin at him and shake my head, because I know exactly what will happen when they *do* finally meet. Especially since she likes to come out at night. I nibble at the bread and give him a sly, alluring look. "And Jesus is she one kinky bitch."

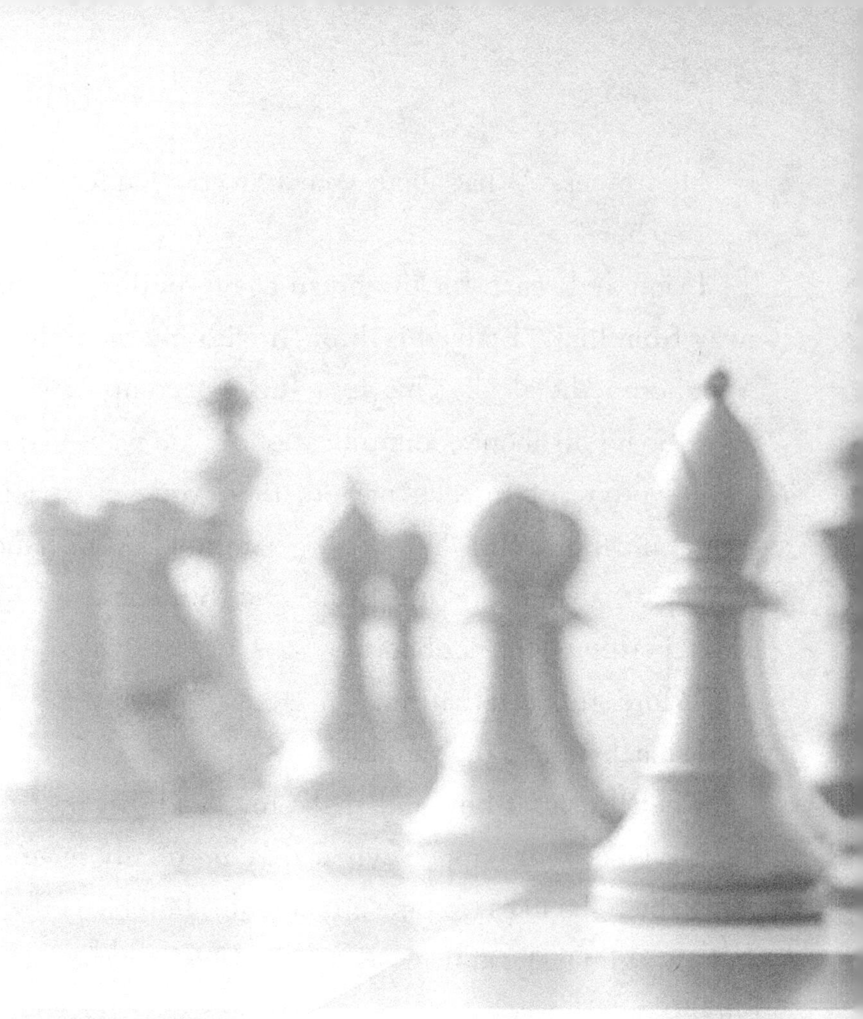

EPILOGUE II

DOMHNALL

We barely make it to the hotel room before I tear all Anna's clothes off again.

She seems sure of what will happen when I meet this alter of hers, but all I know is that I want the girl I've loved since I was seventeen, in any way, shape, or form she comes in.

I push her against the door and snatch both of her wrists, slamming them to the door beside her head.

She grins back at me as I press my groin against hers to pin her there.

"Were you hard all throughout dinner?"

"Of course I fucking was."

Her grin gets bigger.

Fuck, I've missed her. This year without her has been one of the hardest years of my life, and that's fucking saying something.

"What do you feel right now?" I ask.

"Uh... your big dick."

I chuckle. "Not that. I mean your feelings. I'm trying to check in. How are you feeling? Like if you had to name the feeling?"

Her eyebrows pop to her hairline. "Who are you and what have you done with Domhnall Callaghan?"

"Ha ha," I say deadpan. "You aren't the only one who's been in therapy. I still think feelings are fecking annoying as shit but apparently they're important. So name your feelings."

"You first," she says stubbornly, even though she's the one still pinned against the door.

"Fine." I look up at the ceiling, thinking about that stupid fucking feelings wheel my therapist is always having me look at to name my feelings from. It's always more helpful to have the damn thing in front of me. But I'm definitely in the yellow or orange section. I've stared at that damn wheel enough, I've got a lot of the feeling words memorized so I can pick out the ones I need.

"Okay, I'm happy. Excited. Enthusiastic." I smile down at her and massage the pulse point on her wrist with my thumb. "Curious. Impatient. *Aroused.*" I always particularly liked that one, especially now that I get to do something about it more than stare at stolen pictures of Anna.

Her eyebrows bunch as she looks up at me. "How are you so good at this?"

"Come on, don't tell me they haven't busted out the feelings wheel in your therapy sessions?"

She huffs out a breath so hard it makes her hair fluff out of her face. It's fucking adorable and my cock jumps in my pants.

I can't fucking believe she's finally here. I grin so big I think my cheeks are gonna fucking bust.

My Mads and me. After all these goddamn years. We finally made it.

"Marry me."

She gasps, eyes wide, but her smile gets as big as mine.

Then she tugs against where I've got her wrists pinned. "Lemme go."

Alright, not exactly the answer I was hoping for. But I do release her wrists and step back, freeing her.

Then she starts skipping—literally *skipping*—through the large suite towards the bedroom. "C'mon," she calls over her shoulder. "Follow me."

I hurry after her, and when I get to the bedroom, she's opening the accordion closet doors and walking inside.

"What are you *doing*?"

"Close these on me and turn off the light?"

"Mads— Anna. Seriously, what the fuck?" I finally get to the closet and see she's sitting in the very corner with her arms wrapped around her legs. When she looks up at me, she's never looked younger or more vulnerable. I immediately want to yank her out of there and pull her into my arms.

"Pull the doors shut and turn off the light."

"Anna, this is—"

"I want to marry you," she says, shutting me up. "But we need her permission, too."

Fuck.

She was right. This is going to be complicated.

"It doesn't feel right shutting you up in here like this."

She shakes her head, obviously impatient with me. "This is just a shortcut to bring her out. I've done it dozens of times. It's okay. Trust me."

Fucking fuck. She's scared of the dark. It's her worst fear.

"Of course I trust you." I can't say anything else because I know its what she needs from me. And I'll always give her what she needs, no matter how it kills me. Wasn't that what this whole last year was about?

I thought that would be it, though. One great sacrifice, and then I'd be done. Some part of me actually thought, despite the bullshit I spew in therapy, that I could take up the reins again once Anna was back and be master of my own destiny again.

Fuck. This is going to be forever, isn't it? I'm never going to feel that sense of control I did back when I was numbing all emotions and keeping everyone in my life at an arm's length. I was a miserable fucking bastard, but I thought I was in control. Even if it was an illusion, it was a comforting one.

But... being happy is better. Being in the yellow and orange part of the feelings wheel is better. Letting Anna all the way into my fucked up, gnarly little center is fucking *better*. Even if it comes with chaos that's always spinning me off my axis. I want it. I want all of it and all of her.

"Then—" She gestures with her head towards the doors. "What are you waiting for?"

I swallow hard, then close the closet doors on her with her inside.

"Now the lights," comes her muffled voice. "All of them! And shut the curtains!"

Jaysus fecking Christ.

I hurry so I can get it over with. I yank the blackout curtains shut first, then turn off both bedside lamps we'd left on earlier, the only lights in the room. Finally, I shut the door, leaving the room in total darkness.

How long are we supposed to fucking wait? Standing here in the dark is even freaking me the fuck out—

A scream comes from the closet.

Fuck!

I pull the door back open so light streams in from the living room, then run to yank open the closet doors.

I'm not sure what I expected to find on the other side.

Anna in tears? Curled up in a ball, completely whacked out and dissociated like that night I found her in the cage?

Instead, I find her sitting in a yoga pose, looking up at me calmly as the dim light falls upon her face.

"Well hello, Domhnall. I've waited ever so long to meet you."

EPILOGUE III

HER

Domhnall's chest heaves up and down as he breathes, obviously shocked to meet me even though that was the intent of the little game they were playing.

I climb out of the closet, stretching as I go. The Chicago therapist made us—I'm sorry, not *made* us, merely *intensely suggested that we*—take up yoga to help us center ourselves. Even though I've informed her I've never had a problem being off center, thank you very much.

Domhnall's hand comes down immediately to help me up and my breath hitches a little as I take it.

I'm embarrassed at the flush that hits me at the contact of his skin against mine.

But god, I've dreamed of touching this man for so long.

He pulls me up so we're face to face, long dark lashes blinking over those piercing blue eyes of his. I can barely breathe at being this close to him.

"Are you okay?"

My hand reaches out to touch his face. It's him. It's really *him*.

But he flinches backwards before my fingers can make contact with his cheek, and it's like a whip, lashing me. I take a step back from him.

"Playing hide and seek, hmm?" I straighten my shoulders contemptuously. "The girl always was so impatient. I'm sure I would have come out eventually. There's no need to summon me like a ghost. Next thing I know she's going to be pulling out a Ouija board."

Domhnall cracks a smile. "You call Anna *the girl*?"

I glare at him primly. "She is. And I don't see that you've grown up all that much since I last saw you, either."

His eyebrows furrow and then I see pain and shame and devastation wash his features as realization hits him.

"You," he whispers, crumpling in on himself a bit, though he doesn't turn away or even move further back from me. "She saw the once, but the rest of the time... it was *you* stuffed in that old busted-looking footlocker across the room, wasn't it?"

I blink, trying to swallow back sudden, foolish tears.

I'm not the one who cries.

It's the girl that cries.

"I had to protect her," I manage to squeak out. "But I'm fucking sorry—"

My voice breaks, and the tears I swore I'd never cry break through anyway. "I'm so fucking sorry there was no one there to protect you."

I expect him to turn away in disgust. To shun me for the fucking disgusting creature I am. I'm the monster's true daughter.

I took on the sins the girl couldn't bear—shouldn't have ever had to bear. I ate them and took them inside me like the sin eaters in those old Appalachian stories.

Then she stayed pure and innocent.

And I just stay soaked in the putrid muck of the monster's depravity and perversion. The nameless daughter of darkness, rightly shunned by the world. Even by the girl. She hates me, even if lately she claims not to.

I'm a thing no one could love, and I'd cut myself out of her if I could. She deserves better.

So nothing could astonish me more in the world than when Domhnall steps forwards and flings his arms around me, pulling me close to his chest.

"It's gonna be alrigh', love. I swear, it's gonna be alrigh'."

I inhale his scent and absolutely crumple into him. I'll just steal this moment. This one moment with him.

"I'm so fucking sorry," I whisper again.

"It's alrigh'. I mean, fuck. No, some t'ings will never be alrigh', but at least we're toget'er now, love."

He squeezes me harder, and the heart I didn't think I had left shatters into pieces.

It's the girl he's calling love, not you, you dumb bitch.

But I don't fucking care. Because I'm at the helm right now. And I'm the one feeling the arms of the boy I've loved since forever around me. So I don't fucking care if he's confusing me with her or just the body I'm in.

I lift up and kiss him on the lips. Just a peck. Just to see how he'll receive it.

Because I've been waiting for this man my whole goddamned life and I can't not take the chance.

He definitely looks surprised. That's for damn sure. And his chest does that heaving up and down thing again.

But he's hugging me so I can feel his erection suddenly spring to life. I grin and lift my face close again, giving him the choice.

"I want you," I whisper low, shifting slightly against his hard-on.

He frowns, still breathing hard. "Is that alrigh' with—? I mean, have you and Anna discussed—?"

I grin at him. "Oh we've discussed."

It only took about a month in therapy arguing for us to get on the same page. There were mixed feelings, but in the end, the girl decided fair was fair, and we could share. "Why do you think she pulled the hide and seek trick? She was hoping this could happen sooner rather than later."

I drop a hand to slide up his thigh slowly towards his cock.

He immediately snatches my hand away with a firm grip around my wrist, yanking it up towards his chest. He doesn't let go, and I can see his jaw is clenched.

"Oh you discussed, did you?"

He steps into me, forcing me to back up several steps against the wall. I inhale sharply as he cages me in, grabbing my other wrist and forcing them both up to the wall on either side of my head.

I grin. It's the same position he had the girl in. A thrill runs up and down my body at feeling it in the flesh instead of just in a fleeting memory.

"We did. She knows I'm the one who likes it a little rough. She knew you and I would have fun together."

I peek my tongue out through my teeth. Fuck, this is so freeing. I've only dreamed of letting myself play this way. Of letting the darkness run free in a way that doesn't feel bad. I want to be depraved but not evil.

"I want to play in the dark with you," I beg. "I want you to degrade me. I want you to do every perverted thing you can think of to me, and I want you to make it hurt."

His hand drops from my left wrist and comes to my throat, eyes lighting with dark fire. "Let's not run before we can walk, love."

"Why not?" I hiss. "I've been waiting for this my whole goddamn life."

His eyes narrow, hand squeezing a little at my throat in a way that thrills me down to my toes. It's Domhnall. Oh god, it's Domhnall here in front of me. It's his strong, firm hand at my throat. I swear I'm about to come on the spot from the tiniest contact and the command in his hold.

"Have you sought this out before? When Anna didn't know?"

He slides his other hand down my waist to my pussy, giving me plenty of time to pull away. But I don't. Fuck, I'm so hungry for his hand.

"Did you go seek out other men to fuck you and satisfy this need?"

When he finally touches my center, he's not shy about it. His hand firmly palms my pussy, and the pressure after all the anticipation lights the firecracker wick.

I shudder against him as I come. Oh god, my first ever orgasm with Domhnall. Oh god, he's touching my cunt.

He looks so fucking surprised I'm coming from the barest touch, but he doesn't pull away. He massages me more intentionally as I keep shuddering. Oh fuck, the man of my dreams is making me come.

"Choke me," I gasp.

His hand at my throat tightens and my orgasm ratchets even higher. I cry out in bliss, shuddering against the wall.

His hard-on spasms against my belly before I finally go limp, blinking lazily up at him.

"No," I gasp out breathlessly. "I never fucked anyone else.

I just watched a lot of porn and bought some ruthless nipple clamps and obscenely large dildos online to shove in all of my holes while thinking of you."

His hand around my throat squeezes hard before letting go, and his eyes go even darker. "The first you get for free. All the rest, you'll have to work for."

"Am I your little slut?" I blink up at him through my eyelashes.

"Is that what you want to be?" One of his thick eyebrows lifts.

"I'm your filthy little slut, and I need to be punished."

"That, my filthy little slut," he grins at me, "can be arranged."

Ten minutes later, Domhnall's got me tied down naked, bent over one of the fancy dining room chairs. My ankles are tied spread-eagled to the back legs, then I'm bent over the back of the chair and my wrists are tied to the front legs. The rope is soft, made of some sort of silk.

But he's definitely got me in a position where I can't move. My head rests against the seat of the chair, and yeah. I'm totally immobilized.

He's pacing back and forth behind me. I hear the *thwack* of something smacking his hand. A flogger? A cane? I'm not blindfolded but all I can see is the goddamned chair.

I'm wet with anticipation, and I suspect he knows that. But oh my god. It's my first scene with Domhnall. *I finally get to see him as Sir. I finally get to feel his firm hand of control and the sharp bite of pain that can release these fucking demons inside me.*

"Hmm, what does a dirty little slut like you deserve?"

"Everything," I whisper. "Please, Sir," I beg. "Ruin me. Destroy me." Debauch me. Degrade me. Remake me.

Fuck everything the girl's learned in her stupid therapy sessions. I want to worship Domhnall as my god. In this space, in our play here, he *is*.

"I want to worship at your feet," I hiss. "I want to lick your boots. I want to suck on your balls. I want to swallow your cock down my throat and choke on it as you fuck my face. I want to—"

I screech as a paddle smacks my ass, then writhe in the ropes binding my limbs. "Oh fuck, *yes*. More. Please, Sir. More."

"I'm going to make you cry such pretty little tears." His voice is low. Raw.

I giggle. "You can try, sir."

Another smack. Oh *fuck*. That one smarts. I dance in my bonds. "Please may I have another, Sir?"

Oh god, he gives it to me. A paddle right to the bottom of my ass cheek—harder this time but in a way that thrills me so fucking *deep*.

"Yes!" I scream, not caring who else in the hotel might hear. Domhnall's richer than god, right? So fuck it.

Suddenly Domhn's warmth is up against my back as he curls over me, his voice hot in my ear. "This is barely even phasing you, is it?" he mutters darkly.

Fuck, I'm so thrilled by his nearness. And I'm *so* goddamned wet.

"I love every one of Sir's touches. However they come."

"Is that right?" he growls, and a hand drops to squeeze my ass, right where he just paddled me.

I cry out, and almost come again from the pain and his nearness.

He immediately releases me and steps back.

"Fuck you're a live-wire, aren't you?"

Then he steps around to the side and I see his hand right before he reaches and grabs my nipple to twist it.

My mouth drops open at the exquisite pain. He just holds it in the twisted position, ruthlessly. I lift up on my toes, my whole body feeling like it centralizes on the pain he's eliciting in my left breast.

My legs tighten and I let out a little squeak.

"Fuck me," he mutters darkly. "You're going to come the second I let this go, aren't you?

I can only squeak again.

He lets out a huff of a laugh. "And goddamit, I'm so fucking hard right now, my dick could break through a goddamned boulder."

He bends down so his hot breath is right in my ear again, his brogue suddenly coming on deep. "So I tell ya what, love. I'm gonna fuck every hole of yours now, so ya know yur mine, just as much as Anna is. And yur gonna come when I fuck your sweet little cunny. And then when I fuck your face. Because now you've promised you'll swallow my cock like a good little slut, well that's a ticket I'm gonna cash in. And then I'm gonna take yur asshole, because I'm a dirty motherfucker and I want it. So I'm gonna take it. Do ya understand me, slut?"

"As long as you make it hurt, Sir."

"That's the right answer, Pet."

He lets go of my nipple and then spanks me. Hard.

I shudder from the flood of endorphins at him releasing my nipple, but am too distracted by him spanking me to come.

He spanks me once, and then twice.

Then over and over. Unforgiving smacks that have me quickly dancing on my tiptoes again and writhing in my bonds. Especially when he gets me in a spot the paddle already landed. Goddamn, that smarts!

My fingers clench around the ropes binding my wrists as my pussy clenches, so fucking wet. I always suspected it could be like this.

I dreamt about this for years after he was gone. Whenever my father locked me in the closet, or in the box beneath my bed, or in the big barrel out back when it was raining. I'd think of Donny hurting me for my sins and it would make me come in the dark. Just thinking of what his dark touch might feel like. I always thought it meant I was even more fucked up.

But it turns out I'm fucked up just like him.

"Please, Sir," I beg desperately. Because he said I could only come when he fucked my cunt and my face and my ass, and he's not doing any of those things right now.

He's just spanking me like the bad girl I am, making me dance where he's got me bound up so tight.

"Please. *Please—*" I whine.

And then I hear the barest noise of a zipper and then the slightest pressure of his chest at my back, his long, thick cock slipping between my spread legs.

He thrusts in my cunt—*hard*.

The girl has had him all weekend but this is the first time *I—*

I gasp out in such absolute exhilaration and singing freedom and dark pleasure as I clench down all my inner muscles on his cock.

Mine.

He pulls out far too quickly, but then he shoves back in, rougher still.

But not rough enough. He's forgotten who he's fucking. Just because it's the same body, doesn't mean it's the same girl.

"Harder!" I shout. "Fuck me like you mean it, Sir, or don't bother at all," I call from where I'm bent over the chair.

His next thrust comes at me like a battering ram, and I feel him everywhere as he pounds into me. The chair I'm tied to screeches on the wood of the dining room floor as he sends it forwards several inches with the force of his pounding.

"Yes," I cry, holding on to the ropes for dear life as I brace for his next thrust.

It's just as brutal and I love him giving into the monster he always keeps so carefully tucked away inside him. With me he can give into it completely.

"I'm not crying yet, Sir," I taunt.

"You little bitch. You fucking slut!"

I hear the snick of a knife being released and then feel the taut line of the rope binding my left ankle free, then my right. Sir is soon quickly slicing the ropes binding my wrists, too. He doesn't bother undoing the knots, he just grabs me by my waist and bears me down to the floor.

"I wish you were wearing mascara," he mutters.

"It won't matter, Sir." I grin up at him as he climbs on top of me, two knees bracing my shoulders down as he sits on me, positioning his huge cock at my lips. "You won't get me to cr—"

My words are cut off by him shoving his cock past my lips. In spite of what I know he wants, he tries to take it easy at first. Just pushing his bulbous head past my lips before retreating again.

But that's not what either of us are here for.

He's got me pretty severely pinned with his body—careful not to actually lean his weight down in his crouch on top of me—but when he next bobs his cock past my lips, I can lift up just enough to swallow his shaft down my throat.

I look him straight in the eye as I do it and he gasps, likely from how good what I'm doing to him feels.

I wish I had a hand free to squeeze his balls, but that's not the point of this, is it?

Domhnall gets to be in complete and utter control, for once in his life.

So he snarls in pleasure, grasps hold of my hair to hold my head to the floor, and starts to fuck my face. Well, my throat, really.

I choke on his cock. Spittle pours out the side of my mouth.

And goddamn him, my eyes do tear up and water pours down the sides of my cheeks before he finally lets up so I can gasp for air.

"Such beautiful, beautiful fecking tears, lass," he growls. "Now cry some more for me."

He ruthlessly shoves his cock straight back down my throat.

And I take it, pussy clenching in near-bliss as I stare up at him.

My dark-haired god.

My Donny.

He's giving me everything I ever dreamed of.

I stayed so strong my whole life for this.

So I could break completely and for once in my whole existence, be weak and cry and give myself over to the beautiful boy I watched my father destroy, the one I *couldn't* save.

But I can save him now.

Maybe just maybe, all of us can save each other. Together in this twisted knot.

We can play in the dark, and long before I'd die without air because the gentle monster inside Donny is a far, far more benevolent monster than any I've ever known before, he pulls back and lets me drag in huge lungfuls of air.

I'm high with it and I spasm deep with a low, groaning orgasm.

"That's righ', my beautiful feckin' girl," he says, climbing off me and rolling me to my side, hand to my cunt. As he rolls me, he wraps one arm underneath and around my waist.

His middle finger lands right on my swollen clit and his other hand moves up to ruthlessly clamp and twist my right nipple.

I groan low and shudder between his arms wrapped around me, the orgasm only barely begun with the breathplay now amping much higher with the direct stimulation.

His two middle fingers dip inside my sex and I clench around them, but they're gone almost as quickly and I whine at the loss of them.

Only to realize moments later what he intends when I

feel those same fingers rimming my asshole with my own juices.

Domhnall's hiking my leg up with his elbow moments later and dragging more juices down from my cunt to my ass before I feel his cock lining up there.

I expel a loud breath before his thumb comes back to strum at my clit.

He did promise all three holes, didn't he?

"Deep breath in, love," he whispers hot at my ear.

I've only just begun to take my deep breath when Donny thrusts forwards and breaches me. Or tries to, anyway.

The forceful thrust only scoots me forwards on the slick wood flooring several inches to the carpeted living room.

I can feel his frustration in the way he grips me and thrusts uselessly several more times.

"Flip me," I tell him. "Get on top of me and take it. Take everything that's yours."

As if unsure, he lets go a little. So I roll to my chest on the soft carpet and spread my legs as wide as I can.

The next second I hear him spit in his hand, and I shudder with the start of another orgasm as I imagine him coating his cock with his own spittle. Then I feel the weight of him climbing on top of me and his heavy cock swinging between my butt-cheeks.

The next time he shoves forwards, there's nowhere else for me to go.

I take him.

"Yes!" I scream, and then continue howling. In desire. In pain. In release, because yes, the pain has lit the orgasm that started moments ago.

It's Donny fucking my ass, rutting inside me with harsh, rough thrusts. Over and over until I'm sure he's splitting me apart like a log with an ax.

But I meant what I said to him at the start of all this.

I want it to hurt.

Pain is a refuge.

Hurt that's on the outside is something I can scream into and release. Adrenaline follows on its tails and takes me to a higher, sublime place beyond the reach of the dark.

I don't just cry, I wail and sob, exorcising the demons within me.

And now as he fucks me, one hand clenching my hip and the other on my cunt to hold me in place to absolutely just *rut* me like an animal—deeper and *deeper* and *harder* up my ass—I can fucking *feel* him through the thin walls of my ass and into my cunt. He's there in places I have no godly right to be feeling him.

I scream with another orgasm.

Domhnall starts to shout behind me, gibberish and expletives as he thrusts harder than ever, absolutely wild before finally stilling and slumping over on top of me. He's careful to roll slightly to the side so he's not crushing me with his weight, but I love that he's not pulling away.

He's there, holding me, letting me feel his body

completely wrapped around me, and still hard inside me. There is nowhere that I am where Domhnall is not.

"I love you," he whispers into my hair.

I shudder again beneath him.

Does he know what it means to me for him to say that?

Does he have any clue?

I could die right here and be complete. I could disappear, and give Anna the wholeness I know she wants, finally at peace.

But... I blink my eyes several times... I don't think I will.

Or maybe it's because I can't.

Maybe it's not a choice either of us was ever capable of making.

He loves me.

Me and Anna, each just shattered pieces of a fractured whole. In the shards of the mirror, I think I begin to see the light grow brighter on the room that is *us*.

And front and center is our framed picture of the boy.

Donny.

The love of our lives.

You could be called Mads. One of us should be.

I still.

It's so rare for the girl and I to communicate directly without Dr. Kim to facilitate. Usually we're too angry at each other.

But here, with half of Domhnall's weight on top of us, it's easier to be close to her. Just like she felt closer to me when she was with him even when our father had made her forget me entirely.

The boy loves us, I tell her.

I know he does. He asked us a question. You should give him an answer.

Will we ever be enough? What if he deserves better?

We all deserved better. But now I think we all deserve to be extraordinarily wild with happiness, no matter if that means occasional tough times. So that means we deserve each other.

Well fuck. When did you grow up and get so wise?

When you weren't looking.

Domhnall rolls all the way off of me and curves me into his chest. "Fuck, you alrigh'? I was too rough there at the end."

"Yes."

"Fuck. I'm so sorry, I'm so feckin' sorry. I'll never do that to ya again, I swear, I'll—" He drags his hand down his face and tries to move away, but I only haul him closer, shaking my head.

"Don't say that!" I cry, throwing my arms around his waist. "That was the best fuck Mads has ever had. *Yes*, she'll marry you. I mean, we'll marry, you."

My cheeks get hot, which is ridiculous, considering this man literally just fucked me ten ways from Sunday. I've got the memories, but I didn't feel any of the pain. I think that might be more of a Mads-and-Donny thing when they get in a particular mood. I'm a light-pain kind of girl, I think. But I'm happy to let them play in the dark together to let their demons out.

Domhnall's eyes have been dancing back and forth between mine but they finally settle. "Anna?"

I nod.

"Wait, are you serious?"

"She and I just had a little chat. She finally picked a name. *Mads*. We're both the girl you first fell in love with, but it only felt right that some part of us should still have the name. So she's Mads and I'm Anna now."

He blinks, and understandably, this is all going to be a little hard for him to follow at first. Shit, it's happening inside my head, and I barely know what's going on half the time.

"And you both want to marry me?" he says cautiously.

I nod.

"And the rough sex we just had was okay with ya?"

I lift an eyebrow. "More than okay. Though now that I've switched back to Anna, I might demand a massage later."

A grin breaks out on his face. "I'm so fecking in love with all of ya! You've made me happier than I ever coulda hoped 'a bein'!"

He throws his arms around me.

I laugh with total, absolute abandonment and joy, for the first time believing that everything is really going to be all right. "We love you, too."

Don't miss a thing, read Moira's forbidden love story with Father Bane in **UNHOLY OBSESSION HERE**! **Unholy Obsession**, book 2 of Carnal Games is out now, and oh my holy moly this book!!! 🙀😳

So, I meanttttttt to just write a bonus scene to share for more of Anna/Mads and Domhn's life as they all learn to live together… and then it turned out they all had more to say!! 🙈

So now I'm writing their sequel and er-ma-gerd. The intensity. The angst. The obsessive love. The need for therapy. 🤣 If you thought it was intense in this book… um… Let's just say I've been reading too much (and never enough) dramione fanfic. 👀😈 **Catch up and read along as I write the sequel here!**

ALSO BY STASIA BLACK

TABOO SERIES

Daddy's Sweet Girl

Hurt So Good

Taboo: a Boxset Collection (Boxset)

BREAKING BELLES SERIES

Elegant Sins

Beautiful Lies

Opulent Obsession

Inherited Malice

Delicate Revenge

Lavish Corruption

MONSTER'S CONSORTS SERIES

Monster's Bride

Thing

Between Brothers

Hunger

MAVROS BROTHERS SAGA

Who's Your Daddy

Who's Your Baby Daddy

Who's Your Alpha Daddy

Mavros Brothers Saga Boxset

MARRIAGE RAFFLE SERIES

Theirs To Protect

Theirs To Pleasure

Theirs To Wed

Theirs To Defy

Theirs To Ransom

DARK MAFIA SERIES

Innocence

Awakening

Queen of the Underworld

Cruel Obsession (Boxset)

BEAUTY AND THE ROSE SERIES

Beauty's Beast

Beauty and the Thorns

Beauty and the Rose

Billionaire's Captive (Boxset)

LOVE SO DARK DUOLOGY

Cut So Deep

Break So Soft

Love So Dark (Boxset)

STUD RANCH SERIES

The Virgin and the Beast

Hunter

The Virgin Next Door

Reece

Jeremiah

FREEBIE

Indecent: A Taboo Proposal

DRACI ALIEN SERIES

My Alien's Obsession

My Alien's Baby

My Alien's Beast

Alpha Alien Beasts (Boxset)

ABOUT STASIA BLACK

STASIA BLACK grew up in Texas, recently spent a freezing five-year stint in Minnesota, and now is happily planted in sunny California, which she will never, ever leave. She recently got married, is wildly in love, and has the cutest cat on this side of the Mississippi.

Stasia's drawn to romantic stories that don't take the easy way out. She wants to see beneath people's veneer and poke into their dark places to find their twisted motives and deepest desires.

Want to read or listen to an EXCLUSIVE, FREE book/audiobook? Indecent: a Taboo Proposal, that is available ONLY to my newsletter subscribers, along with news about upcoming releases, sales, exclusive giveaways, and more?

Get **Indecent: a Taboo Proposal** at www.stasiablack.com

When Mia's boyfriend takes her out to her favorite restaurant on their six-year anniversary, she's expecting one kind of proposal. What she didn't expect was her boyfriend's longtime rival, Vaughn McBride, to show up and make a completely different sort of offer: all her boyfriend's debts will be wiped clear. The price?

One night with her.
 Get it at stasiablack.com

Website: www.stasiablack.com
Tiktok: @stasiablackauthor
Instagram: @stasiablackauthor
Facebook: facebook.com/StasiaBlackAuthor
Goodreads: goodreads.com/stasiablack
BookBub: bookbub.com/authors/stasia-black

Made in United States
Cleveland, OH
09 May 2025